Tessa Barclay is a former publishing editor and journalist who has written many successful novels, among them the four-part Craigallan Saga — *A Sower Went Forth, The Stony Places, The Good Ground* and *Harvest of Thorns* — and the Wine Widow trilogy — *The Wine Widow, The Champagne Girls* and *The Last Heiress*. She lives in south west London.

Broken Threads

Tessa Barclay

HEADLINE

First published in 1989
by W. H. Allen & Co. Plc

First published in paperback in 1990
by HEADLINE BOOK PUBLISHING PLC

10 9 8 7 6 5 4 3 2

ISBN 0 7472 3554 6

Typeset by Avocet Robinson, Buckingham
Printed and bound in Great Britain by
Collins, Glasgow

HEADLINE BOOK PUBLISHING PLC
Headline House
79 Great Titchfield Street
London W1P 7FN

Broken Threads

Chapter One

For the most part, the citizens of Galashiels were pleased with Miss Jenny Corvill's marriage.

Some there were who, a few years ago at her twenty-first birthday, had written her off as an old maid. After all, when a woman reaches that watershed without showing much desire for the state of matrimony, it is reasonable to suppose she won't change her mind. The more especially as Miss Corvill had plenty to occupy her at the mill.

Her eventual choice of husband was odd. Who else but Jenny Corvill would have taken a man she used to employ in her tweed mill? But then Ronald Armstrong had always been an unusual employee. In these days of expansion and invention in the weaving trade, Ronald Armstrong could have set up on his own at any time. Backers for a master dyer of Ronald's ability would never have been lacking.

He, however, had left the employ of William Corvill and Son without explanation some years ago. 'Just like him,' the local gossips had said with sagely nodding heads. 'Didna care to have a woman ordering him about.'

Whatever the truth of it, he had scarcely shown himself again in Galashiels before Miss Corvill had thrown herself into his arms. It seemed, by all the

1

evidence, that the two had always had a fondness for each other.

When friends and acquaintances tried to fish for details of this hidden romance, no one in the Corvill family appeared to have anything to tell. Jenny's widowed mother simply beamed with pleasure at her daughter's happiness. Her brother Edward had little to say except that he was 'well pleased to have a man like Armstrong as a relative'. Only Edward's wife, the fairy-like little Mrs Lucy Corvill, evinced any dissatisfaction.

And even that was muted. Those who belonged to Lucy's social circle always regarded her as one who loved to please. Approval was as necessary to her as sunshine to a flower. For that reason, she said very little to show displeasure at the forthcoming marriage.

'I'm sure it will all work out very well,' she would remark, when pressed for her opinion.

'But Jenny could have had Simpson. Or Archie Brunton.' This was Mrs Kennet, wife of the town's leading lawyer, naming the most prosperous farmer and the biggest landowner of the district.

Lucy Corvill said nothing, although a faint colour — perhaps of anger — came into her cheeks.

'Aweel, if a lassie doesna fancy a man, she can say no until the right one comes along. The only wonder is,' said Mrs Cairns, stabbing her needle into the sock she was darning, 'that Ronald Armstrong should be the right one. He's always been a pawky lad, fond of his own way. Jenny'll mebbe find him hard to handle.'

'I should think,' blurted Lucy, 'that he would have more sense than to argue with his betters.' She broke off, bit her lip, and tried to smother the words by delving in the pile of garments the Ladies Sewing Circle was mending on behalf of the deserving poor.

'Aha,' thought Mrs Cairns, 'she's no pleased with the marriage though she willna let on.'

If the truth were known, Lucy Corvill was furious about it. To be sister-in-law to a common workman! She, the wife of the best-known mill owner in the Scottish Borders, she who had met Queen Victoria and the Prince Consort in person!

But Jenny was determined, and when Jenny Corvill set her mind on something, it was no use opposing her. Strange and unwomanly though she was, somehow she generally got her way without having to wheedle and coax as Lucy did.

Lucy knew she would never like Ronald, that Ronald would always have that look of hidden amusement when he conversed with her. Uppish, ignorant yokel, who did he think he was?

And God knew, he would have an even higher opinion of himself once he took over as manager of Waterside Mill. Edward Corvill, the 'and Son' of the original firm, had given his prospective brother-in-law the post unhesitatingly, as soon as the engagement was announced.

'But Ned,' Lucy had protested in their bedroom that night, 'you *can't* do that! He's a nobody! You can't hand over the running of the firm to a mere workman!'

Ned paused in unbuttoning the front of his evening shirt. 'My love, he's not a "mere" workman. He's the greatest expert in dyes in the entire Scottish woollen industry. His reputation –'

'All right, he's a master dyer. But how do you know he can manage a mill?'

'Lucy, he's going to be Jenny's husband,' Ned said

simply. 'It wouldn't be fitting to give him an inferior post, and since Jenny as a married woman could scarcely go on as manager, Ronald is the best substitute.'

Lucy felt a little stab of triumph at that. Jenny would no longer be the real head of Waterside Mill. Jenny would have to take her proper place in Galashiels society — wife and mother, sister to the owner of the pre-eminent mill, a country lady like all the rest of them, no more and no less. At least there was that much of a silver lining to this dark cloud: the redoubtable Mistress Jenny Corvill of the weaving industry would cease to exist and her sister-in-law Lucy would no longer have to look up to her.

Cocooned though she was in blissful happiness, Jenny Corvill still retained enough of her normal shrewdness to know that her brother's wife resented the forthcoming marriage. But then, Lucy resented almost everything that didn't serve as an adornment to herself.

Jenny had long accepted the fact. Yet she felt guilty about dragging Ronald into this uneasy situation.

'I ought to warn you what you're taking on,' she said to him one evening as they walked arm in arm in the gloaming of the hill's shadow behind Gatesmuir. 'Were not a very happy family, my dear. What with Ned's drinking and Lucy's snobbery.'

'But Ned's going to take himself in hand.'

'You think so?'

He nodded. 'And as for Lucy; you don't expect me to take Lucy seriously?'

Jenny shivered a little. Behind Lucy's pale, fey exterior there was a sharp and unkind nature. She had had experience of it in the past. But then, in the main

4

Lucy was so anxious to preserve appearances that she held herself well in check. Only extreme emotion drove her to reveal her true self. And if they were lucky, no extremes of emotion would be aroused in the foreseeable future.

Ronald was remarking that his future sister-in-law would probably forget her illwill towards him in the enjoyment of arranging the wedding reception.

'She wants to choose my wedding gown for me,' Jenny murmured.

'Well, let her. What does it matter?'

'But she wants me in virginal white with sheaves of pure lilies. And we both know how inappropriate that would be.'

'I won't tell anyone if you won't,' he replied, looking down at her with a sparkle of amusement under his tawny brows.

'All the same, I feel badly about acting out a lie in church.'

'So do you want to get wed in a scarlet shift?'

She laughed. 'There's no need to go quite that far, Ronald my dear.'

Lucy was full of enthusiasm for paper taffetas and slipper satin and silk voile. Jenny went along with her as far as the fabrics and the style were concerned, but insisted on pale primrose. Lucy frowned inwardly at the choice. Could it be — could it really be — that her calm and upright sister-in-law had some reason to shy away from the symbolism of purity?

'Everyone will expect you to wear white,' she objected.

'Nonsense. I'm nearly twenty-five years old. White is for little girls.'

And with that Lucy had to be content.

The Corvills had a long-standing commitment to the little United Secession Church but for this great occasion Lucy campaigned strongly for the Parish Church of Galashiels. 'Everyone expects it,' she insisted. She had a new gown of cornflower blue repp silk which would be seen to best advantage in the big church.

The reception was held at Gatesmuir, with all the refinements that Lucy had intended — hired waiters in livery, much champagne, bride cake from Ferguson's in Edinburgh, and a string trio to play sentimental tunes.

Her plans were spoilt a little when, after changing into their going-away clothes, the bride and groom insisted on going off to the mill where another celebration was in progress, for the mill workers. Here there were more substantial eatings and drinkings, a fiddle-and-melodeon partnership to provide music for reels and jigs, and a great deal of noise. Lucy wondered that any truly refined person would even dream of going near it on her wedding day.

From here the happy couple departed in the carriage for their honeymoon. The chant of 'poor oot, poor oot', which meant the crowd expected the traditional pouring-out of largesse, was rewarded with a shower of silver coins from the window on Ronald's side. Cheers and blessings were called after them.

'Well, that's that,' Jenny said, as they sank back against the leather cushions.

'Well, that's that so far,' Ronald amended. He put his arm around his bride. 'Mrs Armstrong, are you happy?'

'Don't ask daft questions.'

'That's no way to speak to your husband, my good woman.'

6

She leaned her head against his shoulder. She was happy, no doubt about it. But she had no illusions about the problems that lay ahead.

When they returned from Dunbar to the workaday world, the first and unexpected problem had arisen.

Gowan, the station master, rushed to greet them. His perturbation was so great that he addressed Jenny in the name she had always been known by. 'Mistress Corvill! Michty me, I expected you back lang since!'

'Mr Gowan! What's the matter?'

'Did they no send word to you, mistress? There was an explosion at the mill the morning after you left —'

'An explosion!' Jenny grabbed at Ronald's sleeve for support.

'Aye, they think one o' they mad European anarchists set a bomb —'

Abandoning their luggage on the platform, the newly-weds hurried on foot to Waterside Mill. Later they confided to each other that they had expected to see it in ruins. What they saw was the same old mill building, but silent, with a member of the Galashiels constabulary on guard outside, a few mill girls standing about, a bulge in the ground floor wall some yards from the entrance hall, and timber balks shoring it up.

Ronald's longer stride had taken him there first. He rushed in. Saltley, the acting-manager, was supervising the removal of some twisted metal.

'What the hell's been happening?' Ronald cried.

'What? Oh, Mr Armstrong — so there you are at last —'

'What do you mean, at last! Why wasn't I called back?'

'Well, Mr Armstrong, that wasna up to me, and I thought you'd see it in the newspaper.'

7

Jenny had by now caught up with her husband. At the words, she stopped short. The truth was that during their blissful two weeks at Dunbar they had never so much as opened a newspaper, nor thought of anyone or anything except each other.

'Gowan said something about a bomb,' she put in, gasping for breath.

'Ach, havers! The town's been full of daft rumours ever since it happened.' Saltley, his red face smeared with dust, looked vexed. 'There wasna the least sign of a bomb or siccan a thing. The fact o' the matter is, some drunken fool left a gas tap on with no light in the mantle, and over the night the gas accumulated so that when the town was at church on Sunday morning . . .'

Ronald had stalked past to look at the damage. It was a miserable enough sight in the clear light of the May afternoon. A whole set of carding machines — scribbler, carder and condenser — had been removed. Those on either side were damaged, bent steel and wires hanging loose.

'Good God . . .'

'It's a mercy it happened on a Sunday,' Jenny breathed. 'Think if anyone had been here!'

'McWhin the watchman was here —'

'Was he badly hurt?'

'Not him! Safe at the back of the mill where he fell asleep when the rest o' the revellers went to their beds. He was as fou as a turnip-skin, still had no great hold on his wits when we all ran to see what had happened.'

'What a mess,' groaned Ronald.

'What a homecoming, sir,' said Saltley, shaking his head mournfully. 'I'm sair sorry.'

'Why is the place so silent?' Jenny said, lifting a hand to call attention to the fact.

8

'Well, mistress — we had to get out the wreckage and shore up the wall —'

'But that was ten days ago,' Ronald interrupted.

'Aye, well, the first day we thought — aiblins there might really be a bomb — so Mr Corvill said —'

'Mr Corvill?'

'Of course, Mr Armstrong. I didna like to take responsibility on sic a thing.'

'And the girls?' inquired Jenny.

'They've been laid off — them and all other body.'

'But why?' said Jenny and Ronald, almost in unison.

Ronald walked across the carding room. 'Two sets of machines here are damaged and out of action, but the others seem to be all right.'

'Aye. Mr Armstrong, as far as we can see —'

'Then why aren't they back at work?'

'Well, y'see, we turned off the power —'

'And let the steam boilers out,' Jenny put in. 'Not even the finishing department is working.'

'No, mistress, Mr Corvill said —'

'Get the boiler-room men back, get the steam going,' Ronald said. 'We need a team of cleaners to get the dust off the machines. What was on them when it happened?'

'The dark green yarn for Pattern 401,' Jenny said.

'Oh yes, so it was. That's no problem, there's plenty more of that yarn in the yarn store —' Ronald broke off, and began unbuttoning his frock coat so as to begin work at once. 'Go you home, Jenny, speak to Ned, find out what's been in his mind. I'll get things started here.'

'Yes, dear.'

The shock on the acting-manager's face when she

meekly accepted this command wasn't lost on Jenny. She hurried off, put out that Ronald hadn't couched it as a suggestion, but with more important things to worry about.

At Gatesmuir, she found outward peace and quiet. Her mother and sister-in-law were playing hostess to a meeting of the Welfare and Benevolent Association. Jenny hurried in almost before the parlour maid had got the door open.

'Mother, where's Ned?'

'Oh! Jenny! Oh . . .' Millicent Corvill stumbled to her feet. 'Excuse me, ladies, my daughter . . .'

Jenny heard a murmur of sympathy as her mother hastened out to her in the hall. 'Och, poor thing . . . what a homecoming . . . it'll fair o'erset her . . .'

'Jenny, I'm so glad you're back! I've been at my wits' end, people wanting decisions that I'm not fit to be making —'

'You?' Jenny said, not troubling to hide her astonishment. 'You've been making decisions? About what?'

'The mill, my dear, and many another thing. You see —'

'But Ned should have shouldered all that —'

'Aye, but that's what I'm trying to tell you —'

'Mother, where is Ned?'

Her mother, flushed with shame, looked down at her soft leather house-shoes. 'We don't know, dear.'

'What?'

'We don't know. He . . . well, you know, he . . . took it badly about the explosion.'

Jenny sank down on the hall settle. 'You mean he got drunk?'

Lucy came out of the drawing room, closing the

door that her mother-in-law had left partly a jar. 'Please lower your voices,' she said in reproof. 'Everyone can hear you in there.'

Jenny began to untie the strings of her bonnet. A great weariness threatened to engulf her. For two weeks she had been gone from them. She had forgotten the anxieties and the animosities of her family. But once she set foot inside the door again, they swept towards her like a tidal wave.

'You had better ask the ladies to excuse us, Lucy,' she said. 'We have to talk.'

'You and Mother can talk in the dining room. There's no reason why I should be dragged in.'

'Lucy, we need to talk about Ned.'

'I have nothing to say about Ned.'

'My love, I think our friends would understand if we closed the meeting rather short,' Millicent intervened. 'They ken we're in some trouble, they're weaving folk themselves.'

Lucy looked as if she would resist, but then with a sulky set of her mouth went back into the drawing room. Millicent led the way heavily into the dining room, calling to the maid, 'Bring fresh tea and sandwiches in, Thirley, Mrs Armstrong must be famished.'

There was the muted bustle of departure. About ten minutes later Lucy came in, looking mutinous. Jenny by then had drunk a much needed cup of tea. She had had nothing since a late breakfast at Dunbar.

She had been brought up to date by her mother. The facts, briefly stated, were not pleasing. When news of the explosion was brought to Ned he had hurried to the scene, like most of Galashiels. Mr Saltley had been frightened by the rumour, which seemed to spring up like wildfire, that the Corvills were targets of the anarchists because of the Royal Family's patronage of them.

'It quite unmanned him, Jenny. So Ned took charge and spoke with the police and so on. On the Monday he got workmen in to make the wall safe and later in the day the wrecked machines were taken out. Some talk arose about the boilers being unsafe — the dear knows where it came from — and he decided not to restart any of the machinery.'

'I understand he wouldn't want to use the pressing plant. But that shouldn't have stopped him from resuming with the water power?'

'I don't know, child. He seemed to be in a tither. Then Saltley came to him and said what was to be done about the workforce, who were standing about with nothing to do. So he told Saltley to lay them off.'

'What on earth made him do that?' Jenny demanded, raising her eyes to the ceiling for help.

'I told him to,' Lucy said, as she came in. 'They were just earning wages for standing idle, it was silly. It was clearly going to save money to send them away.'

'Lucy! You could have put them on half-time —'

'So that a pack of girls could stay at home enjoying themselves?'

'It's not just the girls. Ritchie and Ainsley will have gone to the opposition — we'll never get Ritchie back if Begg and Hailes have got him. And he's the best carding-room foreman in Galashiels.'

'Good heavens, you can get him back if he's so important —'

'Why should he come back to a firm that turned him off at a moment's notice? Ned should never have done such a thing.'

'Well, in truth, Jenny, he knew it as soon as it was done because Dick Ainsley picked a fight with him the next morning and then . . . then . . .' Jenny's mother faltered into silence. She was unwilling to describe what had happened next with her only son.

'And then he came home and found comfort in the whisky bottle,' Lucy said with contempt. 'So that's where it all ended, all those good resolutions about never touching another drop and all the rest of it. I could have told your husband he was a fool to believe it when Ned told him he was reformed.'

'But why didn't you send a message?' Jenny cried.

There was an embarrassed silence. Then Millicent said, 'If you remember, my dove, Ronald told only Ned where you were going for your honeymoon. It was so that you could have complete privacy, and at the time it seemed right . . .'

'Then why didn't Ned — ?'

'At first he was too taken up with what happened. We all were. And then, you see, he shut himself up in the reading room, and then on the Thursday he went out and he hasn't been back.'

Jenny was aghast. 'He's been missing *ten days*?'

'I'm afraid so.'

'You've sent to find him, I take it?'

'Oh aye, all over Galashiels and in Hawick and Melrose. We've heard word of him, but so far Mr Kennet's man hasn't been able to catch up with him.'

'In other words, he's out on a drunken hoologh,' said Ronald, when he heard the report from Jenny that evening.

At the blunt words she bent her head. He caught the sparkle of tears on her dark lashes. Aghast at his own tactlessness, he put an arm about the slender

13

shoulders. 'Never you mind, my heart,' he said, 'it's not your fault.'

'When I think what a family I've dragged you into,' she said, in a voice that quavered.

'You didn't drag me, I hurried in with an eager mind. Why, Jenny lass, if you've a brother that isn't fit to be in charge of a Sunday School outing, what does it matter? We'll sort it. I've made a fair start already — the wheels should be turning at Waterside Mill tomorrow morning.'

'But we have to find Ned.'

'It won't be difficult,' he assured her. He was thinking that Ned must be running out of money after ten days, and no one can drink on credit for ever.

Ned Corvill was found two days later in a local lock-up at Romanno Bridge. Due to be taken before the sheriff on a charge of disturbing the peace, he was recognised by a lawyer who had seen him in happier circumstances. A message was sent to Gatesmuir, everything was arranged discreetly, and Ned at his own request went into a private nursing home in Peebles.

'We went through all this before,' Lucy complained, when Ronald came back from shepherding his repentant brother-in-law into the nursing home. 'It won't do a bit of good. He just hasn't any willpower.'

'He wants you to go and stay in Peebles, somewhere near him so you can visit —'

'I shan't go near the place. That awful clinic in Glasgow was enough for me.'

'Sister-in-law, your man needs you,' Ronald said. 'I said the marriage vows recently enough to recall them: "for better, for worse".'

'Oh, it's easy enough for you to talk —'

'Besides,' Ronald went on as if she hadn't spoken,

'Peebles is a very agreeable place. Any spa town has its attractions. There's a band concert every day in the public gardens, the shops are full of summer silks, there's a touring company playing *The Revenge of Adair* at the theatre.'

'Don't try to coax me as if I were a child,' Lucy cried, and flounced out of the room.

Nevertheless, she went to Peebles at the end of the week. Ned began to mend. With that problem taken care of for the moment, Jenny and Ronald were able to concentrate on Waterside Mill.

The original plan had been that Jenny would step down from the role of manager of the mill to make way for Ronald. She would occupy herself instead with designing the plaids with which she had made the firm of William Corvill and Son famous. To this end she had fitted out a room on the top floor of the mill, with a good northern light.

But it was necessary to replace the damaged machinery of the carding room. Since they were having new, they might as well have all the latest improvements and refinements that weaving engineers could provide. Jenny had to go to Yorkshire to see the new machines.

Then there came the problem of the money with which to pay for them. Jenny and Ronald expected it to come from the insurance on the lost machinery, but the Mechanical and Industrial Assurance Company refused to pay up. Jenny had to go to Edinburgh to confront the claims examiner.

'The police are thoroughly satisfied that the damage was caused by the accumulation of coal gas when a tap was left on after a celebration in the works,' Mr Scranton pointed out with stiff politeness. 'I fear my company cannot be held liable for damage caused in that way.'

'I think if you read paragraph 8c of the policy you will see that damage through accidental negligence of the workers is covered.'

'But the implication of that, Mistress Corvill, is that the workers' negligence occurs when the workers are working.'

'That may be your reading of it, but there is no such phrase in the policy, sir.'

'Forgive me, Mistress Corvill, but usage in the insurance business will bear me out —'

'I don't give a bent bawbee for usage in the insurance business, Mr Scranton. The policy covers accidental negligence by the workers and that is what caused the gas explosion.'

'I fear I cannot go along with you on that —'

'I fear you will thereupon hear from my lawyer, Mr Scranton.'

'You should not waste your money on filing suit, mistress —'

'I should not have wasted my money on a policy with a company who intend to welch on it. I bid you good-day, Mr Scranton.'

'Wait, dear lady — let us not part on bad terms —'

'What terms do you offer instead, then, sir?'

And so the fencing went on, the case at last went to arbitration, and in the end William Corvill and Son got a substantial settlement — not enough to pay entirely for the repair of the damage and the replacement of the machines, but more than Jenny had expected at first.

All these additional tasks kept her from stepping aside, as she had sincerely intended to do when Ronald took over. But she took care to leave him the full control of the work at the mill. There, she tried very hard to make everyone call her Mistress Armstrong instead of Mistress Corvill, and continued to keep to her role as designer.

For some time now instinct had been making her turn away from the bright plaids and checks that had reigned supreme in the world of fashion. She found her paint brush mixing the browns and grey and slate-blues of a more sombre world.

'Jenny, lass, you'd think you weren't happy,' Ronald protested as he looked over her shoulder one bright autumn day. 'You don't really want to put those in the pattern book for next spring?

She hesitated, head on one side, examining a check of brown and moss green. 'I think so, Ronald. I think that's what will sell.'

'Ach, you've lost your lamp-wick! Men might buy that, but women always go for the light, bright checks.'

'Yes, you may be right . . . but I think we should put half a dozen or so of my shadowy checks into the pattern book.'

Since she had been right for five or six years running, she had her way. When the cloth buyers came to look at the new plaids, they fingered the samples gingerly, looking askance at the quiet dark colours she was offering at the back of the book. Hardly an order was taken for what had been dubbed her 'shadow checks'.

She shrugged. She wasn't disappointed, for they had orders for the brighter designs, enough to keep them going without regrets for the others.

Besides, she had something to keep her happy no

matter what might happen in the world of trade. She confided her news to Ronald at the end of November, after an evening of planning for a St Andrew's Day party. This was to welcome Ned and Lucy home from a sea voyage that had completely restored his health.

'A bairn?' Ronald said, when she had told him. 'You're sure?'

She nodded.

He picked her up and swung her round. 'My lass, my love,' he carolled, 'it makes everything perfect! We'll have a son, and we'll call him Maxwell after my father, and he'll be the best dyer and weaver in the whole Border country!'

'Ssh,' she warned. 'You'll wake Mother.'

'You haven't told her yet?'

'I wanted you to know first.'

'When's it to be, Jenny my dove?'

'June — a summer baby.'

'Well, that's just right. We'll put him out in his cot in the sunshine so he can see the flowers and hear the birds —'

'He won't be bothered with that at first, husband. Newborn babies sleep most of the time.'

But Ronald continued to picture his baby son waving his fists and cooing at the flowers. Jenny hardly liked to mention the fact that babies often cried, too.

Ned returned, looking bronzed and fit. Gatesmuir was filled with happiness. St Andrew's Day came, the party was held, Lucy sparkled in a new dress à la Turque which she had brought home with her. Ned was greeted with pleasure by all his old acquaintances. The world seemed to glow with the expectation of winter revelry.

All the worse, then, was the dreadful news that

appeared in their black-bordered newspaper on 15 December.

'Yesterday at an early hour His Royal Highness Prince Albert the Prince Consort died of the typhoid fever. Her Majesty the Queen was at his bedside. Arrangements for the funeral will be announced tomorrow. A full year's mourning has been ordered at Court. It is expected that loyal citizens will observe this solemn duty also.'

The shock stunned the country. Prince Albert had not been universally popular but it was known how much the Queen loved him, and for her sake mourning was adopted by everyone who could afford to buy it. The Corvills, who had actually met the Prince, immediately put off light-coloured clothes. Most others did the same.

And so the sombre checks that Jenny had been designing in some instinctive foreknowledge were suddenly in demand. Orders flooded in. Waterside Mill was humming with activity.

'A strange thing,' Jenny said, her face pale, 'that the death of a friend and patron should bring us trade.'

'My dear lass, don't think of that,' her mother soothed. 'Don't think of death — think of new life, think of the coming baby.'

It was an old wisdom. Jenny accepted it. Yet the perfect happiness was gone, try though she might to recapture it.

Chapter Two

Newly returned from a cruise along the Mediterranean coastline, Ned and Lucy should have been the social lions of the winter season. They had stories to tell of the great market in Constantinople, the sunrise behind the Acropolis, the smoke cloud over Vesuvius.

But the death of the Prince Consort changed the social climate. When Lucy brought out the spangled caftans and embroidered silks, she found there was no opportunity to wear them — fashion was totally opposed to the idea.

Ned, on the other hand, was listened to with some respect. On the cruise ship he had made friends with a politician whose family had supported Wilberforce in his campaign to abolish slavery.

'We may have abolished it in this country,' he told the startled worthies of Galashiels, 'but others not only support it, they encourage it to flourish. Why, in Turkey, Michaels pointed out black men being sold — didn't he, my love?'

Lucy, thus appealed to, shuddered. 'Don't speak of it, my dear. I hurried on, if you remember — I didn't wish to be present.'

Ned gave her a fond glance. 'It wasn't fit for a tender heart to see, that's true. They were in chains, you know. Most shocking. Michaels told me that slavery is still rife throughout the Arabian countries. I have joined the organisation to help abolish it.' Ned stared around at the group of friends sharing a fine dinner with him. 'I hope to enlist you all in that task.'

Jenny exchanged a glance across the dinner table with Ronald, who was looking perplexed. Later, when they had said goodnight to their guests and had gone to their room, she explained.

'Ned seems to need some campaign or crusade to throw himself into. You had left Galashiels before he got involved with the Temperance Society, I think.'

'I read about that. He was stravaiging around the Borders, making speeches, was he not?'

'Yes, and very successful at making converts.' She sighed. 'But after he fell from grace himself he could hardly go on haranguing others to give up drink. So I suppose he was ready to be recruited for another great cause.'

'Well, it *is* a great cause, Jenny. You know what Burns says — "Wha sae base as be a slave".'

'Of course. I don't belittle the cause. I just wonder if Ned is really devoted to it, or if it's just that he needs something to fill the gap left by his temperance campaign.'

Ronald went to stir up the fire against the chill of the February night. 'Is it warm enough in here for you, my love? I don't want you taking the shivers, not in your delicate condition.'

'I'm fine, Ronald, fine,' she assured him, laughing. She had never felt so fit in her life, now that the pregnancy was well established.

He put his arms round her. 'I don't want you worrying about Ned,' he admonished. 'Ned has made a good recovery from his lapse and if he needs any

22

shoring up, I'll see to it. You've been too worried about him all your life, if you want my opinion.'

Jenny said nothing. Between her husband and her brother there was a sort of edgy friendship which might one day grow into real warmth, if only Ned would take a better hold on his life. Ever since he was a child, he had been subject to enthusiasms: he had yearned for a university education as if it were the Holy Grail, he had wanted to be a 'gentleman', he had started a learned treatise on Greek philosophy, he had embraced the cause of temperance . . . One by one these great goals had failed to satisfy. It was as if he were trying to escape from himself by entering into enthusiasms that might enlarge and transform him.

This latest enterprise was certainly a worthy one. When she heard Ned speak with reverence of the late John Brown, Jenny thought she heard true conviction in his voice. Brown had been a leader of the anti-slavery cause and had been hanged two years previously by the State of Virginia. To Ned, he seemed almost a martyred saint.

Now, of course, the United States of America was engulfed in civil war, the North against the South, with this very matter of slavery as the main quarrel. Ned threw himself into the business of raising funds for the Union cause, helping to organise meetings and writing to the newspapers.

Ned's wife perforce got caught up in the work. Jenny saw it happen, and couldn't help being glad. For there was no doubt Lucy had felt her nose put out of joint when she came home from her travels. She had thought to amaze the populace with her tales of life in Asia Minor, to tantalise the ladies with her exotic clothes. But what did she find?

She found a society very subdued by the loss of the Prince Consort. Worse, she found a sister-in-law who received all the attention and consideration because she was expecting a baby.

Now, however, she was meeting men of politics and letters. She gave tea parties at which the tables were decked with little Union flags. She helped make shirts and knit scarves for the Union soldiers. On the whole, it was quite enjoyable.

Even so, her attention never seemed to wander far from her sister-in-law. 'Don't you find it very wearisome to have to wear such unfashionable clothes?' she murmured to Jenny, when she came down one morning in a loose mantle.

'Needs must,' said Jenny, glancing down at herself. 'Baird is letting out my gowns. Such is life these days.'

'She's right, Lucy,' said Millicent Corvill. 'I'm strong against women lacing themselves up tight so as to get into their narrow waists at a time like this. It harms the child.' She rose from the breakfast table to go upstairs for bonnet and cape. It was nearly church time.

'You're not going to church?' Lucy said rather enviously to Jenny.

'No, I don't feel like it.'

'I thought you were always saying how well you feel?'

'Yes, I feel well. I just don't feel like church.'

Lucy's lips parted in surprise. Simply to refuse to go was an action quite beyond her. The family expected her attendance: the upright citizens of Galashiels all went to church — therefore it followed Lucy must go.

But oh, how she longed to get out of it. She hated

the boring sermons, the unaccompanied hymns, the kneeling on the bare boards for prayers. If she had to observe the proprieties by attending a service, she would rather have gone to the parish church where at least there was pleasant architecture to look at and the comfort of kneelers.

Resentment rose in her. 'I suppose you don't want to go because you feel so clumsy getting down to pray and lumbering up again,' she said unkindly.

Jenny, about to address herself to baps and butter, looked up in surprise. 'I'm not going because I don't want to,' she said, 'that's all.'

'Oh, I see. You're taking advantage of the tradition that pregnant women can have whims and fancies.'

'Lucy,' said Jenny, 'when it's your turn, I promise not to be envious if you decide to stay at home on a cold March Sunday.'

'My turn! It's never likely to be my turn.'

The maid came in, bearing smoked fish on a server. There was a little silence until she withdrew again.

Then Jenny said in a gentle tone, 'Your turn will come, Lucy. Don't worry about it.'

Lucy pushed aside her plate with unexpected violence. 'No it won't — not ever!'

'But, sister-in-law —'

'You never thought to ask, did you? The years are going by and I've never had another pregnancy since I lost my first baby. No, no, you never thought to ask — but that's what happened, that's what Ned did to me when he knocked me down!'

'Lucy!' cried Jenny, shocked beyond words. She got up and came round the table to Lucy, attempting to take her hands.

Lucy, jumping up, eluded her. 'There's never going

to be a baby for me now,' she said, the words spilling out scarcely above a whisper.

'But . . . are you sure? Did the doctor . . .?'

'He told me. There was damage after my miscarriage.'

Jenny's mind went back to that dark time when Ned had been out of his mind with alcoholic poisoning. As he was taken to the ambulance, he had resisted, and in the ensuing confusion Lucy had fallen. The baby she had been expecting consequently made its entry into the world too young to survive.

But nothing had ever been said to suggest she couldn't have another. Now that it had come out, Jenny understood her sister-in-law's envy. She regretted now that she had been so overflowingly happy about the coming child. How it must have grated on Lucy, all the planning and looking forward, the making of the layette, the choosing of the cradle.

'I wish you'd told me, Lucy,' she said with a sigh. 'It's the kind of thing that one woman should tell another.'

'Oh yes, and have everybody saying I was a poor wife to Ned. And now,' said Lucy, frowning and shivering a little, 'I suppose you'll tattle about it and everyone will know —'

'Of course not! What makes you think I would ever —' Jenny broke off. A thought had struck her. 'But, Lucy, you have in fact told Ned?'

Her sister-in-law was moving to the door of the dining room, head turned away.

'You haven't told him?'

'I don't want to talk about it,' Lucy muttered, and made her escape.

So, it was quite clear that no one except Lucy and

the doctor in Glasgow had ever known this secret. Naturally she wouldn't want to discuss it, but nevertheless, it made a difference.

Because the child Jenny was now carrying would be heir to William Corvill and Son of Waterside Mill.

Ronald was still in the house, though he was preparing to go to St Aidan's, where the service began later and ended earlier than the Secessionist Church. Jenny went upstairs to him. She had protested at Lucy's accusation of 'tattling', but she felt this was something she must discuss with her husband.

He was looking for his gloves as she came in. 'Changed your mind?' he said. 'I don't think you should go out — that wind's biting.'

'No, Ronald, it's something quite different. Put down your hat and coat. I have to tell you something.'

Her serious expression made him pause. He threw the thick black overcoat on the bed, led her to the cushioned chair in which she felt comfortable these days, and looked down at her.

'Lucy been baiting you again?'

'Lucy!' She was taken aback that he should speak her name at once.

'Oh, if there's a cloud on your brow, it's usually that one who's put it there. Dear sakes, I'd love to shake her till her brains rattle, if she has any.'

'Ronald, don't speak like that about her. I know she's difficult —'

'Difficult!'

'She was brought up with different values from ours. She —'

'She never lets a chance go by to prick at you. The way she puts it, you'd think having a baby was a sin against elegance and propriety —'

'There's a reason. Ronald, I've just been talking to her and she blurted it out. She says . . . that she can't have children.'

'What?' He was startled, then second thoughts came. 'But I understood — didn't I hear there had been a baby — ?'

'Yes, that's the point. She lost it, very early in her time. And the doctor told her she would never have another.'

Ronald went to the fireplace to kick at the remains of the morning's bedroom fire. 'Ach,' he said. 'I'm sorry.'

'You see what a lot it explains? No wonder she's been so . . . so . . .'

'So ill-natured. Well, mebbe it's that, though I noticed from the first that she leaped at any chance to take you down a peg or two.' He stared down at the small flicker of life in the fire. 'Are you sure it's true? She's not just saying it to get sympathy and make you feel guilty?'

'Ronald! She wouldn't do that!'

'Oh, would she no? She's been sore put out at the way she's had to take second place ever since she got back from her legendary trip to the Middle East. I wouldn't put it past — '

'No, no, my dear, this was the truth. She didn't mean to tell me, it all came gushing out, and then she was terribly afraid I'd tell everybody and make her look small.'

'And now you've told me.'

'Never let her know I've told you, Ronald. Promise me.'

'I'm not likely to be having little confabs with Mrs Edward Corvill, Jenny.'

'No, but never let it slip out, never — I was going to say, never taunt her, but I know you never would.'

He stooped, picked his wife up out of the chair, and kissed her while they wrapped their arms about each other. 'My lass, you're too tolerant of that girl, but it's like you to be so. However, I know you. Why have you told this secret to me, instead of wrapping it up and putting it away with the other skeletons in the family cupboard?'

'I want your opinion. It's important. You see, husband, I think it's very likely Ned doesn't know.'

'Eh?' said Ronald inelegantly.

'From the way she acted I think, in fact I'm almost sure, she's never told Ned.'

'Mercy on us,' said Ronald, and let Jenny go sufficiently far to look at her troubled face. He smoothed back her dark hair from her brow. 'Well, then, don't fret about it. It's none of our business.'

'But Ronald . . .'

'It's none of our business, Jenny. It's up to Ned and Lucy how much they confide in each other.'

Jenny nodded, resting against him with some relief. But conscience forced her to go on. 'You see, Ronald, Ned owns William Corvill and Son.'

A silence.

'Waterside Mill and all that it implies is legally Ned's.'

Still no reply.

'If what Lucy says is true, and I feel it in my bones to be true, Ned can never have an heir.'

A long indrawn breath. Then Ronald said, 'Dear God. What a mess.'

They stood in silence for a moment. Then Ronald

29

began to untie his cravat, as if preparing to change into less formal clothes.

'What are you doing?'

'I think we ought to sit down and talk about this.'

'No, darling — please!' She looked really alarmed, he noted. 'If you change your mind and stay at home, Lucy will know I've told you and we've talked about it.'

'Oh.' His hand paused in its tugging at the silk bow. 'Aye, you're right.'

'You must go to church as you intended. We'll talk about it this evening.'

Evening, when they had gone to their own room, was a time when they often had long, undirected discussions about the usual problems that came up — at the mill, at the house, in the community.

That evening they went upstairs as soon as Ned's reading from Macaulay ended. It was clear Ronald's mind had been ranging far all through the preceding hours.

'Tell me, Jenny, has Ned made a will?'

'Yes, Mr Kennet insisted on it when Father died. As far as I remember, it leaves the firm to Lucy. In the event of their having children, the will was to be revoked in favour of another. Mr Kennet has the draft. I think it goes to the effect that everything goes to his son or, if no son, to his eldest daughter — something like that.'

'Nothing to you?' Ronald said, shocked.

'Oh yes, you know of course that Mother and I own the house and grounds here, and I was to get — I forget what, a share of the profits throughout my lifetime.'

'It's damnable!' He was angry. 'The ingratitude of

it! You earn every penny he spends on himself and that doll of a wife —'

'Ronald —'

'Don't protest, it's a disgrace and if you hadn't been brought up a strict Huguenot woman you'd feel it. Jenny, where's your business sense?'

She sighed and tried to explain. 'It was always the way in the Huguenot community. The men managed the business and the things of the world, the women ran the home and brought up the children. I never imagined myself inheriting anything to do with the business —'

'But you made it, you built it up, it's yours if it's anyone's.'

'I know, I know, but I never did it for the money, Ronald. It was to be someone, to achieve something — not for the money.'

'I accept that. But things are different now, my lass. You are the moving spirit in William Corvill and Son —'

'No, no, I've stepped aside —'

'Ha!' snorted her husband. He patted her hand with kindly tolerance. 'You're about as capable of stepping aside as an old barge-horse — you'd drown in the canal water if you didn't keep to your well-worn path.'

Jenny felt herself blushing. 'I'm sorry, Ronald, I never meant to get in your way.'

'Did I say you had? Its true I thought to see you keep to the home-place more, but who else could have handled those insurance rascals? Who had dark checks on the loom for when they were needed? And who's drawing up plans for enlarging Waterside to while away her pregnancy?'

'Oh! I didn't know you knew about that.'

'No, I never noticed when you hastily put away sheets of drawings in the desk drawer. Nor did I observe you pacing out the distance to the boundary wall of Messiter's Mill.'

Jenny began to laugh. 'You're gey clever, Ronald Armstrong.'

'I'm not as green as I'm cabbage-looking, as the saying goes. But look you here, lassie. All that just goes to show I'm right in what I say. You have the good of William Corvill and Son at heart, you make it a success — and it's grossly unfair that Ned never makes any acknowledgement of the fact.'

'I don't want Ned's gratitude —'

'But you ought to have justice. Ned ought to pay you a salary, just as he pays me —'

'No, no! I could never ask it!'

'And,' said Ronald, disregarding her protest, 'he should leave the firm to you.'

'It's impossible, Ronald —'

'Because I'll tell you one thing,' he ended, rather grim, 'if anything ever happened to Ned, and Lucy inherited, she'd have us out of there so fast our boots would make sparks on the stones.'

There was enough truth in this to make Jenny very thoughtful. Then she said, 'She wouldn't do anything that might make her look bad in the eyes of society. Nor would she want to damage her own fortunes.'

'I'm glad you see her clearly enough to admit that.'

'And in the first place, Ronald, Ned isn't going to die. He's got forty of his three score years and ten still to come.'

'Yes?' her husband demurred. 'And when he has some setback that tips him over into drink again, can you guarantee he won't fall under a carter's dray?'

Jenny put her hands up to her ears. 'Don't say things like that!'

'Ach, I wish you didn't have such a fondness for the man, Jenny! It hurts you even to think he might scratch himself on his own tie-pin. Well, let's suppose he lives a long and honoured life. The time must come when he realises he's not going to have any children −'

'That's looking too far ahead, my dear. And Ned isn't thinking of things like that.'

'No, his mind is set on raising two thousand pounds for a first aid wagon for the Union Army.' Ronald sighed. 'Nor can we mention any of this to him, I suppose.'

'No.'

'Unless . . .'

'What?'

'Are you really going to expand Waterside Mill?'

Jenny went to the bureau by the window. From the drawer she took out sheets of cartridge paper. She had never been good at representational art but she had drawn up in pencil a careful plan of the mill as it now stood, with a rough sketch of its frontage and a view of the abandoned mill which stood at the back.

'You see, Messiter's goes down to the Old Mill Lead, which never proved satisfactory as regards the flow of water.'

'But that, of course, could be remedied if someone would pay an engineer to construct a proper water gauge.'

'As you say,' Jenny agreed, suppressing a smile. 'My thinking is this. It's time for William Corvill and Son to extend their range into plain tweeds −'

'Plain tweeds?' Ronald said, astounded.

Jenny had had the idea in her head a long time. Once, sitting on the hill above Galashiels, she had looked down at the colours of the town on a cloudy day. She had seen soft, muted tones — slate grey, sandstone red, river-water brown. She had thought then, I could make a tweed cloth, a soft mixture cloth, with those shades. It could be as beautiful in its way as a tartan. One day, I'll make a plain cloth.

'There's a coming market for soft tweed,' she said. 'You'll see.'

'No doubt,' said her husband drily.

'I'm going to get Ned to speak to Mr Kennet about buying Messiter's.'

'Is that a fact?' But there was no real question in the tone. 'Well, while you're speaking to Mr Kennet, it wouldn't be difficult to introduce the notion of a fair share of the firm being put in your name.'

'No, Ronald!'

'But why not? You're not asking for anything unfair. You're only asking for your just deserts.'

'But Ned and I . . . we've never discussed such a thing. We've never had any thought of it . . .'

'Then it's time you did.'

'It sounds so grasping!'

'Jenny,' Ronald said, 'if you won't ask it for yourself, ask it for the boy. When he comes into the world, he deserves to have a share of what his mother has built up.'

His words silenced her objections. Though her upbringing made it impossible for her to insist on rights for herself, she wanted everything that was right and good for Ronald's child.

So in the course of the next few months she put the idea of the expansion of Waterside Mill to her brother.

Once he had been convinced that this was a good and
workable idea, he took the project to their lawyer.

Mr Kennet had been half-expecting something like
this for a long time. He had been the family lawyer
ever since they had come to Galashiels and, moreover,
was part of their social circle. His antennae had been
telling him for almost a year that Mistress Corvill
— or Mistress Armstrong, as he must foree himself
to call her — would want to enlarge their premises
soon.

Ronald Armstrong was called into the discussions,
of course, because the joining of Waterside to the
rebuilt Messiter's concerned him greatly. As the four
of them sat in Mr Kennet's office taking tea after an
hour poring over blueprints, it seemed only natural to
speak of the forthcoming baby.

Mr Kennet had long had his own view on the
injustice of the legal situation concerning William
Corvill and Son. He surprised Ronald by taking
matters into his own hands.

'I suppose, Mr Corvill,' he said to Ned, 'that you'll
wish to make some disposition of the assets to take
notice of your sister's child.'

'What?' Ned said in surprise.

'Of course it's a family matter,' Kennet said in an
apologetic tone, 'and of course you would come to it
after the birth. But your mind is so greatly taken up
at present with the war in America that I take the
liberty of reminding you. I'm sure you wouldn't want
to be remiss on something so important to your sister.'

'Oh . . . ah . . . naturally, I would of course have
. . . What exactly is expected in such a situation?' said
Ned, looking pink with embarrassment. He had never
in this world given a thought to providing anything

for Jenny's child. He never thought about money unless it was linked to one of his enthusiasms.

'This is hardly the time,' Jenny said, equally embarrassed.

'Quite, quite, your brother will wish to see me on another occasion to talk it over. I just felt this was an opportunity to remind you I'm at your service, Mr Corvill.'

Ronald was sipping his tea and grinning to himself behind the cup. What an old fox! But good for him, he had made easy the opening of a discussion that might have been difficult.

What was said between Ned and the lawyer never became public. But privately Ned said to Ronald, 'It crossed my mind, your boy . . . it might turn out he will be the heir to William Corvill and Son.'

'Good heavens, man, that's looking far too far ahead.'

'Well, you know, Ronald, Lucy and I have no children after nearly six years. Who knows? At any rate I thought I'd tell you that . . . well, I've talked to Kennet. Your boy will be well provided for.'

And then Nature, with her usual irony, played her part. Jenny's baby was a girl.

Chapter Three

Jenny was leaning back among her pillows in a mixture of exhaustion, triumph, and tearful apprehension when Ronald was allowed in.

'You won't be too disappointed?' she asked as he tiptoed towards the ribbon-decked cradle at the bedside.

'Disappointed? Why should I be disappointed?' he asked in astonishment.

'Well, you wanted a boy . . . '

'Who ever told you that?'

He leaned over the cradle for his first view of his daughter. She was asleep, fairish hair only hinted at beneath the edge of the crocheted bonnet. Her face was crumpled and flushed like a pink poppy in the bud. One tiny fist was folded against her cheek.

Ronald put his forefinger into the curled fist. Instinctively she grasped it. And like every father, Ronald was captured for ever.

'Ah, my bonnie wee lass,' he whispered to her.

When he turned to kiss Jenny, he was smiling broadly.

'And what's so funny?' she asked, the threatening tears giving way to puzzlement.

'One thing's sure. We canna call her Maxwell!'

Argument went on for a week or two about a name

for the baby. In the meantime the servants called her the bairn, Mrs Corvill Senior called her Baby, and Lucy called her the infant. Jenny suggested names from her grandmothers — Yvonne, Heloise. Ronald thought something typically Scottish would be better; his own mother had been Agnes.

But nothing seemed right for the little slumbering child. In the end her name came by chance. Ronald, allowed to hold her, took her to the window to see the sun on the hills. It was early July, the heather was coming into bloom.

The baby blinked in the light. Some tint or shadow reflected back for a moment on her shawl so that she seemed in a cloud of pale amethyst.

'That's what we'll call her!' exclaimed Ronald.

'What, my love?'

'Heather!'

'Heather?'

'Yes, it just suits her.'

'But nobody is ever called Heather, Ronald.'

'I don't see why not. Little girls are called Rose and Violet — why not Heather?'

There was no reason why not. Somehow it seemed to suit her. Heather Millicent Armstrong she was christened, and a few years later the name was not only accepted but became quite fashionable.

At first Jenny was more than content to stay at home, watching over the baby, supervising her bathing and dressing and sleeping. The nursemaid was tolerant. New mothers were often like this, and so were grandmamas and aunts.

At first Lucy resisted the charms of the baby. She wished to have as little to do with her as possible. But as the weeks went by and Heather spent less time asleep, Lucy could be found leaning over her cradle, cooing at her.

'It's a side of Lucy I never expected to see,' Ronald remarked one afternoon as, from the far side of the lawn, he watched his sister-in-law dangling her silver pendant over the crib under the apple tree.

'And you like her the better for it.'

'Well, anyone who admires Heather must have some good in her, Jenny.'

She laughed and patted his arm. 'You're biased.'

'That might well be. But you must admit she's a lovely little lass.'

'I admit it, I admit it. So much so that I've designed a plaid for her.'

Ronald raised his eyebrows at his wife. 'I thought you weren't going to think about work for at least six months?'

'Oh, it's not work to design a plaid.'

'That's not what you used to say when the pattern book needed filling.'

'This just came to me. I thought we might put it in the book for next spring now that colour is coming back into fashion — it's a blue and brown check on a lavender background.'

'And its name in the pattern book will be — ?'

'Need you ask? Heather!'

Other ideas seemed to follow fast on the new plaid, so that without being aware of it Jenny was soon back in the swing of work. There was the expansion to supervise — the redesigning and rebuilding of Messiter's old mill to unite it with Waterside. She made a ceremony of it. The Provost was asked to unveil a plaque. The town band played. The mill workers were given a half-holiday.

39

The extension was given over to the making of plain or mixed tweeds. The yarn used for the subtle shades in Jenny's designs involved 'doubling', the twisting together of two strands before the weaving began. Ronald was in his element in the new works with a range of dyes at his disposal to produce the tints she needed. As a result, Jenny herself took over some of the management of the firm, or supervising the fastening and winding of the threads for the new 'fancy' tweeds which were generally woven in short runs to specific orders.

It meant that she spent much less time at home. In fact, she was almost as often at Waterside Mill as in the old days. She came home with Ronald for lunch, and enjoyed that — the walk through Galashiels during the working day, the meeting with acquaintances, the casual chat about the morning's routine as they walked. At first Ronald had insisted she take a rest in the afternoon, but within three months this had been forgotten. She would go back with him to Waterside to consider the designs for next season, or entertain buyers, or speak with the auditors.

As winter approached there was the usual conference among the ladies of Gatesmuir about the parties they would give. St Andrew's Day had become a customary highlight and then there was Christmas to consider. Lucy was full of plans.

'We must have a Christmas tree —'

'A tree?' interrupted Mrs Corvill in surprise. 'How do you mean — we should go outdoors into the wood — ?'

'No, no, it's in all the magazines, Mother,' Lucy said, in the patronising tone she sometimes used in response to Millicent's naivety. 'You have a fir tree in a pot indoors, and decorate it with sugar mice and sparkling ornaments. Heather will love it.'

'Oh, it's a children's thing. But is Heather no a bitty young for it?'

'Nonsense, she'll be six months, she'll love something all sparkly and with candles.'

'Candles. Not lit up?'

'Of course.'

'Is that not a dangerous notion?'

'Of course not, we'll be careful. You agree we should have one, don't you, Jenny? For Heather?'

Jenny had nothing against it, so long as the candles were only lit for brief periods and under guard. And truth to tell, it was a beautiful thing, this new Christmas symbol that the late Prince Consort had helped to bring to Britain.

What did trouble her was the number of presents Lucy had bought for Heather. She had gone to Glasgow, and it seemed she had come home with every toy that a little girl could possibly want. Most of them were for a child much older than Heather. There were china dolls, puppets on sticks, tin dogs and monkeys, beads to thread, puzzles to put together.

'Mercy me, girl,' Millicent cried when she saw the gifts unwrapped on Christmas morning, 'you've enough there to keep the bairn occupied until she's ten years old!'

Lucy laughed, kneeling on the floor to offer the baby a fairy doll. 'It's good to have plenty of things to occupy her. You don't realise how quick she is — she's interested in everything that goes on.'

Heather refused to be interested in the doll. Instead she was making determined efforts to roll over on her front so that she might try to squirm towards a length of bright ribbon on the carpet.

'Any minute now she'll be trying to walk,' Lucy said, watching her proudly.

'What, at six months?'

'You don't see as much of her as I do, Jenny. She's dying to get at the things that interest her. Look how she's struggling to get at that ribbon.'

The baby's strength gave out, she collapsed on her face in a muddle of long gowns and her shawl, and began to howl. The nurse, Wilmot, came to bear her off to bed.

The grown-ups went to church, friends came for a Christmas dinner, and then thoughts turned to the really important celebration, Hogmanay. Every house in Galashiels had to be cleaned from top to bottom to welcome in the New Year, supplies of black bun, shortbread, port and whisky had to be laid in, and presents bought for first-footing.

Gatesmuir was open and ablaze with lights when the chimes of midnight rang out. Kisses and hugs were exchanged, and within a few seconds Ronald came in at the front door bearing the obligatory piece of coal to ensure warmth and comfort for another year.

Then the first-footers began to arrive. The ladies of Gatesmuir were in their best gowns, and music was provided by two fiddlers from the mill.

In the midst of the first set of toasts and greetings, Jenny was amazed to see the nurse Wilmot coming downstairs with the baby in her arms. What was more, the baby wasn't in her flannel night-gown but in a 'company robe' of embroidered net over satin.

Jenny threaded her way to her through the crowd. 'Wilmot! What on earth are you doing?'

The nurse looked surprised. She glanced around as if in some confusion. 'But I thought, I was told . . .'

'Told what?' Jenny's voice was sharper than she intended. She saw the colour come up on Wilmot's broad face. 'I'm sorry, nanny, I didn't mean to snap at you. Why have you brought the baby downstairs in the middle of the night?'

'I thought I was meant to, mistress.'

'What gave you that idea?'

'I . . . well . . . Mistress Corvill told me to.'

'Mistress Ned Corvill?'

'Yes, ma'am.'

Jenny was just about to tell her to take Heather back up to her cot when one of the lady visitors caught sight of her. 'Oh, the baby's down to wish us a good New Year. What a little angel. Let me hold her a minute, nanny.'

'No, Mrs Wallace –' But Jenny was too late. Heather was taken out of the nurse's arms to be crooned over like a little doll. Lucy came up to hear the compliments, and in a moment or two all the ladies were clustered round, admiring the marvellous robe which had come, so Lucy said, from the best shop in Glasgow.

Naturally Heather became over-excited and began to cry. Wilmot took her upstairs to bed, but when Jenny went up at two-thirty to check that all was well, the baby was still crying and Wilmot was still trying to soothe her to sleep.

'I cannna do a thing with her, mistress,' she said, with a mixture of distress and irritation.

'I don't wonder at it,' Jenny said, concealing her own annoyance. The baby was crying in that stretched, whining fashion that becomes an established pattern until exhaustion ensues.

43

Wilmot was swallowing her yawns.

'You go to bed. I'll get Heather off.'

'Oh, are you sure, ma'am?'

'Off you go, nanny.'

The nurse went to the alcove that housed her bed. Jenny picked Heather out of her cradle, sat down, and began to rock her to and fro.

> 'This is the way the weaver goes,
> A-rickelty-tick, a rickelty-tick,
> The treadle down with his heel and toes,
> A-rickelty-tick, a-rickelty-tick . . . '

It was a song of her own childhood, with a gentle rhythm and a tune of the utmost simplicity. There were hand-movements that went with it, little pats on the head and the feet to keep the child amused. But for now it was a lulling motion, a voice that brought comfort. To the steady background of snores from the nurse, Jenny sang her child to sleep.

Next day, New Year's Day, was a day of visiting and activity. Nevertheless Jenny managed to keep an eye on her little daughter. It took all day for her to settle back into her usual happy frame of mind after the upset of being wakened and dressed in the middle of the night.

Now Jenny was alerted. She began to see how much Lucy was engrossed by Heather. The trouble was, Lucy had almost nothing else to do but amuse herself with the baby. The house was run by the elder Mrs Corvill, the mill was run by Jenny and Ronald, and there was little companionship to be found with Ned.

Ned was taken up altogether with his work for the anti-slavery movement. In America, the war see-sawed back and forth — the Union army had lost the second battle at Bull Run, but Lincoln had the courage to declare that all slaves in his country would be considered free as from the beginning of this new year, 1863. Ned had barely spared the time to come home from London for New Year — there was work to be done in publicising Lincoln's speech, and in urging Her Majesty's Government to admit liability over the cruiser *Alabama*.

Jenny found his devotion to his cause encouraging. He seemed never to think of taking a drink, his faith in his own abilities was firm, his life was full. But, of course, looked at another way, he was neglecting his wife.

If Lucy had been the least bit interested in helping him, that would have been ideal. But his political friends bored and alarmed her. They discussed matters she thought indelicate — the fate of black women at the hands of Arab slavers, the punishment meted out to escapers.

Lucy preferred the social and domestic round. And, with little left for her to do at Gatesmuir, it was only natural that she should give all her attention to baby Heather.

It was difficult not to feel sympathy with her. Being condemned to a childless marriage had something almost tragic in it, a sense of being excluded from the blessings everyone else enjoyed. Practically all the married women of Lucy's age had children, some three or four; 'a fine young family', as the complimentary phrase had it. It would have been almost impossible for Lucy not to feel as if she had some rights in the pretty, good-tempered baby in her own home.

Yet Heather was on the verge of becoming

hopelessly spoiled. Lucy thought nothing of waking her from sound sleep to play with her. If she so much as whimpered, her doting aunt was ready to pick her up and amuse her.

The convention in upper-class circles was that children should be banished to the nursery except at the set times when they were brought down to be shown off. This was when Jenny herself had the opportunity to play with her baby, to cuddle her and make a fuss of her. But Lucy found away round this — she went up to the nursery to interfere with Wilmot's regime. Wilmot didn't actually say that the younger Mrs Corvill was making a nuisance of herself, but there were little edged remarks, hints that the baby was 'getting above herself' because she got too much attention.

Jenny understood Lucy's feelings. She didn't want to forbid her to spend so much time with the child, nor could she herself be at home more because this was a very busy time at the cloth mill. Besides, it would have meant being in open competition with Lucy over her own daughter — a situation fraught with dangers.

Heaven sent a distraction. In March of that year, the Prince of Wales was to marry the Princess Alexandra of Denmark. Galashiels decided to celebrate the occasion with high festivity. The *Galashiels Record* announced that there would be 'a Public Procession of Magistrates, Police Commissioners, the Manufacturers' Corporation, the Volunteer Regiment, the Freemasons, and other notables'. The town was to be decorated, flowerbeds planted with royal emblems, there would be a firework display on the banks of the Gala Hill, and the town band would give a concert outdoors if the weather was fine.

Naturally all this had to be organised. Without any difficulty, Jenny saw to it that Lucy was well to the fore — and in fact Lucy's love of everything shiny and gilded fitted in very well with the designs of the Decorations Committee.

Later in the year, on their way north for a summer visit to Balmoral, the young royal couple made a tour of the Borders. Prince Edward was handsome in a more robust style than his late father; his skin had more colour and his manner was much more rakish. In his cutaway coat and curly-brimmed bowler hat, he was like some fashion plate.

His bride seemed an ideal fairytale princess. She was beautiful, good-natured, kind, tactful. In the few months since her marriage she had already endeared herself to the population of London, and Galashiels was just as ready to fall under her spell. She allowed almost everyone to be presented, although there were some signs of boredom from her husband at the stream of townsfolk.

When Mr and Mrs Edward Corvill were brought forward, the Prince of Wales brightened. Here at last was a pretty young woman who knew how to dress. As she made her curtsy, he leaned forward.

'Corvill?' he said. He had been briefed by his equerry. 'The makers of the fine tartans?'

'My sister Mrs Armstrong is in charge of the work, Your Highness,' Ned replied, in all honesty. He turned to Jenny, who was next in line with Ronald.

The Prince beamed. *Another* pretty woman! My word, there was something to be said for these Border lasses.

'The Queen has spoken of you,' Princess Alexandra said, having looked at the notes handed to her by her

lady-in-waiting before the audience. 'I am very glad
to make your acquaintance, Mrs Armstrong.'

'Thank you, Your Highness. I hope to have the
honour of sending you a piece of plaid as a memento
of your visit to Galashiels.'

'I shall be pleased to receive it.'

'Yes, indeed,' put in Prince Edward. 'And if ever
you come to London for the season it would be a
pleasure to see you.'

Lucy was in seventh heaven. To be spoken to by the
Prince and Princess! To be more or less invited to
come to London! Nothing could be more splendid.

Except, of course, actually to go to London and be
included in the royal circle of acquaintances.

At first Jenny resisted the notion. But as the year
went on more problems arose in the household. The
baby went into short frocks, which gave Lucy an
opportunity to buy silks and lawns and broderie
anglaise for her. Wilmot was driven to distraction by
orders to change the child's clothes the moment a speck
of dirt appeared. Little Heather became somewhat
nervy and a little wilful at being treated like some kind
of animated doll.

Lucy quite clearly had nothing else to do. Galashiels
had sunk back into its workaday self after the glories
of the royal visit, so everything seemed even more dull
and unfashionable. Ned was in London for meetings
with the Free-the-Slaves Committee, there was no one
to squire Lucy even to a day or two in Peebles or
Edinburgh.

'I don't like to speak ill of anyone,' Millicent Corvill
said to her daughter, 'but I do think Lucy is becoming
very difficult. If one so much as says a word to her,
she snaps your head off, Jenny.'

'She's bored.'

Millicent shook her head. 'I don't understand it. There's so much to be done in the world, there's no time to be bored.'

But not from Lucy's point of view, thought Jenny.

She spent three or four days thinking it over. And then she decided that after all it might not be a bad thing to take a house in London in time for the winter season. After all, Ned spent a great deal of time there, living in hotels — it would be no bad thing to have a proper residence. And then, William Corvill and Son were a firm of considerable consequence; it would look well if the Corvills had a London home for entertaining the overseas businessmen who didn't care to make the trip to Galashiels.

It would reunite Lucy with her husband. It would take her away from the nursery at Gatesmuir. It would give her something to do, for what could be more entertaining than staying in a good hotel while she looked for a suitable house?

So next time Ned returned to London on Abolitionist business, Lucy went with him. She wrote enthusiastically of the shops, the concerts, the exhibitions — but not at all, Jenny noted with amusement, of any meetings with Ned's colleagues.

Early in October she came back to Galashiels to say that she had looked at a house in Belgravia which seemed to her ideal. If Jenny would come to inspect it and give her approval, the lawyers could draw up the lease.

The difference in Lucy was extraordinary. She was aglow with vivacity and happiness. She gossiped of the new friends she had made. Every morning letters came, as evidence of those friendships.

Jenny couldn't help noticing how her sister-in-law would snatch up one particular letter out of the collection on the salver. But it was almost a week before the significance sank in. The special letters were always in the same handwriting — a strong, dashing hand. A man's hand. And that daydreaming look when she sat with it in her hand afterwards . . .

She's in love, thought Jenny, with a sudden sinking of the heart. What have I done? I sent her to London to make life easier here at home, and now . . . now . . .

She didn't want to believe it. She was reading too much into what she saw, she was misjudging her sister-in-law. Just because Lucy was elated over one particular letter, that didn't necessarily mean anything special.

What was best to do? Cancel all thoughts of a house in London? But that was hardly fair on such scant evidence, and besides, how would she account for such a sudden change of heart? It seemed best to go ahead. She would go to London with Lucy to look at the house and perhaps get a better idea of how things stood.

She said nothing of this to anyone. If she was wrong, least said was soonest mended. And she prayed she was wrong, because otherwise trouble loomed ahead. Lucy could be so self-centred, so blinkered, when something caught her fancy. It was with some foreboding that she left Galashiels with her sister-in-law on the south-bound train one bright cold morning in late autumn.

Chapter Four

The house which Lucy had chosen was in Eaton Square, on the west side, facing St Peter's Church. Lucy was more eager to show it off than the clerk from the lawyer's office.

'You see, very spacious, and one of course uses the big room on the first floor as the drawing room so that one can have a view of the gardens from the windows. And plenty of bedrooms, although I fear the night nursery may have to be in the attic —'

Jenny caught up with her sister-in-law so as not to have to call after her in the hearing of their escort. 'I shan't be bringing Heather to London, Lucy.'

'What?' Lucy swung round, crinoline swaying under the impetus of her startled movement. 'Why not?'

'It would be too much of an upset for her, I think. Besides, I shan't be in London so very much myself.'

'You won't?' Lucy looked put out at first, then perplexed. 'Then I don't see . . . '

'Oh, I shall come — perhaps once a month or so. And Ronald may be here at other times. He's said more than once that he'd like to attend various lectures at the Royal Institute and so forth. But in the main, I think you and Ned will be the residents at Eaton Square.'

Lucy brightened. It was easy to see her picturing

herseIf acting hostess to all kinds of charming people, having little at-homes, soirées, congeries.

'Ned's income is quite considerable these days, the profits from the mill being so high,' Jenny went on. 'And, of course, he has spent very little in the last year or so —'

'Apart from the absurdly large donations he's made to the Abolitionist Society.'

'Well, I suppose so. He never mentioned the actual sums to me. What I'm saying, Lucy, is that you ought to be able to run the place and entertain up to a reasonable standard — although you won't be expected to do as much as a society hostess, thank heaven.'

Lucy went into the dining room. This was a room she admired particularly. It had been fitted up after the style recommended by Ruskin: 'Where you can rest, there decorate.' The walls were covered in flock paper of a rich dark red, a mantelpiece of carved brown marble held porcelain figures and two matching lamps with crystal pendant shades, festoons of maroon velvet draped the windows, and an oval walnut table stood on a Turkey carpet.

She could picture it with her guests around it, with the silver and cut glass glimmering, the hothouse flowers scenting the air, footmen in well-cut livery gliding about with serving dishes of French food. And one particular guest would be there. She smiled to herself as she thought of him.

Jenny had no difficulty in picking him out when they at last met. Lucy and Ned had taken her to a performance of Mr Dion Boucicault's, recently returned from the United States. There was a fashionable attendance at the Adelphi Theatre-Royal to welcome him back, and at the first interval, after the attendant had brought refreshments, visiting from box to box was the thing to do.

Harvil Massiter appeared, very elegant in his evening clothes. He was a little this side of thirty, with dark eyes under medium-brown brows and a somewhat romantic mop of brown hair.

'Dear lady,' he said, bowing over Lucy's hand. 'How delightful to see you again.' He straightened, and gave a friendly nod towards Ned. 'Corvill, old man − this isn't your usual kind of thing − no little blackamoors here to take pity on.'

This was an allusion to a previous theatrical event, at which Ned had caused an upset by complaining loudly over the exploitation of four little negro acrobats. Ned blushed a little, and to cover his embarrassment turned the subject.

'We're here to give my sister a taste of the comic genius of Mr Boucicault,' he murmured. 'Jenny, allow me to present Mr Massiter, who came to one of our charity events when His Royal Highness was good enough to give us his patronage.'

Mr Massiter bowed over Jenny's gloved fingers. She had a feeling he held them too long, but perhaps that was just imagination.

'Mr Massiter is on friendly terms with the Prince,' Lucy said proudly. 'They have interests in common.'

'Indeed? Matters of state?' inquired Jenny, and would have been very surprised had the answer been in the affirmative.

'Good lord, no − horses! Teddy loves to see his horses run. Are you interested in horse racing, Mrs Armstrong?'

'I'm afraid not.'

'What a pity. I should have enjoyed showing you the glories of Newmarket.'

Other visitors arrived at that moment, which was perhaps just as well since Lucy was looking faintly annoyed at the attention Jenny was receiving. Conversation became general, Jenny preferring to listen rather than talk. She was startled to hear a reference to 'Mrs Massiter'.

She sat up. 'Is she here?' she asked Ned, under cover of some banter among the others.

'Who?'

'Mrs Massiter.'

'Oh, yes, she's yonder, in the box under the chandelier.' Jenny put her opera glasses to her eyes, glanced idly about, and without being noticed studied Harvil Massiter's wife. Mrs Massiter was as elegant as her husband, but the effect was marred by lack of subtlety in the use of rouge and rice powder. Clearly Mrs Massiter wanted to be as young as her spouse, but it wasn't easy to disguise the ten-year difference in their ages.

The interval ended, the visitors left the box, and Jenny settled back to enjoy the second act of the comedy. But her mind wasn't entirely on it.

Lucy's admirer was not the kind of man to be under-rated. Perhaps after all it would be better to change the plan and decide against the house in Eaton Square. What reason she could give, she hardly knew. She would have to make up her mind soon, because the lawyer wanted to know whether or not to draw up a lease.

Next morning the problem was solved for her. As they sat at a leisurely breakfast in their suite at the Hyde Park Hotel, a note was delivered to Lucy. Jenny saw her sister-in-law colour up with vexation, quickly veiled.

'Anything important, my love?' asked Ned from behind his copy of *The Times*.

'From Mrs Massiter. She sends apologies for not being able to call and make your acquaintance this morning, Jenny, but they are off to the country for the shooting.'

Of course, the winter shooting – the ducks and the geese and the partridges. Silently Jenny blessed them. And she blessed Mrs Massiter too, who clearly had her wits about her. Perhaps the forty-year-old wife of a handsome, lighthearted thirty-year-old husband had to be on the alert at all times.

It was reassuring. Lucy might be romantically inclined towards Harvil, but so long as Maud Massiter remained on guard nothing serious was likely to come of it.

Much encouraged by this little sidelight, Jenny sent a message to Prym, Lightfoot and Sivier to say that she would like to have the lease of Number Forty-one Eaton Square made ready as soon as convenient.

Although the place was taken ready-furnished, there were nevertheless changes and improvements to be made. Lucy found solace in busying herself with these. Jenny left her to it, having first reminded her that all items put in store from the house must be returned when the inventory was checked at the end of their tenure and that, although money was in fact no object, it would be as well to stay within certain guidelines of expense.

'You needn't worry about any of that, Jenny, it's not fashionable to be ostentatious. The Princess of Wales was quite poor before her marriage, you know

— she's set a fashion for rather simple entertaining. And as for not having our own carriage . . . Well, certainly there's no lack of hackneys but perhaps by and by we might think about it.'

Jenny went home to the Borders quite determined not to think about private carriages for London or any other such extraneous matter. She had weaving designs to set down on paper for the spring pattern book, there were difficulties about exporting to the United States in view of the Civil War, and in Europe the German princes had been meeting to reform their confederation, which might mean new taxes on imports. In view of these problems manufacturers had been setting up consultation groups, some of which she would have to attend.

When talking to Ronald and her mother about her London visit, she said nothing to single out Harvil Massiter from the rest of the new London friends she'd met. If Lucy wanted to flirt with him, that was no one's business but her own. Jenny's worries about it had been much relieved on noting that Harvil's wife could look after herself.

Lucy wrote regularly. At first it was to boast, in her usual uncertain spelling, about the improvements she was making.

'I have set aside a study for Ned, so that he can have his Political Friends to see him without interfering with the household arangments and if I have guests to tea or a cosery, he doesn't feel he has to come and be polyte because in fact I notice in London that Husbands and Wives have their own Seprate Interests a great deel more than in Galashiels whitch I find much more Agreeable

56

and allows me to have the morning room decorrated with lace vallences to make it much more Femanine for morning visitors who of course are mostly ladies as you will apresiate.'

As Christmas drew near again, she announced that she was planning alterations to provide a small conservatory 'which is all the raige since HRH is so fond of hothouse flowers'. She therefore would return home to Galashiels while the workmen would be 'clumping about and hamering'. Moreover, she would be able to bring with her all the wonderful presents she had bought for little Heather. 'I miss Heather grately. I'm sure she mises me too.'

Jenny couldn't honestly reply that her little daughter missed her aunt. The baby was now eighteen months old, a bubbling, happy child, ready to hold out her arms to anyone who would pick her up and talk to her, ready for nursery rhymes and singing games of 'This is the Way the Lady Rides' or 'Rickelty-tick'. But it did no harm to say she was sure Heather would be glad to see Lucy again.

Events fell out quite conveniently. Jenny had to go to London to give evidence to a parliamentary committee about exports to America. Lucy would take her to one or two evening parties: 'It will be an opurtunity for you to get to know the princess, who is gracousness itself. We can then travvel home together whitch find much more Agreeable than travling Alone because one needs someone to talk to.'

Jenny had Baird pack some evening finery as well as the dark day clothes thought suitable (if anything could really be suitable) for a woman of business. Ronald saw her off at the station. 'Explain to those parliamentary eedjits that trade has to go on, Jenny. A nervous crisis between British and American admirals is no help.'

'I'll do my best. And for your part, make Ritchie find that fault in the scribbling machines —'

'Yes, yes, and bring back those statistics from the Board of Trade for Muir —'

'I've made a note of it. Don't forget the special delivery from the wool stapler in Hamburg —'

'And in the intervals of fitting it all in,' Ronald said, laughing as the train began to move, 'have a good time!'

She intended to. She was going primarily for business reasons but there was no law against enjoying the opportunities for dressing up, for meeting new people.

At the end of her first day of appointments there was a quiet dinner party for ten at Eaton Square followed by cards. To Jenny's surprise, they played for real money, though the stakes weren't high. Ned did rather well, but immediately put his winnings in a box labelled 'Free the Slaves'.

Lucy looked vexed. 'It makes people *uncomfortable*,' she explained to Jenny in a whisper.

Next day being Saturday, the parliamentarians weren't available. Jenny amused herself with some shopping, and collected tickets from Cramers in Regent Street for a concert that evening at Exeter Hall off the Strand.

'But we can't go to a concert!' Lucy cried, when Jenny produced the tickets. 'Were going to a party for the Bulwer-Lyttons in honour of his latest novel.'

'I know, Lucy, I remembered. But you said we shouldn't turn up at the party until about ten o'clock.'

'Quite so, it's provincial to arrive too early – '

'So we can go to the concert and then on to Audley Street – '

'Good heavens, how naive you are, sister-in-law! Of course we can't 'go on' to an important party from a concert hall. In the first place, our gowns would be all crushed from sitting in the stalls, and in any case, it would be *most* unsuitable to go to Exeter Hall in the kind of gown you'll be wearing for the party.'

'Oh?' Jenny said, at a loss. 'I thought it was a quiet affair. No dancing or anything of that kind?'

'Quiet, yes . . . but one must always be perfectly turned out if the Prince is coming.'

Now Jenny understood it all. 'You never mentioned the Royals.'

'Well, it's not certain. Teddy likes Bulwer-Lytton but one gathers Alex isn't so keen. You know, there's a theatrical connection – Bulwer-Lytton has had plays on at Covent Garden, and though Alex goes to the theatre, of course, she doesn't like to mix with the theatrical crowd.'

Her sister-in-law explained all this to Jenny with the satisfaction of someone who knows all the latest gossip. Jenny, far off in the Borders, had nevertheless heard the rumours that the Prince of Wales was not a faithful husband to Alexandra. It was whispered that he had a weakness for actresses. So it would be quite understandable if Her Royal Highness found some good reason for not attending a party where actors and actresses might be among the guests.

Jenny also understood now why the Corvills would not want to arrive early. It was apparently Prince Edward's habit to arrive late. People said it was because his wife liked to retire early, so that he felt he could then go out alone with an easy conscience.

In a word, the affair this evening was an opportunity for Teddy and his cronies to meet theatrical people, to relax in a way that would be impossible if Alexandra were with him.

Jenny couldn't help being intrigued. She herself never met any actors, and though she had met one or two authors none had had the popularity of Sir Edward Bulwer-Lytton, author of the amazing epic novel, *The Last Days of Pompeii*. He was in addition notable for his political work and for being Chancellor of Glasgow University.

Such a man was worth meeting, even if the Prince of Wales didn't put in an appearance. Jenny reconciled herself to giving up the duets by Signorina Sinico and Signor Foli. Instead she dressed with particular care, putting on the sapphire blue velvet that showed off her brunette looks to perfection, and wore with it the necklace of enamel medallions on silver given to her by Ronald as a wedding anniversary present.

'My!' said her brother as she came downstairs to dinner. 'I've never seen you look better, Jenny.'

'Thank you, Ned. May I ask — am I supposed to eat a hearty meal now, or shall we be offered refreshments at Audley Street?'

Lucy replied for him, coming into the dining room in a sweep of silvered satin and pale blue lace. 'It depends on whether you want to be bothered with food at a party. Personally I think it's such a risk to one's gown, trying to eat canapés with one's fingers.'

Canapés were a recent invention of party hostesses, little titbits on toast or biscuit intended to be eaten while sitting on a canapé or French sofa. Jenny abhorred them, so made a good meal from among the five courses Lucy thought obligatory at even the simplest occasion.

The Truscotts' house in Audley Street already had carriages lined up as they arrived. Indoors Jenny found a scene of considerable grace and charm — a lighter, airier decor than their own at Eaton Square. A pianist was playing Schumann as background music to the conversation. There were rather more ladies than gentlemen in the gathering, all very pretty or striking.

'The tall fair one is Mrs Lander,' Lucy whispered, after they had greeted their hostess and begun to glance about. 'She's in *Elizabeth of England* at the St James'. And the lady in shot silk is Mrs Newnes or Nownes, I forget which, she does the modelling of the portrait heads at Tussaud's. And there's — oh, I declare, that's going too far! That's Madame Rowalla, the ballet-dancer.'

'Point out Lord Lytton to me, Lucy.'

'Who? Oh, of course. The man in the dark green broadcloth, talking to a naval officer. And there's Berthold Tours, the song-writer. And there's —' The little whispering voice broke off.

Jenny turned to look over her shoulder at her sister-in-law. Lucy had just stopped short in her survey of the room and was gazing down at her silver fan.

'What's the matter?'

'Nothing. Look, there's a lady wearing one of the new embroidered opera mantles, Jenny.'

They made their way in among the gathering. Lucy made introductions here and there, or was in her turn introduced. Ned paused to join a group with Bulwer-Lytton, deep in politics. It seemed to Jenny that her sister-in-law was trying very hard to get rid of her, and in due course she succeeded. She left Jenny with a group poring over an album of illustrations by Gustav Doré.

She was listening with interest to criticisms of that artist's dark humour when a voice at her elbow said, 'Good-evening, Mrs Armstrong. I didn't expect to see you here tonight.'

She turned. Harvil Massiter was at her side.

'Good-evening,' she replied. 'I thought you were in the country?'

'Oh, I was,' he agreed. 'But one can't stay there all the time — don't you find? A certain amount of country discomfort is good for the character, no doubt, but after a week or two one bush begins to look much like another.'

Jenny, after smiling at the quip, turned back to the Doré album. 'Would you like me to introduce you to the Prince?' Harvil persisted, touching her gently on her gloved wrist.

'I don't believe His Royal Highness is coming — it's getting rather late.'

'Oh, he's here — I came in the carriage with him a few minutes ago. We came on from Astley's, don't you know. Shall I take you across to him?'

'I don't think so, thank you, Mr Massiter. We have in fact already met on another occasion.'

'Oh yes, Lucy mentioned it — some rustic revelry in your home town, I seem to recall.'

Lucy? So they were on first name terms. Jenny frowned.

'Is something wrong?' inquired Massiter.

'Nothing, thank you. Perhaps you should rejoin the royal party, Mr Massiter?'

'No, no, he don't need anyone to play guardian on

him. Let me fetch you some refreshments, Mrs Armstrong.'

She shook her head, turning back as definitely as she could to the group with the album of illustrations.

'I say, don't waste your time on those dull things, dear lady,' he urged. 'Black and white engravings are dreary, I always think. The Truscotts have some awfully decent paintings in the library — let me take you there —'

At that moment Lucy appeared from behind the crowd.

'Harvil,' she exclaimed, 'I saw you come in.'

'Good-evening, Lucy, how beautiful you look. Just like one of those enchanting silvery figures they put atop the Christmas tree.'

Lucy smiled, and then looked doubtful — and in fact Jenny wasn't quite sure the remark was entirely complimentary. The more she knew of Mr Massiter, the less she liked him. And yet Lucy seemed to find him irresistible. She was leaning towards him now, whispering close to his cheek so that the soft brown lock just above his ear trembled at her breath.

'Shall we go and find something cool to drink?' Jenny suggested brightly.

'You go, Jenny, I have something I want to say to Harvil.'

'To *Harvil*?' Jenny echoed, not troubling to hide her astonishment.

'I mean, it's a message for Maud . . . his wife . . .'

Sighing, Jenny moved off. As she accepted a glass of chilled wine, she glanced back. The guests sauntered to and fro, obscuring her view, but from time to time she could distinguish Lucy and Massiter leaning close to each other in intimate conversation.

She knew she would have to go back and break up
the tête-à-tête. It was very unsuitable, even in the
relaxed atmosphere of a London literary party. People
would notice — or, she reminded herself wryly,
perhaps not, because most eyes were turned towards
the Prince of Wales. He was setting a very bad example
by laughing uproariously with the dancer Rowalla.

Nevertheless, what was permissible to the Prince of
Wales was not permissible to the young wife of a
respectable Scottish wool manufacturer. Jenny braced
herself to push her way through the crowd, a foolish
excuse to go home ready on her lips.

Too late. A slight commotion at the open doors of
the drawing room had caught the attention of the
guests. They turned towards the newcomer.

It was Mrs Massiter, pink with anger and still with
her outdoor wrap about her. And her gaze was fixed
in fury on her husband whispering secrets to Mrs
Edward Corvill.

Chapter Five

Mrs Harvil Massiter moved forward, escorted by an anxious butler. The hostess, scenting trouble, came to greet her.

'Maud! How delightful!' beamed Mrs Truscott. 'Won't you let Lawson take your cape?'

'No, thank you, Alice, I only dropped in on my way home from Baroness Tanbeck to collect my husband.'

'You've been to Magda's? How charming! Did Herr Ludwig play?'

Mrs Massiter was moving inexorably across the room towards her husband. Mrs Truscott was fighting a delaying action. Massiter saw it was time to intervene.

'Maud my dear, how sweet of you to come for me. But I can't go until the Prince decides to leave, you know.'

'I'm sure if you tell him I have a dreadful headache and need your assistance, he'll excuse you.'

He came close and spoke in a low tone, so that the words were for her alone.

She stiffened away from him, adamant. 'I don't need to be told that. It was the reason you begged off Baroness Tanbeck — that the Prince wanted to talk to you. You didn't mention who *you* wanted to talk to.' Her angry glance went past him to Lucy, who was

65

trying to shrink back into a small group of which Jenny was one.

Jenny felt it was time to restore things to normality, if she could. She came forward. 'Allow me to introduce myself, Mrs Massiter. I'm Ned Corvill's sister, Mrs Ronald Armstrong. We missed each other on my last London visit.'

Maud Massiter checked herself, took a deep breath, and gave Jenny a bow. 'Charmed,' she said. Then, after the introduction had sunk in, 'I didn't realise you were here as well.'

Jenny couldn't hide her surprise. 'I beg your pardon?'

'Mrs Culworth told me . . . she left just as the Prince was arriving . . . she told me Mrs Corvill was here . . .'

Jenny saw it all. Some busy gossip had hurried to the Baroness Tanbeck's soirée on purpose to tell Mrs Massiter that her husband had arrived with the Prince of Wales at a party where Mrs Corvill was also present.

So it was talked of to that extent. Jenny said in a very calm tone, 'My brother and his wife were so kind as to bring me to meet Lord Lytton. It's a new experience for me. We don't have this kind of literary party in my home town.'

Mrs Massiter understood very well what Jenny was doing. She was telling her that Lucy had been under her eye most of the time and that nothing untoward could have happened. Some of the indignation ebbed out of her.

Her husband, sensing it, said playfully, 'My dear, do take off your wrap, it's much too hot in here for sables.'

He was quite right, and if he had worded it differently she might have given in enough to accept a few moments' hospitality and leave. But he made her aware of the spectacle she was making — wrapped about with a cape of violet satin trimmed with sable and beaded edging in a roomful of women with bare shoulders. True enough, she was too hot. Perspiration stood on her skin, showing up the patches of rice powder.

'I'm leaving!' she said. 'And if you want the money for that new horse you'll give up the pleasure of chit-chat with your latest light-o'-love and come home.'

She turned and sailed out, her satin skirts dragging on the Aubusson carpet.

'Maud dear,' urged Alice Truscott, hurrying after her, 'do stay and have at least a glass —'

But Mrs Massiter was out the door and going through the hall by that time.

Jenny felt her face must be scarlet with embarrassment. She took a little glance around. Luckily her brother was at the far side of the room where conversation was still going on in ignorance of the battle just played out.

But certain eyes had been watching. A tall gentleman approached. Jenny knew him to be one of the Prince's aides.

'I say, Massiter, bad form, eh? Raised voices in public! HRH don't like it.'

Massiter managed a smile. 'Can't say I care for it myself, Prior.'

Mrs Truscott was back. 'I do think, Harvil . . . Perhaps you had better . . . She's very upset . . . '

'But —'

'Cut along, old man,' said Prior, in a tone of cool

sympathy. 'I'll explain to Teddy — he's a married man himself, after all.'

With an expression that showed he knew he was momentarily out of favour, Massiter made brief farewells to his hostess and took his leave. As soon as he was out of the room a buzz of talk broke out.

'My dear Mrs Corvill,' said Mrs Truscott to Lucy, with politeness but very little friendship, 'let me take you to the buffet table. I'm sure you would like some negus.'

Lucy, pale and shaken, allowed herself to be led off. Jenny quietly sank back through the ranks of guests to a chair by the wall. She sat down, perturbed by what she had just witnessed.

'She's a dreadful woman,' said the lady in the next chair from behind her fan. 'Quite unreasonable.'

She was elderly, portly, in a fine gown and pearls. She waved her feather fan a time or two, then added: 'That was very brave of you, to step between the lioness and her prey. It almost worked, too.'

'I thought . . . I thought some natural conversation might calm her down.'

'Splendid idea, but foolhardy. She's quite liable to bite, Maud Massiter.'

'You know her well?'

'Oh, we see each other here and there. I'm Cecily Grimsdale, you know — run the East End Charities events.'

Jenny murmured her name. Mrs Grimsdale hardly listened. 'No, apart from that husband of hers, she's quite an acceptable acquaintance.'

'You don't like Mr Massiter?'

'Harvil? Oh, he's a charmer! Of course I like him,

he's a scape-grace but he can twist you round his little finger. He's losing the knack with Maud, though. What I meant was that she's obsessed with him these days. She's sure he's off canoodling if he isn't actually under her eye.'

'And is he?' Jenny inquired, out of need to know more about the situation.

'Very likely. He's a lot younger than poor Maud, you see. Married her for her money, of course. But, poor soul, what a howler that turned out to be.'

'You mean, she has no money?'

'Good lord, pots, absolutely pots! But you see, they married against Papa's wishes — Papa thought Harvil a bad lot, and when he died he left everything to Maud but tied up with trusts and managements so that Harvil can't get at it.'

'But surely a married woman's property —'

'Oh, Harvil gets a very comfortable income from her stocks but for any of the extras — and poor dear Harvil likes the extras — he's got to ask her. And she has to go to the trustees. If she goes, they generally say yes, I believe. But that gives her the whip-hand, do you see? If she's cross with him she won't ask the trustees for extra funds. It keeps poor Harvil very jumpy.'

Jenny could well understand that. He didn't seem the kind of man to enjoy being kept subordinate.

'Will Mr Massiter fall in with his wife's wishes?' she ventured.

'You mean about *la petite écossaise*? Shouldn't think so. It's clear he likes her. But you know, she's outclassed — too much of a provincial to play the game right.' Here Mrs Grimsdale paused. 'You're a provincial yourself, aren't you — no offence intended.

69

But London manners are different and that little creature simply doesn't understand the rules.'

'You may be right.'

'You know her well? A friend, relative?'

'I'm her sister-in-law.'

'Ah. Well, if you have any influence with her I'd get her back to the bonnie bonnie banks. Maud can be very unpleasant when she sets her mind to it. She showed that tonight, sailing in when she knew HRH was here. Your little mountain sprite is no match for her.'

Jenny nodded. 'I appreciate your advice.'

'Costs me nothing. Anyone'll tell you — Cecily Grimsdale likes to poke her nose in. But I'm right most of the time. It comes of dealing with committees of ladies trying to run a charity.'

A moment later Ned came along to say that he would introduce her to Lord Lytton if she wished. She excused herself to Mrs Grimsdale, but the old lady's words stayed with her through the rest of the evening.

When at last the Prince of Wales took himself off and the rest of the guests could leave, it was close on two o'clock. A very light covering of snow had fallen. 'I do hope,' Lucy said, as they stepped down from the hackney in Eaton Square, 'that it will melt before church time. I do hate getting my skirts draggled.'

'We're going to church?' gasped Jenny. She was sure that when she got to bed she would sleep till midday.

'Certainly.' And as they went upstairs together while Ned supervised the locking-up, Lucy whispered, 'I'm not going to let anyone say Maud Massiter scared me into staying at home!'

At home in Galashiels the Corvill's attended the

United Secessionist Church, chiefly to please the elder
Mrs Corvill. The younger generation had no deep
religious convictions — Ned, in fact, had lost his faith
under the onslaught of Darwin's theories about
evolution.

Here in London, Jenny found, her sister-in-law
insisted they attend the church across the square, the
fashionable St Peter's. Here the Rev. Mr Wilkinson,
later to become a bishop, preached entertaining
sermons to the lighthearted Belgravians and the
organist regarded the service as an opportunity to play
Mendelssohn.

Heads turned when the Corvills came in. There was
no doubt gossip had got abroad in the few hours since
last night. Lucy, her face shaded by a scuttle-shaped
bonnet of blue velour, stared ahead but could find no
voice to sing the hymns. Afterwards, in the porch,
there seemed some reluctance on the part of the ladies
to pause for chat, although the men were friendly
enough to Ned.

Jenny didn't know how much to infer from this
occasion. She didn't know what the ladies of Belgravia
believed about Lucy and Massiter, nor how much truth
there was in it. One thing was certain — discretion was
the better part of valour. As they sat down to lunch
she said, 'If you'll get packed, Lucy, we can travel
back on Tuesday.'

'Tuesday? But I thought you were staying until the
end of the week.'

'No, I shall go to the Board of Trade tomorrow
morning and see the MPs' committee in the
afternoon —'

'But weren't you going to see the factor, Jenny?'
Ned put in.

Wilson, the cloth merchant who handled their London orders, had Thameside premises. Jenny always enjoyed a visit to this rascal and the game of wits that ensued. But on this trip she had decided to deny herself the pleasure.

'Ronald is coming down after New Year for lectures at the College of Science on anilines. He can see Wilson then. I'd like to get back, Lucy, particularly as it looks as if the weather is breaking up.'

This was true enough. Grey clouds reflected a dim light into the dining room, so much so that the table candles were lit for the midday meal. Snow in London was a matter of draggled skirts and thicker boots. In the Borders it could mean real problems.

'It would be very inconvenient,' Lucy objected. 'There are things I want to do. And I've invited people for Wednesday, and we have tickets for —'

'You can write notes this afternoon,' Jenny broke in. 'If you explain you've been called out of town, no one can object.'

'But people will think —' Lucy fell silent. In front of her husband she couldn't say, 'People will think I've left because of Maud Massiter,' because that opened up a subject of which he was ignorant.

'I certainly think it would be best to go as soon as possible,' Ned remarked. 'If the weather is really turning wintry at last, it's best to get up to Gatesmuir and be snug and comfortable with Mother and little Heather before it breaks.'

Lucy looked mutinous, but she always gave in in the end. Jenny knew her sister-in-law well. Open rebellion was beyond her.

Obediently, Lucy wrote notes of apology that afternoon. She ordered her maid to begin packing. But

when Jenny came home from the day's business on
Monday, it was to find Lucy had gone out. There was,
perhaps, nothing unusual in that; Lucy had many
social engagements.

When Lucy came in there was something secretive
about her entry. She started back in surprise when
Jenny came out of the morning room to greet her in
the hall. 'Oh! Jenny! I didn't think you'd be back until
six.'

'Things went more quickly than I expected. I see it's
still snowing.'

Lucy gave her cloak to the parlour maid. 'Shake that
well, Gibbons, and hang it in the warm.'

'Not the best choice for a cold day like this,' Jenny
observed, watching the maid carry off the light cloak
trimmed with watered silk.

'Heavy cloth is so unbecoming,' Lucy said, going
into the morning room to warm her hands at the fire.

Jenny understood the truth that lay beneath the
remark. Lucy had wanted to look her best this
afternoon so had put on a pale, light cloak in which
she looked fragile and appealing.

It was an easy guess she had been to meet Massiter.

They settled by the fire. Jenny poured the tea which
had been brought just before Lucy came in. 'Sister-
in-law,' she said conversationally as she handed Lucy
her cup, 'I'm glad to have this chance for a quiet little
chat. When we go up to Galashiels I want it
understood that you'll be staying on there for a month
or two after New Year —'

'That wasn't the arrangement —'

'It is now. I want you to stay until any little
problems here in London have faded away.'

'There are no problems —'

'What was the meaning of that little episode on Saturday night, then?'

'Oh, I knew you'd blame *me* for that! As if it's my fault if that absurd woman —'

'This conversation isn't about blame, it's about discretion. I don't ask the reasons Mrs Massiter behaved so badly the other night. All I say is that it will be better if you are not present when she loses her temper next time.'

Lucy's mouth trembled. 'I won't be spoken to like this. You've no right . . .'

'The one who has the right is Ned. One day even he will come down out of the clouds and notice what is going on. Do you want that?'

'Ned is far too busy with his good works to —'

'Quite. And so you'd better come back to the safety of the Borders for a long stay.'

'But it's so dull there!' It was a cry of despair.

Jenny sighed, eyeing her sister-in-law over her teacup. What was to be done with Lucy? She needed to be amused, entertained, made much of, admired. She needed activities that came easily — parties, picnics, shopping, theatres. She needed male companionship. It wasn't the first time Lucy had been involved with a man — there had been occasions before now when Jenny had feared for her reputation.

But it was better not to speak of that. Better to stick to the present problem. 'Look on the bright side, Lucy. Christmas will be here almost as soon as we get home, and then there are all the parties for Hogmanay, and the Burns Nichts . . .'

Lucy began to cry, but in a quiet manner. She knew she had to accept Jenny's dictum. But that didn't mean she would do nothing on her own behalf.

After they had had tea, Jenny went upstairs to attend to her packing. She thought Ned had come home a little while later but when she went down to speak to him, she found it wasn't so. Yet the front door had opened and closed, she was sure.

'Did Mrs Corvill go out?' she asked the maid.

'Yes, ma'am, a quarter of an hour ago.'

'Did she say where she was going?'

'No, ma'am.'

The family sat down to dinner at eight. Lucy was ready with the information that she had slipped out to buy the new ribbon she was wearing round her throat, a piece of expensive French embroidered moiré. It would have been convincing except that Jenny had seen her sister-in-law wear it the last time she had been in London.

There was no need to ask where she had been. She had slipped out again to see Massiter or to get a message to him, to let him know she was being taken home a prisoner for the next few months. From her composure, it seemed that Massiter had been able to assure her he would never cease to think of her while she was in durance vile.

The hills were clothed with snow when the train steamed stolidly into Galashiels. It was dark, street-lamps gleamed, and stars twinkled overhead in a black frosty sky. The little town presented a pretty picture.

But Lucy refused to be cheered until, on going indoors, she found that the baby had been kept up so as to welcome her mother home. The little girl was clad in a warm short frock of white flannel liberally decked with lace, and with at least four layers of lace-edged petticoat underneath. Her feet were in little kid boots. When the travellers arrived, she turned from her nurse and took two or three determined steps towards them in the hall.

'She can walk!' Lucy cried in delight. 'Why didn't you tell me? I had no idea! Oh, precious, so you come running to welcome your Aunt Lucy? There's my angel!' She swept her up in a hug.

Heather, delighted to be made much of, crowed and waved her arms and legs. Jenny stood by, trying not to be put out at being made to wait. After all, what did it matter? Heather was an outgoing child, ready to love everyone. One day soon she would understand that Jenny was the one she should love most.

At Christmas there was a cornucopia of goodies from Lucy, though she bewailed the fact that she hadn't bought wheeled toys for the toddler to trundle to and fro.

Jenny spent as much time as she could with her daughter, playing the simple games she loved.

'This is the way the weaver goes,
A-rickelty-tick, a-rickelty-tick,
The treadle down with his heel and toes,
A-rickelty-tick, a-rickelty-tick . . .'

Heather giggled as her mother took her hand and with it patted her heel and then her toe, first one foot and then the other as the verse was repeated.

'This is the way the weaver goes,
A-rickelty-tick, a-rickelty-tick,
The wool on his ears and on his nose —'

'I do wish you wouldn't teach the child those vulgar songs,' Lucy interrupted, her manner full of reproach.

'It's just so she'll learn the name of her heels and toes and so forth –'

'It's the kind of thing suitable for a workman's children. Come along, Heather, play with your lovely drummer boy.'

The toddler's father watched all this with some perplexity. 'You'll no doubt correct me if I'm wrong,' he said to Jenny, 'but I thought the whole idea of taking the house in London was to get Lucy away at a safe distance from the bairn?'

Jenny looked up from the book she was reading. She frowned at Ronald. 'When did you work that out?'

'It came to me as a voice out of the burning bush,' he said, amused. 'Will you explain to me why she's not only back for Hogmanay but talking as if she's here till spring?'

'She's here to mend a broken heart.'

'Is that a fact? Whose heart got broken?'

She drew him down beside her in the quiet of her father's old reading-room. She liked to come here sometimes, to think and plan, to look at his books, to let tranquillity seep into her.

'Lucy has a heart, Ronald, though you don't seem to think so. She wants to love someone –'

'There's always Ned,' Ronald put in. 'You do remember Ned, don't you?'

She shook her head. 'She was never in love with Ned. He was an escape from being poor and having to help her mother run a boarding-house. Sometimes I think she even bears him a grudge – when she first came here she expected a fine country estate.'

Ronald glanced out of the window at the winter trees on the hillside. 'Well, it's not a bad estate, at that.'

'But she expected grouse moors and liveried footmen. We're a lot more workaday than she'd imagined. It's difficult to explain. But she's never really happy, never content — except perhaps when she's in love.'

'And who is she in love with at the moment?'

'His name is Harvil Massiter. Very much the man-about-town. It was really very important to get her away from him, even though . . . Well, she needs someone to spend her affection on, and at the moment it's Heather, I'm afraid.'

'Humph. Heather's got to be spoiled to death to help keep Lucy happy? Have I got it right?'

'It's not for long, Ronald. Just a month or two. When the London season begins, I'll go back there with Lucy.'

He looked discontented at that. 'You mean you're going to stay there, acting collie-dog to keep her out of mischief?'

'I've a sort of a plan . . . I haven't done anything about it, but I think of asking Lucy if she'd like to be presented at court.'

'Eh?' Ronald said. 'That's only for eighteen-year-old lassies.'

'No, I believe married ladies can be presented too, wives of the county gentry and the town gentry as well as the military and the aristocracy. I'd have to find someone willing to sponsor Lucy — there are society ladies who have the right to present others at court, I'm not sure of the ins and outs but I think I've heard something along those lines.'

'Presentation at court . . . Lucy would love that.'

'Yes, and you see, the sponsor has to supervise her and guarantee her — I believe the Palace is quite strict

about status and behaviour. So I could deliver Lucy
to the general overseeing of some elderly dragon and
leave her with an easy mind for two or three months.'

'All this, of course, would cost money,' Ronald
said, with a look of cynicism on his long face.

'We're not short of money, my dear. What we're
short of where Lucy is concerned is peace of mind.'

'Aye. It might work. You'd better put out feelers
as soon as you can. Maybe there's a waiting list for
a place under the wing of these old society hens?'

'Just let me get Hogmanay over and one or two
other things.'

'Perhaps I could take a letter with me to London
when I go next week?'

'No, this is women's business, my love.'

'I might run into Lucy's sweetheart — wouldn't
mind a look at him.'

'You'll find him at Tattersall's, I imagine.'

'Not at the College of Science lectures?'

'Only if the lecturer is a young and elegant woman.'

'No such luck,' said Ronald.

After the festivities of New Year the world settled
down to routine. Ronald went to London for ten days,
Ned was in Liverpool welcoming an American
delegation concerned with funds for educating freed
slaves, and Jenny had to go to Newcastle-upon-Tyne
over the non-arrival of a cargo of valuable wool.

The weather was cold but the snow had for the
moment gone away. Instead a period of rain set in.
Coming back on the train from Newcastle, Jenny
looked out at the dripping landscape. She was
depressed, she had been unsuccessful in tracing the lost
cargo, and by the time she got to Gatesmuir it would
be late and Heather would be in bed.

Worse yet, the rain caused a landslip at Coldstream. The line was blocked for several hours while men called out from the soldiers' barracks worked by lantern light to clear it.

By the time Jenny got to Galashiels it was well past midnight. The station was still open but all the hackney cab drivers had gone home for the night.

'I'll send someone up to Gatesmuir to fetch out your carriage, Mistress Armstrong,' the station-master offered.

She shook her head. The idea of sitting yet longer, waiting, was anathema. The rain had stopped, though there was still a cold breeze.

'I'll walk up, Mr Gowan. Keep my luggage here till the morning, will you? I'll send for it.'

'I'll put someone with you to light the way, mistress.'

'No, no, I know the way fine. Never you trouble yourself, Mr Gowan, I'll be home in a quarter of an hour.'

She set off, glad of the exercise after so many hours in the train. Buffeted by the wind, she struggled along High Street and up the slope towards Gatesmuir, the night air reviving her as she battled against it.

The road outside Gatesmuir was awash from the rain. She trod carefully through the puddles glinting in the faint light from the flying clouds. She paused a moment inside the gateposts, to get her breath back for the steep curve of the drive.

She was leaning forward into the slope when her foot hit something in the middle of the drive. She drew back in alarm, almost losing her balance. She leaned down, trying to discern what it could be. Something longish and low-lying, but . . . she touched it with her foot . . . not a log, not a tree trunk, something soft.

She stooped, put out a hand.

Soft woollen clothing . . . flannel . . . cotton lawn . . . someone in night clothes was lying in the middle of the drive.

She knelt down in the mud. 'Who's there?' she said in a quavering voice.

Her hand touched lace, a lace cap. She recognised the shape of the lappets — it was her mother's nightcap.

'Mother!'

Now the flying clouds released enough starlight to let her see that her mother was lying face down in the path. She put her arms about her, turned her over so that she was lying over Jenny's own knees.

'Mother! Mother! What happened? Mother, for God's sake —'

She made a faint sound, a moan of returning consciousness. 'Jenny . . .?'

'My darling, what are you doing out here? Mother —'

'Jenny . . . Jenny, the baby . . .'

'What?'

'Jenny . . . ahh . . . I tried to stop her . . . Forgive me, I couldn't . . .'

'What?' Jenny cried, baffled. 'What are you saying, Mother?'

But Millicent Corvill had lost consciousness again.

Chapter Six

Jenny never recalled the events of the next hour or so. Her personal maid, Baird, told her what happened.

She and Thirley, the parlour maid, were roused from sleep by a hammering on the front door and a voice screaming, 'Let me in! Let me in!'

Very scared, they went downstairs, clutching each other. Baird recognised Jenny's voice when she heard her own name being called. They unbolted and opened the front door.

Their flickering candle revealed a dishevelled, mud stained figure.

'Quick — fetch the gardener and his boy — send Coachman for the doctor. Tell Cook to rouse the fire —'

'Mistress, mistress, what ever has come to you? Your clothes —'

'Never mind that, you fool! Run for McKeith and the boy. They have to carry my mother in —'

'Your mother? But mistress —'

'Blankets! Run up and get blankets, Baird. Thirley, why haven't you gone for McKeith?'

Next moment Mistress Armstrong had plunged back into the darkness. Bewildered, Thirley and Baird gaped at each other. Then Baird, who knew her employer very well, pulled herself together. 'Do as she says.'

'But she's lost her mind — she said Mrs Corvill had to be carried —'

'Go for the gardener. God knows why, but *go*! Use the back path, it's quickest.'

Baird whirled round, ran upstairs to the upper floor, and called to the cook, who slept at the far back of the house. When she heard sounds of arousal from her she shouted instructions. 'Go down, get the kitchen fire going. I don't know why, just do it!'

Flying back down, she had a sudden thought. She looked into the bedroom of the elder Mrs Corvill, the door standing ajar. Millicent Corvill's bed was empty.

Still bewildered but beginning to understand that there was method in the mistress's madness, Baird snatched up the quilt and the top blanket before hurrying downstairs.

The front door stood wide. Someone, presumably Jenny, had lit the gas lamps so that the light spilled out. About ten yards away down the slope of the drive, heads were bobbing. She could hear the mistress's voice. 'No, don't — look at her leg, I think it's broken. You'll damage her if you pick her up in your arms, McKeith.'

Baird flew out with the bedclothes. Mistress Armstrong, McKeith, and John the boy were kneeling by a prostrate figure.

The gardener took the blanket from Baird. He laid it on the ground alongside the unconscious woman. He had had experience, in his long career as a workman, of injuries to limbs. He stationed the boy and Mistress Armstrong at one side of Mrs Corvill, himself and Baird at the other.

'Take hold of her dressing-gown at the sides. When

I say move, raise her gey gently but as fast as you can. Lay her on the blanket softly. Ready? Move!'

On a stretched blanket they carried Millicent Corvill indoors. There Jenny darted into the drawing room, coming back with the folding screen that helped shield its occupants from draughts. With that as a stretcher they carried Millicent upstairs, and with infinite care transferred her to her bed.

By this time Cook, having obeyed orders, had roused up the fire in the kitchen range, and now came halfway upstairs to see what was required of her.

'Hot pigs,' said Baird, running down to her, 'and mebbe tea or hot toddy — get the kettle singing, at any rate.'

'But what's ado?'

'The Lord knows. It looks as if the old mistress was sleepwalking and had a fall outdoors.'

'Outdoors? In this weather?'

Shocked, Cook hurried away. Baird returned upstairs to help strip the soaked nightclothes off Mrs Corvill. She moaned as they handled her, no matter how gentle they tried to be, and in the end Jenny said, 'Cut them off her. It's less hurt to her.'

Hot stone water bottles were brought by Cook, well shielded in flannel to keep them from scorching the skin. Millicent was wrapped in blankets. Now and again her eyes flickered open as she was touched.

'Jenny?'

'I'm here, Mother.'

'Jenny, my darling . . . Oh, what will you say . . .'

'Ssh, ssh, rest now. You've had a fall —'

'No, no. I —'

'Now, Mother, be good. The doctor will be here in a moment.' Baird noticed that the nursemaid, Wilmot,

85

had come to the door, struggling into her dressing-gown. Wilmot was a notoriously heavy sleeper but at last the hubbub had roused her.

'What's happening?' she muttered to Baird.

'Never you mind, go and make sure the baby isn't woken by all this collieshangie.'

Wilmot vanished.

Thirley ushered in Dr Lauder with his hair awry, his nightshirt tucked into his trousers and his greatcoat wrapped round him unfastened. 'What's happened? Your coachman knew nothing except that he had to fetch me at once — ' He broke off when he saw Jenny. 'Oh, from what he said, I thought it was you that was injured, Mistress Armstrong.'

'I found my mother in the drive. Her clothes were soaked, God knows how long she was lying there. I think her right leg is broken.'

'Go you and sit down. Take some hot tea, with mebbe a little whisky in it.'

'No, no, I — '

'Go and let me examine my patient, Mrs Armstrong.'

'Oh . . . yes . . .'

With Baird's hand under her elbow, Jenny went downstairs to the kitchen. Cook had tea made, Baird fetched whisky from the dining room.

The time was then about two in the morning. The comparative quiet and security of the kitchen brought Jenny back to herself. She took a sip of the tea.

Then she paused and frowned. 'You'd think all the noise would have — '

The kitchen door burst open. Wilmot came in, hands outstretched, her face distorted with fear and dismay.

'Mistress! Mistress!'

'What Wilmot?' Jenny was on her feet, swaying.

'The bairn — she's gone!'

The world stood still. Jenny's vision clouded. Next moment she was being held up by her maid, then helped back towards her chair.

'No!' she cried, thrusting off the sheltering arms.

She raced through the hall, up the stairs. She burst into the night nursery. The tiny glow of the nightlight flickered in its shallow glass container. She ran to the crib, threw herself upon it.

The little bedclothes with their frills and tucks were thrown back. The bed was empty.

'Wilmot! Wilmot!'

The nursemaid came in, already sobbing and crying out in dismay. 'I never saw she wasna there! I ran out to see what all the noise was for, I just took it she was there —'

'She climbed out, mebbe,' Thirley suggested, desperately looking about.

They lit all the gas lamps, they brought candles, they searched the house. Heather was not there.

Jenny's head was whirling. She could feel her heart pounding through every nerve in her body. Her breath seemed to come very shallow and fast, insufficient to keep her alive. She was stifling, she was losing her grip on the world.

Then a sudden thought struck her. All the stifling warmth left her. She was cold, icy cold, shivering with cold.

She looked at the maidservants. 'Where is young Mrs Corvill?' she asked.

The women gaped, then looked from one to the other. 'I suppose . . . . suppose in her room, mistress.'

Like a flock of swooping birds they ran along the landing. The door of the room occupied by Ned and Lucy, the garden side bedroom, was closed.

Jenny knocked. No reply.

She was terribly frightened. What could it mean?

Gulping down a sobbing breath, she turned the knob and thrust the door open.

The room was dark. Baird came in holding a candle high. Thirley lit the gas lamp. The bed, turned down by Thirley at eight o'clock, had not been slept in. Everything was in perfect order.

Except that it had no occupant at some ten minutes past two of a winter's morning.

Jenny felt as if the nightmare would overwhelm her. She was so cold her teeth were chattering. Her maid picked up the ornamental shawl from the back of a chair, wrapped it around her. Jenny clutched it to draw it close, then stopped to look at it.

'Is anything gone, Baird?'

'Gone?'

'Any of Mrs Lucy's clothes.'

The maid served all three ladies of the Corvill household. Her experienced eye ran over the items on the dressing table. She looked in the big wardrobe.

'Mrs Lucy's hairbrush and comb are missing, and a small valise from the bottom of the wardrobe. There's some underwear and two pairs of shoes I can't see.'

The mistress and the household staff stared at each other. They all knew what it meant.

'When did you last see Mrs Lucy?' Jenny asked.

'At dinner,' Thirley said.

'About ten o'clock, mistress,' said Baird, from her

own stand-point. 'She went upstairs early. She said the house was dull with everyone except Mrs Corvill away.'

Jenny made a grasp after logic. 'When did you lock up, Thirley?'

'About eleven, mistress.'

'Yes, you had to unbolt the door to let me in. So how — ?'

'The side door, Mistress Armstrong! I noticed it when I ran for McKeith. The side door is open.'

Jenny darted out of the bedroom and down the back stairs. The maids all followed her. She didn't even stop to think how absurd it was. The side door, which opened on to a paved path, was allowing the night breeze to sway the curtains of the lobby.

If you walked round the side of the house on the path, you came to the drive. Lucy must have crept down the servants' staircase some time after the house was quiet, let herself out, and —

And what? Gone where?

Jenny went through to the front of the hall, and up the main staircase. Dr Lauder was coming out of her mother's bedroom.

'I've given her a sedative. She'll sleep for five or six hours, I hope. Then we must set that leg but we'll do that under chloroform, though I wish your mother had a better pulse for it.'

'Doctor —'

'Try not to worry, Mistress Armstrong. We'll do all we can —'

'Is Mother asleep already?'

'Well, drowsing off —'

'Oh, God,' cried Jenny, and ran past him into the bedroom.

She knelt beside her mother's bed, and gripped her hand. 'Mother! Mother!'

Millicent half-opened her eyes. Her lips formed her daughter's name, but almost no sound came out.

Dr Lauder came in, shocked at the violence of Jenny's action. 'My dear young woman, what on earth —'

'Wake her! Wake her, doctor!'

'I can't do that!'

'You must, you must. She has something to tell me —'

'Don't be absurd. I'm shamed at you, Mistress Corvill, I never thought you would take the hysterics —'

'Dr Lauder!' Jenny's voice was almost a shout. 'Wake my mother up! My baby is missing, my brother's wife has left the house in the middle of the night! Mother knows something of it — wake her, wake her!'

But it was no use. The bromide had taken effect. Millicent Corvill could not be roused without stimulants which Dr Lauder refused to apply.

So when the police came an hour later, there was nothing to learn except the information offered by the empty bed and the empty cot.

Their first action was a thorough search of the house and grounds.

'There's ower much rain to show traces,' the sergeant said, troubled and ill at ease in the elegance of the drawing room, 'but it looks as if a carriage stood for a time down the road a wee bit from the gates. You can see where the horses got impatient and howked wi' their hooves.'

'Who was in it?'

'There's no way of telling that, Mistress Armstrong.' He ran a finger round the stiff collar of his uniform jacket. 'Did the leddy leave a letter of any kind? Leddies usually leave a wee letter or a note when they . . . if they . . .'

'If they run away from home?' Jenny ended for him.

'Aye, well, ye see, mistress, we have to think she went o' her own free will, for of the fact that she packed her wee bag wi' one or two things.'

'She could have been forced to do that.'

'Wi' no sound being made the while?' Sergeant Johnson said, shaking his head. 'Na, na, it's no likely. She packed the bag herself, the maid didna do it. She did it after she went up to her bed, supposedly. She wouldna have to be quiet about it. Who would think anything of hearing her move about her own room opening and closing drawers? Then sat herself doon, fully dressed, and waited till the house was quiet.'

'And meanwhile there was a carriage waiting for her outside on the road?'

'Aye.' He paused, considering. 'It's just the greatest bad luck your train was delayed. If it had been on time, you might have seen the carriage.' His thought travelled on. 'I marvel that, if she went of her own free will, she chose a night when you might happen on her.'

'No — I wasn't expected back for another two days. But everything in Newcastle was a waste of time so I just packed up and came home.'

He looked at Jenny with anxiety. Her voice was weak with exhaustion. She was sitting in a chair by one of the little occasional tables, an untasted cup of coffee at her hand. She had changed out of the muddied clothes of last night, but she had not bothered to have her hair re-dressed. Her face was white. Out of it her dark eyes stared, seeking answers, looking for help.

The sergeant wasn't accustomed to dealing with the gentry, nor with women. He cleared his throat. 'Will your husband be back soon?'

'I sent a telegraphic message. The reply came half an hour ago. He's on the train now.'

'Aha.' That was no help. The London train wouldn't be in at Galashiels until early evening. 'And your brother?'

'He's coming from Liverpool.' Suddenly the great eyes shone with tears. 'What am I going to tell them when they walk in?'

'Now, now, Mistress Armstrong, dinna fash yourself. We'll find the both of them.' But he didn't believe it, because he couldn't understand what had happened. Ladies ran away from their husbands — that was not uncommon. But to hamper yourself with a baby, and someone else's baby at that . . .

And yet it couldn't be two separate events. It was impossible that there could be a runaway wife and a baby abducted by criminals on the same night in the same house. No, the one was connected with the other.

'Have you any idea where the leddy might have gone?' he ventured.

Jenny shook her head.

'Was she . . . Was there . . . Excuse the impertinence, mistress, but was there . . . ye know . . . a gentleman in the case?'

'Yes, but he's in London.'

'Do ye say so?' This was the first piece of useful

information. 'She could have gone to London, then.'

'She'd have gone by train.'

'Mebbe no. A body would know her at the station, and she'd want to avoid notice, do ye no think so?'

'I don't know,' Jenny said, putting her hands up to her head as if to force her brain to act. 'I don't know. I can't understand any of it.'

'Well, I think I'll go back to the station and send a wee telegraphic inquiry as to whether a lady of the given description got on the train further down the line. And I'll inquire about the hiring o' the carriage. See then, it wasna hired in the toon. It must have come from somewhere else, and if it was a post-carriage there'll be a record of when it was handed over or the horses were changed.'

'Yes,' Jenny said, grasping at the idea. 'Yes, the inns where the horses are changed . . .'

'That's just it. So I'll away and do that. And Mistress Armstrong — ?'

'Yes?'

'Would you go upstairs wi' my constable and look at the leddy's belongings? Because you see, if she went on her own to meet someone, she'd need funds to pay for the carriage and so on. Would you look and see if she's taken her valuables?'

'Yes, of course.' She should have thought of that herself. She made herself pay heed to the sergeant. 'Anything else?'

'Would you look and see if any of the baby's clothes are missing? Ye see, if they are, it means that the leddy might have premeditated the taking of the child.'

'But Wilmot would have heard her if she moved about collecting clothes in the nursery.'

'Do ye say so? I thought you told me Wilmot was

the last to come down when all the upset was going on about your mother.'

'Yes.' Jenny tried to remember what had happened, what had been said. It all whirled in her mind like leaves in the wind. 'She didn't know Heather was missing at first. Yet I feel . . . if someone had been moving about in the room . . .'

'No one seems to have heard anything.'

'My mother,' Jenny insisted. 'My mother heard something. Why else was she outside in her night things?'

'Aye, but your mother is drugged asleep.'

Jenny glanced at the clock. Close to seven. 'Dr Lauder said she would wake after five or six hours. It could be any time now.'

'Then go you, mistress, and sit by the bed. The minute she wakes up try to get from her what she knows. It's gey important. I'll away, then.'

Leaving matters underway at Gatesmuir, he hurried back to the police station. It was his intention to get word to the Police Commissioner at once. This case was quite beyond his ken, and needed extraordinary measures. Besides, the sergeant knew that if in his uneasiness he made mistakes, his head was likely to roll.

Jenny went upstairs with the constable. A second examination of Lucy's room revealed that she had taken her jewels. The little japanned cabinet in which she kept them was closed and locked, but opened easily to the constable's pen-knife to show empty trays.

'Would that amount to a wheen of money?' the policeman inquired, his notebook out.

Jenny tried to recall the presents that Ned had given his wife. 'Pearls, diamond drop earrings, a gold chain with an emerald pendant . . . ' She enumerated them.

'Coming to how much in guineas, would you say?'

'I don't know. A thousand?'

He drew in a gasping breath. 'Ach, she could get to the ends o' the earth wi' that!'

In the nursery Wilmot was sitting with her apron over her face. When Jenny spoke her name sharply she uncovered red, distorted features, wet with tears.

'Are any of Heather's clothes missing?'

'Not a stitch, Mistress Armstrong.'

'You're sure?'

'Am I not! I flew here the minute the police were sent for and looked in every press and drawer. Nothing's gone except the clothes she . . . she . . . ' Wilmot's face blubbered into silence.

'Her nightgown and her bara coat, then?'

Wilmot nodded her head, her apron up to her eyes again.

Jenny turned to the constable. 'Is there anything else we should see to?'

'No, I'll just call the man at the gate and ask him to take this information to Mr Johnson. Excuse me, mistress.'

When he had gone Wilmot ran to Jenny, taking her hand in both of hers. 'Mistress, forgive me! Don't hate me for sleeping-on! I would gie my life for it not to have happened.'

'I know, Wilmot.'

'Say you dinna hate me!'

'Let go my hand.'

'Mistress Armstrong, I canna live with myself if you dinna say —'

'Let go, Wilmot, let go — I've enough to bear!'

She snatched herself free. Outside she stopped short,

hardly knowing what she was supposed to do next. Then she remembered the sergeant's instructions.

She dragged herself along to Millicent's bedroom. Baird was in attendance, but nothing needed doing — Millicent slept, the daylight was shut out by the heavy curtains, the lamp was turned low.

'Go and get some breakfast, Baird. I'll take over.'

'I couldn't eat a morsel —'

'Go all the same —'

'Would you no take a rest yourself, mistress? You're blanched as a willow wand.'

'I can't rest — oh, I can't rest!' She felt her control going. She hid her face against her arm.

'There now, there now,' murmured Baird, taking her by the shoulders and pulling her close. 'Greet, lassie, greet and let the tears ease you.'

'No, I mustn't — we have to find out —'

'We'll find out, never you fear. We'll get back the bairn. Your man will be here in a few hours. Take heart, we'll help you.'

They stood close in silence, the arms of the older woman around the younger. After some moments Baird led her to a chair.

'Ach, you look unlike yourself wi' your hair in a connach. I'll fetch the brushes and combs and see to it while you sit here.'

So they spent the next half hour, Baird soothingly brushing and combing the long dark hair, winding it into the coils that made a chignon on top, turning wisps round her finger to soften the cheek-line. She was placing the final tortoiseshell comb when Millicent murmured and moved a hand on the coverlet.

'She's waking!' Jenny cried, jerking herself away

from her maid's ministrations. 'Quick, Baird, draw back the curtains.'

The cold light of a January morning flooded into the room. The wind had died, taking the clouds with it. By and by the sun would come from behind the hill to brighten the room, but as yet everything was coolly illuminated.

Millicent moved her head. 'Jenny . . . Jenny . . .'

'I'm here, Mother.'

She sat by the bed, her two hands holding Millicent's one. There was a long pause while her mother breathed in long, almost weary sighs.

'Is it daytime?'

'It's almost eight o'clock in the morning.'

'Eight o'clock . . .' A silence. Then the hand Jenny was holding clutched at her.

'Did you get her back?'

Jenny went cold, then hot. 'Who, Mother? Who?'

'The baby! Did you get her back?'

The negative almost slipped out. Then she caught it back. It would be bad for her mother to know the truth yet. 'Did you see Heather last night, Mother?'

'In her arms . . . I tried to stop her, Jenny . . .'

'What happened?'

'Is she all right? She'd take a cold, the wee lamb.'

'Tell me what happened.'

Millicent's voice was husky. 'I'm dry,' she said.

The doctor had prescribed brandy in milk for when she awoke. It was in a glass on the bedside table. Jenny raised her mother's head a little and gave her sips of the mixture.

'You know I sleep lightly since your father died,' Millicent began. 'I heard a sound. I couldn't think what it could be at first, then . . .'

'Yes?'

'I thought it sounded like the side door being opened. Then I thought, no thief could open the door, it's bolted on the inside. So I thought . . .'

The words faded. Jenny gave her another sip of brandy and milk.

'I thought it must be somebody going out. But I looked at my clock and it said ten minutes past midnight. I couldn't understand it. So I put on my dressing-gown and slippers and went down the back stairs . . .'

'And the side door was open?'

'Aye, so I went out for I could hear light footsteps on the paving — ' She broke off, panting a little under the emotion of her memories. Jenny brushed the hair back from her brow, soothed her, offered the drink again. Millicent shook her head.

'It was gey dark out there, and the rain coming down across the wind. I was frichted, daughter. Then I put my trust in the Lord and went out, and I saw a shape against the clouds for a minute — just the outline, but I knew it, it was the new fur cape with the upstanding collar that Ned gave to Lucy for her Christmas.'

Behind her Jenny heard Baird draw in her breath. Baird knew that cape only too well, she had had to alter the fastening at the neck to make it fit better.

'I knew then. It was your sister-in-law, Jenny. I was sore astounded. I went after her and cried her name, and she turned in surprise.'

'Quiet, now, Mother, quiet. Don't upset yourself.'

Tears were dropping down her mother's cheeks. 'I canna help myself. I was staggered at the sight. She had your bairn in her arms! I ran at her — ' A sob shook her, she broke off. 'Jenny, I ran at her, and she thrust out her free arm that had a bag or a case in it, and I went over — stupid fool that I was, I lost my balance and went over, and I think I hit my head for everything went swirling round me and I couldn't tell where I was.' She paused and added, 'And I think I twisted my leg for it's aching sore.'

It was like a description of a nightmare dream being made reality. Jenny murmured, 'Dr Lauder is coming in a little while to see to your leg, Mother.'

'But the baby? Did she take no harm? The last I saw, Lucy was vanishing down the drive with her. At least I think so — unless it was a confusion from hitting my head.'

Millicent gazed inquiringly into her daughter's face. Caught without her mask, Jenny's misery and exhaustion were clear to see.

Millicent Corvill gave a shuddering gasp. 'It's true, then. Ned's wife has taken away your baby.'

Chapter Seven

When Ronald Armstrong stepped off the train at Galashiels Station he could tell at once that things were as bad as he had suspected from Jenny's terse message: 'Come at once, very bad news.'

Gowan the station-master came hastening to him with a porter eager to take his portmanteau. They treated him as if he were some kind of delicate invalid.

'What is it? Has there been an accident at the mill?'

'Na, na, nothing like that. The carriage is waiting for you, sir.'

He hurried out. The coachman opened the carriage door for him. 'Dunlop, what the devil is the matter?'

'They're in sore trouble, sir — we'll hasten hame.'

He threw himself into the coach, angry with the man for not saying more and made even more anxious by the fact that whatever was wrong could scarcely be talked about.

They went through the main street of Galashiels with the street lamps shining on them. He thought the few passers-by turned to look after the carriage. He began to think there must be a death in the family. His mother-in-law? But Millicent, though not burgeoning with health, had been quite well when he left home.

As the carriage turned in at the gate, he glimpsed

101

a uniformed policeman on watch. They breasted the steep drive. At the sound of the wheels the front door burst open. A flying figure rushed to him. Jenny was in his arms, sobbing, clasping him, uttering his name as if he were the rock of salvation.

He looked at the open door. There was no crepe bow on the knocker. No one had died.

'Jenny, dear heart — Jenny — what's happened?'

'I don't know how . . . I don't know how to tell you. Ronald, Ronald . . . our baby is gone!'

He was sure he had misheard it. 'Wait now — say it clearly, my lassie. What is it?'

'Heather's gone . . . gone . . . taken away!'

He was holding her fast. He looked over her head. In the doorway hovered Thirley. One look at the parlour maid's white and frightened face told him it was true. He felt everything waver before his gaze. But Jenny was clutching him, he had to stand upright and hold her.

'Come indoors and tell me,' he said, through lips that would hardly form the words.

In the hall was another police constable, bare-headed, his helmet and gloves on the table. The familiar drawing room had the curtains closed and the fire made up, safe and comfortable, totally at odds with the idea of policemen and missing children.

He drew Jenny down beside him on the sofa. Thirley closed the door on them.

'Now,' he said, 'tell me.'

In a voice totally unlike the one he loved so well, she told him the story. His sense of disorientation grew as he listened. He simply couldn't take it in.

She ended with the latest news. A lady answering Lucy's description was seen in a post chaise at

Hexham, waiting for fresh horses. Attempts by the police to trace her further had met with no success so far. There was no word whatever of a child being with her.

'What you're saying,' Ronald said, after staring at her in dismay for a long moment, 'is that Lucy ran off last night to join this man —'

'Harvil Massiter.'

'*And took Heather with her?*'

She said nothing. Her breath was coming unevenly, shaken by suppressed sobs.

'It can't be true.'

'Mother saw her.'

'She took Heather with her to join her lover? Jenny, it doesn't make sense.'

'But Heather's gone, Ronald. And Lucy's gone. And Mother saw them.'

He got up, and paced about the room a moment, his hand going up to his mouth to keep back the flood of frightened oaths. That damned little bitch! He had always disliked her, always distrusted her!

After a moment he came to Jenny and sat down. 'She was last seen at Hexham.'

'Yes.'

'She was heading for the railway.'

'That seems likely. She could have got on a train at several stations. If only they can find someone who saw her!'

Ronald felt stifled. He began to undo the buttons of his greatcoat, and shrugged it off. 'Who's in charge of the hunt?'

'The Police Commissioner has taken charge personally. He's sent an inspector to Hexham. But it's so long since the sighting — eighteen hours or more.'

'She'll be in London by now! With her lover.' An additional horror struck Ronald. 'Is Ned here?'

'No, I sent for him at the same time as my message to you but his journey home is more difficult — he has to wait for a connection twice, I think.' Jenny sank her face into the cloth of her husband's jacket. 'Ronald, what are we going to say to him when he comes in?'

Ronald had no idea. He put his arms around his wife and sat rocking her to and fro in stricken silence.

After a time they went over the story again, and yet again. Then he thought to ask after his mother-in-law. She told him the broken leg had been set but that Millicent was in pain, softened by laudanum drops. 'She's very poorly, husband. She was lying out there for perhaps two hours, with a slight concussion and unable to move because of the injury to her leg.'

'And that damned little cat did it to her! When they catch her I hope they lock her up for a thousand years.'

'Please, Ronald . . . don't speak like that in front of Ned. He adores Lucy.'

'Not after this,' Ronald said grimly.

'No. Oh, how could she do it?'

'I'll tell you how! By closing her eyes to everything but her own desires, that's how! She never gives a toss about anyone but herself. Well, we'll see how she likes what she's got when Ned divorces her.'

'Ronald!'

'What else can he do? And I'll make sure they press every charge against her that can possibly be devised. Abduction of a child, assault, theft —'

'Don't, don't — all I want is to get Heather back, I don't care about anything else.'

He was silenced. Anger was no use. What was

needed was good sense, calm organisation. The police must be given every possible help in finding Lucy.

'Have you told them about Massiter?' he challenged.

'Not by name. I hoped they would find Lucy between here and London, if that's where she's headed.'

'I think we're past that point. You must give them Massiter's name and address.'

'Ronald, Lucy isn't likely to have gone to Massiter's London house —'

'But the police can go there and ask questions. After all, who else can we suppose she's going to?'

'Yes, I see.' She shivered. 'I'd better tell the constable to take a message to the police station.'

'Yes, at once. The sooner the better.'

He went with her to the hall. The constable, on hearing Jenny's information, wrote it down in his notebook, then went to take the torn-out page to his partner at the gate.

'You must have something to eat,' Jenny said to her husband. 'Everything's at sixes and sevens —' Her voice broke.

'Have you eaten?'

'Yes — no — I don't remember.'

'We'll have something together.'

They were picking at a meal of hot stew and vegetables when they heard the carriage again in the drive. With a glance of reluctance at each other they rose.

Ned was in the hall, giving his coat to Thirley. He swung round on them. 'What's wrong? At the station they said something about Mother.'

'She's had an accident, Ned —'

'She was attacked,' Ronald interrupted, 'last night in the drive, and left lying there to live or die.'

Ned's face went white. 'My God! How is she?'

'Ronald, how could you! Ned, my poor lad, Mother is in bed, the doctor has seen to her and she's resting. But you see . . .' Jenny faltered into silence.

'I'll say it if you won't. The person who attacked her was your precious wife Lucy.'

Ned drew back as if he had been struck. Then a flush came up into his fine-skinned features. 'Watch your mouth, Armstrong! How dare you make a mad accusation like —'

Jenny went up to him and took his sleeve in her fingers. She was trembling. She didn't want to hurt her brother but he had to be told the truth. 'Don't be angry with him, Ned — he has good cause. What he says is true. Lucy struck our mother down when she tried to stop her from running away in the middle of the night.'

'That's insane!'

'No, it's true. Lucy is gone. And' — she stared up into her brother's face — 'she took my baby with her.'

The only defence against the news was disbelief. Ned swept aside everything they told him. 'You can't mean any of this! Is it some kind of joke? Lucy would never harm anyone! She's sweet and gentle . . .'

They let him rage through a defence of his wife. Then Ronald said, 'If it's not true, then where is Lucy?'

Ned drew up in a start of alarm. 'She's here.'

'No.'

'My wife is here.'

'No.'

'I tell you —'

106

'Go and look for her, then,' Jenny said in helpless distress. 'See if you can find her. And find Heather too. Find my baby for me.'

Ned stalked away from them, up the stairs. They heard him go to the garden-side room, which was the bedroom of himself and Lucy. They heard his footsteps become muffled on the thick carpet inside.

After a moment he could be heard moving along the landing. He went into the night nursery. No nightlight glowed there. He went into the day nursery. That too was dark and silent.

'He'll go in to Mother,' Jenny cried, and picking up her skirts ran up to prevent him. Ned had his hand on the knob of her door.

'No, Ned. She's resting. Baird is watching by her bed. Don't wake her — she must sleep.'

'But I must ask her —'

'There's no need to ask her. She told me, I had it from her in so many words. Lucy hit her, and ran off with Heather in her arms past the gates.'

'No, no, I won't believe it.' He turned back into his own bedroom, closing the door with a kind of finality. Jenny went back down to Ronald.

A little later a visitor arrived, Herbert Muir, the chief clerk from Waterside Mill. He came in looking extremely distressed and embarrassed. 'Mistress, maister,' he said, touching his hat. 'I know this is a kittle thing to be asking now, but are there any instructions for the morn?'

Next day was Saturday, the day the weavers were paid. Jenny had forgotten all about it. She looked at Muir in consternation.

'If you'll give a letter of authority, mistress, I'll go to the bank first thing for the money. The workers'll be late getting their pay because of the delay in filling their pay tins, but they'll understand.'

'Yes, Mr Muir. I'll write a line for you now.'

'And Mr Armstrong, what's to be done about the doubling for the green fleck tweed?'

Ronald looked as if he had never heard of it. 'Tell Ritchie to do the best he can,' he said.

'Very good, sir. Will I tell him you'll be in on Monday for the approval of the colours for setting up Leuchar's order?'

'Tell him what you like!' shouted Ronald.

Jenny, at the writing desk, turned. Her glance reproved him. He took a grip on himself and said, 'Mr Muir, tell Ritchie that until things here at Gatesmuir are sorted, he's to regard himself as in charge. It's to be hoped I'll be back in a day or two. Until we know more of what's to happen Mistress Armstrong and I can't be sure of coming to the mill.'

'Yes, maister, I understand.' He was clutching his hard hat across his breast. He half-raised it now in a kind of salute. 'The workers asked me to say, sir and madam, that we're a' thinking of you and wishing you well.'

'Thank you, Muir,' Jenny said.

'Yes, thank you,' said Ronald.

Muir had hardly left when the Commissioner of Police, Major Wishart, arrived. He was an ex-soldier, a stout, generally jovial man with a great gift for organisation. The police force in the Borders was still in course of being established, but in Galashiels there was a small and efficient body.

'I've come in person,' he said, 'to give you such news as I have. I sent a message by the telegraph to the London force, asking them to call on Mr Harvil Massiter. The reply is that they have done so, that Mr

Massiter is from home, but Mrs Massiter asserts she knows for certain that he is in Suffolk at their country house.'

Ronald looked at Jenny. 'You've met her, Jenny. Would you say she'd know where he is?'

'I'd say not. And, what's more,' Jenny said, thinking of that proud, angry woman at the Truscotts' party, 'I think she would lie to save face.'

Major Wishart nodded, pulling at his beard. 'So if I request the London detectives to go back and ask again, they may get better information?'

Jenny sighed. 'I don't know. She may not know where he is at all. I don't see that it will help us.'

'Can you suggest anything else to try, dear lady?'

They talked it over, but there seemed no other lead to Lucy's whereabouts. Wishart took his leave, promising action first thing in the morning.

A little later Ned came into the drawing room. 'Where do you think she has gone?' he asked without preliminaries.

His brother-in-law shrugged at him. 'So you've come to the conclusion we weren't inventing things?'

Ned went a slow, painful red. 'I saw the jewel box left standing empty. So I looked for a few things of my own — oh, nothing much, but you know I kept Father's gold watch, and there were some pearl shirt studs and a seal ring.'

Jenny and Ronald looked at him. 'They've gone,' Jenny said, as a statement and not a question.

'Yes.'

'We'll have to tell the police. If she sells them it may help in tracing her.'

'Jenny, how could she? How could she? And why? We were always so happy . . .'

He turned away, and to the utter dismay of his sister and brother-in-law, began to weep. Next moment he had fled to the sanctuary of the bedroom he had shared with his wife.

Jenny and her husband stayed up very late but no further news came. At length they went to bed, and such was Jenny's state of exhaustion that she slept soundly, only waking when Baird came in at seven-thirty to say that Major Wishart had come.

Ronald was already downstairs. Jenny dressed hastily and descended. Wishart was pacing about the drawing room with his heavy step. He waited for Jenny to seat herself before beginning.

'I got a long telegraph message this morning. Inspector Dancy went first thing to Mrs Massiter. It seems she repeated the same story as yesterday until Dancy mentioned Mrs Corvill. Then I regret to say she went into a tirade, the gist of which Dancy gives, although a written report is coming on the next train.'

'What did she say?'

'It appears that after the first visit from the police she looked about, and it's quite clear that Massiter has cleared out, taking with him his wife's diamonds and a fair sum in cash, and leaving a great many debts.'

'My God,' groaned Ronald.

While Wishart was speaking, Ned had come in, looking wan and red-eyed. He said now, 'Why are we speaking of Mrs Massiter? She's only a casual London acquaintance of ours.'

All heads turned to him. Wishart darted a glance at Jenny, who sighed and by a slight shrug told him that as yet Ned hadn't learned about Massiter. There was a silence. Then Wishart, who needed to be able to get information and could never do it if there wasn't total openness, took the initiative.

'There is reason to believe that Mrs Corvill left this house to go to Mr Massiter, I understand.'

'*What*?' Ned cried.

'You didn't know of this relationship?'

'What relationship? Are you out of your mind? Lucy scarcely knows Massiter.'

'I infer from what I have heard from Mrs Armstrong that Mrs Corvill and Mr Massiter were more than slightly acquainted.'

'Jenny! What have you been saying?'

Ronald sprang up. 'Don't shout at Jenny! If you had had the brains you were born with you'd have known that Lucy was bored to death with you and ready for a romance with anybody that would smile at her.'

'Don't you dare — '

'Gentlemen, gentlemen, this is no help at all,' Wishart said, in the tone that had rebuked rowdy messrooms.

When Ronald had sat down again and Ned looked ready to listen, Wishart resumed. 'It seems more than a coincidence that your wife should run away from home and that at the same time a man with whom she had a close . . . er . . . friendship should cut and run. Is that an unreasonable idea?'

'Of course it is! You don't know Lucy! What you're suggesting is impossible.'

Major Wishart had in fact met Lucy, but only at social events. He recalled her as an angelic creature, all milk and roses. Yet experience had taught him that even with angelic creatures nothing was impossible. And the evidence was inescapable.

'Can you suggest any other possibility, Corvill? Any

111

other reason why she would have gone from home without warning, without any message?'

Ned was silent.

'Can you suggest anywhere she might have gone?'

A shake of the head.

'You hadn't quarrelled?'

'With Lucy?' Ned murmured, as if the idea were ludicrous. 'Lucy isn't quarrelsome. She's shy, reticent . . .'

The major felt in his breast pocket for a slip of paper, examined it, then said, 'When the idea of the missing little girl was broached to Mrs Massiter she found it −' he glanced at the paper − 'I quote, "laughable".' He looked at Jenny.

'Yes,' she said in a stifled voice. 'I would say he's not a man who cares for children.'

'Don't you see?' Ned broke out. 'That means Lucy never intended to go to Massiter!'

'No, it only means she stole our little girl and injured your mother,' Ronald snarled.

Wishart frowned at him, but couldn't find it in his heart to rebuke him. 'It's very puzzling.'

'Where can she be?' Jenny moaned. 'Heather, oh, my little lass . . .'

'Lucy loves Heather,' Ned insisted. 'Lucy will look after her, don't be afraid, Jenny −'

'Look after her! My God, brother, she doesn't know the first thing about looking after a child! She only ever played with Heather and spoiled her. She doesn't know how to give her her breakfast or wash her face for her. If Heather got a speck on her dress, Lucy handed her to Wilmot to tidy up. Look after her!'

And to her own dismay Jenny burst into tears. She covered her face with her hands, turned in among the sofa cushions, and leaned there, weeping as if the flood gates had opened for ever.

Wishart hesitated, nodded in understanding, then moved out into the hall, beckoning the men to follow him. 'My wife would say it's best for her to have her cry out. Is there someone who can look after her? Another woman?'

'Her mother — but her mother is lying injured in bed,' Ronald said. He shook his head despairingly. 'I'll get Baird for her.' He rang the bell.

'Tell me,' the major resumed, 'is there anything more to be told? Have you found a note — because ladies usually leave a note, you see.'

Ronald hesitated, then looked at Ned. His brother-in-law, very unwilling, said, 'I discovered that . . . that one or two of my belongings have gone, as well as the jewellery.' He gave Wishart a description. As he spoke, the major pursed up his lips and sighed inwardly. A selfish girl, Mrs Corvill. A bad lot, it seemed.

After he had gone, the normal day began. Slowly, inevitably, the household of Gatesmuir began to recover a little from the shock of Lucy's actions. Friends began to call, and though they were turned back by the policeman at the gates they left messages of goodwill and hope.

Ronald dismissed Wilmot that morning. 'I can't have her in the house,' he said.

Jenny was too dazed and confused to defend the nursemaid, even if there was much defence to make. Perhaps the girl's only crime had been that she had drunk too large a glass of port with Cook before going to bed and, always a heavy sleeper, had snored through the kidnapping.

Wilmot left in tears, knowing full well she could

never get another post after this shameful event, and not daring to beg Jenny for a character reference — though had she but known, she might have got it. Through her haze of misery Jenny might have admitted she had nothing against Wilmot's character. It was Lucy who was to blame — how could any nursemaid have been expected to stand guard against *Lucy*?

For that day and the next Ronald stayed at home, trying to comfort Jenny, avoiding Ned, staring out of the window in hopes of a messenger to say his little daughter had been found. Anger and frustration mounted in him. He wanted to smash something, to hurt someone — but none of that would do any good.

At length he went back to the mill. At least there was something to do there. He couldn't concentrate on the work, not even on the problem of how to get a vermilion dye to fix for a new lightweight tweed. His normal wry good humour had deserted him. His workforce found him short-tempered, over-critical — but they forgave him everything.

'Poor soul,' they murmured to each other, 'look how thin he's getting — and he never had much flesh on him. And think what it must be like for the mistress . . .'

Jenny promised she would send a message the moment any news came to Gatesmuir. For her part, she spent most of her time in her mother's bedroom.

Millicent Corvill wasn't making a good recovery from the shock of the attack nor from the broken limb. She was in pain all the time, although Dr Lauder kept it subdued with laudanum drops. Jenny began to worry about that treatment. 'It seems to make her so listless, doctor. And she hardly eats a morsel.'

'Time, my dear lady, time — it takes time at Mrs Corvill's age to recover from such a stramash. Let you be thinking of the end of February before much will improve.'

Ned tried to share in the task of watching in the sickroom. He was silent most of the time, white with strain. Once Jenny passed the open door of his bedroom, and saw him standing with one of Lucy's favourite fans in his hand, holding it closed against his face, almost as if by this he could conjure her up in the flesh. Jenny must have made some sound, for Ned looked up, then darted to the door and slammed it in her face. He didn't want even his sister, who loved him, to see his pain.

The one thing that Jenny could be thankful for was that Ned hadn't turned to the bottle for consolation. Or at least, not so far . . .

When ten days had gone by Major Wishart came flurrying up the drive in a fly. He almost fell out of it in his eagerness to speak as Thirley threw open the door to him. Jenny ran downstairs, hearing his voice in the hall.

'Major Wishart! There's news?'

'My dear Mrs Armstrong! I believe we have found her!'

The daylight suddenly blazed, then dimmed. Jenny felt herself falling. She grasped the banister. 'Oh, thank God! Is she well — safe and well?'

'Oh yes, quite well —'

'Where is she? Oh, God, my baby —'

All the animation went out of Major Wishart. 'Wishart, you fool!' he said, smiting himself on the forehead. He was red with shame. 'I only meant — we've found Mrs Corvill.'

'But Heather is with her?'

She watched in horror as he shook his head.

Chapter Eight

Dr Lauder happened to be in the house. He came downstairs at Wishart's exclamation of alarm, and restoratives brought Jenny out of the momentary faintness.

'Tell me — quickly — Major Wishart —'

The little that could be told in a telegraphic message from another police force was soon conveyed. 'Mrs Corvill has been found in Dover —'

'Dover!'

'A pawnbroker recognised her from the description —'

'She was trying to sell her jewellery?' Jenny broke in.

'No, that's the strange thing. She was trying to sell a piece of fine lace — a collar, I believe.'

'A piece of lace? I don't understand it. And Heather — ?'

'Is not with her, I very much regret to say.'

'Dear God,' Jenny whispered. 'What has that she-devil done with my baby?'

'They don't say anything about that in the message. Their phrase is, "Suspect does not respond to questions." '

'Massiter?'

'No word of him.'

Jenny pulled her hair back from her face, as if to pare away anything that might distract her. 'She's alone. She's without money — or else why was she trying to sell her lace collar?'

'That seems to be the case.'

'She won't say what's happened?'

'They can get nothing out of her. But she was in a small hotel by the harbour, and the proprietor was pressing her to pay her bill.'

'We must go there at once,' Jenny said, getting up from her chair.

'Mrs Armstrong, I advise against it,' Dr Lauder said. 'These perpetual anxieties — your husband would be more suited —'

'Dr Lauder, if you think these "perpetual anxieties" will be eased by staying at home while the woman who took my baby is in Dover —!'

Jenny's brother came slowly into the drawing room. When Dr Lauder quitted the sick room at the alarm on the stairs, he had come out to the landing. There he had stood, hidden from view, but listening.

'I told you she wasn't with Massiter,' he said, in a kind of resentful triumph.

Major Wishart looked at him. There was pity in his glance, to see the man so diminished. He said as kindly as he could, 'The innkeeper told the police, as far as I can gather from the report, that there had been a gentleman with her but he had left.'

'No!'

'Sir,' the major said, still kind but firm, 'open your eyes. Your wife ran away with another man. And he, it seems, has abandoned her.'

Ned put his hands over his ears. 'I refuse to listen to lies like that!'

'You can't refuse to accept the truth. And the truth is that your wife is in Dover, destitute.'

'Lucy, my poor little Lucy.' Ned turned to the door. 'I'm going to her.'

'No –' cried Jenny.

But the major put his hand on her arm. 'He has the right to go. In fact, it is his duty. But God knows how he'll acquit himself.'

The gardener's boy was sent with a message to Ronald. He came home at once. Jenny was already packing. Within an hour they were off to the station, leaving Baird in charge of Jenny's mother.

Lucy was being kept under the charge of a police constable at the little inn on the road above the harbour. The detective sergeant who met them at the railway station took them there at once.

'We thought it best to keep her there. We've no facilities for keeping a lady in the police lock-up.'

When they arrived at the White Boar, Ned insisted on being shown up to the room alone. Jenny didn't know what to say, and while she was still trying to think of a way to prevent it, he had gone up the wooden staircase with the sergeant.

In a moment there was an outcry, screams and protests, Ned's voice trying to calm Lucy down. After a minute or two the two men came back, Ned white and very shaken. The sergeant said, 'The lady's hysterical, ma'am. I wonder if you . . .'

'My God, are you asking my wife to look after that little trollop?' Ronald cried.

'She needs a woman to handle her, sir,' the sergeant said. 'We don't have no women on the police force, so she's been all alone for three days now, and very distressed.'

'I don't give a damn if she's broken in pieces! My wife isn't — '

'Ronald, she and I have got to meet some time. I'm going up.'

'No, Jenny — '

'I think it would be best, sir. We can't get not a word out of her, y'see.'

On limbs that trembled Jenny went up the stairs. The constable opened the door for her.

Lucy was sitting in a wooden armchair with a handkerchief up to her face. Her head was thrown back. Her pretty blond hair was in a tangle, hairpins falling out, the decorative ribbon reduced to a rat's tail. Her travelling gown of soft lilac wool was stained at the hem with mud. There was a tear in her sleeve. Her shoes had not been cleaned for many a day.

The room was in disorder, the few articles of clothing scattered about, a cup overturned in a saucer on the table, the washbasin unemptied.

'Lucy,' Jenny said.

The figure in the wooden chair stiffened.

'Lucy, look at me.'

Lucy turned away her head.

Jenny went to her, took hold of her hands, and pulled them from her face. The wet and dirty handkerchief revealed red-rimmed eyes, a quivering mouth.

Lucy began to wail, a wordless, meaningless cry of misery.

'Stop that. You're only making things worse, Lucy.' And, since there seemed nothing else to do, Jenny hit her hard on the cheek with the palm of her hand.

Lucy stopped wailing. She gasped, choked, went into a spluttering paroxysm. The constable hurried forward. But by the tine he had got close enough to intervene between, as he imagined, two fighting women, she had recovered enough to draw a quieter breath. She sat up straight.

'I don't want you here!' she cried to Jenny.

'What have you done with Heather?'

'Go away, I don't want you here. Nobody must see me like this.'

'Tell me where Heather is!'

Lucy shook her head from side to side. 'Don't talk to me like that! I know why you've come! You want to laugh at me — that's all it is, you want to see me brought low —'

'Stop thinking about yourself for once, you empty-headed little fool, and tell me what you've done with my daughter!'

'You shouldn't have brought Ned! I don't want to see Ned! He looks at me . . . I don't want him to look at me like that!'

Jenny took a grip on herself. Somehow she must get through to this unbalanced, self-centred girl. And the only way seemed to be through her vanity.

She brought a chair opposite and sat down, so that she could take hold of Lucy's hands. Lucy tried to withdraw them but she held firm.

'Lucy, you have to tell us what has happened. You have a choice — you can either speak to me, or you can be committed to an asylum, because the way you're going on, you're losing your wits.'

'No!' wailed Lucy.

'You want to be looked after? You want proper clothes and a pretty room?'

The other girl looked at her, her gaze vacant and yet with some intelligence beginning to return.

'I sold my cape,' she mourned. 'It was new but I only got a few shillings for it. Did you bring my blue silk dress?'

'I'll send for it, Lucy. You'd like that.'

'Yes. And stockings and shoes — I've no clean stockings left.'

'They'll be here tomorrow. But only if you tell me what happened.'

Lucy looked away. 'You'll be angry with me.'

'No I won't. Tell me, Lucy.'

After a quavering start, out it all tumbled. Harvil had had a hard time with his wife, who wouldn't put up the money to pay his debts. Harvil had decided that if she wouldn't part with it willingly, he'd take it anyway. 'It served her right, you know — a wife's property really belongs to her husband, doesn't it?'

The deciding factor was Mrs Massiter's outburst at the Truscotts' house. Before Lucy was packed off to Galashiels they decided to run away. Lucy promised to bring her jewellery and anything else she could.

They had to wait for a night when her flight would be easy. Ned was often away, and they had known when Ronald would be in London. Fortune favoured them even more — Jenny went to Newcastle.

Harvil had arranged for the post chaise to be waiting. Everything had been arranged by letter. 'You didn't realise we wrote to each other regularly, did you?' Lucy asked, with a gleam of something like triumph in her blue eyes.

Jenny had noticed the envelopes in what she guessed was Massiter's handwriting. But she had been sure that he would get bored with writing love letters after a few weeks. It had never occurred to her they were planning an elopement.

The arrangement was for Lucy to drive to Newcastle for the mainline train to London at six in the morning. She had no fear of meeting Jenny because according to Jenny's plans she hadn't intended to leave Newcastle until two days later and would hardly be up and about in the railway station at six.

'It was exciting at first. I packed a few things and was ready to slip out to the carriage at midnight. Then as I went out, I thought — I felt —'

'Go on,' Jenny prompted, keeping her tone calm so as not to frighten her into silence.

'I thought I'd just go in and kiss Heather goodbye. You see, I knew I wasn't —' her voice broke ' — I wasn't going to see her again. And so I tiptoed in, and leaned over her, and she woke up. And she just put her arms up, the way she does, and twined them round my neck, and smiled at me, and I picked her up, and she snuggled against me, half asleep. And I couldn't put her down again, I just couldn't.'

Lucy paused for a long moment. She was reliving that moment. 'You see, I was going away — for ever. It was a bit frightening. And Heather was part of the familiar things, and it was comforting to have her holding on to me, the way she always does.'

'I see.'

'So then,' Lucy said, with something almost like a toss of her head, 'I thought, why shouldn't I take her — I'm the one who loves her most, after all —'

'Lucy!'

'Well, it's true, you never pay her enough attention, you're always off at Waterside Mill or looking over the accounts or drawing designs. *I* was the one who was always there for her. So I just went out as quiet as a mouse and got downstairs with no trouble and opened the side door and I was on my way down the drive — almost safe away from you all — and your mother called my name and caught at me. And I swung round, and I don't know how . . .' She broke off, frightened at the recollection.

'Well, anyhow, she fell, and I thought she'd make an outcry, but she didn't make a sound after that once when she called me. And I thought, she's fainted, good, she can't stop me. And I was in the carriage the next moment and the postilion was shaking up the horses, and we were away!'

Jenny held her breath. She dared not ask any questions for fear of disturbing Lucy's train of thought.

'We were lucky to get good horses, we made good time . . .'

'But,' Jenny burst out, 'no one saw Heather when you changed at Hexham.'

'No, she was asleep in the corner. She was so good then. Not a sound out of her, she slept like a little angel. And when we got on the train at Newcastle she was pleased, she waved her arms and gurgled. But then she began to cry. I suppose she was hungry. I got some bread and milk for her at one of the stops and she went to sleep again, so that was fine and I got a hackney to take me to the inn in Holborn where Harvil was to meet me.'

'He was waiting for you?'

'No, it was very lucky, really, I was able to buy a frock for Heather and though she was very naughty about letting me put it on she looked quite nice and she ate some minced chicken and seemed to like it and then Harvil came.'

'Yes. And what did he say when he saw Heather?'

'He was . . . he was surprised.' Lucy bent her head so that the words were muffled and her face was hidden by the tangle of her hair. 'He was cross.'

'Didn't you think of that, Lucy? That he wouldn't like it?'

'I don't know . . . She's so good as a rule, I thought she wouldn't be any trouble . . . And we could get a girl to look after her in Rome —'

'Rome! Was that where you were going?'

Lucy looked up at that, her cheeks flushing with pleasure. 'Oh, it would have been so wonderful! It's a beautiful city, everybody says so, and the sun shines there, and there are palaces and gardens with fountains, and Harvil and I would have strolled by the sea — or I think it's a river — and Heather would have been no trouble, and the sunshine would have been so good for her, better than the damp and cold of the Borders . . .'

'What happened, Lucy?'

The sheen of happy expectation left her face. She sighed and drooped. 'Harvil was so angry. He just refused . . . He refused to take me if I insisted on bringing Heather. He told me I'd have to go back. And you know, I couldn't do that. Not after . . . after . . .'

Not after stealing her husband's watch and ring and after knocking her mother-in-law down. Not after running away in the middle of the night with her sister-in-law's baby.

'So Heather was crying because she was frightened by the raised voices, I suppose. And she was sick down the front of her new dress. And Harvil said she was disgusting, and she was being so kittle, you know. So after a lot of arguing he said that he really loved me and he wanted me to go with him but I'd have to leave

Heather. And I said . . . I really did, Jenny . . . I said I couldn't leave her, I couldn't just abandon her. So Harvil said not to worry my little head about it, he'd see to it that she got safely back to you.'

'How was that to be done?'

'He took Heather downstairs and when he came back he said he'd paid a very respectable young woman who was waiting for the stagecoach north to take Heather and deliver her back to Gatesmuir. He gave her a guinea as well as paying for her seat on the coach.'

'And you believed him?'

'Yes of course!' Lucy gave a sudden gasp. 'You mean, he didn't do it?'

'I've no way of knowing. All I know is, Heather has not been seen since you took her away.'

'But that's impossible,' Lucy protested. 'He told me, a very respectable young woman — he gave her a guinea!'

The constable, who had been listening to all this without speaking or moving, now left the room very quietly. Jenny had no doubt he was reporting the facts, true or false, of the 'respectable young woman' at Holborn to the sergeant.

Lucy was rubbing her forehead with her fingers. 'I don't understand,' she said. 'You can't mean Heather is missing?'

'Yes.'

'But she should have reached home — I forget what day it was — but by now. I mean, I know I've been in Dover for at least a week and we sent her back before we left London.'

'Why didn't you go to Rome, Lucy?'

Tears welled up in the forget-me-not eyes, welled

126

over, and flowed down the grimy cheeks. 'He left me
here,' she said, choking on her sobs. 'He said he was
going to check that we had berths on the packet for
Calais and he went out and . . . and . . . he never came
back.'

'When was that? What day?'

'I think it was Thursday. A week ago, it must be.'

Jenny sighed. 'And before he left, he asked you for
your jewellery, I suppose.'

'How did you know that?' Lucy said in surprise.
'Of course, as he explained, he had to sell it to pay
for the steamer tickets. He said he would give me some
of the money at once to buy some clothes, because I
hadn't brought much, you see, and I felt I wasn't
looking my best, and after the disagreement about
Heather I wanted him to be pleased with me so I said
if I could have enough for a ready-made dress which
of course wouldn't have been very fashionable but
there are some dressmakers here with modes in the
window — did you notice, Jenny? Quite smart, and
I thought one of them would probably fit me with a
little alteration, and then perhaps just gloves and
stockings, because of course we were going to travel
via Paris and I could have bought such nice things
there . . .' Her voice wavered into silence.

'Do you really think he's gone to Rome?'

'Of course, he said he was. You don't think he was
lying to me?' Lucy said, as if the notion were shocking.

There was no way of knowing. Harvil Massiter
might really have intended to take Lucy with him to
a new life in Rome. Perhaps he had been put off by
her stupidity in burdening them with a baby girl, and
had changed his mind at the last moment. Certainly,
if a man was planning a romantic escape to Latin skies,

Lucy was beautiful enough to seem the ideal companion. But she had made their future together much more dangerous. Baby-stealing was likely to cause them a lot of trouble.

'I don't know why he went like that,' Lucy went on, shaking her head in bewilderment. 'After all, I gave in about Heather. And I came all this way, and he promised . . . he *promised* . . .'

The constable came back as quietly as he had left. He raised his eyebrows at Jenny.

'I don't think there's anything more to be learnt,' she said. 'Massiter seems to have gone about a week ago, taking everything of value with him. As far as Mrs Corvill knows, he was taking the steam packet to Calais.'

'We knew about the steam packet, ma'am. The innkeeper told us that. He did actually go on it.'

'He went without me!' Lucy wailed.

The constable stared at her. Without taking his eyes off her he said to Jenny, 'What's to be done with her now, ma'am?'

'Is she to be charged with anything?'

'She hasn't committed any offence in Dover, Mrs Armstrong. The London police want to see her on account of the matter with the little girl. There may have been an offence against a minor within the jurisdiction of the London magistrates, that's to say the selling of a child for money.'

Lucy cried out in protest. 'Harvil didn't sell her! It's quite the opposite — he gave money to the young woman to take Heather home!'

'What was the name of this young woman, ma'am?'

She stared at him, a blankness in her eyes. 'How do I know? Harvil saw to it all. It was the kind of thing that a man has to see to.'

'We can have inquiries made at the London inn. The coachdriver may remember her, or the ticket seller.'

He turned to go. As Jenny was about to follow him, Lucy snatched at her sleeve. 'Don't go, Jenny! Don't leave me here alone! I'll go mad if you leave me!'

Jenny pulled herself free. Her whole being shuddered away from any contact with her sister-in-law.

'No, no! Don't go! They lock me in! They question me and I don't know what they want me to say! You promised, Jenny — you promised I should have a clean dress and stockings — you promised!'

The constable had intervened to unhook the clutching hand from Jenny's jacket. He pushed Lucy back into the room without gentleness. 'Sit down and control yourself, lady,' he said.

Outside, after the door had been locked on the sobbing girl, he said to Jenny, 'She's right, though, she's going out of her mind. Something'll have to be done about her, ma'am — I've seen it before.'

The sergeant was with Ronald and Ned in the innkeeper's private parlour. They all rose as she was shown in by the constable.

'I've sent word to London to try to find the woman Mrs Corvill mentioned,' the sergeant said. 'But I don't hold out much hope. It was over a week ago now, and the Mitre is a busy place, I imagine.'

Ned shouldered his way between the two others to get to his sister. 'How is she now?' he demanded. 'When can I see her? I must see her —'

'She hardly knows where she is or what's happening.'

'Is it true, what the constable said — she gave

Heather away to some stranger?' Ronald sounded dazed, incredulous.

Jenny sank down on a chair. 'It seems so, Ronald. It seems so. She's muddled and weak in her nerves, but I think she's telling the truth. Harvil Massiter took Heather downstairs and when he came back he said he'd given her to a passenger on the coach to take home.'

'There's some mistake,' Ned insisted. 'She wouldn't do that. She's talking wildly. She was hysterical when I saw her —'

'I'll kill her,' Ronald said. 'If ever I lay hands on her, I'll kill her.'

'Now now, sir,' said the sergeant, laying a broad hand on his arm, 'you don't mean that —'

'You don't think so? If ever she and I are in the same room —'

'You're doing no good like that, sir. Think of your poor wife, it's no help to her.' Ronald turned to look at Jenny. He found her leaning back in her chair with an arm over her eyes. At once he forgot his anger. He rushed to kneel at her side, an arm about her, words of comfort ready to whisper to her. 'It will be all right. We'll find the woman who has her. My dearest lass, you've been so brave — don't give way now.'

Later that night the sergeant came back to say that there were no grounds for any charges against Mrs Corvill, but that a member of the Metropolitan force would be here next day to escort her to London. 'She's wanted for questioning there, but the big problem is she goes into a hysterical attack if we attempt to move her. I wanted to warn you — it'll have to be done by force.'

'No!' shouted Ned. 'Don't dare to —'

'Sir, what else are we to do? She cries out if anyone even comes in the door, something about her dress —'

'I promised her a new dress,' Jenny said. 'She's always set a lot of importance on how she looks.'

'Well, we could get a dress from a secondhand shop if that would quieten her.'

'I'll buy her a dress,' Jenny said, getting up. 'A dress, and stockings and shoes. I promised.'

'You'll do no such thing,' Ronald cried. 'Don't ever do anything for that woman —'

'It's not for her, it's for Heather. We want her in London, where perhaps she can help trace the woman she spoke of. She mentioned a modiste — I noticed one as we drove by in the High Street. Send for a cab, please, Ronald.'

When the inn was at last settling down for the night, there was a knock on the door of Lucy's room. It was unlocked. As she drew back in dread, her sister-in-law came in with an armful of parcels.

'Your new dress, Lucy. Look, it's blue velvet. You like velvet, don't you? And the bonnet matches. And here are stockings — only cotton yarn, I couldn't get silk at this hour, but they're quite fine. And a cloak, because it's very cold outside.'

Lucy came forward, her eyes on the clothes that were coming out of the paper wrappings. 'Where are the shoes?'

'I couldn't get any. But we'll have that pair cleaned and they'll look almost as good as ever, and besides, they're mostly hidden under your skirts.'

The words, softly spoken as if to a child, were soothing. Lucy picked up the velvet gown and held it against herself. 'It's too big!' she complained. 'It won't do!'

131

'We'll have it altered when we get to London.'

'We're going to London?'

'Yes, tomorrow. And there are shoes there, in your room at Eaton Square.'

Lucy was unhooking the fastening of her soiled gown. 'Quick, help me. I must put it on — '

'No, Lucy, it's time to go to bed now.'

'I want to put on my new dress! I want to put it on!'

'Put on your nightgown instead. You must get some sleep. We'll be leaving for London early in the morning.'

'No, no,' cried Lucy, her fingers fumbling with the hooks of her bodice. 'You don't understand — it's important — I must wear it — I'll look pretty in it — everything will be all right if I have something pretty to wear.'

There was no avoiding it. Jenny helped the other girl put on the new dress. When it was fastened and tied, she found the lace bertha she had attempted to sell to the pawnbroker. She draped it round her shoulders. 'It's not much too big,' she said, turning to examine herself in the small mirror that was all the room afforded. 'The colour's too bright, but it will do until I get to London. I think my amethyst silk is at Eaton Square, and there's a dark blue wool voile . . .'

She talked on, her world suddenly changed by the thought of pretty dresses and clean underwear, of silk stockings and kid shoes.

When Jenny, dropping with exhaustion, eventually left her, she was sitting upright on a chair in the middle of the room, fully clad, eyes staring ahead, glorying in her new gown.

Ronald had taken two private carriages on the

London train for next day. Lucy and the police sergeant occupied one, and though Ned wanted to be with her that proved impossible — the mere sight of her husband drove Lucy to hysterics. He sat with his sister and her husband, white-faced, bewildered.

A closed carriage took them to Eaton Square. A gentleman in a dark suit was waiting when they came in; an inspector from the Central District of the Metropolitan Force.

Lucy was put in the morning room with the sergeant on guard. Inspector Simmons went with the others into the library.

'The report from Dover came by the morning post,' he said, waving a manila envelope. 'May I just go over it to be sure I have the facts? The lady travelled south by post chaise and train to London, where she met her lover — '

'No,' Ned groaned.

'I beg your pardon, sir?'

'My wife would never enter into an illicit affair.'

The inspector, a man of about forty who had seen everything, raised his eyebrows but didn't attempt to argue. 'Mrs Corvill came to the Mitre Inn in Holborn and there Mr Harvil Massiter was also present. At some point Massiter took Heather Armstrong, the child of Ronald and Genevieve Armstrong, to the general waiting room. When he returned he told Mrs Corvill that he had sent the child home to Galashiels in the care of a woman passenger on the northern coach. That is correct?'

'So she told me,' Jenny said wearily. 'I think it's true.'

'Have you traced this woman?' Ronald put in with anxious eagerness.

Inspector Simmons shook his head. 'Not at all. In fact, madam and gentlemen, it's difficult to be sure the child was ever there.'

'What?' cried Jenny, staggering under the shock of the words.

'But Lucy said —'

'From all I hear, she's scarcely responsible for what she says or does. No one at the Mitre actually saw the child, although one of the chambermaids did say something about being asked to buy a short frock, which she did.'

'Then she would be able to say —'

'Unfortunately she's left her employment. The owner of the inn, Mr Treadgold, says she was a flighty piece and he's glad to be rid of her. We haven't been able to find her.'

'The woman who promised to take care of Heather?' Ronald demanded. 'You've traced her?'

'I'm afraid not. The ticket seller has no recollection of her, and the driver says he's had several women or families with children as passengers. You must realise, sir, that though the stage doesn't get anything like the custom it used to before the railways, it's still very busy — it still serves places the railway has bypassed, and in one week the routes handle a great many passengers.'

He left them to go and interview Lucy. When he returned he was shaking his head. 'I don't know if she understands the situation at all. She keeps talking about sending for a milliner. I can't get anything of use from her.'

Jenny was now under attack from a blinding headache. The housekeeper helped her up to bed. Inspector Simmons took Ronald aside.

'Mr Armstrong, I didn't like to say any of this while your wife was present. But that lady in there —' he nodded towards the morning room '— isn't responsible for her actions. If she really did take the child from your home in Galashiels, she may have got rid of it on the way south.'

'What are you saying?' Ronald cried in horror. 'Whatever her faults, Lucy loves the baby —'

'That's as may be, sir, but I can't be sure she had the baby with her when she was at the Mitre.'

'But she says Massiter —'

'That may be true or it may not. She may only be putting it onto him. But if he took the child away from her, sir, I think you have to accept the possibility that he didn't hand it to any convenient woman passenger on the stage.'

'I don't understand you.'

The inspector looked grim. 'I think you've got to be prepared for the worst, sir. Your baby may well be at the bottom of the Thames.'

Chapter Nine

A new factor entered the case next day. A silver-haired gentleman called at the house in Eaton Square, sending up his card and asking to speak to either Mr or Mrs Armstrong 'on behalf of Mrs Massiter'. Since Ronald was out with officers of the police force, trying to trace the chambermaid from the Mitre, Jenny received Mr Giles.

'Mrs Armstrong, I realise that you are under a very great strain at present and I offer apologies for breaking in upon your anxieties. Before I go further I must ask if what I hear is true — that young Mrs Corvill is supposed to have abducted your daughter?'

Jenny, turned to ice by his cruel question, bowed slightly. By now, she knew, it must be common gossip. And the newspapers had printed veiled hints about runaway wives and missing gentlemen.

'Mrs Massiter has been approached by the police for news of her husband —'

'Has she sent you to tell me where he is?' Jenny cried in startled eagerness. Massiter alone knew the truth of the story about the 'respectable young woman'.

'Indeed no. Mrs Massiter has no idea where her erring husband may be. It is unlikely that he will communicate with her, since he took with him some very valuable gems and a large sum of money in gold sovereigns.'

'Then I don't understand —'

'Am I right in believing young Mrs Corvill has been found?'

'Yes.'

'She is to be prosecuted, of course.'

Jenny frowned and hesitated. 'We don't know — not here in London, certainly, because there seems to be no case to bring against her.'

'Theft! She took part in the robbery of Mrs Massiter's diamonds.'

In all fairness Jenny had to counter that accusation. 'There's no proof she knew Mr Massiter planned to take the diamonds, Mr Giles.'

'Then she will be tried for the abduction of your child.'

She shook her head. 'No witnesses saw her with Heather except my mother.'

'She, I believe, is in Scotland?'

'Yes.' She forbore to tell this high-handed stranger that her mother was very ill in bed.

'So the prosecution will be brought in Scotland.'

'Mr Giles, I fail to see what it is you wish to achieve by these questions.'

'I wish to convey the interest of Mrs Massiter. I will tell her that the prosecution is to take place under Scottish law, for which I have the greatest respect, but I am sure Mrs Massiter would want me to say that if there is anything she can do to further your case against Mrs Corvill — if you wish to have inquiries made here in London or elsewhere in England, if you wish to have evidence sought, if you can use letters from Mrs Corvill left behind by Mr Massiter — Mrs Massiter stands ready to help.'

'Are you saying,' Jenny asked in horror, 'that Mrs

Massiter has sent you here to ask for help in getting revenge against Lucy?'

'Justice, dear lady, justice! Mrs Corvill tempted away Mrs Massiter's husband —'

Jenny rose. 'Sir, I must ask you to leave.' She rang the bell.

The lawyer, looking surprised, rose too, but made no move to go. 'Surely you wish to see Mrs Corvill punished?'

'Please go.'

'One moment. Am I to understand you would help to shield this wicked young woman?'

'No, but I've no wish to be involved in Mrs Massiter's vendetta.'

'Your brother, Mr Corvill, would presumably have different views about a wife who has betrayed him. He would surely like to see the very revealing letters the lady wrote to her lover. Is your brother at home, Mrs Armstrong?'

'No,' lied Jenny, 'and I assure you you're quite wrong in your notions. Ned is grieved for Lucy, not vindictive. Graham, the gentleman's hat.'

'Your brother must be a very strange young man. But you, Mrs Armstrong — surely you feel strongly against the woman who stole your child? You must want revenge!'

'I want my baby back, that's all,' Jenny said, struggling for control in face of this insistent probe.

'And if you don't get her back?'

'I want you to go!'

Mr Giles moved in stately fashion to the door. 'I believe you will change your mind. When you do, remember that Mrs Massiter is your friend and ally.'

When he had gone out, Jenny slammed the door

behind him. To the butler she cried, 'Never let that man in again!'

Ned was in Lucy's room during this interview. Lucy, now under the care of a doctor, had been given an opiate to calm her nerves. Under its influence she slept, a fragile figure in a lace-trimmed nightgown against lace-trimmed pillows. Her husband sat at her bedside murmuring soothing phrases. But the sounds of Mr Giles's peremptory dismissal had reached his ears. He came downstairs.

'Who was that?'

'Some minion from Mrs Massiter, who wants Lucy prosecuted for every crime she can think of.'

'Jenny, I know things look very black against my poor little wife, but you must believe me — she's incapable of the things the police have been suggesting.'

'Don't let's discuss it, Ned.'

'But I want you to understand — Lucy would never harm anyone —'

'She took Heather away, Ned.'

'But she never meant to harm her — it was Massiter —'

'Yes, Massiter! Face it, brother. Lucy ran away to be with Harvil Massiter!'

He had had time to think of a way to live with this dreadful fact. 'You have to understand that Lucy is a victim, not a criminal. Massiter *used* her. She's more to be pitied than condemned —'

'Pitied! God, pity is what she will batten on now! She'll use it like a shield to keep from being made responsible. Ned, she struck down our mother —'

'She never *meant* to!'

Jenny walked away, trembling with the anger that

kept coming up in a senseless wave inside her. What was the use? Everyone wanted to look at the facts from a different viewpoint: Ned wanted to see only what could exculpate his wife, Mrs Massiter wanted to punish and annihilate her, the police wanted evidence, a case . . . No one understood that the only important thing was Heather, Heather; a little girl of eighteen months taken from everything she loved. Heather, lost now, somewhere in the wilderness of London.

Ronald came home about nine in the evening, exhausted, soaked by the rain that had been falling steadily all day. Jenny didn't even have to ask if he had had any success. He looked beaten, broken.

'Inspector Simmons has offered more men tomorrow. We'll go out first thing.'

She nodded. She knew she should tell him that he needed rest and should stay at home, but she wanted him to help in the search, she wanted the whole world to search for her daughter. And find her. *Find* her.

The doctor came once more to look at Lucy and satisfy himself she was resting quietly. The household retired early. At three in the morning Jenny started awake. There was a sound downstairs, the bell of the outer door was ringing, had been ringing for some minutes.

She threw on a dressing-gown. Ronald was already at the bedroom door, wrenching it open. They flew down the stairs. Graham the butler, in rumpled nightclothes, was letting in a man in the uniform of the Metropolitan police.

'You've got news? You've found her?'

The officer came forward. In the light of the hall lamp silver buttons gleamed on his tunic. 'No, ma'am,

I'm sorry. It's something quite different. I'm from the local station, Sergeant Luxby.

'Yes? What is it?' Jenny, at the foot of the stairs, drew back at the seriousness of his face. 'It's bad news of some kind.'

'We received a message by telegraph from a Mr Lauder in Galashiels —'

'Dr Lauder!'

'He didn't know quite where you might be, so he asked the Galashiels police to get in touch with the Met. I've been sent to tell you — he asks Mrs Armstrong to return at once.'

'My mother — something wrong with my mother. What else did he say?'

'That's all the message, ma'am. "Please contact Mrs Armstrong, tell her to return at once." '

Ned had come down. He said, as if remembering it from a long time ago, 'Of course, Mother is ill . . .'

'There's a train in a little over an hour, ma'am,' the sergeant said. 'I have a carriage outside — if you would like to dress and come at once?'

'Of course.' She turned, began to climb the first step, stumbled, and almost fell. Ronald put his arms about her to help her up.

'I'll come too —'

'No, stay here! Stay here and find Heather!'

'But you can't go alone.'

'I'll go with you,' Ned put in.

Her impulse was to shout at him to stay out of her way. Her brother, whom she had loved since childhood, had become like a stranger to her now that his wife had wrecked their lives.

Yet while she was hesitating, holding back the angry refusal, he said, 'She's my mother too, Jenny.'

When they reached Galashiels in the grey light of morning, Dr Lauder was waiting on the platform. One look at his face told them the news was the worst.

'She's gone,' he said. 'At about four this morning.'

Jenny was past all tears. She stood on the draughty platform, the wind catching at her winter cloak and the ribbons of her bonnet. She felt her brother's hand on her arm, but shook it off.

'Mrs Armstrong, you look far from well,' the doctor said.

'I'm all right. Is the carriage here?'

'Yes, we had word by telegraph from the London police that you were on your way.' He glanced at Ned. 'Have you any luggage?'

'No, we just pulled on our clothes and —' Ned's voice was wavering out of control. He dropped behind as Lauder took Jenny's arm to lead her out of the station. He was trying to come to terms with the fact that he had almost forgotten his own mother in the last few days.

'How did it happen?' Jenny asked, when they were in the carriage.

'A pneumonic fever. That was always a danger after the exposure she suffered lying out in wet clothes that night. She simply hadn't the strength to fight it.'

'She was never robust.'

'When I saw the crisis approaching yesterday evening I sent word to fetch you. Unfortunately I thought you were still in Dover. But even if you had come at once . . .'

The house was arranged for mourning — the blinds down, the wreath of evergreen leaves bound with black crepe on the door, the hall mirror covered with a black shawl. Jenny threw off her cloak and went

143

slowly upstairs. She stood by her mother's bed in silence.

'She asked for you,' Dr Lauder said.

'And me?' Ned asked, from behind him.

Dr Lauder looked embarrassed. 'She asked only for Jenny. But she spoke very little at any time. The growing infection in her lungs made it difficult for her to speak.'

Jenny had never felt so alone. Her mother was dead. Her brother was here, but the affection that had once bound her to him had turned to contempt. Ronald was in London, miles away. Her daughter was missing. It seemed there was no one, nothing, by which to find her way through life.

The well-established traditions of mourning took over. Friends called, leaving black-edged cards of condolence. The funeral was announced. Ronald arrived the next day, and the day after that the men followed the coffin to the graveside. All the men of Galashiels — neighbours, friends, fellow textile manufacturers, officials, workmen — every man who could walk and had black to wear even if it were only an armband, came out to do honour to the mother of the mistress of Waterside Mill. After the funeral Ronald noticed that no one spoke to Ned. They shook hands on leaving the grave-yard, as custom demanded, but no one seemed to want to pause with comforting words. In fact, as they later walked back to the carriage to go home, Ronald heard hisses from some of the workmen.

Next day Ned came uncertainly into the drawing room, where Jenny and Ronald sat signing formal cards of thanks to neighbours' messages.

'I want to speak to you,' he began, looking from

one to the other. 'I ought to go back to London, to take care of my wife.'

His sister and his brother-in-law looked at him. Neither spoke.

'I want to bring her home.'

Jenny put out a hand as if to ward off the words. Ronald captured it in his.

'You're not bringing her here,' he said.

Ned stiffened, thrust out his chin. 'This is our home!'

'If you bring that woman across the threshold, I'll —'

'You've said that kind of thing before, Ronald. I let it go by because you're under a great strain —'

'Ned,' Jenny said.

He stopped, looking at her.

'Lucy cannot come into this house.'

Her brother stared, then opened his mouth to challenge the statement.

'Wait. This is my house.'

'What?'

'Have you forgotten? When father died he left the business to you. He left the house to Mother and me, so that we would always have a roof over our heads. Now that Mother is gone, the house belongs to me. And I will never, *never* allow Lucy to enter it.'

It was clear that he had not thought of any of this. He coloured in futile indignation, but had more sense than to argue against the embargo.

'In any case, I imagine that the Procurator Fiscal will decide where Lucy is to stay,' Ronald said in a hard tone.

'The Fiscal!'

'She has charges to answer.'

'But she's not fit to be charged with anything —'

'She won't go on for ever living in a twilight world of chlorolhydrate. She'll end up in court — and after that, I imagine, in prison.'

Ned put a faltering hand to his shirt collar, pulling at it as if he were stifling. 'You hate her,' he whispered, 'you really hate her.'

'Yes.'

'I won't let you hound her! She didn't mean to harm anyone — you know she wouldn't harm anyone!'

'Only a fool like you could really believe that, Corvill.'

Ned turned for the door. 'I'm going to London. She needs me. And I'll find her a good lawyer so that you can't trap her into a prison sentence! I'll protect her from you, Ronald Armstrong!'

He almost ran out of the room. There came a bitter silence. Then Jenny said with a deep sigh, 'What has it come to, that we can only think of hurting each other?'

Ronald had no answer to that. He had long ago gone past hope of anything but retribution.

A few days later, after a troubled conversation with Mr Kennet, the family lawyer, he went by appointment to see the Procurator Fiscal Depute in Edinburgh, Andrew McArder. The advocate had the documents of the Corvill case in front of him. He was a youngish man, with a clever, fox-like face.

'Well now, Mr Armstrong, I've agreed to see you because this is a most difficult and delicate business. Mr Kennet of Galashiels writes to my superior Mr Gladwell that he hopes there may be no long delay in bringing Mrs Corvill to justice.'

'Yes, that is our aim, Mr McArder. The lady is sheltering behind a claim of poor health, but – '

'Her health would matter gey little, Mr Armstrong, if we had a good case against her. But I have to tell you we probably will not prosecute.'

Ronald gasped. Words of protest clogged his throat.

'I see you're surprised,' the Depute said, playing with a paper-knife on his oak desk. 'I don't blame you. But from the legal point of view, there is no case to be brought.'

'But she took our daughter, she carried her off to London – she let her lover give her away – '

'Mr Armstrong, no one saw Mrs Corvill with your daughter.'

'You mean at the London hotel, but we hope to find the chambermaid – '

'Even if you do, you know perhaps that in Scottish law we prefer to have two direct witnesses.'

'My mother-in-law, the elder Mrs Corvill – '

'The elder Mrs Corvill is dead.'

'But she saw Lucy with Heather – she told my wife so.'

'I don't wish to sound a note of levity, Mr Armstrong, but you may have heard the phrase coined by Mr Dickens: "What the soldier said is not evidence." '

'I don't understand.'

'What your wife was told is not evidence.'

'But her own mother – !'

McArder nodded, as if he had heard the tone a great many times before. 'It makes you indignant, sir. I understand you. You know your wife is a woman of probity and your mother-in-law would only speak the truth to her. Nevertheless, it is not admissible in court as evidence.'

Ronald leapt up, towering over the advocate. 'I don't believe this!'

'Calm yourself, Mr Armstrong.' The man was so gaunt, so tall and thin, he was alarming in the sedate office. 'I'm afraid you must believe me on a point of law. There are no witnesses in the case against Lucy Corvill for the abduction of your daughter.'

'But she herself confessed to it!' Ronald shouted, hitting the desk with his hand. 'She admitted it all!'

To his incredulous amazement, the advocate was shaking his head. 'No, sir, she did not.'

'But she did! In Dover! She told Jenny —'

'Your wife?'

'Yes, my wife Jenny —'

'I repeat, Mr Armstrong. What Lucy Corvill told Jenny is not evidence.'

'But how else did we know which inn in Holborn to go to? Only because Lucy told us —'

'You may have gone to every inn in Holborn and the Fleet. There is no proof that Mrs Corvill ever took a child there. She made no statement to the police, signed no paper —'

'God in Heaven! She was hysterical — too hysterical to be questioned by a police officer, so my wife —'

'Your wife heard this information. Exactly.'

'And a police constable was in the room —'

'But took no notes which she might have signed afterwards. Believe me, Mr Armstrong, it gives me no pleasure to tell you this, but there is no evidence against Mrs Corvill except her own admissions, which were never written down and signed by her, and which in any case she now denies.'

'Denies!'

'At least, she has sent a statement through her lawyer that she remembers nothing.'

Ronald twisted one hand in the other, as if he were wringing the neck of Lucy Corvill. 'A convenient loss of memory, is that it?'

'She was ill, confused, she remembers nothing. That is the gist of the statement she has now made to her lawyer.'

Ronald folded slowly on to the chair behind him. He ran fingers through his sandy hair. 'Wait,' he said. 'The attack on my mother-in-law, from the results of which she has since died —'

'There is no evidence that the young Mrs Corvill had anything to do with that. It could have been a simple accident.'

'But —' He broke off. Only Millicent could prove the contrary. And Millicent was dead.

After a pause he said, 'There could be a charge of simple theft. That would be better than nothing.

'What did Mrs Corvill steal? She says she knows nothing of Mrs Massiter's diamonds, and as for the jewels and some other items —' he glanced through his papers '— a gold watch and shirt studs and etcetera, her husband says she took those with his permission.'

Ronald felt as if a mighty hand had smitten him. His breath seemed to have deserted him. After a long moment he said, 'Are you telling me that this wicked little bitch is going to get off scot-free?'

McArder smiled. 'Well, ah, hardly scot-free. Her husband will of course divorce her, she will be left penniless and cut off from good society. I think you may say —'

'I may say that you're quite wrong,' Ronald interrupted harshly. 'Her husband's shown you what he feels by claiming he gave permission for her to run off with her jewels and his belongings.'

'Oh, that's different. He doesn't want her to face a criminal charge. But on the marital charge —'

'He won't bring it.'

'But he must, Mr Armstrong. After such a flagrant episode —'

'He won't, you'll see. He's already forgiven her.'

'That's not possible.'

'The only way she's going to be made to suffer for what she's done is if we bring her to court for abduction or assault or manslaughter. *We* have to do it, Mr McArder.'

Now it was the advocate's turn to fall silent. At length he said, 'I can only tell you what the law allows. The evidence we have against Mrs Corvill is negligible. We cannot prosecute.'

With this news Ronald had to go back to Galashiels. But when he reported it to Jenny she didn't cry out against it. She listened in silence, then nodded without comment.

'Don't you care?' he shouted at her. 'Doesn't it matter to you that that selfish guiser is going to live and be happy after what she's done?'

'It matters less to me than it does to you, my dear —'

'I want her punished! She ought to swing at the end of a rope!'

'Ronald, man, how would that help? Would it bring Heather back?'

He realised all at once that they were strongly at odds, that they might very well quarrel if he didn't mind what he said. He fell silent, but it broke something in him to think she didn't feel as he did over this bitter defeat.

Ned turned up at Gatesmuir the following evening, when Jenny and Ronald were picking at a dinner for which they neither of them had any appetite. Thirley came to announce she had shown him into the drawing room. He awaited them there with obvious trepidation, but with his words rehearsed.

'I've come to say goodbye,' he began. 'The Procurator Fiscal has let us know that no charges are to be brought against Lucy, so we're going away.'

'Are you, my bucko,' said Ronald. 'Take her to Italy. She wanted to go to Italy.'

His brother-in-law went red at the sneer. 'We're going to the West Indies. To tell the truth, we have had some hints that Lucy wouldn't be safe if she went out and about in London −'

'That will be from Mrs Massiter,' Jenny said, with ironic amusement. 'Mrs Massiter is a good hater.'

'I think she's demented,' Ned remarked in a chill tone. 'But I didn't come here to speak of that. I came to say that you won't be seeing me again for a very long time. I wanted to ask, Jenny, if we might say goodbye without hard words −'

'If you imagine we're going to wish you and your wife well, you're out of your senses,' Ronald said.

'I don't expect your good wishes. But we are members of the same family, after all.'

'Blood is thicker than water, you mean.'

'After all, Ronald, there's truth in that −'

'But blood has been *shed*. Lucy killed your own mother −'

'I don't think we can be sure of that. Lucy denies she ever saw Mother.'

'Carefully coached by the lawyer you hired, I take it.'

Jenny had listened in silence to most of the exchange between the two men. She spoke now. 'There's one thing I should like to ask, Ned.'

'What?'

'Has Lucy ever uttered a word of contrition?'

He looked confused and flustered. 'She's sorry, of course she's sorry Heather went missing — she loves the child. Do you think she hasn't suffered?'

'But has she sent you here to ask for forgiveness?'

'She . . . I . . .'

'I see she has not,' Jenny said, feeling once again that wild anger that often threatened her these days. 'Very well. There's no more to be said on that score.'

'I don't want us to be enemies, Jenny.'

'You just intend to leave, is that it? Just walk away?'

'There seems nothing else to do.'

'You've forgotten something, brother. You are the owner of Waterside Mill, of William Corvill and Son. There are always papers that need your signature, agreements that await your approval.'

'Och, you know I never played any real part in the business, Jenny.'

'Quite so. But if you are in the West Indies, who is to sign the papers that need your name?'

'You can do that.'

'That wouldn't be legal.' Jenny stared at him, her eyes dark. 'I need your power of attorney, Ned.'

'Of course. You shall have it.'

'I need a legal agreement giving me full control of William Corvill and Son.'

'Yes, I understand. I'm willing to give you that.'

'We'll go to see Mr Kennet this evening. He'll draw

up the papers in the morning and you'll sign them.'

'Yes.'

'After that you go to the West Indies and you never interfere in anything to do with the mill.'

'Yes, yes, you don't need to labour the point. I agree, of course I agree.'

'Very well.' She rang for Thirley to bring her brother's hat and coat. She went upstairs to fetch her cloak. Ronald followed her.

'What is this? Do you think it's some compensation for our daughter, to make him give up what he never cared for?'

She was tying her cloak as she turned. 'It's going to make me rich. And I'm going to spend every penny profit we ever make on finding our little girl, Ronald. I'll find her, if she's been taken to the ends of the earth.'

In his mind, Ronald amended that to 'if she's still alive'. Taken on his search through London by the members of the Metropolitan Police, he had been shown evils he could never have imagined.

If Heather had been abandoned among those wild and cruel dwellers in the criminal 'rookeries', she was probably already dead. And if she was still alive, she was the more to be pitied.

Chapter Ten

For a time after her little girl was lost it seemed as if Jenny's emotions ruled her. She was sometimes overwhelmed by grief when she was alone, and when others were with her a baffled undirected anger would seize her. The only defence had been to make herself feel nothing.

But now her intelligence had reasserted itself. A month had gone by since Lucy Corvill took Heather away. Police inquiries had had no effect. No trace of the child could be found, no one remembered Lucy with her in London or en route to the capital from Galashiels. The one person of whom the police had slight hopes — the chambermaid of the Mitre Inn — remained obdurately missing.

Inquiries went on, and would continue to do so. But Jenny understood that the police were convinced they were wasting their efforts.

It was time for her to act. And, having thought the thing through, she decided to act in a different way. The Metropolitan police were the force equipped to find a missing person in London, if anyone could. But, besides the chambermaid, there was someone who might shed light on Heather's fate.

That someone was Harvil Massiter.

He might be said to have disappeared as thoroughly

as the chambermaid. But to Jenny's mind, he might prove possible to find.

'But he's gone abroad, Jenny,' Ronald objected, when she told him her thoughts.

'That doesn't mean we can't track him down.'

'You don't have the least idea where he went.'

'He actually sailed on the Calais packet. The Dover police ascertained that much.'

'But from there, Jenny? He might have gone anywhere.'

They were in the office at Waterside Mill. Jenny, having spent the morning in the design studio on the top floor, had been planning while she worked. She had come down to tell him her conclusions.

In her mourning, with her flesh thinned down by grief and anxiety, she seemed too slight to be planning a campaign of any kind. Her husband studied her with alarm. He wondered if it might not be kinder to convince her that the task was hopeless. Heather was gone, probably dead. Perhaps it would be best if Jenny could accept that fact and let it become part of the past.

'We might be able to find out where he went, and get some information —'

'You're not thinking of rushing about all over Europe, Jenny? I forbid it!'

She half-smiled. She knew as well as he did that if she really wanted to go, he couldn't prevent her. Although as a wife she was subject to her husband's will, they didn't have that kind of marriage.

'I didn't think of going myself. It requires someone with experience of investigation.'

'That means a policeman, but the British police could hardly —'

'I saw an advertisement in the *Times* yesterday —
a Private Inquiry Office in Paddington.'

'But you've no way of knowing if they're reliable.'

'I could check with Inspector Simmons in London.'

It wasn't after all a hare-brained scheme. There
might be something in it. At any rate, it brought back
some of the animation to her eyes. Ronald didn't feel
entitled to argue her out of it.

So Jenny went to London, to speak to Inspector
Simmons in his sombre little office in the second
Metropolitan Police District. He had been dreading
her visit, because he had nothing to report, and he
expected tears and recriminations.

But no, Mrs Armstrong was calm and businesslike.
She explained her idea. Simmons couldn't fault it.

'If you want to go to Pollaky, the inquiry agency
in Paddington, I have nothing against it,' he said. 'But
I would say they restrict themselves to inquiries in this
country. What you want is a man who would work
for you on a full-time basis, travelling wherever he saw
a chance of success.'

Jenny nodded. 'Can you recommend such a man?'

'Well, in fact, there's a man who retired from this
station last year. His name is Baxter, Sergeant David
Baxter. And it so happens . . .'

'Yes?'

'He speaks some French. He married a
Frenchwoman, you see.'

Jenny drew in a breath. She hesitated to believe that
fate had sent her this man, but it seemed a good omen.
'Do you think he'll undertake the work?'

'I'll send him to see you,' Simmons said, drawing
a pad of paper towards him and beginning to write.
'I'll send word immediately. He does some work for

a legal firm in Theobald's Road so he's kept his hand in.'

That afternoon Sergeant Baxter presented himself in Eaton Square. He was a tall, portly man, grey-haired and whiskered, very respectably clad in navy broadcloth and a spotless shirt. His cravat was dark blue poplin. The one sign of individuality was a silver cravat pin in the shape of a horseshoe. When he saw Jenny glancing at it he said in an easy manner, 'My good luck charm. You need all the luck you can get in investigation.'

'Inspector Simmons sent you. Did he tell you what I need?'

'I went to see him, ma'am, before coming here. If you don't mind me saying so, it has to be something worth the wormwood to make me cross the Channel in a March gale.'

His forthright manner pleased her. 'It is very important to me to get in touch with Mr Massiter.'

'So I gathered from Inspector Simmons. I should warn you, though, that it may cost more than a tanner or two. Foreign travel isn't cheap, and there'll be bribes and *pourboires*.'

'I understand that. There's no problem about money.'

He had already guessed that from her address and the appearance of the house. There was money in plenty. 'Perhaps you could tell me the story in your own words, Mrs Armstrong.'

Briefly, and as unemotionally as she could, she related the events that had ended with the disappearance of Heather. Sergeant Baxter listened attentively, noting that it was almost identical with Inspector Simmons' account. The lady knew how to organise facts.

'So what we want to know is, first, if Massiter actually gave the little girl to some other person – ' He heard her draw in a gasping breath and paused. 'Mrs Armstrong.'

'Yes?' she said unwillingly.

'You have faced the fact that he may just have done away with the child?'

She took a long time replying. She was gazing over his head, at the sky beyond the window. 'I only know Harvil Massiter slightly,' she said. 'I think he is a vain, frivolous man. I don't think he's a murderer.'

'Very good. Then the second thing we want to know is, who was this "respectable woman" who's supposed to have taken the kid? Where was she actually going? On the northern stage-coach, so we gather, but how far up the route? If he asked her name and destination, we're off to a good start.'

'If he could tell us that . . .!'

'First we have to find him. As far as the other lady knew, they were going to Rome.'

'Yes.'

'Well, you can be sure of one thing. A jemmy like him wouldn't go to Rome after he left that poor silly woman in the lurch, all ready to squawk it out to anybody who rescued her. So that's a place *not* to look.'

Jenny nodded. His reasoning seemed sound.

'Have you any idea where he might head, Mrs Armstrong?'

She tried to remember all she knew about Massiter. 'I would think he would head for the sun. What I mean is, there are German spas and there are casinos in northern countries, but he left England in January. He would go towards the sun.'

TESSA BARCLAY

'Right you are!' But though he sounded enthusiastic he was thinking, that only leaves the rest of Italy outside Rome, and southern France, and Spain, and Portugal, and Greece, and Turkey . . .

He stood, saying he would make some inquiries among Harvil Massiter's London acquaintances, to see if he could learn if the gentleman had expressed a particular liking as regards foreign parts.

'His wife might know something,' Jenny said with reluctance. 'But whether she would tell you anything . . .'

He tugged at his side whiskers. 'Can hardly go to a lady and say, "Excuse me, where's your runaway husband gone to?" No, in any case, he's more likely to have pattered to his chums about it. I'll have a discreet word with the servants — if I can track down his valet it would help. A feller often says things to his valet he wouldn't say to anyone else.'

'When will you begin?'

'Straight away, ma'am. I've got something on hand at the moment for Peabody and Grant, but I'll give it to a colleague to finish. I'll come back in a day or two to let you know if I've come across anything.'

'Thank you.' She rang for Graham. As Baxter turned to the door she said, 'Do you think there's any chance of finding Massiter?'

'Why not?' he said with optimism. 'A mutcher like that probably leaves a trail of debts behind him.'

On the Sunday he returned to say that he had found Massiter's valet. Kitling felt hard done by, having been turned off without notice. But he could only say his master had spoken of Italy. One or two gentlemen, members of Massiter's club, had agreed on that point.

'That's not so handy,' Baxter mused, 'what with all

160

the unrest over unification and protests and stuff. But I'll see if I can pick up his trail in Calais.'

'When will you go?'

'Tomorrow, ma'am. That means I shall need cash money to take with me, and letters of credit. Can you get all that ready by tomorrow midday?'

'Certainly!' she cried, on the sudden surge of hope that came with action. 'I shall have everything ready if you call at noon.'

'It would be better if you brought it to the station; I'm taking the train to catch the six o'clock steamer.'

'Very well. I'll meet you at the barrier. When shall I hear from you?'

'I'll write at the end of my first day in Calais, to let you know if I've found a trace. After that you'll have to expect letters when you get them. Shall I write to you at this address, Mrs Armstrong?'

'Of course.'

'But, excuse me, I understood your home was in the Scottish Borders.'

'I'll arrange for letters to be sent on at once. If you send any information that can be acted on, I'll come back to London immediately.'

'Very good, ma'am. I think if he really headed for Italy, it ought not to be impossible to track him down. There are only two or three routes through the Alps, after all.'

'He may have taken ship —'

'I'll cover that possibility too.'

She offered him her hand. 'I believe in you, Mr Baxter.'

'Thank you, ma'am.'

The promised letter came. No one by the name of Massiter had stayed in the likely hotels in Calais but

161

a gentleman called Rollins sounded very like Massiter. Mr Rollins had gone to Paris. Baxter was off after him.

Jenny groaned inwardly as she read it. Paris! The chance of tracking his movements in Paris was as slight as the chance of finding the missing chambermaid in London.

Hope deserted her. The wild, vague anger welled up in her. She jumped up, seized a china shepherdess from her place on the lace-trimmed chiffonnier, and threw it with all her might against the wall. Her simpering partner followed. She picked up the brass-headed poker and with its heavy knob she attacked the Landseer of spaniels and children on the opposite wall.

The door flew open. Graham the butler hurried in. Astonishment froze him on the threshold.

'I hate it! I hate it! I hate everything,' Jenny screamed. 'It's all hideous — it's hers, *hers*, she put it all here!'

'Mrs Armstrong!'

She swung the heavy poker at the ornate mirror above the mantelpiece. Graham, shocked, caught her arm. The poker was carried by its momentum, the mirror cracked, pieces of silvered glass fell into the fireplace.

'Madam,' he exclaimed, 'you're beside yourself!'

She let the poker fall, threw herself down on a sofa, and began to weep. She didn't know what to do. Everything was all wrong, and nothing she could do would alter it. She hated this room, with all its echoes of Lucy. She hated the sentimental pictures, the decorative china, the lace and fringes and bows and flounces, the rows of silver-framed pictures, the knickknacks, the heavy wall-paper, the carved furniture, the velvet upholstery.

When she looked up again, Graham had tactfully withdrawn. Her personal maid, Baird, had appeared. 'Bring me a cloak,' she said. 'I'm going out. I'm going to hire a man to take all this rubbish away. If there are any clothes belonging to Mrs Corvill in her room, I want them burned. While I'm out, pack our bags — we're going home to Galashiels. Next time I come back, this place won't remind me of Lucy Corvill.'

'I dinna wonder you hate the place, mistress,' said Baird, glancing at the damage. 'Would you no rather surrender the lease?'

Jenny hesitated. Why should she ever set foot in this house again? It was taken only to please Lucy, to keep her out of mischief.

How ironic . . .

Nevertheless, if Baxter had any success in his inquiries, she might need a London base again.

'No,' she said curtly, 'we'll keep it. It may have its uses.'

If Baird had any thoughts about useless expense, she kept them to herself. Mistress Armstrong was in no mood to be argued with these days.

Her journey home next day was dogged by depression. She felt sure she had wasted time and money in hiring Baxter. Ronald didn't say, 'I told you so,' but she felt it was in the air.

Yet eight days later a letter was forwarded from London. Marvel of marvels, Baxter had found the hotel in Paris where Massiter had stayed. 'Not much problem, I traced him back through the gaming house he had been frequenting,' she read, amazed at how he could work his way into another man's mind.

Massiter had left by train for Italy. Baxter was on his way to the station to follow him as he put this present letter in the post. 'All in all, madam, I am not unhopeful,' he ended his report.

And hope revived in Jenny, like a fountain nourished by spring rains. It was possible, after all. Baxter might find Harvil Massiter.

Other letters came. From Venice: Massiter had stayed there for some days, enjoying the carnival. From Milan: here Massiter had sold his wife's diamonds for a very handsome sum. Florence: some trouble here over a drunken brawl. Perugia: it appeared Massiter had friends here, at the University. He stayed some time, but then temporarily vanished.

'I have reason to believe he went south again via Rome,' Baxter wrote. 'Though for the moment he eludes me, I beg you will not be too perturbed. An English "milor" is noticed by the Italians.'

Harvil Massiter was sitting at ease outside a wine-shop in Naples when Baxter caught up with him. Baxter was feeding the pigeons in the Piazza San Bernardo, an occupation that allowed him to watch without being too obvious.

Nevertheless, Massiter sensed the gaze upon him. He turned in his wrought-iron chair. He saw an elderly man in a cloth suit much too heavy for the Neapolitan sunshine, for though it was early June the temperature in the piazza was like the finest August day in England.

He himself was in a well-made suit of grey poplin. His wide-brimmed hat and his cane lay on the chair next to him. As their eyes met, the stranger seemed to take it as an invitation to join him. He strolled across the square, throwing the last of the hard Italian bread to the birds. After a moment's hesitation,

Massiter removed hat and cane so that the other could sit down. After all, he looked like a fellow-Englishman — rare enough in Naples.

'May I join you? The name's Baxter.'

'Rollins,' Massiter said, nodding invitation.

The waiter hurried out. Baxter looked at the empty wine glass in front of Massiter. 'Another of the same? And one for me.'

'Si, signore.'

'A fine day,' Baxter said to Massiter. 'Hot.'

'It will be cooler in an hour or so when the evening breeze comes in off the bay.'

'A beautiful bay — a beautiful city.'

'The women are beautiful too,' Massiter said with a wink.

His new-found friend didn't seem amused by the remark. Oh lord, thought Massiter, he's one of those strait-laced Methodists or Baptists that have come over to convert the Italians away from Catholicism. To test the matter he said, 'Are you here on business or pleasure, sir?'

'Oh, business, business.'

'Really? What line of business are you in?'

'I travel on behalf of others. What do you do, Mr Rollins?'

'Oh,' said Massiter, leaning back to let the waiter put down the wine, 'I travel to please myself.'

They sat in silence a moment, sipping the dark, metallic-tasting wine from the slopes of Vesuvius. 'You travel, I think you said,' Baxter took it up. 'Have you been here long?'

'A couple of weeks. I may stay here. I like it here.'

'A large English community?'

'Oh, not large. A consul, one or two merchants,

some artists and students of architecture . . . You know the kind of thing. But the Italians are convivial.' He debated whether to add, 'Especially the women'. But since the previous remark hadn't gone down well, he decided against it. 'Do you know anyone here?' he asked.

'Not a soul. But that doesn't matter, I don't expect to stay long.'

'A pity. There are pleasures to enjoy in Naples.'

'No doubt.' The burly gentleman sipped his wine, and looked at the shadows lengthening towards the fountain. 'And so, Massiter, what did you do with the baby?'

Massiter gasped. He turned to ice.

'You remember the baby?' Baxter went on, leaning forward across the table. 'A female, nineteen months old, fair hair, hazel eyes, baptised Heather. We need to know what happened to her, Massiter.'

Massiter's tongue seemed cloven to the roof of his mouth. He dragged it free to say, in a slurred fashion, 'My name's Rollins.'

'Your name's Massiter, and you're wanted in England for the theft of your wife's diamonds. However, I'm not here about that. Diamonds don't interest me, missing children do. Where is Heather Armstrong?'

'I don't know what you're talking about,' Massiter panted, fear making his heart lurch about in his chest.

'Don't waste my time. Just tell me what I want to know before I lose my temper with you.'

'I don't know what you're talking about! Who do you think you are, walking up to me out of nowhere with these mad accusations?'

'Massiter, you're cornered now, so just —'

'*Camariere, camariere*!' shouted Massiter. The waiter came running. In Italian Massiter said, 'This man is annoying me, he must be a madman — throw him out.'

The waiter knew Massiter, who had been coming regularly to the wine-shop for a week or two and tipped well. Baxter was a stranger to him. He seized him by the collar of his cloth jacket and pulled him sideways out of his chair.

Taken by surprise, Baxter went over. At once Massiter threw money on the table and took to his heels. By the time the detective had righted himself, soothed the waiter in a mixture of French and English, tipped him lavishly and been allowed to leave, Massiter had made his escape in the lanes behind the piazza.

In his hotel he fell on his bed and let his breathing go back to normal. My God, a hired man on his tracks! Well, he would find it hard going to find him in the maze of streets that made up Naples — the more especially since he probably spoke no Italian.

Shadows fell, and the world outside began to wake up as taverns and restaurants lighted their outdoor lanterns and the musicians began to tune up.

Massiter was hungry. Time for dinner. He washed and changed and went out.

On the pavement outside the hotel, a burly figure lounged.

'Good evening, Mr Massiter.'

'Good God!'

'Thought you'd got rid of me? Not at all, not at all. Easy to find you even if I can't speak the lingo. Well, where are we going?'

'I'm not going with you!'

'Come now, why not? Time for a nice plate of fish

and another glass of that red wine. You know the restaurants, I expect. Where do you recommend?'

'Let me go!'

'Listen, Massiter, you might as well talk to me now. I'll be on your heels for ever if you don't tell me what I want to know. So come on — let's sit down and be comfortable and then we can have a chat.'

The muscular arm round his shoulders guided Massiter along the pavement. They came to a restaurant with tables in front under an awning hung with little coloured lamps. 'Here?' suggested Baxter, and without waiting for a reply pushed Massiter into a chair.

It was a little too early for the Neopolitans to be eating their evening meal. They received the attention of a waiter at once. Massiter was stricken to silence, so Baxter ordered fish stew, bread, and table wine.

'Now,' he said, looking at Massiter with great composure, 'tell me what you did with the baby.'

Massiter said nothing, his eyes blank.

'Did you kill her?'

'No!' The response was immediate. Life came back into the blank stare. 'What kind of a monster do you think I am?'

'The kind of monster that takes a child away from its mother,' Baxter said.

'I didn't! Lucy did that.'

'Right. We agree on that. Lucy Corvill did the actual abduction. But you got rid of the baby.'

The waiter came with a carafe of wine, and poured two full glasses. Massiter seized his and gulped some down.

'Feel better?' Baxter said, in a soothing tone. 'Good, now tell me what happened.'

There was a long hesitation during which Baxter could see his victim was trying to decide whether to speak or not. In the end he said, 'I never meant to have that brat with us in the first place.'

'No, of course not.'

'I was utterly taken aback when I walked in and found Lucy with her. I mean to say, who wants to take a squalling kid along on a romantic escapade?'

'Just so.'

'So I told her she had to leave it. And she took on as if I'd insulted her. So in the end I said I'd make arrangements for her to go back to her family — the baby, I mean.'

'I understand.'

'And that's what I did.'

'Excuse me, Mr Massiter, I need a little more than that. This arrangement — what did it consist of?'

Massiter paused. He seemed to be looking back at a very distant past.

'Well, I took the baby from Lucy and went downstairs. I gave her to a woman who was waiting to board the northbound coach.'

'Indeed? What was her name?'

'Mrs Dyer.'

'Mrs Dyer. Her address?'

'I . . . er . . . I didn't get her actual address.'

'Where was she travelling to on the coach?'

'Er . . . Durham.'

'Durham. And you asked her to take the baby.'

'Yes.'

'And she agreed.'

'Yes.'

'Although it meant travelling on much further than she intended?'

'She . . . well, I paid her for her trouble, of course. I paid for her ticket on the stagecoach and gave her five pounds in gold.'

'Wouldn't it have been more considerate to have given her money for a rail ticket? The stage coach doesn't go anywhere near Galashiels.'

'I didn't have time to think of all that. I'd left Lucy — Mrs Corvill — upstairs crying, and I was afraid she'd come down and make some kind of scene. And anyhow,' Massiter added in morose tones, 'she never stopped snivelling after that, and I can tell you it took the gilt off the gingerbread completely. There's nothing so unattractive as a face all blotched with tears.'

Baxter nodded. 'Disappointing for you, sir. And so this woman — Mrs Dickson — she agreed to take the baby home. You were quite satisfied she would do so?'

'Oh, of course. A very respectable woman.'

'I see.'

The food came. The waiter set a basket of bread between them, with several little dishes of saladings. The table became cluttered. Massiter, in trying to clear a space, jogged his glass so that wine slopped over on to his trouser leg.

'Oh, damn! Now look! It'll make a hell of a stain — this red wine's got iron in it. I'll just go and rinse it out with cold water.' He rose, nodding towards a sign that pointed to the cloakroom.

Baxter sat back, sipping his wine. Time went by. Massiter didn't reappear. After fifteen minutes Baxter went to the cloakroom. No sign of Massiter.

Smiling to himself, Baxter went back, ate his food, paid the bill, and went to stand guard outside Massiter's hotel.

But his calculations weren't quite good enough, for

Massiter didn't reappear up to the time that Baxter gave up and went to his own bed.

Next morning, he went to the hotel to inquire for his quarry. The *signor inglese* had left that very morning at dawn.

With no trouble at all, Baxter learnt that Massiter had taken passage on one of the regular ferries plying between Naples and Athens. He went back to the inn, packed his valise, boarded the next boat, and landed in Athens next morning.

In Athens he had to call in some help. Here people spoke only Greek or Turkish, of which he had not a word. The British consul provided him with an interpreter. Before dusk that evening he had found Massiter again, in a hotel much patronised by British enthusiasts for Greek antiquities.

He was shown up to Massiter's room. The man-servant knocked and called, 'Effendi?'

Massiter opened the door. At sight of Baxter he threw up an arm as if he expected to be hit. 'You!' he gasped.

'Thank you, my boy,' Baxter said to the servant, tossing him a coin. He walked into the room, closing the door firmly behind him.

'Now, my lad,' he said, 'let's have the truth.'

'How did you find me?' Massiter groaned.

'You've no idea how easy it is,' said Baxter. 'And I'll find you wherever you go, so why don't you just tell me the real story and be done with it.'

'But I've told you —'

'No you haven't. You made up the name of the woman that you were supposed to have given the baby to. You didn't correct me when I said Dickson instead of Dyer.'

Massiter sat down on the edge of his bed. He drooped his head.

'Who did you give her to? A passing dollymop? A kidman?'

'No, no . . . What do you take me for?'

'I dunno why you ask me that — you ought to know you'll get a rude answer. Come on now, sir, be a good man and tell me the truth.'

Massiter made a sound that was almost a sob. 'If I tell you, will you promise to let me alone?'

'Yes.'

'You won't inform the authorities?'

'I've no jurisdiction here, if that's what you mean. You're safe from me, whatever you tell me.'

'What I meant was, you won't tell them where I am when you get back to England?'

'Wouldn't matter if I did. They can't drag you back.'

'Are you sure of that?'

'Stop thinking about yourself, Massiter. Think about the kid. What did you do with her?'

'I gave her to the chambermaid.'

'The chambermaid. Ah!' The missing chambermaid. He ought to have thought of that before.

'Alice, her name was. I could tell she was "open to offers", as the saying goes. I caught her tampering with the locks on my portmanteau a bit earlier, but we settled that amicably — a pretty enough girl, though too much of a Cockney for my taste.'

Baxter knew the type well. London was full of them. Good-looking, quick-tongued, always on the lookout to make a shilling or two. 'The landlord said he wasn't sorry to see the back of her,' he mused aloud.

'Oh, she was ready enough to go,' Massiter agreed.

'I think she was well out of favour. When I came downstairs with the brat she was in the lobby. I asked for a word in private, she took me into a sort of pantry off the main passage. I think she thought I was going to arrange to see her later that night, but she caught on readily enough when I told her I wanted her to get rid of the baby.'

'You weren't silly enough to use those words to her?' Baxter said in alarm.

'No, no, I said she was to take the little nuisance home to Galashiels. If she asked there, anyone would tell her where the Corvill house was, and she'd get a good reward for her trouble. I gave her five pounds in gold, and all the silver I had about me — six or seven florins.'

'I'll ask you again what I asked before: did you think she would do it?'

Massiter gave it some consideration. 'I thought there was an even chance,' he said seriously. 'I thought the idea of the reward would tempt her.'

And the idea of a journey to the wilds would put her off, thought Baxter. These Cockney girls, born and bred in the streets of London, they scorned the rest of the country, thought it was peopled by savages. One pickpocket had said to Baxter, 'I tell yer, guv, it's no pleasure workin' the lay norf of St Albans, yer can't get a civil word from nobody.'

'Is there anything else you can tell me? Did she say when she would be travelling, whether she'd take the train?'

'I hadn't time for all that. I had to get back upstairs to Lucy before she changed her mind about letting the brat go. I wanted to be off for Dover — the longer we stayed in London the more chance that someone would catch up with us.'

They talked for some little time but Baxter's experience told him the man really had nothing more to relate. Baxter couldn't help being sorry that Massiter and Mrs Corvill had parted company. From all he could gather, they had been made for each other.

Athens was ill-equipped for sending urgent messages back to London. Baxter took ship for Ostia, and from Rome sent cables to the Metropolitan Police prompting further search for Alice Yates. He also sent word to Mrs Armstrong that he would be in London within the week.

When he called at Eaton Square at the beginning of the second week in June, he found her with her husband waiting for him in a different setting. The drawing room was uncluttered, there had been a change in the colours of curtains and chair covers. Mr and Mrs Armstrong in their mourning were in stark contrast to the lightness of the room.

He told them quickly what he had learnt in Athens and what he had been told by Inspector Simmons since his return. 'We know now that Alice Yates took Heather. But we still don't know the whereabouts of Alice Yates.'

'Why didn't she bring her home?' Ronald cried. 'She could have asked for anything by way of reward!'

'What kind of girl is she?' Jenny asked. 'Is she the kind who'd take good care of my baby?'

'We don't know, Mrs Armstrong. The landlord at the Mitre had employed her for four or five months but was beginning to have doubts of her. He says she was a good worker but had some worrying friends.'

'Worrying?'

'Well, you see, these girls . . . If she was a pilferer, she probably handed on what she took to somebody else for disposal. There are all kinds of gangs in the rookeries, who organise thefts and fence the dibs. What follows from that is, she mightn't have been a free agent. It was all right for Massiter to tell her to go to Galashiels, but she might not have been able to do it without asking permission.'

The Armstrongs gazed at him. The view from this window on the criminal side of London had shaken them.

'Do you think she asked permission and was refused?'

'More likely she never intended to go in the first place. A girl like that, a man hands her five sovs, she doesn't say no thank you, sir. She pockets it and pleases herself.'

Neither Jenny nor Ronald dared to ask the next question. Baxter guessed what was going through their minds. 'She's a pretty baby,' he remarked. He had a copy of the tinted photograph taken on her first birthday, held proudly on her mother's lap. 'There are people in London who are on what we call the kidman lay — they rear kids for various kinds of work, to take round for begging, and of course the prettier the child the more money they earn. Or girls are brought up to about ten, at which time they can be sent as maid-of-all-work to some good family, and pass the word about portable property.'

He stopped there, deciding that information about the next possibility for a pretty little girl was not likely to help the Armstrongs.

What he had already said was enough to drive the blood from Jenny's heart. 'No,' she gasped. 'Oh no . . .'

'I know it's hard,' the detective said, shifting

uneasily in his chair. 'No use blinking the facts, though. She's been missing for almost six months. If she's alive, it's because Alice Yates and her friends could see a use for her.'

'Where is she — where would they keep her?'

'With some family, probably in the rookeries.'

'Can you find her?'

'I can try, Mrs Armstrong. If she's still alive, I can probably track her down. But it might take a while.'

'Do it! I don't care how long it takes — I'll never give up until I find her!'

Ronald accompanied David Baxter out on to the pavement when he left. 'Tell me frankly,' he said, 'do you think my daughter's alive?'

Baxter tugged his whiskers. 'It's quite possible.'

'Probable?'

'Yes, I'd even say probable, except you've got to allow for run-of-the-mill childish ailments. I mean, if little Heather happened to get the whooping cough or a fever, her keepers might not bother too much to save her.'

Ronald blenched. 'Goddammit, man — don't talk like that!'

'You wanted the truth, I'm giving it to you. But from all you told me, your daughter was a healthy, happy little girl. She might stand up quite well to her situation. In that case, she's probably still alive.'

'And you can find her? Or are you just going on with it to indulge my wife?'

'A bit of both, you might say, sir. I think that poor lady needs something to cling to.'

Ronald sighed. There was no gainsaying that.

Jenny insisted on remaining in London. She had the feeling that Baxter might call on her for information or help. Or he might come to the house bringing Heather with him – she couldn't bear to think she might be in the north if that happened.

Ronald parted from her with misgivings. The wild swings between hope and despair to which she was subject were very worrying. Her emotional balance was precarious. Sometimes she was desperately in need of him, sometimes she seemed hardly aware of his existence.

Their lovemaking had been strange since they lost Heather. Jenny would be consumed by an urgent passion but then afterwards she would be ashamed, unhappy. He couldn't understand it. And she could never explain it to him, for it arose from a feeling of disloyalty to her lost child. If she were to have another baby, it would be like replacing Heather, displacing her.

Between herself and Ronald there was still a strong bond. Yet now what held them together was shared loss, shared tragedy. The first close and careless love had gone, perhaps for ever.

When Ronald went north, more than distance separated them.

Chapter Eleven

The weeks went by. David Baxter came back from time to time to give his report. It was very difficult, he explained — Alice Yates had sunk out of sight at the very beginning of the inquiry, and now he was having to go over old tracks. People were warier than ever.

'At first the police were looking for a missing chambermaid to ask her a few questions. Now, you see, we're looking for her as a participator in an abduction. That's a hanging matter — and word's got round so your normal rampsman don't want to talk to me.'

'But you won't give up,' Jenny begged.

'Not so long as you want me to go on.'

She looked at him with anxiety. Was he saying she ought not to go on?

'She isn't dead, you know,' she said, clasping her hands in fervour. 'I'd feel it if she were dead.'

He nodded. It wasn't so unlikely as some might think. But what he couldn't bring himself to say was, she may be alive but we may never find her.

'Keep trying,' she urged. 'Please.'

'All right.' He left with his faltering determination renewed.

And two days later he was back. 'Mrs Armstrong, would you come with me to look at a child?'

She went utterly white. He thought for a moment she was going to faint. She swayed slightly in her armchair. Then she said, 'Where? When?'

'This evening. Wear something plain, not to attract attention. Were going into a rough neighbourhood.'

'You'll come for me?'

'About eight.'

'Can't we go now?'

He shook his head. 'No, the party I want to see won't be home until the evening. I'll come about eight.'

'I'll be ready.'

It was September. At eight daylight was thin and without strength on the London streets. The lights on the cab flickered in the gloom as she came out to join Baxter, in a plain black poplin gown and cape, with a bonnet heavily veiled.

As soon as she had entered the hansom, the driver moved off. He had already had his instructions, had been well-paid to go into the district where they were headed. It was a neighbourhood he avoided.

They rattled over the paved road into Grosvenor Place and then to the new and handsome Victoria Street. They seemed to be heading towards Westminster. 'Where are we going?' Jenny demanded in surprise.

'It's an area known as Devil's Acre — behind the Houses of Parliament.'

'Behind *Parliament*?'

'You'd be surprised, ma'am. I dare say when you go out and about you go in a carriage or, if you go on foot, you stick to the high-class roads. But if you just turn down an alley off the Charing Cross, or take a walk behind St Pauls . . .'

The cab was moving more slowly now. Westminster Abbey was behind them, they were passing Sir Charles Barry's House of Commons whose stone was still new enough to glow in the evening light. But darker buildings loomed, they turned one way and another, street lamps became fewer, the noise increased, and the driver pulled on the reins.

'You said I didn't have to go no further, guv'ner.'

'Right you are.' To Jenny, Baxter said, 'We get out here, ma'am.' After they were on the roadside he said to the driver, 'Now, remember, you got ten shillings for bringing us here and waiting. If you're still here when we get back you get a sovereign.'

'It's a bargain, guv — but don't be long 'cos they'll steal the ears off my hoss if you're more than a quarter of an hour.'

Baxter took Jenny's arm and began to walk up a narrow, muddy lane. Shops and taverns were open for business, people were pressing by on either side of them.

'Now the situation's this,' Baxter said into Jenny's ear. 'We're going to wait for a woman to come home — she generally gets in about half-past eight. She'll have a baby with her. I want you to look at the baby. If it's Heather, press my arm. We'll go in after her. Don't say a word —'

'But if it's Heather I —'

'Don't say a *word*, Mrs Armstrong! If they know you have a particular interest they'll put the price sky high.'

'The price? We're going to buy the child?'

'Why not? She was probably bought or hired off somebody else in the first place.'

'What?' Jenny said, aghast.

'This woman — her name's Mrs Thomas — she's on what they call the wurdy-woman lay: that's to say, she gives herself out to be a worthy woman, widow of a decent tradesman, left destitute with a baby to provide for. She begs in the toff part of the town. Naturally she has to look a bit decent and it helps if the baby's small and pretty. So she changes kids every year or so.'

'Oh, God,' breathed Jenny.

'Shocking, you think. They do a lot worse, ma'am. But my point is, this kid she's recently got is a looker, so she won't want to part with her for a low price. But if you let on you think it's Heather, not only will she put the price up — she'll have you followed when you leave and might even take the kiddie away again in the night.'

'Don't!' Jenny cried, putting her hands over her ears. 'Don't. No one would be so wicked!'

'Think not? There was a grocer had his little boy taken a couple of years ago. The police got him back, but the kidmen took him off twice more. They sent demands for money and the poor cove paid up. In the end he had to sell up and move, to be in a safe place.'

By now they had passed a grog-shop where the light spilled out and the noise of raucous singing filled the air. Smoke and the smell of cooking battled with the odour of spilled beer and unwashed humanity.

Baxter stopped at a corner. Two tall houses made a narrow entry, over which a ramshackle bridge had been built to allow access between upper stories. On most floors there was what was called a nethersken, a low lodging house run by a landlord who rented space from some other man, who in his turn rented the building from another, who rented it from the owner who well might be a rich and reputable gentleman.

In these crumbling tenements there was little or no proper sanitation, lighting was poor, cooking facilities meant only a fire stoked with what wood the inhabitants could steal or scrounge, beds were on the floor and shared by two or three. The upper mob, the heads of the gangs, might have a room for themselves and immediate family. But a common thief, a pickpocket or someone on the smatter lay, had only a corner.

Mrs Thomas lived in a building whose doorway was the club-house of a gang of children, aged between eight and twelve. They were gambling for ha'pennies with a pack of greasy cards. There were girls among them as well as boys. From behind her veil Jenny stared at them in horror. To this Heather might come, if they didn't find her.

Baxter nudged her arm. A woman in a dark skirt and grey shawl was trudging towards the door, dragging after her a toddler who trotted as fast as she could to prevent being pulled over on her face.

Let it be Heather, prayed Jenny. Oh, please, let it be Heather. The child was small, in sturdy little boots but no stockings. Her frock had once been of good smocked linen but it was torn now, one sleeve coming out of its shoulder. Her hair was golden, curling up in a soft mass held back by a draggled blue ribbon.

As they reached the doorway, Mrs Thomas kicked right and left to clear a path among the gamblers. They scuttled out of her way, knocking into the baby. The child fell over, banged its head on the cobbles, and yelled in pain and fright.

Jenny started forward to pick her up. Baxter

grabbed her arm. Mrs Thomas took hold of a part of the child's dress, yanked her upright, threw her up to her shoulder, and carried her indoors.

But before she vanished into the dark entry Jenny had a full-face view of the child weeping over the woman's shoulder.

It wasn't Heather.

'Well?' said Baxter.

She shook her head, unable to speak.

'You sure? Bear in mind that eight months have gone by — children change a lot in that time.'

She went on shaking her head. She was sure. Heather's hair grew high on her forehead, that child's hair curled close down towards the brows. Heather's eyes were set wide apart, that child's eyes were closer together. A pretty child.

But not Heather.

They turned to go. The young gamblers, sensing profit, closed in on them. 'Hi, lady, give's a downer! Give's a gen! Look, Dickie — flash clob — ain't she the swell! Give's a gen, lady!'

'Clear off,' growled Baxter.

'Who're you? Think you're ream, don't you? Come on, guv, part with it — give's a duce!'

Knocking aside the first two, Baxter led Jenny along the alley. The children followed, shouting, begging, clutching at their clothes. Jenny felt the edge of her cape being dragged at — it only needed the fastening to part at the neck and it would be gone into the hands of the beggars.

Baxter produced from an inner pocket a handful of coins. 'Here,' he called. With all his might he threw them back the way they had come. With a yell the children turned and ran for them. A moment later they were scrabbling in the road like mongrels over a bone.

Walking quickly, Jenny and her escort came out on to the broader street. The hansom was still there, the driver sitting forward with the brake off, ready to flee.

They fell into it, Baxter closed the cover. In a moment they were off. Jenny turned her face into the corner and began to weep convulsively.

'There,' the detective said, patting her shoulder with a clumsy hand, 'don't be disappointed. It was just a chance it might be her.'

But it wasn't only the disappointment. It was the horror, the fear of what might have happened to her daughter, the feeling that Heather might be suffering as that two-year-old was, at the mercy of a heartless stranger.

By the time they got back to her house she had recovered enough to invite Baxter in. She ordered drinks — she took spirits only occasionally but tonight she felt she needed brandy.

'What put you on to Mrs Thomas?' she asked, when they were sitting with their restoratives.

'Well, I wasn't doing much good in tracking Alice Yates so I started from the other end. I put out the word I wanted to know if anyone had got hold of a pretty genteel-looking child — a strange child, not from one of their own families. Mrs Thomas's name came up, I went and had a look, I thought it *might* be Heather.'

Jenny sighed.

'You're sure it isn't?'

'Completely certain.'

He accepted the defeat. 'Keep trying, then, eh? I've got other irons in the fire.'

'Thank you, Mr Baxter.'

'Not much to thank me for, was it? A rotten experience for you.'

'Are there — are there many places like that?'

'Heavens, yes. In and throughout London, and every other big city. One of the pamphleteers calls them the plague spots of our civilisation. Certainly very little good ever comes out of 'em.'

'And the children — they're treated like that —'

'You have to realise that the adults were treated like that before them. Parents often regard their children as just one more mouth to feed until they're old enough to be sent out to earn a penny or two. But they're capable of affection sometimes. Not all the women are as hard as Mrs Thomas.'

'And the little girl. It seems too terrible to leave her there. She may be someone's lost child . . .' The tears welled up behind her eyes as she remembered the toddler being dragged along like a worthless rag doll.

'It's more likely she's a little by-blow of some poor young woman who put her out to be looked after. But then she couldn't keep up the payments — fell on hard times or got ill, mebbe even died. Or mebbe she got married to a man she was scared to tell about her little mistake. So there's this baby in a baby farm and nobody paying for her upkeep. So Mrs Thomas snaps her up cheap, I dare say.'

'It's unbearable. What will her life be?'

Nasty, brutish and short, Baxter might have replied. Instead he remarked, 'You can't take on everybody else's grief, Mrs Armstrong. You've enough of your own.'

'But she's so young and defenceless.' She frowned,

shaking her head to detach the memory of the weeping child. Then she said, 'Couldn't she be put in a foundlings' home?'

'Perhaps, if you could prise her loose from Mrs Thomas. But she'd probably claim the kid's her niece or something like that.'

'Could you go and see her?'

'What? That wouldn't be a good idea. I don't want to attract any attention.' He could see she was intent on helping the little girl but he didn't want it to queer his pitch.

'You could send someone.'

'Well, one of the street missionaries could take it on,' he mused, as he tugged at his beard. 'Yes, it could be done. The Quakers'd probably take it on. They know Mrs Thomas and her like.'

'Will you see to it? I'll give you the money before you go. Do it tomorrow. I can't bear to think of her spending many more days with that woman.'

'I'll see to it.'

When he had gone Jenny went to bed, exhausted. But her dreams were haunted by images of the weeping child dragged by the gaunt, angry woman. Only the face she saw was Heather's.

Ronald came to London partly on business and partly to beg her to come home. He was shocked when he saw her. She was so thin the bones showed. When he took her out in the evening she had to wear a lace shawl to hide the almost skeletal shoulders.

'You're not doing any good here,' he urged. 'It's bad for you. You're wasting away.'

'I can't go home without Heather.'

'If there was any real chance you'd find her —'

'There is a chance, there is, there is! Don't say it's

hopeless.' The colour ran up over her cheekbones. Her great dark eyes reproached him.

'I don't want to hurt you, my dearest,' he said gently. 'But there's not been the slightest hint of — '

'There was a chance. I wrote to you about that little girl.'

'But it wasn't Heather. And all it's done is upset you. Come home, Jenny. I miss you. We all do.'

Once again she felt that looming anger and resentment. Why couldn't he understand that if once she went home again without her baby, it was as if she had given up all hope? She clenched her fists among the folds of her crinoline.

'How is everything at Waterside Mill?' she inquired.

'So-so. Our pattern book for the spring is out now. I included the designs you sent but it lacks something — everybody says so. Come home and do some proper work for us, Jenny. You'll lose the feel for it if you stay in London.'

But when he returned to Galashiels he went alone. The best he could do was extract a half-promise that she would come home for Hogmanay.

December began with a series of hard frosts. Baxter presented himself again one morning in greatcoat and woollen muffler. She hurried down from her room to greet him.

'Have you some news?' she demanded before she had crossed the threshold of the drawing room.

'I want you to come and look at another child, Mrs Armstrong.'

She repressed a shudder. 'In . . . one of those places?'

'This time it's an infant asylum. There's a little girl there — right age, right appearance as far as one can tell.'

'An infant asylum? What does that mean?'

'It's on the lines of an orphanage, for abandoned children or children whose parents have had to go into the workhouse. I have to warn you, it's kind of a grim place.'

'When do you want us to go?'

'Now, if it's convenient.'

She turned back towards the door. 'Am I to dress plainly again?'

'That's not so important this time. Mr Drouet isn't a criminal. At least, he claims to be respectable.'

'Mr Drouet?'

'He runs the place. You'll meet him. Wrap up well, it's cold — and there's precious little heating at the asylum.'

She came down moments later in a thick grey cloak and a felt bonnet. Since she was now in only half-mourning for her mother she was allowed to wear sombre colours. Her muff was trimmed with silk violets of a rich purple and her bonnet had purple ribbons. She looked extremely elegant yet uninterested in her own appearance.

The carriage Baxter had brought wasn't a fly or a hansom but a more comfortable four-wheeler. 'How far are we going?' she inquired when she saw it.

'It's some way out, ma'am. South of the city, a district called Tooting. Mr Drouet's asylum is the far side of the common — I don't know if you know it at all.'

She only knew the area of London where she lived, and the parks in which she took the air. As they journeyed south Baxter tried to prepare her for the forthcoming encounter.

'I don't want you to be too depressed by the

building, ma'am. It's like a barracks, and the sight of some fourteen hundred children is a bit overpowering.'

'Fourteen hundred? In one home?'

'Yes, ma'am. It's an economical way to do it, you see.' His tone was grim.

'Economical! Fourteen hundred girls?'

'Boys and girls, from walking age to fourteen. They get a bit of schooling and learn their prayers. What else they learn I won't vouch for. I have to tell you, I didn't care for what I saw.'

She shivered, drawing her cloak about her. 'What makes you think Heather is there?'

'The story I got hold of is this. Alice Yates had a baby for a few days but her scurf — that's to say, her protector, her gentleman-friend — had another lark laid on for her so she had to give the kid to another woman, Mrs Scribbons. Mrs Scribbons was neighbours with Alice's folk in Aldersgate. She was a streetsinger, had a good voice by all I can learn. She took the kid round with her to help jog up the earnings. Not a bad sort, it seems.'

Jenny studied him. 'You're speaking of her as if she's dead.'

'That's it, Mrs Armstrong. Seems she got more and more sick — terrible pains when she ate, sick all the time. She took the little girl with her when she left Aldersgate to live with a relation in South London. And then in early summer, I gather she passed on and her relations seem to sink out of sight — there may be a strain of didiki there, I mean, they may have been gipsies. Anyhow, in August this little girl was found at Drouet's gates not long after a party of travellers had gone through on their way to Epsom for the races.'

After a moment's consideration of the story Jenny said, 'You've seen her?'

'Yes, ma'am.'

'Does she resemble the photograph?'

'It's hard to say. When you see how the children are dressed, you'll understand. And besides, that little girl in Devil's Acre looked like the photograph.'

She said no more. She was steeling herself for the ordeal to come.

The building was frightening; dark brick and peeling stucco, with a drive up to the main door through frozen laurel bushes. The windows were uncurtained and blank. When a little maidservant opened the door to them it was to reveal a large hall floored in brown linoleum, with brown-painted walls grained to look like oak and an uncarpeted staircase going up.

Mr Drouet came forward to greet them. He was a tallish man in a greasy suit, his shirt collar creased where it could be seen above the stained lapels. Behind his spectacles his eyes looked like slate. He bowed politely to Jenny.

'Mr Baxter said you would be calling,' he said, without much welcome in his tone. 'You've come just as we're serving the midday meal.'

'I'm sorry — is it inconvenient?' Jenny faltered. She was intimidated by the whole atmosphere. The place was very chill, with a strange odour in the air — dampness and decay, perhaps.

'Not at all, the children are well drilled in how to take their meals. If you'll come this way?'

They followed him into a long hall. To Jenny's utter astonishment, there were no tables or chairs. Rows of children stood facing in one direction, towards the grimy windows. Each had a tin plate on which there was a slice of bread and room for a mug alongside. As the visitors entered heads turned, but not a sound was uttered.

A woman clad in black and wearing a large coarse apron banged on a desk at the far end of the room. 'Begin,' she commanded.

Immediately the children picked up the bread and began to wolf it down.

It was a nightmare scene. They were arranged so that the shortest and youngest were at the far end, the tallest and oldest nearest the door. Their hands unanimously brought the tin plate up to chin level. They shoved in the slice of bread, half of it vanishing in one bite. They drank greedily at the contents of the tin mugs. The rest of the bread followed. Their movements were like ripples on a restless sea.

They were all clad in grey, the girls in shapeless smocks, the boys in ill-fitting trousers and blouses. Their heads were shaven, although some of the older ones had hair growing again unchecked as if to prepare them for going out into the normal world. They were bare legged, in clogs with wooden soles and straps of rough leather across the instep.

When the bread was gone, some even licked the plate like cats, gathering up the smallest morsel. Then the arms fell to their sides, one hand holding the plate, the other the mug.

Silence.

'What do they have next?' Jenny inquired, looking at the hungry faces.

'Next?' repeated Mr Drouet, taken aback.

'Is that the whole of the midday meal?'

'Madam, at midday we don't want to interrupt their work routine for too long.'

'I see. So they eat more sustainingly in the evening? What is the menu then?'

'They have soup, madam. And another slice of bread.'

'And what else?'

'What else? On four shillings and sixpence a week maintenance money?'

Jenny was about to argue, but Baxter put a restraining hand on her sleeve. 'Let's see the child first,' he said in her ear.

Controlling herself with an effort, she fell silent.

Mr Drouet moved off to stand by the woman in the apron. 'Infant June Smith, stand forward,' he called.

No one moved.

'Infant Smith, forward.'

Still no reaction.

With a grunt of irritation Drouet moved between the lines of children, to the far end, where the small children stood.

'Infant June Smith!'

No one responded. Drouet took one of the children by the shoulder and shook him. 'Which is Smith?'

Jenny hurried to stop him. The child he was grasping turned his head and pointed with a dirty finger. 'Her, sir.'

Other heads had turned. The children were looking at one of the smallest of their number, who stood with her head drooped down and her shoulders averted.

'Are you Infant June Smith?' Drouet demanded, coming to tower over her.

She nodded without looking up.

'Why didn't you answer when I called you?'

No reply.

Drouet stooped, took her chin in his hand, and

turned her face up. 'Is this the child you are inquiring for?' he said to Jenny.

Jenny almost turned away in despair. This couldn't possibly be Heather, her laughing, bubbling child of happiness. The little girl's scalp showed grey and unwashed through the stubble of hair. Her face was thin and dirty. She stared up into Drouet's face with eyes that looked like frozen brown leaves.

But the eyes were hazel, and though the hair was shaved away the growth line showed high on her brow.

'Heather?' breathed Jenny.

The child didn't look round at her. In fact, she seemed to be trying to get her face out of Drouet's grasp so she could hang her head again.

'Heather?' Jenny asked again.

No response.

Jenny turned to Baxter. 'I don't think so . . .'

'Hard to tell, with her little head shaved like a convict.'

Drouet heard the accusation in the words. He said stiffly, 'We have an acute water shortage here, Mr Baxter. We have to draw every drop from our own well. Naturally we don't want to waste it on continually washing children's hair — and besides, the newcomers bring infestation with them.'

'No doubt,' Baxter soothed. He looked from the tiny figure to Jenny. The other children were gaping at the tableau in utter silence.

'Perhaps if we could go somewhere private?' he suggested.

'Certainly.' Drouet let go of the little girl, and nodded at the aproned woman by the desk. She rapped the desk and said, 'Dismiss.' The children filed out, leaving their plates and mugs in two separate wicker hampers by the desk. As Drouet led the way out, the children stood aside like sentries to let them pass.

The keeper of the infant asylum herded the child in front of him. She trotted on, head down, shoulders hunched, like a dog that expects a beating. 'Office!' Drouet barked. The child took a line across the hall, and came to a door with the word office painted on it in black letters. She waited there until he threw the door open. 'Inside!' She went in.

The grown-ups followed her. The room was small, ill-lit by a small window. There were ledgers ranged on end on a shelf. There was a chair behind the desk, a chair to one side. On a peg hung a slender cane. The child turned her eyes toward it for a moment, then looked down again.

'There you are, madam,' Drouet said. 'Privacy.'

Jenny nodded. She crouched down to be on the child's level. 'What's your name, sweetheart?'

The little girl would not look at her. She kept her head down. She made no reply.

'Come come, tell the lady your name!'

'Don't speak to her like that!' Jenny flared. Then, collecting herself, she took the child's hand. 'Are you called Heather?'

No answer.

'Are you called June Smith?'

'That's the name we assigned her,' Drouet put in. 'She was left at our gate in June, and we normally give a common name such as Smith or Jones as a surname.'

'What's your name, then, lovie?'

Silence.

'It's stubbornness, sheer stubbornness!' exclaimed Drouet. 'Your name's Infant June Smith, isn't it?'

The child nodded.

'Where do you live, June?'

The child remained mute.

'Come along now, speak up when you're spoken to! You live at the infant asylum, say that to the lady!'

'Surely she isn't able to say hard words like asylum, at her age,' Jenny suggested.

'Madam, children in this home have to answer when they're spoken to.'

'I think, sir,' Baxter intervened, red with suppressed anger, 'that it would be better if we could leave Mrs Armstrong alone for a while with the child.' Unspoken was the criticism: you're frightening her to death.

'Alone?' Drouet looked about his office, as if wondering what Jenny might steal if he left her there unsupervised. Then he shrugged. 'The Commissioner of Police for Surrey, a noted patron of ours, has asked me to afford you every civility. I'm happy to leave my office to you, madam.'

He went out. Baxter followed, giving an encouraging nod to Jenny.

She was still kneeling by the child. She got up now, picked her up, and sat down on the chair by Drouet's desk. 'Don't be frightened, darling,' she said in a soft murmur. 'I'm not going to harm you. Tell me your name.'

The little girl said nothing.

'Do you remember your mama?'

Still nothing.

'I had a little girl,' Jenny said. 'Her name was Heather.'

She bent sideways to gaze into the child's face as she said the name, but there was no visible reaction.

'She lived in our house in Galashiels. She had a nurse called Wilmot. She had a doll with brown curls.'

But there was no answering interest in the little body sitting so stiffly on her lap.

She curved her arm round her, drew her closer. Almost automatically she began to rock. It was an ancient reflex, mother and child, protector and protected. Jenny sang,

> 'Bye Baby Bunting,
> Daddy's gone a-hunting,
> To fetch a little rabbit skin
> To dress poor Baby Bunting in.'

There was just the faintest softening in the child's attitude. Almost, almost, her head seemed to droop towards Jenny's shoulder.

> 'This is the way the weaver goes,
> A-rickelty-tick, a-rickelty-tick,
> The treadle down with his heel and toes,
> A-rickelty-tick, a-rickelty-tick.'

The little girl raised her head, looking up at Jenny from her place near her shoulders.

Jenny smiled down at her. 'Do you know the song, Heather? Do you remember it?'

The child said not a word.

> 'This is the way the weaver goes,
> A-rickelty-tick, a-rickelty-tick,
> The wool on his ears and on his nose,
> A-rickelty-tick, a-rickelty-tick.'

The little girl put up a wavering hand. She almost, not quite, touched a little pink-rimmed ear.

'Yes,' said Jenny, 'yes. That's what you do, Heather.' And once again she began the song.

> 'This is the way the weaver goes,
> A-rickelty-tick, a-rickelty-tick.
> The treadle down . . .'

The little girl put her hand down towards her foot.
'With his heel and toes . . .'
She patted her bare heel and then her toes. Then she raised her hand towards Jenny.

Jenny patted it with her own in rhythm as she ended, 'A-rickelty-tick, a-rickelty-tick.'

She sang the second verse. This time the little girl was ahead of her, her hand moving to her ear and her nose and then waiting to be patted twice in the slow rhythm of the ending.

'That's it,' whispered Jenny, 'that's it. Oh, darling, I've *found* you.'

She hugged the little girl. The little body squirmed at the sudden movement. Jenny let her go and looked into her face. Terror was contorting it. In this place, to be taken hold of suddenly didn't mean love, but hurt.

'No, no, Heather! I wasn't going to hurt you! No one is ever going to hurt you again!'

She stood up, carrying her daughter. She went to the door and looked out. Drouet and Baxter were standing in the passage in stilted conversation.

'This little girl is my daughter,' Jenny said.

Baxter started, then raised his eyebrows. His lips formed the silent word, 'Sure?'

'I'm quite sure,' she said in a firm tone. 'Her eyes are the right colour and the shape of her head and the way her hair grows are the same as Heather. Moreover, she recognises a game we used to play. May I take her home at once?'

The warden of the place looked surprised. 'Well, of course, if you're sure . . .' He cared little one way or the other. If he lost four shillings and sixpence a week by the departure of Infant June Smith, the loss would be made good very shortly by the arrival of another stray.

'There are a few formalities to attend to,' he ventured. 'And some slight legal costs . . .'

'Of course,' Baxter agreed. A guinea or two would soon see the back of this greasy scoundrel.

When Jenny had signed a document agreeing that she took the child on the understanding of its being her own, and promising to have her husband write a letter of authority, they were free to go. The fees for the legal stamp came to ten shillings. Baxter added some other coins, which Drouet didn't refuse.

'Can I have a shawl to wrap her in? It's very cold outside.'

'A shawl,' he echoed, at a loss.

'A blanket, then.'

'Oh, well, madam, every blanket in the place is needed.' He wanted her to offer payment for it.

'Never mind,' said Baxter, and went out to the coach. He came back with a carriage rug. The little girl was wrapped in it and carried out. As they went they could see little thinly-clad figures in a field across the road, walking and stooping, walking and stooping, gathering up potatoes. The rest of the children were no doubt bestowed elsewhere in the grounds, at work on tasks suitable to their age.

With a look of absolute wonder Jenny's daughter

surveyed the inside of the carriage as they drove off. It was ordinary enough, but she seemed fascinated by the shine of the woodwork, the polish of the leather, the glow of the padded satin headrest.

When they reached Eaton Square Baird was hovering in the hall. At sight of the little girl she cried, 'Michty me! Is that our Heather?'

Jenny disregarded the question. 'Run a bath, put out one of my chemises to dress her in. Send out Dorothy to buy nightgowns, frocks, underwear, slippers — tell her to ask the draper for two complete sets to fit a little girl of two and a half. And caps — for God's sake buy some pretty caps for her poor little head.'

Upstairs in Jenny's room were some of the toys from Heather's nursery at home. Jenny set her daughter down on the carpeted floor, put the doll with the brown curls into her hands, and set one or two others nearby. The child sat bewildered, not daring to touch anything.

Between them Jenny and Baird bathed her. Baird swore horrible Scottish oaths at the shaved head. Gently they rubbed away the grime that had built up due to the shortage of water at the infant asylum. They dried her in soft towels. They put the fine lawn chemise over her head, directed her arms through the armholes, and tied it about her with a satin ribbon.

Then, set down in front of the fire with the faint glow of soap on her skin, she looked a little more like a normal child. Jenny had had thick chicken soup brought up, and stewed apples with curds and whey. The child ate hungrily at first, but soon let her spoon drop from her hand into the bowl.

Her eyelids began to droop. Jenny picked her up

and put her on her bed. She brought the china doll again, and a toy made from sheepskin to look like a little Eskimo.

After a long, dreamy pause, a hand stretched out. The Eskimo was touched tentatively, as if the little girl expected it to be snatched away.

'Mo-mo,' she murmured.

It was the first sound she had made since Jenny saw her. And it was the right one, for that had been Heather's name for the toy.

A little later she was asleep on Jenny's bed, the quilt tucked around her and the Eskimo clutched to her cheek.

Jenny sat beside the bed, her arm stretched out over the sleeping child.

'Heather,' she kept saying to herself in tremulous thanksgiving. 'Heather, Heather . . .'

Chapter Twelve

Ronald Armstrong travelled full of joyous anticipation in response to the message: 'Heather found.' He almost threw himself through the doorway before Graham had the door open.

Jenny came running downstairs to greet him.

'Where is she? Let me see her! How did you find her?'

He began by following Jenny up to their bedroom, but had soon passed her while she was pausing on the stairs, trying to warn him, to prepare him.

He rushed into the bedroom. The child was sitting on the hearth rug before the bedroom fire, a little to one side and protected by the mesh of the fireguard. Her gaze was fixed on the dancing flames. The flickering light outlined her strange little body — the stick-like arms and legs, the baby's cap close against her head so that it was like a skull.

For a moment he thought his eyesight was playing him false. He started forward. She looked round, and shrank back at the figure of a tall man in dark clothes, so like Mr Drouet in essence.

Ronald almost recoiled in horror.

Had his wife accepted this — *this* — as their beautiful, golden baby girl? Where were the tawny curls? Where was the ready smile?

He turned to protest to Jenny. She was at his elbow saying quietly, 'Don't startle her, Ronald. She's very easily frightened.'

'But she's not —'

'Not harmed, no. She's been half-starved and kept in terror, but the doctor says she'll be all right.'

'But her hair — ?'

She explained about the infant asylum, about the dreadful regime there. She tried, in a half-whisper, to tell him all the facts he needed. But he wasn't convinced. He knew his poor, grief-stricken wife had made a terrible mistake.

He had pictured himself catching Heather up into his arms, covering her with kisses, listening to her cooing with happiness. He found he couldn't bring himself to touch this little stranger.

Jenny led him out. He felt it only fair to let her tell him the facts as she believed them. She related the tale of the nursery game that Heather had recognised. He thought, Of course, when she said heel and toe, the child knew what she meant. And when she told how Heather had known Mo-mo, he thought that the sound was one a sleepy little girl might easily make.

Yet he found he couldn't say outright, 'You're wrong — this isn't Heather.' Jenny was so certain, so uplifted by the happiness of having her baby again. And Ronald discovered that the rest of the world accepted this little changeling as Heather Armstrong. Mr Baxter accepted her, the doctor too, and friends who were beginning to send messages of congratulation, and newspapermen who called for details to publish in their pages.

He should have spoken at once, the moment he saw the child. He debated with himself what to do, and thought it would be best to wait a week or so, when everything had settled down to something like normal.

The doctor had advised against moving Heather for the present. She was under-nourished, dehydrated, and suffering from exhaustion, both physical and mental. 'A month or so here in the place she's got used to,' he advised, 'and then we'll see. I do feel that the country will be better for her — fresh air, good food, a quiet life.'

As the week passed Ronald found he couldn't tell Jenny he didn't accept the baby. It sounded too cruel, Herod-like in its harshness. And as the next week went by and the next, he began to see that Jenny was right and he was wrong.

The stick-like limbs became more rounded. Fawn curls began to peep from under the baby cap. The child sometimes smiled — not directly at him nor, in fact, at any man. But sometimes as he watched her he saw her lips curve over some silent game with her doll, or some encounter with the kitchen cat.

The child really was Heather. But it would have been more true to say she was Heather's shade, a kind of tracing of Heather on grey paper — fainter, less defined, and utterly quiet.

'Isn't she able to speak?' he asked Jenny one day, when he had spent more than ten minutes trying to coax a word out of her.

'She can speak. She just doesn't want to.'

'But why not? Why shouldn't she want to speak to her own mother and father?'

'I don't know, Ronald.' His wife shook her head, wondering if she would ever be able to make Ronald understand what Heather had been through. No one who had not seen the infant asylum could fathom the depths of fear in which Heather had lived there. And what had gone before? There was no way of knowing.

Ronald felt shut out. The only people with whom Heather seemed to have anything like a normal relationship were her mother and, to a lesser extent, her mother's maid, Baird. Baird had taken over the role of nursemaid for the present. As she herself said, 'It's easier to look after one quiet wee lassie than a grown lady, and the bairn seems easy wi' me.'

A complex harness of emotions held Ronald in check. He didn't know how to handle his little daughter, nor did she seem to want to be handled by him. Moreover, he felt a terrible, gnawing guilt at having failed to recognise her. He had almost denied his own child! It was too awful to think of. It made him uncertain in any overtures he made to her.

Beyond that, he felt unwanted. Jenny's entire attention was taken up with the baby. He kept telling himself it was only natural — the child had been snatched away from her, missing for nearly a year, found again under circumstances of deep distress. Naturally Jenny thought and worried about Heather to the exclusion of everyone else.

The best thing was to go home to Galashiels and get back to work, instead of hanging about in London being useless. Ronald put this to Jenny, perhaps half-hoping she'd say, 'No, no, don't leave me — I need you to help me with Heather.'

She only said, 'I suppose you'd better go, dear. It will soon be time to get out the spring pattern book.'

'When do you expect to come home?' he asked, wanting to hear her say, As soon as ever I can.

'We'll leave that to the doctor. I don't want to risk moving Heather if Dr Mainbridge is against it.'

'Of course,' he agreed.

Of course. The child must come first. He hated himself for feeling even the faintest twinge of irritation on that score.

So he went home to Waterside Mill and the empty house of Gatesmuir, to bury himself in the work. Jenny wrote regularly, full of news about Heather. 'We took her out for her first walk in the park today.' Or, 'When weighed yesterday Heather was one-and-a-half stones, which Doctor says is very satisfactory considering the check she received.' Or, 'Today we discarded the baby's cap since the weather was warm and there was no fear of her taking a chill without it.'

March came, then April and May. In June the days were long, the sun shone, and Dr Mainbridge decreed that Heather was fit to make the journey to the Borders.

At Gatesmuir everyone was thrown into a flurry of activity. The mistress had been gone so long! Nothing must seem amiss when she walked in again. Everything was polished, everything smelt of beeswax or black lead. The gardener furnished sweet-scabious and veronica without grudging them, so that there were flowers in every room.

Ronald went to the station to welcome them home. There was a small, discreet crowd of towns folk also, wanting to show goodwill and interest without being intrusive. The stationmaster hurried to help down the travellers, Ronald moved forward trembling with anxiety, and the Armstrongs were united in their home town once more.

Heather was walking now at her mother's side. It was to be noticed that she never let go her grasp on Jenny's hand unless Jenny needed to use it, and even then the little girl held fast to a fold of her skirt.

The onlookers noted with satisfaction that she was dressed in a pretty frock of blue muslin over white silk, and a bonnet to match. Her hair was now long enough to show in a fringe of curls on her brow. She was small for her age, pale, and with an air of timidity.

At the end of this month she would have her third birthday. Out of the two others in her short life, one had been spent with strangers, only one in safety with her parents.

Next day, friends and neighbours began to call, in hopes of being introduced to this celebrity, this child who had been stolen away and now returned as if after a year in Elfland.

But little was seen of her, and still less was heard. She began to have the reputation of being deaf-and-dumb, although when people stopped to think about it they knew this wasn't so — call her name and she would look up, so her hearing was excellent. It was her power of speech that seemed lacking.

There were those who claimed to have heard her talk. But when cross-questioned, they would hesitate. 'I canna let on that she said much. I heard her say "yes please" when the Mistress asked her if she would like lemonade. But it was scarce above a whisper.'

Kind neighbours invited the little girl to come for tea and games with their own offspring. It was never a success. The other children would rush about in their usual rowdy fashion. Heather would sit by, clutching a shapeless doll, watching them as if marvelling but taking no part.

'She's backward, poor lamb. No wonder, is it, after what happened?'

The murmur, when it reached Ronald's ear, vexed and hurt him. No child of his ought ever to be described as 'backward'. And as to her ability to speak — he could have given evidence of it, for sleep at Gatesmuir was broken most nights by an outcry from Heather, struggling with nightmares. She would call out in terror — broken words of distress, of fear, of appeal. Mostly, her cry was for Mama.

Jenny and her maid took turns sitting by her at night. But even when Jenny was not on duty, she would be only lightly asleep, ready to leap up if the baby needed her, and often summoned when Heather refused to settle down again until she had seen Mama.

Marital life was almost impossible under these conditions. On the rare occasions when Ronald had Jenny to himself all night, their lovemaking had lost its certainty and joy. He felt almost as if Jenny gave herself in duty-bound. Gone were the moments of shared ecstasy, the long embraces afterwards when they lay in each other's arms murmuring in shared contentment.

The problems of their own life almost excluded awareness of the outside world. But that world was changing dramatically. The American Civil War had ended, followed later by the assassination of Lincoln — an act which would have horrified Jenny if she had really given it consideration. In December of that year, an amendment to the constitution of the United States at last abolished slavery.

At the end of the following January, a letter arrived from Jenny's brother Ned. She went pale when she recognised the handwriting on the envelope. Her little exclamation of surprise caused Ronald to look at her across the breakfast table.

'What is it?'

She held up the envelope. 'From Ned.'

He frowned. If he could possibly avoid it, he never thought of Ned, nor of his wife Lucy whose actions had brought Heather to her present state. 'Are you going to open it?'

'Do you think I should?'

'Throw it on the fire.'

'Yes.' But she didn't do so. She sat looking at it. Heather, who took breakfast with them — who in fact was never parted from her mother if she could possibly avoid it — glanced from one to the other, then busied herself offering porridge to her shapeless doll.

'I think I ought to open it, Ronald.'

'For God's sake, why? We agreed we never wanted to see or hear from either of them again.'

'But he may be ill . . .'

He grunted. He cared nothing for that.

Jenny was thinking to herself that she couldn't hate Ned. Now that she had Heather back again, she was so grateful to the world in general that she couldn't even hate Lucy. She certainly didn't want to see either of them — yet if Ned had taken the trouble to write, ought she not at least to read the letter?

'I think I'll open it, Ronald.'

'No.'

She hesitated. 'Do you forbid me?'

It was seldom that Ronald behaved as the traditional 'head of the house'. In this respect he was very different from most of the men they knew, for it was accepted and expected that men should exert authority over their wives and families. He, however, had a wife different from most. And as to a family . . . the situation in his household was so strange he sometimes wondered if he even belonged there.

After a moment he said, 'Open it, then. You'll be unhappy if you burn it.'

'I just feel . . .' She didn't finish the sentence, but instead picked up the letter-opener and slit open the envelope.

'Dear Sister,' she read, 'the great news of the abolition of slavery in the United States of America has roused me to feel that life after all can take a fresh start.

'Moreover, an item in an English newspaper, recently come to hand, tells me that Heather has been found safe and well. In view of that I felt I must write to offer my congratulations and good wishes. I hope the condition of safety in which she was apparently found will at last diminish your resentment towards my poor little wife who, as I am sure you know and will now acknowledge, never meant any harm to the child.

'The climate and circumstances here do not quite agree with Lucy. She finds the heat enervating. That being so, and the peace now being assured in America, I have accepted a post there to help in the education of the freed slaves. I will send my address once we are settled there. I think we shall be in or near Richmond, Virginia.

'We go first to Washington so that I can meet my colleagues in this good work. The cost of removal and our expenses in settling in a new home will be considerable, so I should like you to instruct Mr Kennet to arrange for an advance on my allowance – and indeed, I think it would be reasonable to ask for

211

an increase in it, as living in Washington or Richmond is bound to be more expensive than here in Kingston and the stipend I shall receive is only nominal.

'Such news as I can glean of the woollen industry in Scotland is excellent — expansion and prosperity seem to be the rule. My best wishes for Waterside Mill and for the New Year, which by the time you receive this will be well begun.

'If you would write to me once we have taken up our new abode, it would be a great blessing and consolation to me.

'Your affectionate brother, Ned.'

To read his words summoned him up before her: apparently benevolent towards the world but in reality self-engrossed, and still blind to any fault in Lucy.

She raised her eyes, blinking back a tear, to find Ronald watching her. He held out his hand. She had no choice but to give him the letter. He read it in a silence that grew more and more grim.

'Well, if that is not completely typical,' he snorted when he laid it down. 'Safe and well — he got that phrase from a newspaper, but does he bother to inquire as to the real situation? Not he!'

'You can quite understand he didn't want to write too much on that point, Ronald.'

'No, the real point was to ask for more money. First he tells us he's taking up this philanthropic post, then he tells us his allowance is too low, then he congratulates us on how well the mill is doing. In other words, we're being tightfisted if we say no.'

'But after all, my dear, it is his money —'

'The hell it is! He never did a hand's turn to earn it, and after the way he and that cat of a wife of his behaved he doesn't deserve a penny! Why you ever told Kennet to arrange that income — '

'Ronald, please don't raise your voice — '

'Dammit, I have a right to raise my voice in my own house! I want you to ignore this letter — '

'I certainly shan't reply to it — '

'But you're not to increase his allowance — '

'Please don't shout. You're frightening Heather.'

Ronald leapt up from the table. 'What the hell is she doing eating with us instead of in the nursery like other children? Why do we have to have her hanging round our coat tails all the time?'

'Ronald — '

'And another thing! I won't have that disgusting object at table with us one more time! It's enough to put anybody off his food.'

'Ronald, you know she needs it — '

'Needs it? Don't talk rubbish! How can she need a lump of dirty old sheepskin?'

'It's not dirty, Ronald, we wash it from time to time.'

'My God, I'm not talking about laundry! I'm talking about my daughter dragging around with her a piece of tattered, grubby leather when she has dressed dolls and German toys by the score.'

'But Mo-mo is special, Ronald. He seems to be a sort of link with her past — he makes her feel she belongs here.'

Ronald glared down at his wife. The pent-up irritation of past weeks erupted as he saw her, flushed and upset, trying to defend what he knew for certain was silly waywardness.

'I want that doll thrown out,' he commanded. 'We've had enough of this nonsense about the world revolving around a little girl. We've got to have some sense and discipline in the house. Heather's to have the same kind of routine as any other child —'

'No, Ronald! Don't be cruel —'

'Cruel? What's cruel about trying to behave sensibly? As it is, you're spoiling her beyond belief. She's a law unto herself at the moment and she'll grow up totally uncontrollable. I tell you, Jenny, enough is enough. You'll do as I say. That doll goes in the dustbin —'

Heather had been following all this with a tense interest that now brought her into a protective crouch around the sheepskin toy. She made a whimper of protest.

Infuriated, Ronald snatched the sheepskin Eskimo out of her arms, and with an angry movement tossed it into the dining room fire.

The little girl watched the flames take the toy. Then she opened her mouth and uttered a wail of misery and loss.

Jenny, who had darted from her place to try to retrieve the toy, turned back to take her daughter in her arms. She gathered her close, hid her face against her breast, and rocked her to and fro.

'Never mind, my dove, never mind, it's all right, my lamb, don't cry. Don't cry, baby, Mama will look after you, it's all right . . .'

Ronald was stricken to silent immobility. He couldn't believe what he had done. For a long moment he stood looking down at mother and child. He wanted Jenny to raise her eyes to him so that he could show her he was sorry.

But her entire attention was on the child. And after a pause which seemed to him to last an eternity, he turned and left the room.

He didn't go home for lunch because he still hadn't worked out how to apologise for his action. At the end of the day he delayed his return to purchase a fine new doll in Galashiels' only toy shop. When he went indoors he gave the parcel to Thirley. 'Put it in the cloak cupboard for the moment,' he said.

His intention was to go up to the nursery, try to make friends anew with his little girl, and then lead her downstairs to find the new doll in the cupboard. He opened the nursery door, and put his head round.

Heather was sitting on the hearthrug before the fire – her favourite spot, for she loved the generous warmth of a fire. Jenny was sitting beside her reading from a book of nursery rhymes.

But what struck Ronald at once was that Heather had her sheep-skin toy in her arms, hugged close.

He couldn't believe his eyes. He came in, walked slowly towards them, and stooped to kiss first his wife and then his daughter. It seemed to him that Heather drew back a little from this customary kiss, but his attention was all on the Eskimo doll.

'I see you've got your friend with you,' he remarked, in a too jovial tone that hid his perplexity.

'Yes, isn't it wonderful,' Jenny rejoined, nodding at him to warn him he must take part. 'Poor Mo-mo was getting so worn out that he had to go through the fire to Toyland, where they washed him and dressed him and made him new again – and here he is, back home and full of his adventures.'

All the courage to make his apology ebbed out of Ronald. His wife had solved the problem, had made good the damage. He would only renew the original hurt by going over it again. And as for his fine china

doll with her satin dress and lace-trimmed bonnet . . .
He didn't even mention that.

Later Jenny explained that she had gone
immediately after breakfast to the retired shepherd
who made the sheepskin toys and bought a new one.
He had a cupboard full of them, all as like the first
Mo-mo as made no difference. The charred and smelly
remains of the original had been taken out with a pair
of tongs and given a secret burial while Baird dressed
Heather for her morning walk, and at lunchtime there
had been the new Mo-mo, sitting by Heather's place.

The drama was over, the crisis had gone by. But
Ronald felt only too deeply that he had not behaved
well. Other men would have scoffed: 'Good Lord, if
a man isn't master in his own home, things have come
to a sorry pass . . .' But to be master, to snatch a
beloved toy from a child — that was not what he
wanted.

He didn't mention the letter from Ned. He never
asked what Jenny did about it. He didn't want to
allude to that awful scene in any way whatever. But
he was sure she had increased Ned's allowance, and
he was secretly angry at that. It rankled to think that
he, in the office at Waterside Mill, wrestled with the
problems and found the solutions which supplied the
money Ned would spend so blithely.

Although the woollen industry was flourishing, it
wasn't without its problems. New machinery meant
new work routines. Although the weavers of the
Borders were the aristocrats of the industry, they had
to comply with new regulations. Informality in the
work place couldn't be allowed any more: fines were
introduced for lateness or drunkenness.

Waterside had 'modernised' twice in the last three

years, but Ronald had resisted the move towards greater strictness.

'I can't bring myself to fine a man for being late if he has a sore head,' he remarked to Jenny. 'I was a workman myself, I know what it's like to wake up the morning after a night out.'

'Have the others all introduced the rules?' she asked, although she knew it was so — dinner guests had mentioned it over the last year.

'Aye, and it causes friction between us because, you see, workers tend to wait for a chance to move to Waterside when there's a vacancy.'

'That makes an awkwardness.' The fact was, good workers in the Borders were in great demand, so that no manufacturer liked to lose any to a rival.

They each went back to their own pursuits. Jenny was sketching an idea for a marled tweed, Ronald was reading a technical journal. The silence grew.

'Ach,' he grunted, 'I suppose I'll have to introduce the fines system.'

She hid a smile. 'But, Ronald man, make sure the fines are paid — no letting a lassie get away with it if she slips off before the tea-time bell.'

'I hate the whole idea. Ah well, I can have a notice put up to say the fines will start next week, and as I'm away to the wool auctions in London then, they'll not be able to reproach me.'

'Ritchie and Ainsley will have it all running by the time you get back. You'll see that the new "tailor's tartan" is set up before you go?'

'Jenny, I never take any part in that these days! I seem to spend all my time attending meetings, seeing factors and buyers, talking to the bank manager . . . I haven't had my hands on a dye tube for weeks.'

She looked at her sketch with her head on one side, but her thoughts were elsewhere. 'Times are changing, Ronald. These days a manager has to spend his time managing.'

'But I'm not a manager!' he burst out. 'I'm a dye-master! I hate all this fiddle-faddle about rates of pay and definition of practice. And I'm not even all that keen to be consulted about the joining of the Galashiels and Peebles Railway —'

'But all the manufacturers were consulted about the volume of business —'

'The volume of business! That's book-keeping! My field is dyestuffs.'

This would have been the beginning of something he had long wanted to confide — that he wasn't comfortable any longer in the role of manager now that the job was becoming so specialised. But at that moment there was a sound from upstairs. Heather, who had been put to bed about an hour ago, had awakened.

Jenny threw down her sketchboard and hurried out. She came back thirty minutes later, peace restored. But the moment had gone by, the opportunity to talk about his problems had passed.

In London Ronald found yet more to contend with. The Saxony fleeces from this year's German growers happened to be less abundant than usual because of drought on the sheep pastures. The alternative, the excellent Saxony-merino from Australia, were not plentiful either, because the great London merchants were buying them at the source, in New South Wales. After a week's hard bargaining Ronald went home, angry and disheartened.

'I bought enough, but by God the competition

from the Yorkshire factories was *fierce*. I tell you, Jenny, that agent of ours in Sydney is worse than useless.'

Jenny nodded. Henry Chalmers, wool factor, was unknown to them. They had hired him by letter when it became clear that the London mercantile houses had their own men out there ready to do business on the spot. But against the plentiful credit the big merchants could supply, it was very hard for freelance agents to hold their own.

'I read in the *Textile Recorder* that the London houses are even beginning to buy their own sheep-farms,' she remarked.

'That's damned unfair!'

'It's just good business. If you have a continuing need of a product and you can buy into the production of it, that's good sense.'

'Meantime supplies are tied up so that manu-facturers can't get at them.'

'Well, that's not entirely true. We did actually get what we wanted.'

'This time. But I tell you this, Jenny, I'm not looking forward to having to go through that every year. Suppose we came up short in supplies? We've orders to fill — if we can't get the right wool we'd have to renege on our commitments.'

'It's never happened yet, my love.'

'You weren't there, Jenny. You didn't see the infighting. There were dealers there from America and Canada as well as from Italy and Turkey and God knows where.'

She listened to his worried and irritated recollections of the auction. Then she said, 'You'd better write to Chalmers and ask him to send us a proper report of how the deals are done in Sydney. Perhaps we need to review how we buy our wools.'

Somehow he felt she didn't take it quite seriously. Her main attention was always on Heather, and recently she'd been involved in a campaign to help vagabond children. Most of her free time was spent in correspondence to do with that.

Jenny had never forgotten the scenes in the infant asylum. She had hired David Baxter to find out more about the place. He had helped unearth the awful fact that forty-one children had died over a short period of time under Mr Drouet's reign. With others, he and Jenny had urged an inquiry. At length that had been held, Drouet had been censured, the home closed down and its inmates dispersed among other, healthier institutions.

But still the methods of helping children in need were limited. The Boards of Guardians regarded them as lesser citizens, the main problem being to deal with destitute adults.

One man had put forward a new idea. With financial help from supporters such as Jenny Armstrong, Dr Barnardo had just opened his first home for waifs in Stepney.

Jenny felt that her own little girl was now strong enough to undertake a journey. Now that Ronald was at home again, she and Heather set out for London, where Jenny would visit the new home for children and meet some of the friends with whom she had corresponded over the last year.

The house in London seemed infinitely strange when she went into it. More than a year had gone by since Jenny had last been there, though Ronald had been there intermittently on business. She walked through the downstairs rooms, went slowly up the stairs to the drawing room, and looked out over the gardens of the square. Heather, at her side as usual, stared about with interest. No memory seemed to visit her of her homecoming here after the reunion with her mother in the infant asylum.

They spent ten days in London. Baird urged Jenny to order some new clothes. 'You're a sair sicht these days, you havena bought a single new gown for almost two years. And while you're at it, get some stylish hats — the fashion's going right away from the wee set-back bonnet.'

They shopped, they went for outings on the Thames and to the Zoo in Regent's Park. When Jenny went to her meetings concerning the welfare of children, Baird sat with Heather. They were a self-sufficient trio, and it struck Jenny that Heather often seemed happy these days — almost on the verge of happy speech.

Unfortunately on the way home the little girl caught cold. It was nothing serious but Jenny took alarm at once. So the homecoming was marred by immediate demands for hot-water bottles, camphorated oil, flannel chest pads. Ronald watched his wife and the maid bustling about, directing operations, seeing to the little girl's needs, and realised they were absolutely oblivious of him.

So the year wore round, Hogmanay came, Heather was allowed, sleepy-eyed, to stay up until the New Year came in with a pealing of bells and a skirl of pipes. She had been home for eighteen months and in that time had scarcely said eighteen words. She couldn't even be brought to speak the ancient greeting to guests, A guid New Year.

Her father busied himself seeing to the first footers,

as hospitality demanded. But his heart wasn't in it. The new year stretched before him, with little to beckon him forward.

He was trapped in a job for which he felt himself unsuited. Day by day he had to play-act, to convince himself he was really the right man for the role. At home he seemed almost as much a misfit. His marriage had somehow gone sour. Jenny had drifted away from him, his child was a stranger to him.

During January the long-awaited report came from Chalmers in Sydney. He tabulated the prices paid by local merchants financed by London houses, compared these with prices paid first in Sydney auctions and then at the London auctions. He then drew his conclusions, which he set out at length.

First, he asked for larger funds to be made available to him on the spot so as to get in on equal footing with the agents of the big London merchants. Then he put out the suggestion that he should be allowed to hire an assistant who would travel on his behalf to look at the wool while it was still on the sheep, and perhaps make a bid for it at that point.

Both Ronald and Jenny read and re-read it. They discussed it intermittently. Then they set aside an evening when they would talk the matter through.

'It seems to me,' Jenny remarked, 'that it would be a good idea to send someone out to Australia to see if Chalmers is talking sense or simply building himself up to a better salary.'

'Apart from that, it would be a good idea to have a fresh view. Someone from the Borders who knows exactly what our problems are. For instance, it would be a help to know what the shipping facilities are like in both Sydney and Hobart. The shipping agents fix the rates, but does anybody know whether it's possible to do it cheaper and faster?'

'It would be a worthwhile investment, the money for his passage out and back,' Jenny mused. 'But it would have to be someone we could rely on.' She thought about it. 'Kennet has a young assistant — he might take it on.'

'He's only a laddie — not yet twenty.'

'Yes, that's a drawback.'

'I tell you what . . .'

'What?'

Ronald took a breath. 'I think I'll go myself.'

Chapter Thirteen

The townsfolk of Galashiels were greatly intrigued by the news of Ronald Armstrong's project. The longheaded businessmen thought it very astute.

'He'll get a first-hand view of the wool sales the tither side of the world. Pringle have done it already, you know — sent a man to learn the inside o' it.'

'But is Armstrong the right man?' wondered some. 'He never seems to know whose side he's on — many's the time I've heard him arguing against economic sense.'

'But that's only where the workforce are concerned. He's as good a man as any when it comes to valuing the wool.'

'I wonder,' said the ambitious underlings, 'who they'll put in as manager?'

'Ach, the mistress will have men queuing up from all over Scotland. Don't get your hopes up.'

'Aiblins she'll go back to managing Waterside herself. I always wondered that she handed it on to her man when she can do it better herself.'

'Aye, but she'd find it hard to do now, would she no? Now that she's got a wee simple-minded lassie to look after. Na, na, she'll have to put in a manager.'

And so hopes ran high among those looking for a chance to better themselves in the textile industry.

Those who were more interested in matters of the heart rather than matters of trade were equally intrigued.

'He was aye a footloose kind,' the women said to each other at their sewing parties and whist tables. 'The wonder is he's stayed so long.'

'Australia's a long way, though. Up to now he's been all round Scotland and in foreign parts on the Continent. But Australia . . .'

'She won't miss him, in my opinion. Short-tempered and sombre, I've thought him recently − all his sense of humour seems to have left him.'

'It's the bairn, of course. Somebody telt me that he didna really think it was his own when Jenny brought it home.'

'Not his? When she's got his hair and his eyes? Havers!'

'Aye, but . . . She's lacking, you know. That's what he doesna like.'

'So he takes himself off to the tither side o' the world. Well, absence makes the heart grow fonder. A month or two in a clipper ship and six among the rowdies of the colonies will teach him to value his home.'

Between Jenny and Ronald themselves, a frigid peace had grown up after a loud, lengthy and hurtful quarrel. At first Jenny had been unable to take his remark seriously.

'Go yourself? To Sydney? Don't talk nonsense, dear.'

'Where's the nonsense? We need someone to go and see how the wool is grown and sold − and I know as much about that as any man we're likely to hire.'

'But you can't go.'

'Who says I can't?'

'But . . . but . . .'

If she had said, 'But I need you here,' the matter might have ended then and there. But because they were talking about the business she said, 'You're the manager of William Corvill and Son. You can't go stravaiging round Sydney.'

'You can soon hire another manager,' he said curtly.

'But I can't understand why you even *think* of going! There's plenty here that needs your –'

'Plenty of what? People? *You* don't need me, you've made that very plain –'

'Ronald!'

'Don't pretend to be shocked and surprised! We both know very well that in the first instance you only thought of marrying me because you were afraid of being an old maid –'

'What are you saying?' she gasped, starting up from her chair with the report from Chalmers still clutched in her ferocious grasp. 'You know very well that you and I –'

'Oh, we made love, and we seemed to mean it, but you soon got tired of that once the novelty wore off –'

'Be quiet! Don't you dare say things like that to me, Ronald Armstrong!'

'It's time it was said. You know damn fine you never want to come to bed with me these days – you're always listening for Heather's crying –'

'Heather!' she broke in. 'That's what this is all about really, isn't it? You can't bear to think Heather is your daughter! Oh –' she threw up her hand to demand silence ' – don't think I didn't understand your feelings the first time you saw her after I brought her back. You didn't want to accept her as your child.'

'That's not true,' Ronald shouted. His voice was all the louder because he knew it was so.

'And you're ashamed of her now. When people look after us in the street or at church, and whisper about "the wee dummie", you're ashamed. You're ashamed of your own daughter.'

'I'm nothing of the kind, I'm simply tired of watching you turn her into a spoiled, ill-natured little brat. You give in to her all the time, you never raise a hand to her even when she deserves a good skelping —'

'Hit her, is that it? After all she's been through, you think she needs beating? You're so *stupid* —'

'If I'm so stupid, why do you want to keep me here at home being a burden to you? I'd think you'd be glad to get rid of me without a scandal. Australia is a long way off — we couldn't get on each other's nerves if I was there.'

'All right,' she said, nodding with angry finality. 'You're right. It will be better if you go, especially after the things we've just been saying. I don't really think I want to share my bed with a man who feels I married him from ulterior motives.'

'That's quite plain, thank you. I'll have my things moved into the dressing room — and I'll arrange for a passage on the first available ship.'

If things had just been normal next day, they might have retracted all their harsh words. A night alone after four years of marriage can be a splendid lesson in what really matters in life.

But as luck would have it Heather began to sicken with a fever and a runny nose. The doctor diagnosed the beginnings of measles. The child was much more ill than was normal in a simple case of that kind

228

because her resistance was lower than most children due to a long period of malnutrition. Jenny's mind was too taken up with fears and anxieties to feel any weakening towards Ronald. The more so as, after hearing the word 'measles', he refused to take Jenny's anxiety seriously. 'Measles! Children all get measles, you're working yourself into a state about nothing — as usual!'

He arranged a passage on the *Commodore Perry* sailing from Liverpool in two weeks' time, one of the James Baines ships which were famous for their speedy voyages to the Antipodes. It was done, the major step had been taken; now it wasn't 'just talk', the berth had been booked and Ronald Armstrong's name figured on the passenger list of a clipper bound for Sydney.

Jenny went to see him off, partly for appearances' sake because Baird had relayed to her some of the gossip flying around Galashiels. Moreover, after ten long days of high fever Heather was at last taking a turn for the better, and Jenny had time to realise that she was actually going to lose her husband — lose him for at least a year, an idea that had hardly been a reality until now.

Liverpool, that small, bustling port, had one or two good hotels. The Armstrong's booked two rooms. Neither could make the first step towards a reconciliation. They were polite to each other at dinner and at breakfast next morning. Ronald's luggage was already aboard when they went down to the docks for the parting.

The splendid harbour was crowded. The masts of fast sailing ships, the more squat spars of sailing steamers, the funnels of the steam packets now

229

becoming the rule rather than the exception on the trans-Atlantic run: it should have been a colourful sight, but it was almost extinguished by a sky low and full of scudding cloud.

Suddenly it was borne in upon Jenny that her husband, whom she loved, was about to put his life at hazard on a wide ocean where clouds could rain a deluge and winds could drive a ship to its death.

'Ronald . . .'

'Yes?'

'I don't want us . . . I don't want us to part so coldly. Perhaps we should think what we're doing.'

'I know what I'm doing,' he replied.

For him it was different. He always liked movement, travel, new challenges. Now he was about to go on a long journey, freed from trivia, facing the elements, a man among men. He was excited, new blood seemed to thrill in his veins. He no longer remembered he was leaving because of a quarrel with his wife. He was being called by that most seductive of temptresses — Adventure. And the call was the more insistent to him because he felt this was his last chance to go to meet her. He was nearly forty years old. If he turned his back on this chance, he might not get another.

All the same, when he and Jenny kissed goodbye before he walked up the gangplank, emotion stirred him. He wrapped her in his arms, hugged her before letting her go, and murmured, 'Write to me often. I'll send letters by every ship.'

'Take care of yourself, my love.'

'You too. And the lassie. Goodbye, Jenny.'

'Goodbye.'

She stood watching while the hawsers were taken off the bollards, the breeze ruffled the sails, the pilot-boat curtseyed ahead to take the clipper out of the Mersey. The rain came slanting across from the Welsh hills. Cloud scuttered across, falling low as the heavy moisture weighed it down. Within ten minutes the *Commodore Perry* was lost to view in a cloak of mist and rain.

The crowd on the dock slowly dispersed. Jenny returned to the hotel, collected her luggage, paid the bill, and took the train home.

Baird came to greet her in the hall with the news that Heather was sitting up eating arrowroot and looking much better. Throwing off her spring wrap and flower-decked bonnet, Jenny went up to the nursery. At her entrance Heather pushed aside the tray with the food and held out her arms to be picked up.

Wrapping the quilt about her, her mother took her up, and went to sit in the low armchair by the fire. The child snuggled against her, giving a sigh of contentment. For the last two days Baird had managed to account for Jenny's absence with various little loving fictions: 'Mama's gone to ask the elves to take away all your measles spots, Mama's gone to buy you a cowslip cushion and a primrose pocket.'

Over her head Jenny stared into the fire, seeing again the ship heading out into the grey distances of the Irish Sea.

Her vision blurred, her throat ached. But for fear of distressing her little girl Jenny drank up her tears.

Mindful of gossip, Jenny appointed as manager of Waterside Mill an elderly man, married with grown children. His name was Charlie Gaines, who had managed Begg and Hailes, the weavers with whom William Corvill and Son had shared premises on first coming to Galashiels.

Charlie Gaines had held several posts since Corvill's took over the whole of the Waterside Mill, but always in and around Galashiels. He knew Jenny slightly, and was thoroughly familiar with her reputation as a moving spirit in the weaving trade. He was not only willing to take orders from her, he expected to do so.

Jenny had generally been consulted by Ronald about any problems, and had always kept her role as the main designer of their cloths. But she had got out of the way of taking the major decisions. Nevertheless, as Gaines continued to seek her instructions, she found herself giving them.

In fact, everyone soon understood the situation. Jenny was managing William Corvill and Son, Charlie Gaines was acting as her deputy. She was often in the mill, but not in the office. She would be in the design studio up on the top floor, and here Gaines would seek her out.

At first he was taken aback to find her little girl there also. But within a week or two it became a commonplace. Little Heather Armstrong would be sitting in a small chair alongside her mother, carefully colouring charts which Jenny had discarded. Or she would be dressing her dolls in the little scraps of cloth taken from out-of-date pattern books.

At lunchtime the two would go back to Gatesmuir. Afterwards Jenny would return alone, for the little girl would be having an afternoon nap. But she would come with Baird to have tea at four, and then there would be a walk or some outdoor activity for her until it was time to go home with Mama.

The people of Galashiels were used to the mistress being a law unto herself. They soon accepted the idea that she took her child to the mill each day. 'Mebbe she's trying to teach the wee one to be a weaver like her mother,' they observed to one another with a grin. 'But she'll have to be quicker on the uptake if she's going to be as good at it as the mistress.'

The first letters began to come from Ronald. The *Commodore Perry* touched at various ports to take on fresh supplies or deliver goods. He wrote that he had seen whales through the captain's glass, that the landscape around Cape Town was surpassingly beautiful, that at Colombo he had been to see the temple dancers perform. After the first two or three which were full of the excitement of seeing new things, he began to sound a little wistful for what he had left behind.

'I regret now that we came to hard words with each other, my dear, and when I return we must make a fresh start. The long stretches of ocean, with little to see and nothing to do, have given me ample time for reflection, with the result that I can now understand how we came to be at odds. I trust that when you write to me, dearest wife, you will tell me that you forgive me my lack of understanding.'

Jenny's replies were full of goodwill. And then, five months after he had set out, the letter came announcing his arrival in Sydney.

This was a totally different kind of letter — full of enthusiasm, energy, and reports of action. 'Sydney Harbour stretches some eight or ten miles inland. The slopes of the hills are clad in trees whose names I haven't yet learned, but intend to. Surprisingly to me, there are some very fine villas here, with gardens that surpass anything in the Borders. I have put up for the time being at the Australia Hotel, where letters can be addressed as well as to the care of Henry Chalmers at his office in Pitt Street.

'Chalmers is a good enough laddie but I can see he is indolent. When I questioned him about the sheep farmers he had to admit he had met very few. Within a week or two I hope to have him stirred up enough to introduce me to some of these men. The wool staplers I can soon enough find for myself at the Sydney Club, and will report to you on them soon.'

These were the purposes for which he had gone, so Jenny had no right to feel a little disappointed at finding almost no personal references in the letter. She passed on some of the information to the other Galashiels woolmakers, enough to let them know that Ronald had arrived and was carrying out their plan.

'There now,' said the businessmen, 'didn't I tell you it was a good idea?'

The junior men, who had had hopes of the manager's job, were asking themselves how Ronald Armstrong would feel if he knew his wife had taken over the reins again. 'I'll wager she doesn't tell him that when she replies to his letters. His nose'll be gey out of joint when he gets back,' they remarked.

The gossips didn't quite know what to make of it. Jenny Armstrong and her husband writing to each other regularly — it hardly looked like a marriage that was breaking up.

But their hopes revived unexpectedly when something entirely new came into the situation.

Archibald Brunton Esq. returned to his estate at Bowden, south of Melrose. Anyone who had any kind of a memory recalled that soon after the Corvills came to Galashiels, it had been generally expected that Jenny Corvill, as she then was, would marry Archie Brunton.

Archie Brunton, the gossips soon learned, was still unwed. And within a few weeks of his return it became clear he was still very interested in Jenny.

What the gossips wanted to know was: did Jenny still feel anything for Archie?

Chapter Fourteen

It was perfectly true that Jenny Armstrong had once intended to be Jenny Brunton. In the somewhat business-like way of a young lady from a family who could give a considerable dowry, she had fixed on Archie Brunton as her future husband.

He was about six years her senior, and the owner of a very large estate which brought him in a fine income. He was goodlooking, with light brown hair and laughing eyes. He was the most agreeable man in the district — lighthearted, amusing, intelligent.

What made it more likely as a match was that his widowed mother, a lady of good sense and energy, came to approve of it. At first she had not been very keen on these Corvills who had come so recently into the Borders whereas her late husband's family had been here for generations. But then, Archie needed to settle down. His roving eye was constantly leading him into trouble. And Mrs Brunton, once she got to know the Corvills, found she liked them.

She particularly liked Jenny, despite the extraordinary fact that Jenny, a young unmarried girl, practically ran the family business. Jenny went to the mill office every day — it was unheard of. She argued with men, she carried out negotiations, she was in every respect a strange being.

But Mrs Brunton came to believe she was the very one who might keep Archie in order. She gave her tacit support to the proposed match.

Galashiels was on the whole delighted. Young ladies who had hoped to capture Archie resigned themselves to being mere members of the congregation at his wedding.

Then, very suddenly and without explanation, his mother had sent Archie off for a long stay with relations in Canada. He was reportedly to study agricultural methods, but anyone who knew Archie Brunton found that hard to believe.

No one except Jenny and Mrs Brunton knew the real reason. It was a very serious one. Jenny had found out that Archie and her sister-in-law, Ned's wife Lucy, were lovers.

Once that was known to her it was impossible to think of marrying Archie. If she had loved him passionately it might have been different — she might have been ready to resort to all kinds of strategems to make the marriage work.

But, as things stood, she felt nothing but revulsion. And to marry Archie, bring him into close contact with the family so that it might be even easier for him to meet Lucy — that was heading for trouble. Archie, she felt reasonably sure, would give up Lucy without much struggle. But Lucy would not have given up Archie. Lucy needed to be loved, to be loved in a more romantic and demonstrative fashion than poor Ned Corvill could imagine.

So Lucy wouldn't have given up Archie. The only way for Jenny to help the situation was to put an end to any match between herself and Lucy's lover.

Mrs Brunton wouldn't be satisfied until she had

forced Jenny to explain the situation. Shocked but not surprised by her son's behaviour, the old lady banished him at once, before he could wreak any more havoc. It had been a long time before Lucy recovered. For Jenny, too, it had been a troubled time — the only man who was thought 'good enough' for Miss Corvill to marry had gone.

Now he was back. Since his mother's death he had been something of a rover, travelling for pleasure, staying sometimes in Paris, sometimes in Vienna, sometimes coming back to Edinburgh or Glasgow, but never so far returning to his family home. Now, Jenny gathered, the lease he had given to the tenant of The Mains had run out.

'He's come back to meet the Queen,' the locals said with a shrug.

This was quite possible. Queen Victoria had decided to make a visit to Abbotsford, former home of one of her favourite authors, Sir Walter Scott. She would be en route as usual to Balmoral in the early autumn, and all summer the Borders had been making ready for her coming.

Galashiels had a new Town Hall in that year, as it so happened, a fine building of local stone that had cost the burgh the unheard of sum of £2,200. The whole town was in festivity, the mill owners granted a day's holiday with pay so that the workpeople could go to watch the Queen at Abbotsford, which was just down the road.

Naturally all the worthies of the nearby towns expected to be presented to Her Majesty. New clothes were bought, preparations were made for parties, picnics, and expeditions by carriage or on foot.

'You'll be going to Abbotsford, mistress?' Charlie

Gaines inquired in a tone that took it for granted.

'I don't know that I shall, Mr Gaines. My little girl doesn't like crowds, you see.'

'Och, but Mistress Armstrong, this is such a special occasion! Can you no explain to her that the Queen will be there?'

Jenny felt an impulse of annoyance. 'Explain to her that the Queen will be there' — as if the child wasn't as well aware of it as anyone else. Heather was now five years old, and already reading eagerly to herself from the nursery books that Jenny provided. With help from her mother she had read the reports in the local paper about the Queen's proposed visit.

'She knows about the Queen,' she said shortly.

'Well then . . . surely she'll want to see Her Majesty? It's not often we get a chance to see her in person.'

Jenny had inwardly decided not to go. But her decision had to be set aside when she received a letter from the Queen's private secretary inviting her to be present. That was the equivalent of a royal summons.

And to tell the truth, she was pleased. To be remembered by the Queen was an honour.

She debated with herself what to do about Heather. Should she take her? It would certainly scare the little girl to be among crowds. Heather hated crowds — it was some shadow left from her days in the infant asylum, perhaps.

But on the other hand to go out, leaving her with Baird, probably for several hours . . .

'I want to talk to you, my dove,' she said to Heather one day as they were walking to the mill in the soft glow of a September morning. 'You know the Queen is coming next week?'

Heather nodded emphatically.

'She's asked me to go and meet her. There, now, precious, that's a great thing, isn't it, to have the Queen send for me.'

Heather smiled and nodded again.

'I want to go. There will be a great many other people there. A lot of people.'

'Braw Lads?' suggested Heather in the low, unwilling tones that were so seldom heard, even by her mother.

'Yes, like the Braw Lads gathering at the Mercat Cross, but more than that — people from other towns as well as Galashiels. More people than you've seen before. And carriages and horses. And a band, I hear — one of the regimental bands is to play.'

Heather trotted along at her side, face upturned to take it all in.

'Would you like to go too, Heather?'

The little girl's face clouded. She drooped her head.

'You don't want to go?'

There was a long pause. Jenny stopped walking, stooped, and tried to look at her daughter's face. 'I feel I must go, little lamb. The Queen has invited me. I had a special letter — I'll show it to you.'

With her head still averted, Heather nodded.

'If you're afraid of all the people, you'll have to stay at home with Baird. It might be all day, so I want you to understand: the mill will be closed, everybody will be on holiday, you'll be at home with Baird.'

Heather shrugged and swung her body this way and that, as if to show nonchalant acceptance.

'All right. That's agreed. You won't fret if I'm away all day?'

Heather shook her head.

When they reached the mill there was correspondence to see to, and a problem with parcelling for the goods train. When that was settled, Jenny went up to the studio with Heather. They settled down with their sketching. Jenny was busy on a design she wanted to finalise for the book of spring patterns, so her attention was taken up with setting down watercolour lines until she found the mix she wanted.

Heather was, as usual, silent. She was also busy. When at lunchtime they put down their work and went to wash the watercolour off their hands in the washbasin, Heather offered a piece of cartridge paper to her mother.

It held one of those out-of-proportion paintings that children make. A lady in a fine green crinoline was curtseying to another in a chair with a high, lopsided back. One could tell this was the Queen because of a smudge of yellow paint on her head, representing her crown.

But the interesting point was that at the side of the curtseying lady there was another diminutive figure. She was wearing a pink frock. An elongated arm joined her to the curtseying lady.

Heather watched her mother. Jenny looked up. 'Is this me meeting the Queen?'

Heather nodded.

'This is the Queen?'

A nod for yes.

'And who is this?' Jenny inquired, pointing to the small pink clad figure.

Heather put her index finger against her chest.

So it was agreed: Heather would go to Abbotsford to see the Queen.

In honour of the occasion Jenny had Baird quickly make a frock for her daughter — a short length of Swiss voile-brodée over silk, with a broad silk sash and a ribbon of the same shade to trim her straw hat. The little girl submitted to the fittings with frowning obedience. It was as if when she put the frock on, she knew she was preparing for the ordeal to come.

In the event, the crowds were very little problem to the distinguished visitors who were summoned to make up the Queen's party. The ordinary folk were kept at a distance behind white ropes and posts, happy enough to be there and to listen to the band play while they waited for their glimpses of the notables.

As the Queen approached, Jenny thought she had changed a great deal since she last saw her. Then, Prince Albert had still been alive. She had been a compact, alert little personage. Now she seemed heavier in build, her face was pale, with lines deepening from nose to mouth. Her dress was completely black, as always.

'Mrs Armstrong,' she said, as she came opposite Jenny and Jenny curtseyed. 'I am pleased to see you again. Your husband is here?'

'He's abroad, Ma'am — in Australia on business.'

'Ah. You feel the separation, no doubt.' Victoria's face clouded at the idea. Then her glance fell on Heather. 'Your little girl?'

'Yes, Ma'am. Heather.'

'Heather? What an unusual name. A pretty child. You have other children?'

'No, Ma'am, only one.'

The Queen summoned a smile for the little girl. To Jenny she said, 'You made a beautiful piece of cloth for the Princess of Wales.'

'Thank you, Your Majesty.'

The Queen moved on down the line of waiting dignitaries. Those left behind the royal progress fell into step in her train.

Jenny found herself walking next to Archie Brunton.

She had been at some pains to avoid him. He had left a card a week or two after his return to his home at Bowden, but this had needed no acknowledgement. A married lady temporarily living alone because of her husband's absence on business was not obliged to return calls.

Since in the usual run of engagements she controlled who came to the house, she took care not to invite him. Everyone who knew her on social terms understood that she didn't care to go out in the evenings because it meant leaving her little girl. Most people met her in her own home. Businessmen on their travels were frequent dinner guests, she gave small parties such as at New Year, on the day of the Braw Lads, and St Andrew's Day. Some of these were informal enough that he might have walked in with some other acquaintance, but luckily there had been no such parties since his return in August.

Now she was trapped alongside him. But there were others present, and there was a Royal Personage only a few yards ahead.

Archie was already bare-headed in the proximity of the Queen. He bowed with a ready smile. 'Good afternoon, Mrs Armstrong.'

'Good afternoon.'

'The weather isn't particularly suitable for such a great occasion.'

244

'Perhaps not.' It was in fact a calm autumn day with heavy cloud.

Mr Beaton, the newly appointed Superintendent of the town's force of thirteen police, spoke from Jenny's other side. 'A real delight to see you here, Mrs Armstrong. And your wee lass.'

'Thank you. You seem to have managed everything very well, Mr Beaton.

'Oh, we've joined forces, all the towns have sent their constables. If a thief had a wish to break into a house in Selkirk the day, he'd find nobody to stop him!' Mr Beaton laughed in appreciation of this sally, flourished his top hat, and set off to keep an eye on his royal charge.

'This is your little girl,' Archie said. He stooped to bring himself on Heather's level. 'Howdedo, Miss Armstrong.' He put out his hand as if to take hers.

Heather drew back in alarm. Jenny said, 'She's rather shy with strangers.'

He straightened. 'I heard you tell Her Majesty that your husband is away.'

She let the remark pass. She knew very well that he'd been aware of Ronald's absence – the town talk would have been handed on to him as soon as he dropped in at the Gentlemen's Club.

'What are you doing after the Queen leaves?' he inquired.

'Going home.'

'You must let me escort you.'

'No thank you, my carriage is nearby.'

'But I should like to ride –'

Luckily one of the mill owners from Hawick joined them at that moment, absolving her from the need to put him off more forcefully.

They all walked on, in groups, in the wake of the Queen and her ladies in waiting. They saw Her Majesty sign a special page of the Visitors' Book, they waited respectfully while she was shown the novelist's desk and his books and all the other relics. Tea was provided under an awning on the lawn. The band played selections from *The Fair Maid of Perth*. Deputations from the local industries were allowed to offer presentations — a fine checkered shawl, an ornament of carved ram's horn, a silver badge with the arms of Sir Walter Scott.

Heather sat quietly on the druggeted ground by Jenny's chair, drinking milky tea and nibbling shortbread. The marquee was crowded, but she seemed relatively unconcerned. Jenny felt that this was the greatest event of the day as far as she was concerned. Heather had taken a big step forward.

Two years and three months had gone by since she came home to Galashiels. Although she was still not the same easy-natured child that had been snatched away, there had been a marked improvement. The nightmares had died away almost completely, although they had resumed for a short time in the spring when Ronald went away — it was almost as if the loss of that presence, grown familiar, had rekindled fears that had been diminishing.

If only she would join in the activities of other children. Perhaps it was time to try again. There was a small school for young children run by a sister of the minister of Galashiels Parish Church — perhaps she could be tried out in that calm, restrained atmosphere.

But even as she thought of it, Jenny knew it would

be a mistake. Heather never spoke willingly, and never at all to anyone except her mother or Baird. If a stranger, even the kindly Miss McDowell, asked her questions, she would freeze into utter silence. The other children might tease her. Sighing, Jenny put the thought away.

Signals were being given — the Queen was ready to leave. The visitors lined up to applaud and wave handkerchiefs. To Jenny's astonishment she heard from somewhere in the region of her elbow a little voice saying, 'Hurrah! Hurrah!' as Victoria walked past.

But that was the last sound out of the child for several days.

Archie Brunton had been pleased in every way with the day of Queen Victoria's visit. He had met the Queen herself, which was an honour and let the rest of the world see that he was a gentleman of standing. But, more important, he had at last been able to meet and speak a word to Jenny Corvill.

Or Jenny Armstrong, as he must learn to call her.

He had seen her from a distance several times since he came home. Once had been at an afternoon lecture in Melrose, once had been at a display of architectural photographs in Torrance House. On one occasion he had actually stood behind a hollybush in the churchyard to take a good look at her as she came out after the service.

He was astonished to find her still beautiful. Her dark, almost Mediterranean colouring had not changed, and if her face was thinner that only made her dark eyes seem the larger. He calculated she was now just past thirty, when most women were subsiding into mediocrity, having decided there was no need to be too careful of their appearance now a husband was safely landed.

From what he could gather, Jenny's marriage had been a disaster. She'd married much beneath her, and the man, Ronald Armstrong, had not proved much of a husband. There was something wrong with the child he gave her, and now he was off 'to Australia', which was a *façon de parler*, he was sure: it meant the man had got tired of the marriage.

So here she was, alone and presumably lonely, still as attractive as ever and perhaps even more so. There had been a time when her intelligence and ability had scared him. Seen in the setting of a small provincial town, she had been too startling. But travel had broadened Archie's mind. He had met women in Paris and Vienna who were like Jenny — not business-women, of course, but leaders of fashion, hostesses of literary salons, women with whom Jenny could have congregated without feeling out of place.

He wanted to be friends with Jenny Armstrong — friends at least, and as much more as he could manage. The whole thing could be so extremely simple: she was a woman needing masculine companionship and he was a man more than willing to provide it. Companionship in this instance meant whatever he chose it to mean. The husband was absent, the lady was beautiful — it was a heaven-sent opportunity.

But though he'd been back for almost two months she had eluded him. He was sure she was doing it on purpose.

Well, of course, it probably still rankled with her that he had upped stakes and gone to Canada without giving her the slightest warning. In a way, he had jilted her. There had been no official engagement but everyone had taken it for granted that they would be married, so she probably held a grudge against him.

Certainly it was because he had left her in the lurch that she'd made this absurd marriage with Armstrong. Armstrong — so far as he could learn, the man hadn't had a penny to his name. What a match for the great Miss Corvill of Gatesmuir and Waterside Mill! She must have been desperate to take such a nothing of a fellow.

Archie didn't know how long Armstrong was likely to stay in Australia. But from all that he could hear, he wasn't expected back soon. If he had written to say he was returning, word would have got around. And as it took between seventy and eighty days on the fastest clipper, that gave him probably three months at the very least — and more if the man was busy on some scheme at the back of beyond.

He might need all the time he could get. Jenny was showing herself very unwilling to know him. The fact that it wasn't going to be an easy conquest made it all the more stimulating. He would win in the end. He had very few failures in his history.

But September ended and October came. He still hadn't had any further conversation with Jenny Armstrong. On two occasions they were at the same place at the same time, but there were others present, so she avoided him by simply staying inside a group where she could ignore him.

Halloween came, and with it the traditional family parties with bobbing for apples and forfeits. There was to be a party at Gatesmuir, but Archie had not received an invitation. Still, Halloween was an occasion when you could get in almost anywhere by turning up with a turnip lantern and a seasonal gift.

Archie presented himself at the front door of Gatesmuir with the largest turnip lantern ever seen in the town — a work of art made for him by his head gardener. When, as tradition demanded, the housemaid had let him in and carried the lantern ahead of him into the main room, Archie stepped from behind her with a gift basket of fruit direct from Edinburgh that morning.

Jenny had come forward in welcome. He saw how she froze when she saw who it was. He was shocked. What was more, to his own amazement he was hurt.

She couldn't really dislike him that much?

'Thank you for your lantern, Mr Brunton,' she said, after a hesitation. 'We'll put it on the mantelpiece in the place of honour.'

'I hope you'll accept my gift, too, Mrs Armstrong, with wishes for the protection of this house on All Hallows Eve.'

She smiled thanks, found a place for him on a sofa with the Maitlands, and busied herself with supervising the children in their game with the apples in a tub. Heather was playing no part. But, on the other hand, she hadn't withdrawn into a corner. She was sitting on a tabouret watching with amused interest.

It was a good party, held early so that the children wouldn't have to go to bed too late, and full of merriment and foolish pranks. Only when everyone at last dispersed did Archie realise he had scarcely been able to exchange a word with his hostess and that, moreover, the hothouse fruit in his gift basket had been distributed among the home-going children.

Next day was 1 November, the opening of the

foxhunting season. Archie hunted, although he wasn't as devoted to the sport as some. On this particular opening day, however, he decided to attend, because the hunt was going to draw on Mossilee Hill to the southwest of the Corvill property.

Archie found no trouble in detaching himself and one or two others from the direct tracks of the hounds, so that to get back on the scent they had to make a detour along the edge of the wood that sheltered Gatesmuir from the easterly winds. Catching a glimpse of the rest of the field streaming away towards Clovenfords, his two companions dashed in pursuit.

Well content, Archie Brunton set his horse at a fence, jumped it well enough to come to no harm, and then deliberately came off so as to get his breeches and jacket well smeared with mud. His hat came off. He left it in the dirt. Then, leading his horse, he picked his way through the wood, came along the footpath that led to the back gate of Gatesmuir, and limped piteously to the stables.

Tam Dunlop, the coachman, was working on some harness. 'Guid sakes, Mr Brunton, you've taen a tumble!'

'I have. It comes of being abroad so long, Tam. Out of practice for the hard country.'

'Set you down, set you down, and I'll fetch you a dram.'

'Thank you. And if I could stay here a while till the mud dries so that you could brush me down and make me respectable . . .'

'No trouble at all, sir. And I'll give your horse a bit of a rub and a blanket till he cools down. I'll be back in a minute.'

He sent word to the house that Mr Brunton had had a tumble and would be the better of a dram of whisky. Likewise a bandage for his ankle, which he seemed to have wrenched, and a brush for his muddy clothes. In a few minutes the kitchen maid arrived with the requirements.

Archie drank the whisky, refused the bandage, sat for a little, then tidied himself up. Then he went to the front door and knocked.

'Mr Brunton!' said Thirley, when she opened to him.

'Would you tell your mistress how grateful I am for her kindness?'

Thirley smiled and dipped a curtsey. 'I will, sir, when she comes in.'

'She's not at home?'

'She's at the mill, sir, as usual.'

He'd forgotten that in his planning. He'd arranged to be at Gatesmuir on a pretext that would give him a good opportunity to speak to her direct when no one else was by. But the lady was literally not at home.

He glanced at the hall clock. A quarter to twelve. She probably came home soon after twelve.

He swayed realistically and grasped at a nearby chair. 'I think I'll sit down for a minute,' he murmured. 'I think I must have hit my head when I came off.'

'Surely, sir, surely. But come into the drawing room. I'm sure the mistress wouldn't wish you to sit out in the hall.'

He allowed himself to be persuaded into the drawing room. He sank down on a chair. Thirley fluttered round him. 'Can I fetch you anything, sir?'

'A hot drink, I think — tea or coffee — if Cook wouldn't mind.'

'Mind, sir! What an idea!' Off she hurried, thrilled to have the handsome, rich Mr Brunton in need of her ministrations.

So when Jenny came in at twelve fifteen, it was to find Archie Brunton sitting in her drawing room with one foot on a footstool, drinking coffee and looking very much at home.

Thirley had explained his presence when she opened the front door to her mistress. 'Hunting . . . a fall . . . a bit dizzy . . . thought it best . . .'

'Quite right, Thirley,' Jenny agreed. To her daughter she said, 'Run upstairs, lambkin, and wash your hands for lunch.'

When she went into the drawing room Archie made a show of trying to get to his feet. Jenny surveyed him. He certainly looked as if he had had a fall. But on the other hand his voice sounded perfectly unshaken as he said, 'Forgive the intrusion, Mrs Armstrong.'

'How are you feeling?' she inquired.

'Not bad, not bad. Foolish business, eh? But I'm out of practice, as I was saying to your coachman. I've not been hunting in over a year.'

She nodded. She made no attempt to sit down, and in fact seemed on the verge of leaving the room. 'I've blundered in upon your lunch hour,' he said in apologetic tones. 'I'm so sorry.'

He hoped she would say, 'Stay and eat with us.' But she merely smiled and replied, 'It's no matter. I can eat later — the routine is quite elastic.'

'You go back to the mill afterwards?'

She nodded.

'I'm being a nuisance to you, then. Please don't feel

you have to stay and be polite — I'll just sit quietly until I recover enough to ride home.'

'Do you feel you need a doctor?' she inquired. 'I can easily send for Dr Lauder.'

'Oh, no, no — I'm quite all right, just shaken up, that's all.' The devil with all this pretence, he thought. He got up, and went towards her. 'I'm glad to have this opportunity to speak to you, Jenny. We never seem to exchange a word these days.'

She drew away from him as he came near. 'No, and that's because we have nothing to say to each other, I suspect.'

'I have something to say to you,' he took it up. 'I want to tell you that when I left so suddenly all those years ago, it was because my mother commanded me to go. It wasn't by my own wish.'

'I really don't think there's any point in going over the past, Mr Brunton.'

'Mr Brunton! Surely old acquaintances should call each other by their Christian names.'

She shook her head, untouched by the wistful appeal he had put into his voice.

'Jenny, what's the matter? You don't still have any anger towards me for the past?'

'Which past are we speaking about?' she asked. 'The one you are trying to sketch in, or the real one?'

'What?'

'I wasn't perturbed when you went away. I was very glad.'

He was so astounded that his mouth almost fell open. 'What do you mean?'

'Let's not discuss it. Please feel free to rest until you are well enough to leave, Mr Brunton.'

'But Jenny — what are you saying? You were glad

when my mother sent me away?'

'Yes.'

'But I don't understand! I never understood it then — she never would explain why she suddenly decided to pack me off to the Colonies.'

Jenny shrugged. 'She probably couldn't bring herself to discuss it with you. And nor shall I.'

'But look here — I can't have this — you seem to be saying you know something about it.'

'Yes.'

'I demand to be told.'

'You demand?' She drew herself up. 'What right have you to demand anything? You trick your way into my house by pretending to have hurt yourself out hunting, you try to inveigle yourself into my good graces at every chance — what is it for? What do you think you're going to achieve? Do you think I'm another Lucy?'

Archie flinched at the name. Then he went first red, then white. 'Lucy?' he muttered.

Jenny sighed. 'I knew I should never have entered into conversation with you. But you wouldn't be put off.'

'Lucy! You knew about Lucy?'

'Yes.'

'But that's impossible —'

'You overestimate your own discretion. I saw you together.'

His mind was working overtime. 'And . . . and you told my mother?' He went stiff with anger. 'That was a very mean thing to do, Mrs Armstrong!'

'It was a very mean thing to do on your part — the seduction of a silly, vain little girl. But I didn't tell your mother about it willingly. She insisted on a reason for my not wishing to see you any more, and in the end I had to tell her. I may say,' Jenny added, knowing it was cruel, 'she wasn't surprised. She was angered but not surprised.'

Archie felt for a chair and lowered himself into it. He looked as shaken as if he really had had a bad hunting fall.

'She never said a word of it to me.'

'I imagine she felt a distaste —'

'She often used to lay down the law to me, but this time she simply ordered me to go on my travels.'

'And you went, without asking any questions!'

'Of course I went! Glad to go! Everybody in the neighbourhood was edging me into matrimony. People kept asking me if we'd named the day — I didn't *want* to be a married man! So when Mother said —' He broke off abruptly.

Jenny made a little gesture of impatience. 'You were desperately anxious to get away from me then. But now that I'm safely married to someone else, you want to get close to me. Do you think I'm a fool, Mr Brunton?'

'I . . . I only want to be friends . . .'

'You're incapable of being friends with a woman, in my opinion —'

He started to his feet again, straightening his shoulders. 'You've made your opinion quite plain, and now that you've told me the reason, I quite understand. Thank you for your hospitality, Mrs Armstrong.'

She rang for the maid, gave him a slight bow, and stood aside as he went into the hall. Thirley was there with his hat, which had been found by the fence. His horse, refreshed, was waiting outside.

As he reached the doorway to the porch, Archie Brunton turned back for a moment. 'Mrs Armstrong,' he said, as if the words were forced out of him, 'this has been the most extraordinary conversation I ever had in my life.'

His face, as he looked at her, was different. For the first time, she thought to herself, he looked fully adult — the boyish charm had gone, and perhaps for good.

Chapter Fifteen

Eating lunch with Heather, Jenny gave only part of her attention to her little girl. She was chiding herself for losing her temper enough to mention Lucy. But perhaps it had needed that to drive off Archie Brunton.

If she thought he was driven off, she was mistaken. Their confrontation had taken place on a Friday. On Sunday morning a manservant arrived from The Mains Farm, bearing a burden wrapped in fine tissue paper. Thirley brought this into the drawing room, where Jenny and Heather were passing the time with a book before setting out for church.

Surprised, Jenny accepted the package. She untied the tape and folded back the tissue paper. Within was a porcelain plate on which were arranged glacé fruits in little sugar cases, protected by a sheet of waxed paper. The effect was colourful and attractive. Heather gave a little coo of pleasure.

Tied across the plate was a ribbon. Attached to the ribbon was a little envelope. Jenny opened it and drew out a folded card. On one side of the fold was engraved Archibald Brunton's name. On the other a message was written.

'Dear Mrs Armstrong, This is to convey my thanks for your hospitality on Friday. It is also to beg you to receive me this afternoon, if only for a quarter of

259

an hour. I promise the interview will be entirely calm.'

Thirley was waiting inside the drawing room door, agog.

'I was to ask for an answer, mistress.' Jenny's impulse was to say no. But she had an awful feeling that there would be a stream of such gifts and notes until she said yes. The man wanted to see her to justify himself, or to restore his own image of himself — some such folly. So she might as well get it over with.

'Tell the servant the answer is yes.'

'Very good, mistress.' Thirley went out all smiles. There was nothing she wanted more than a pretty flirtation between these two notable people, which she could relate to all her friends on her day off.

At church Jenny's mind was not on the service. She was regretting that she had allowed Mr Brunton's visit. But she felt to some extent secure — other friends would be calling, she could easily end any tête-à-tête with this troublesome man.

The Corvills had originally been Huguenots, and her dead father had had strict views on how Sunday should be employed. But now that Jenny had only herself to consider, she had changed the routine a little. She went to the parish church for the morning service, she had a light lunch, and then in the afternoon she received visitors. The evening meal was the big meal of the day, to which guests were often invited, especially businessmen who travelled on Sunday so as to get an early start on mill visits on the Monday.

When Archie Brunton presented himself that afternoon, he was vexed to see other coats and hats over the settle in the hall. The maid let him in with a bright, welcoming smile. He was ushered into the drawing room, where he found Mr and Mrs Barkworth and their half-grown-up daughter showing off a collection of pressed flowers.

Jenny welcomed her visitor, showed him to a seat, inquired if he had recovered from his injuries. This immediately brought forth exclamations of anxiety from Cecilia Barkworth: had he hurt himself badly, where did it happen, had he seen a doctor?

Archie said, 'I'm quite well, thank you, Miss Barkworth. It was just a tumble.'

'Shall you be well enough for the St Andrew's Day Ball?'

'I'm well enough for it now.'

Miss Barkworth held her breath. She wanted him to ask if she was going and if so, whether she would save him a dance. Archie did neither of these things. He was waiting anxiously for these pestiferous people to go.

When Jenny said she would ring for tea, the Barkworths arose. 'Thank you, Mrs Armstrong, but we promised to take tea with Miss Menzies — she is Cecilia's godmother, you know. You won't mind if we rush away? Delightful to see you. Sorry the little girl was asleep — should have loved to see her. Goodbye, goodbye —' And off they went in a flurry of capes and mufflers.

When the sound of their footsteps on the drive had died away, Jenny returned to her seat. Archie was about to begin the speech he had rehearsed, but she held up her hand. 'The maid will be here with the tea in a moment.'

Feeling an utter fool, he shut his mouth. Thirley came in, set the tea-tray, lit the little spirit lamp under the kettle for extra hot water, eyed everything complacently, and went out.

'Will you have some tea, Mr Brunton?'

'Mrs Armstrong, I didn't come here to drink tea!'

'I suppose not.' With well-acted composure Jenny poured tea for herself.

'I came . . . I came . . . ' Everything he had rehearsed went out of his head. 'I seem to remember being gey tactless on Friday. I said I was glad to get out of marrying you.'

'Tactless, but also honest.'

'Aye, that's true. I've never fancied the married state. The fact that I got so near it with you is a . . . it's a kind of backhanded compliment.'

Jenny smiled to herself. 'Very gallant,' she observed.

'Oh, dammit — I'm making an utter mess of this! I thought I'd be marvellously polite and apologetic and you'd understand . . .'

'What is it you want me to understand? You were almost engaged to me, you took my sister-in-law to bed, you were found out, and the engagement was off. Those are the facts, aren't they?'

He flushed. 'Well, yes . . . Put like that . . . I suppose it was inexcusable. And I haven't come to make excuses. I came to say that if I had known you were aware of all that, I would never have . . . never have tried now to . . .'

'To make advances?'

'I didn't get very far, did I?' He gave a short laugh. 'You can be very cool. I understand now that I was wasting my time, and I'm sorry not only for my actions but for the . . . the insult to you that's implied in them.'

'Thank you. I accept the apology.'

'And I wanted to explain to you about Lucy.'

At the name she stiffened. 'I don't want to discuss Lucy.'

'Is it true what they say,' he plunged on, disregarding her statement, 'that Lucy took your little girl away?'

'Please don't let us talk about that.'

'I've heard all sorts of odd stories since I came back. Lucy ran away with some man? Is that it?'

Jenny said nothing. She stared into her teacup.

Archie seemed to take hold on himself for something difficult. 'In a way, that is typical of Lucy as I remember her. She wanted something out of life that I don't think she was equipped to handle – something grand and fulfilling in which she would play the leading role. And you have to understand that she's very pretty – at least she was when I knew her. Men find her kind of prettiness very . . . very enticing.'

'Enticing?'

'The little Dresden shepherdess – will she break if you take her in your arms? The little fairy princess – will she take you into wonderland if you make love to her?' He fell silent.

Jenny set down her teacup with a rattle. 'You know, Mr Brunton, all you're saying is you were tempted and you gave in.'

'Yes. But she did throw herself at my head, you know.'

'I know.' She rose and moved restlessly towards the window. 'It didn't occur to you to wonder why?'

'Well, because she had these absurd notions about herself . . .'

'And also because you were the man I was supposed to marry.'

'What?'

'She wanted you because to take you away from me would serve me right.'

Archie gaped at her, the laughing eyes very serious and concerned. 'Are you saying she hated you?'

'Yes. Still does.'

'Is that why she . . . about the little girl . . .'

'No, that was just an impulse. She was leaving home to go to her lover and it suddenly seemed a good idea to take Heather. I believe,' Jenny said in a voice that was laden with sadness and regret, 'that insofar as Lucy is capable of love, she loved Heather.'

He was sorry now that he had come. He had stumbled into something much bigger and more important than his own amours of the past. He got up, came to Jenny, and held out his hand.

'I'm very sorry, Mrs Armstrong. Of course I've only been seeing this from my point of view, from the outside. I realise now that you must have thought me a selfish idiot. I'm sorry I mentioned Lucy, or tried to excuse myself there.'

She looked at him. Her glance fell to his outstretched hand.

'Can we be friends?' he asked, uncertain of her response. 'It would be on a different basis. Respect, on my part.'

'I told you before. I don't think you can be friends with a woman.'

'You're wrong. I can be friends with *you*, if you'll let me. I'm not asking for anything special — just to be one of your circle of acquaintances.'

She made a little shrugging movement that seemed to say, 'Why should I bother?'

'It would matter a lot to me,' he insisted. 'I'd feel I was making a new start. It suddenly seems to me I've been playing the fool too long.'

She smiled. He was astonished to see how it lit up

her sombre face. 'The reformed rake?' she inquired.

He smiled, but he was colouring up again. She had a perfect talent for making him blush. 'Call it that if you like. But the thing about a rake is that in the end he has to reform. Either that, or he begins to get bored with himself.'

'Oh, to save you from boredom I had better agree.' She took his hand for a moment, but let it go at once.

He knew she wasn't going to believe in his reformation − if that was what it was − without good evidence. He was trying to frame a sentence or two that might impress her with his good intentions when the sound of carriage wheels on the drive stopped him short.

'Mr and Mrs Strang,' announced Thirley. The newcomers bustled in, glad to get close to a fire on this raw November day, glad to be offered tea immediately.

After a few exchanges, Archie took his leave. He felt very strange. It was as if someone had taken hold of his life and shaken it, like one of those paperweights in which a snowstorm whirls. What the landscape would be like when the snow cleared, he wasn't quite sure.

To Jenny's relief he didn't follow up this encounter with more gifts from Edinburgh emporiums. They happened to meet at a charity concert, were civilised to each other, and that was all. Thirley was quite disappointed. She'd hoped to see Mr Brunton calling at Gatesmuir frequently.

'It's a strange thing,' she confided to Cook, 'she doesna seem to fancy him at all. And him the handsomest man in the Borders.'

'She's a married woman!' said Cook, making indignant punches at the bread dough.

'And where's her man?' riposted Thirley. 'Oceans away! I daresay it's good business sense, but I wouldna care for it if I were a married woman.' She made a little pattern in the floured board with her finger. 'The mistress has been sad a long time. A wee fling would do her the world of good.'

'Much good it did the young Mrs Corvill,' grunted Cook.

Thirley pouted. The shame brought on the household by the young Mrs Corvill had been hard to bear.

Certainly Jenny brought no shame on her house. She had too much to occupy her mind for any little flirtations. Winter brought the usual crop of colds and coughs among her staff, both at home and at the mill. Heather succumbed to a bout of bronchitis. Dr Lauder assured her there was no need to worry, yet she worried all the same.

Then the letters from Ronald began to trouble her. At first he had been very businesslike. He visited woolstores, he took temporary membership in the associations concerned with the gathering and selling of the wool, he spent many hours in shipping offices. But when he began to travel out into what was called The Riverina, the tone of his letters changed. A touch of unaccustomed lyricism began to glow in them.

'I wish I could describe to you how rich this countryside is. It gleams under the sun among the rivers. The rivers and creeks have the strangest, most appealing names — the Murrumbidgee, the Waakool, Moolamein. These come, of course, from the Aborigine language, and the Aborigines are very expert sheep-herders. Not at all like our Scottish shepherds

— they work from horseback and tend perhaps a hundred thousand sheep.

'The distances, the open skies, the feeling of freedom — it's so exhilarating! I wish you could see it all with your own eyes . . .'

And so on: descriptions of travels that took him far from Sydney and more towards Melbourne and Adelaide, accounts of long talks with the squatters, the herders. Sometimes he enclosed photographs — stiffly posed waggoners alongside carts laden with fleeces and drawn by oxen, or the children of a sheep station standing proudly beside a newly purchased piano.

When Jenny replied she always expressed pleasure and interest in these reports. But she always asked practical questions: how much wool would the farmer expect to get from a hundred thousand sheep? How long did the shearing take? Did the wool get to collection points by the farmer's own transport, or was it organised by a waggoner?

Sometimes the questions were answered, sometimes not. It seemed to her that Ronald's attention was not concentrated on the business of wool for the weaving trade.

Here at home there were other worries. In the previous August, the Reform Act had come into being, extending regulations for factory work. Added to that was a subsidiary act which made provision for maximum hours of work and conditions in workshops for children, young persons and women.

The manufacturers of the Borders had not been troubled by the debates in Parliament. In the first place they were sure the Acts would never be passed. Then, when they were passed, they were sure they couldn't apply to them. Everyone knew that the Border weavers had the best conditions in Britain.

And yet . . . there were thirteen-year-old boys in the mills, whose activities must now be strictly supervised. Most of the employees were women, and though they were well-treated and well-rewarded, the factory inspectors began to point out improvements that must be made.

'Whatna way is that to run a business?' complained Herbert Cairns at Jenny's dinner table one evening. 'The women were perfectly content the way things were. It's all added expense, pandering to these fools in Parliament.'

'But there's fines if you don't abide by the new regulations,' pointed out Mr Begg in mournful tones.

'Are you going to take notice of these new hours of work, Jenny?' Cairns asked.

'I think we must, gentlemen. The reputation of the Board of Manufacturers has always been excellent. We don't want to blot its escutcheon now.'

'In the name of God, why do they want a place to hang their coats and shawls? They've always been happy enough to hang their shawls on the end of the loom —'

'But it *is* dangerous, Herbert. And besides, in wet weather they need somewhere to dry their outer clothes —'

'It implies they're less hardy than their mothers and fathers. It's all rubbish!'

And so the disgruntled argument went on. Jenny, however, had decided from the first to comply with the new regulations. She felt that Ronald would have wanted it. Besides, there was little that needed doing at Waterside. Her workforce had good conditions to begin with. An earlier 'loosing time', a row of hooks for coats, more protection from the working of the machines — these were easy enough to give.

The other manufacturers grumbled and delayed, on principle. They and their workforce were not on bad terms. They felt they didn't need members of parliament to tell them how to run things.

By the spring of 1868 the new regulations had been accepted. But the long rumbling argument, the continual meetings and persuading and reasonings, had been very tiring.

As if that weren't enough, someone in Yorkshire produced an almost instant copy of one of Jenny's new cloths. She had no doubt that one of the London warehouses had shown her pattern to a mill owner willing to make it from cheaper materials. It was vexatious in the extreme to have telegrams and cables of complaint that her new 'Bracken' tweed was on sale at a much lower price in rival establishments.

No amount of investigation or complaint would bring the culprit to justice. Nor would finding him make amends unless, with positive proof, she took him to court and sued him. She knew it would cost a tremendous outlay of time, money and energy so she wrote it off. But it hurt her. She had loved that new tweed, the more so since one of Heather's lopsided designs had given her the idea for it.

One May afternoon she was with her maid in her bedroom, looking through the summer clothes newly unpacked from storage, trying to decide on refurbishments for the coming season. A letter was brought up by Thirley.

'From the maister, mistress,' she mentioned, having recognised the stamps.

'Thank you. Go on, Baird, I'll just glance through this for now. Do what you can with that gown — but try to save it if you can, I don't want to part with it.'

Baird went on with the work of unpicking the frayed hem. A new gown, that was what was needed. But she knew fine the mistress would keep this one if she could, for Mr Armstrong had aye been fond of it.

A gasp from Jenny. Baird looked up. Jenny's face was white.

'Bad news?' asked the maid, scrambling up from her knees.

'He says . . . he says he never wants to come back to Scotland, Baird! He says he wants me to go out with Heather, to live there!'

Chapter Sixteen

The shock of the letter was all the greater because Jenny had expected it to contain news of his imminent return home. He had been gone a year now. In the discussions before he left it had always been taken for granted that he would stay in New South Wales for six months or so; he had been there now over nine months.

Jenny was made unwell by the letter. She was overcome by a sick headache that drove her to her bed in a darkened room. Baird ministered to her while inwardly uttering terrible Scottish oaths towards this dunderheaded man off in the wilds of Australia. Heather sat by the bed, clutching the counterpane, very distressed at this unheard-of calamity – her stalwart, dependable mother laid low like any common mortal.

In thirty-six hours the misery was over but the anxiety remained. Jenny had no one to discuss it with except Baird.

'It's perhaps my own fault,' she mourned. 'Heather had that bad cough when I wrote one of my recent letters. Dr Lauder told me it would pass but I probably made too much of it.'

'I'm not sure I understand, Mistress Armstrong.'

'Well, you see, my husband says the climate out

there is so exceptionally good — it would be much better for Heather — it's an understandable reaction.'

Baird thought, but didn't say, that in the past the master hadn't seemed too concerned about his daughter's childish ailments.

'It seems a long way to go to cure a cough,' she remarked.

Jenny laughed despite her anxieties. 'It's not just that, of course. He finds the country very much to his taste, and he likes the people — hard-working and reliable, he says, and with a gritty common sense.'

'I've no doubt they're the salt of the earth. The question is, mistress — why is he asking you to go and live among them?'

'I've just explained —'

'Na, na, you've told me the weather's good and he likes the place, but why are you expected to give up your home and the mill and everything you've built up here?'

Jenny hesitated. It was the big question — but she had no real answer to it. She sidestepped. 'He says there is great scope for a good woollen mill in New South Wales. The wool, of course, would be much cheaper — no transport costs worth speaking of. Ample water supplies. I imagine it would mean building from the ground, but then that can be an advantage — we could have all the latest machinery —'

'And it would all have to be taken out from England at vast expense,' ended Baird.

Jenny sighed.

'Mistress Armstrong, forgive me if this is a daft

thing to say, but is it no true that Scottish woollens have the best name in the world?'

'Well, yes, I suppose so.'

'Scottish tweed is wanted everywhere? America, Russia, Germany, Peru, Timbuctoo?'

'Yes,' Jenny agreed, smiling at the list.

'Tell me this. Who wants Australian tweed?'

Since Jenny didn't know, she made no direct answer. She took another aspect. 'My reputation would stand for something. If we set up again in Sydney or Melbourne —'

'Your name would be a help, I quite see that. But I canna understand why you should be asked to do it. You've a thriving business here, the mills are working to capacity, you have a full order book, your designs are wanted by all the buyers. Why should you uproot yourself and start all over again at a disadvantage?'

'But you see, Baird, you see . . . a wife's place is with her husband.'

Baird considered this. ' "Whither thou goest, I will go",' she quoted. 'But that lassie was speaking to her mither-in-law, if I recall my Scriptures correctly. I wouldn't argue against what you say about a wife's place, all the same. All I'm asking is, where is your husband's place?'

Jenny frowned. 'What does that mean?'

'He's in Melbourne the now. Last year he was here in Galashiels. A few years afore that he was in Perth. Afore that it was Berlin or one of the German towns. He never settles long in one place by all I've ever heard. Can you be sure when you've upped stakes and gone out there, he won't want to move again in a year or two?'

'Baird, Baird,' Jenny murmured, rubbing her eyes with her thumb and forefinger, 'don't say things like that.'

'Well, I'm old enough to be your mother, near enough, and I canna stand by and see you torturing yourself wi' ideas about dragging yourself up by the roots just because your man has a sudden notion. Do you not think you ought to write and ask if he's of a serious mind afore you start selling up the property?'

It was good advice, and Jenny took it. She wrote at length to her husband asking if he was serious in what he said. She reminded him of the problems, not the least of which was that though she had power of attorney from her brother, she had no right to sell his property. If they were to start a new weaving mill in New South Wales it would have to be after they had persuaded Ned and he had always said he didn't wish to speak to Ned ever again.

On the other hand, if they were to start entirely on their own, they would need capital. There was some money put by out of the salary she now paid herself and Ronald from the profits, and Heather of course would inherit something one day. But it wouldn't be nearly enough. They would have to go to the banks or the merchants, and gamble on their own abilities to be able to pay off the loan.

She ended by assuring him that she wanted to be at one with him on this important matter but she needed to know if he had thought it through to the end. She suggested they wait until he got home again to Galashiels, and then they could discuss it thoroughly. She signed it, Your loving and anxious wife, Jenny.

The letter would take something over two months to reach him, and it would be as long again before she had his answer, unless he had meanwhile set off for home. But somehow she felt he had not.

While she was still wondering if she had done the right thing another letter came, this time from Chalmers, the agent of William Corvill and Son in Sydney. It was full of statistics and information about the wool he had bought for her at recent auctions, but the last paragraph was something quite different.

'According to Mr Armstrong's instructions I have set in hand the inquiry for a sheep station to buy. At present there is nothing on the market that would be worth your interest so while I wait for a good property, I wonder if you would be so kind as to put in writing the exact requirements? It would help me very much, although you may be here yourself to make the final choice.'

'Dear God!' Jenny exclaimed, clutching her two hands together around the paper. 'A sheep station? Without even consulting me?'

Now she was angry. It wasn't enough that Ronald expected her to come rushing to the other side of the globe, he was making decisions that meant a great expense – and without even asking her opinion.

She sat down immediately and sent a message by cable and telegraph, to be passed on as a written directive to the first ship en route for Sydney. By this means short messages could reach the destination in about six weeks instead of eleven. 'William Corvill and Son to H. Chalmers Esq, Bridge Place, Sydney, New South Wales. No intention of buying a sheep farm. Do nothing at all until you hear further from me.'

At the same time she wrote again to Ronald. It was in a different tone from the last letter. She said rather tersely that the news from Mr Chalmers about the sheep station had surprised her very much, especially as it was the first she had heard of it. 'I believe that is another matter we ought to discuss when you are home again, my dear.' When she signed it she still called herself his affectionate wife, but there was precious little affection in the letter itself. Afterwards she was sorry. But she had been made very angry.

It was difficult to keep her mind on the day to day business of the mill. She was often inattentive when she was with her friends. Archie Brunton remarked on it. 'There's something very serious on your mind these days,' he remarked, as they waited to take their places at a formal charity dinner in Selkirk.

'Not at all, Mr Brunton.'

'Tell the truth, Mrs Armstrong. I've got to know you quite well over the last six months — I can tell when you are worried.'

'I assure you, I'm not in the least worried.'

'If it's anything to do with money . . .'

'No, really —'

'I mean it, Mrs Armstrong. You know I am a wealthy man. If your firm needs money, you have only to ask.'

'In all seriousness, Mr Brunton, business has never been better at Waterside Mill. But I thank you for the offer.'

He sighed. 'Ah, Jenny, Jenny, you'll never let me be a real friend, I know. But I must be thankful we can at least speak to each other without sharpness now.'

She smiled and nodded. She knew he was in earnest. Whether it was only a temporary change or not, he wasn't the same man who had first come home to the Borders. There hadn't been a whisper of amorous scandal about him. He seemed to have given up the pursuit of pretty ladies. It was even possible to be with him and hear only the usual compliments that gentlemen were supposed to offer ladies — and to tell the truth some of the ladies were quite disappointed at the change in him.

The dinner was for the Weavers' Benefit Fund. At its end, a signal honour was bestowed on Jenny. She was elected a member of the Manufacturers' Corporation. It was something she had often longed for in the past, the mark of equality with the other mill owners, withheld until now because she was a woman. But her good advice on the introduction of the Reform Act had impressed them. She was forgiven for being a woman, she was welcomed into the fold.

It should have made her feel triumphant. Instead, it made her feel old.

Congratulations flooded in over the next week or two. She pretended to be very pleased. Inwardly she was saying, 'What does all this matter, if my husband insists we leave home and start again?'

In November came another letter from Henry Chalmers, a long letter from the feel of the folded paper in the envelope.

Dear Mrs Armstrong,
    Thank you for your express message concerning the purchase of a sheep station. In any case I had withdrawn from the negotiations for reasons

277

which I feel it my duty to lay before you. Forgive me if the facts give you pain, but I believe I am doing right.

I was in error in thinking Mr Armstrong wished to buy a sheep station. Further inquiry on my part ascertained that he was seeking a small farm for his own occupation. His letter to me had not made it quite clear and sometimes his travels through the Riverina have made it difficult to keep in communication.

He returned to Sydney before the arrival of your express message. When he heard I had written to you on the matter of the sheep station, he was angry, although at the time I could not understand why. He told me he wished to buy a small property. I was at a loss.

Subsequently rumour has made his intentions clearer. People are saying he has an attachment to a young woman on one of the stations. I have no way of ascertaining the truth of this but it seems to be borne out by his wish to buy what one might call a 'family property'.

If you know better than I do on this point and are satisfied that Mr Armstrong's actions are on your behalf or on behalf of William Corvill and Son, then I can only make the most abject apologies. But the rumours here are very strong, and since my loyalty is to William Corvill and Son I have ceased to act for Mr Armstrong and shall continue in this unless I hear from you to the contrary.

I enclose some reports on the quality of the wool from recent shearings, and a piece from the local paper on farmers' incomes. Your humble and obedient servant, Henry T. Chalmers, Buying and Shipping Agent.

If Ronald's letter about moving to Australia had shocked Jenny, this one shattered her.

Luckily it had come to the mill office. She let it fall from her fingers on to the desk, covered her eyes, and shut out the world for a long moment.

Heather, sitting in a small chair by the window doing 'sums', looked round. Mama was perturbed. She got up, came over, put her hand on Jenny's arm, and leaned against her.

Jenny took the deepest breath she'd ever taken, to force life back into her deadened body. She uncovered her face. Heather was staring at her in alarm. She knew she was as white as chalk.

'It's all right, my pet. It's all right.'

Heather put a hand up to Jenny's brow, as she had seen Baird do when her mother had the headache. Her hand was warm and sticky. Jenny captured it, kissed it with foolish fervour, and hugged the little girl to her. 'It's all right. I haven't got a headache. Come, let's go out for some fresh air.'

Heather was astonished. She had recently learned to tell the time so she knew the wall clock said only nine in the morning. At nine Mama looked through the morning mail, dictated letters to the clerk, surveyed the order book, listened to any problems from the foremen. Somewhere between ten and eleven they would go up to the studio on the top floor. Mama would work on her designs, or look at samples of wool, or survey past pattern books in search of a nuance, a shade.

But they never went out until they set out for Gatesmuir at lunchtime.

Yet it was exciting to be going out at an unusual time. She ran to get her serge jacket while Mama wrapped her cape around her. Outside, everything seemed different — the light at nine was different from the light at noon, the grey sheen of a November morning was resting on the red sandstone façades, the cobbles glistened in a different way.

They walked to the new bridge over the Gala. It was close to the railway station, a fine object for a walk because one could drop sticks into the river at the same time as keeping an eye open for the plume of steam from an approaching train.

But the place was busy, a train was just in and passengers were hurrying to and fro. Mama led her further up the slope of Buckholm Hill. Soon they could look back past the cottages of Buckholmside to the roofs of the town, grey slates shining with the remains of morning mist, trees with late autumn branches specked with a few green leaves, the hum of industry from the mills.

Heather forgot that Mama had seemed upset. She ran to and fro picking up treasures — acorns, a pigeon feather, a metal ring from some gentleman's walking stick.

Jenny stood in the shelter of the bare oak trees. The letter from Chalmers was in her pocket. She took it out, reread it.

Another woman. She should have guessed.

Despite the hesitancies of Chalmers' letter, she knew the rumours in Sydney were true. All the things that had puzzled her were made clear by this shocking fact.

There had been no letter from Ronald for some time. She'd thought she had offended him by the tartness of her reaction to the supposed buying of the sheep farm. She realised now that she had silenced him because he didn't know what to say in reply.

And all that had gone before; the strange, urgent summons for her to come out and start again with him in a new land — she should have said yes, she should have replied that she was coming at once. Because that had been his plea for help. She could guess at it, feel it in herself — he had known he was falling in love with someone else and had made a last attempt to shore up their marriage.

And she had failed him.

She reminded herself with horror that she had received the letter in May, he had probably written it in March, and now it was November. November! Eight months had gone by. God alone knew what had happened since then.

She looked at the date on Chalmers' letter. September 4. Two months ago it was a well-known piece of gossip in Sydney that Ronald Armstrong was involved with a young woman from one of the sheep stations of the Riverina. Involved enough to be wanting a home for the two of them, a farm they could handle themselves, perhaps. By now he might have found it. They might be living together.

She took refuge in movement, walking suddenly to and fro under the oak branches. Heather ran up, looking at her and rubbing her hands against her arms to signify that it was cold standing still, that she understood why Mama was walking about.

Jenny took her hand. They went on up the hill. At the top the air was cold and moist. Sheep moved among the tussocks of tough grass. In the distance a dog barked. Buckholm village lay on the far side, but it was too long a walk for a little girl of six.

What was she to do? The question rose up in front of Jenny, like a wall she must scale. What could she do? She was so far away from the man she loved, separated by oceans and by time. If she wrote begging him to remember her, to remember their little girl and the love they had shared, it would be months before the desperate words reached him.

In any case, were those the words to write? She couldn't help remembering that it was over Heather they had quarrelled. Everything had begun to go wrong from the moment Heather was taken away.

She tried to examine Ronald's behaviour, without rancour but without excusing him either. At first he had been as stricken by Heather's loss as Jenny. But he had been willing to accept that the child was dead long before Jenny would even consider it. He had wanted her to give up the search.

She understood that when she at last found the missing child he had been glad, but he had been unhappy too − full of guilt for his own lack of faith, full of guilt for his moment of rejection when he first saw Heather again.

Had there been some resentment towards herself too? She had been proved right, he had been proved wrong − perhaps it was too much to expect a man to feel total love and acceptance of a woman who had put him in the wrong.

And then, her own behaviour . . . She had forgotten everything except Heather, Heather and her needs. The wounded child − wounded in her spirit, in her faith in humanity − had taken up all Jenny's attention.

To her it seemed natural, right, necessary. But how had it seemed to Ronald? He had said, in so many words, that she was too indulgent to the child. His view was the one shared by most of the world — that children should be strictly brought up, that they should know their place, that they should be seen and not heard. In the last respect Heather was an ideal child, for she hardly uttered a word. But that too had been thought of as stubbornness rather than as the scar of a deep wound. And it had led to Ronald's sense of shame when others thought the little girl mentally damaged.

Jenny had gone by her own instincts. She might have spoiled Heather — only time would tell. But as she walked on the hillside with her daughter's hand in hers, she felt she had not done badly. Heather was still very silent, and still clung to her mother. But she had gained some confidence, some gaiety, some lightness. She was quick and clever no matter what the rest of the world might think.

Even so, even so . . . No husband likes to be put so much in second place, even by his own child. She had heard other women speak of the problem — the irritation of the man when his wife had to give her time and energy to the children instead of to himself. In the course of family life the thing resolved itself naturally — the child wormed its way into the father's heart and he ceased to feel any resentment. Heather, alas, had not regained her father's love. He had been at a loss how to handle her.

When she looked so far back, Jenny's mistakes seemed plentiful. For years she had been neglecting Ronald. He had seized on the idea of travelling to Australia as a way to be a man to himself again, instead of merely husband to Jenny Corvill, father to the dimwitted child, manager of the firm he had married into but had no share in. The cry rose up within her: How could I have been such a fool?

Yet at the time she had done what she felt she had to do. Heather had been her first thought. Heather had needed her in a way that Ronald did not.

For God's sake, she exclaimed, in her own defence, he was a grown man! Surely he could see that the child came first?

Yes, he could see. He had accepted her course of action. But that didn't make it easier for him. Their love for each other had suffered. She had to be honest and admit it. After Heather was kidnapped she and Ronald had ceased to be close physically. She had often been too anxious or too tired to want to make love. And when they did, it had not been like the old days.

The old days. At the words her thoughts turned back to the time when Ronald had first taken her in his arms. They had been happy, confident lovers. With him there had been none of the near-desperation that had sometimes haunted Jenny. They seemed right together. Time and separation had taught them that they needed each other.

At least . . . it had taught her that she needed Ronald. The day that she saw him again had been like a new dawn. She had needed him, wanted him, been enraptured by his mere presence — that tall angular body, the long face with its glinting smile, his dry manner of speech.

Had he needed and wanted Jenny? Yes, of course, why else had he come back to her from Perth? Yet perhaps he hadn't wanted a marriage.

Certainly she'd given him no time to think about it. Within months they had been man and wife. Now that she came to look at it, with unbiased vision, she wondered if perhaps she'd been selfish and precipitate – and Ronald had been too kindhearted to draw back once she'd shown her need of him.

As she walked on the hill Jenny tried to be completely fair. It might really be that she had rushed Ronald into marrying her. But if that were so – and that having been admitted – he was now in fact her husband. He had taken the vows at the marriage ceremony, he had signed the parish register. Just as it was her duty to try to be a good wife to him, it was his duty to be a good husband.

A good husband doesn't want to reject his own daughter. He doesn't resent her. He doesn't leave home to get away from her.

And he doesn't take up with another woman.

The thought hurt her so much that she had to bite her lip to keep from sobbing. She couldn't bear to think of Ronald in someone else's arms. It stormed over her like a tidal wave – she missed him, she missed him. All this past year while he had been gone she had been growing more and more colourless, more sad-minded. Without him there to mirror back humour and wit and intelligence, she was diminished. The days seemed long without him there to hear her news and tell her his thoughts.

And the nights . . . Her body recalled the touch of his hands, the warmth of his skin against hers. Even when they didn't make love but simply lay in companionship with arms about each other, there was a joyful contentment. But when passion took them, life was changed – they entered a different universe where auroras flamed and galaxies wheeled.

She had lost that with his going, and even before

his going. She had retreated from that wonderland into her shell of anxiety over the child. She said to herself, I denied him that — no wonder he ceased to love me.

The grey of the day was being touched with a faint pearly sunshine, but it was still cold. Heather came running up, tugging at her hand in a suggestion that it was time to go back to the warmth of the mill.

Sighing, she led the little girl down the hill path to the bridge and the streets of the town. Her mind was still whirling. But at least this much had been accomplished: she had recovered from the first shock, she was fit to meet her manager and her workpeople without breaking down.

If she thought she was completely herself again, she was wrong. Everyone noticed that something ailed her. Gaines decided to handle the problem over the late rail collection by himself, and the dye-master withdrew from an argument about his new light blue without forcing a decision.

They knew her well. If something troubled her so much, they felt they must be kind to her. Among her friends something of the same spirit prevailed. At a party at the Misses Wilsons' she was poor company and lost continually at cards, yet no one scolded her.

Word went round: Mrs Armstrong was unhappy. Two and two were put together — there had been a letter from her Australian agent, she was downcast, it had contained bad news. Money lost? Wool shipments astray? But it must be more than that, they felt. In the face of business problems, Jenny Armstrong was generally full of fight. Now, for the first time, she seemed beaten.

At the end of that week Jenny had guests to dinner – nothing elaborate, just good food and wine and the opportunity for talk. The guests were Mr Kennet and his wife, the textile agent for one of the Hamburg warehouses and his wife, Mr McCardie of the Dighton Mill, Miss Lambert of Highton Rise, and Archie Brunton.

Jenny roused herself to be a good hostess. After dinner they had some music; Miss Lambert played well. The men talked politics, the ladies talked fashion, and by ten o'clock they were all ready to go home, for Galashiels kept early hours.

Archie Brunton had to linger. His gig had been put up in the stables and the horse unharnessed, so that there was a slight delay while Jenny's groom got them ready. Archie took Jenny into her drawing room, drew her down beside him on the sofa, and said gently, 'Tell me what's wrong.'

She shook her head. 'Nothing's wrong.'

'Don't lie about it, Jenny. You're like a ghost these days, and even worse this evening than last time I saw you.'

'It's nothing, I assure you.'

'If it's business worries –'

'No.' As soon as she'd said it she was sorry, for it opened the way to questions about her personal life.

'Is it about the little girl?'

'Heather? Oh no.'

'Are you ill? Is that it? Has the doctor –'

'No, my health is excellent, thank you.'

'Jenny,' he said, taking both her hands, 'please tell me. Please. I want to be a friend to you. I want to help you. Tell me what's wrong so I can put it right.'

Silly, treacherous tears welled up at the kindness in his voice. 'It's nothing you can put right, Archie,' she said.

'So there is something, and it's serious. Is it — did you have word from Australia?'

She tried to smile. 'News travels fast, doesn't it. Yes, I had word from Australia.'

He made a guess. 'It's not business. Your husband?'

She gave a stifled gasp.

'He's ill? Been injured?'

'No, no —'

Thirley came in. 'Your carriage is ready, sir.'

'Let it wait.'

'Yes, sir,' Thirley said, surprised at the sharpness of his manner.

As soon as the door had closed on her Archie tried to pick up the impetus of his attack, but he had lost his moment. Jenny had recovered herself.

'You're very kind to be so concerned, Archie, but I really must insist that though I have worries, they are my own business.'

'I admit that, my dear. I don't mean to pry. But when I see you look so wan and hear you sound so listless, I can't bear it. If that foolish man of yours has done something to hurt you —'

'Don't speak of him like that!'

Archie grunted in exasperation. 'How do you expect me to speak of him? He was never good enough for you in the first place, and now he's gone cavorting off to the Antipodes and left you languishing here with a —' He was about to say 'dimwitted child' but caught the words back. He resumed at once. 'Everybody expected him back by now. What on earth is he doing out there?'

'He's . . . it's business . . . you don't understand . . .'

'Then explain it to me. I only want to understand and to help. If you can prove to me it's nothing of importance I'll hold my tongue. But I only have to look at you to know —'

'There's nothing to know!'

'Yes there is, and it's something your husband has done —'

'No, you're wrong, you don't know anything about it!'

His own experience led Archie to an answer that startled him so much he blurted it out. 'It's another woman!'

'No!'

But the force of the denial told him the truth.

'Ronald has taken up with some woman.'

Unable to speak, Jenny was shaking her head from side to side.

'Good God, Jenny, that's it! Nothing else would make you so miserable! That donnart man has taken a mistress.'

'You mustn't say that! I won't let you —'

'What's he done, written to tell you? Or someone else has?'

This time she didn't make any denial. She put her handkerchief over her face and wept.

'Holy saints in Heaven! I never liked Ronald Armstrong but I never thought he was such a full-fledged idiot as this! Do you know how long it's been going on?'

She made a muffled sound.

'How long? Months, I suppose, because mail takes such a long time — Jenny, is this what was troubling

289

you last time I tried to get you to confide?'

'No, not this, but . . .'

'But this is worse. This is definite, I take it — you could get proof if you wanted it.'

'Oh, dear God, I don't want proof!' Jenny whispered. 'I want it not to have happened.'

He put an arm round her in an effort to comfort her. 'It's no use asking for what can't be. The man has betrayed you, my dear. And do you know what you should do now?'

She moved restlessly, to signify she was at a loss.

'You should divorce him.'

'Divorce him!' Her reaction was shock, utter negation. '*Divorce*?'

'Why not? I know it's a big step, but for heaven's sake, Jenny, he deserted you, he's been gone over a year, and now he's unfaithful. You have good grounds for a divorce. You could get an agent in Sydney to furnish an affidavit —'

'But I don't *want* a divorce!'

'I understand, my sweet,' he rushed on, 'it seems a terrible step to take. But reflect — it's not such a blot on a woman's reputation in Scotland as it is in England. Our laws are civilised, our view of the marriage tie is more reasonable. You could —'

'I could never survive it —'

'But no one need ever know about it, Jenny! Ronald is out there in the wilds, the proof for divorce could be sent by document, the hearing could be heard very quietly, it could all be arranged most discreetly. And then if you like you could give yourself out to be a widow — who would be able to contradict you if you said Ronald had died in some accident?'

'I could never do such a thing!' she cried, aghast.

'If I ever took steps to end the marriage, I wouldn't want to lie about it! As to saying Ronald had died –'

'But it happens, my sweet girl, it happens all the time. Haven't you ever heard the phrase, a Colonial funeral? The black sheep of the family is sent off to Africa or Australia, and after a decent interval he's given out as dead –'

'But suppose Ronald came back –'

'Oh, we'd make it worth his while not to! It would probably end as a financial arrangement –'

'But you're racing too far ahead, Archie!'

'No, I'm not! All at once I see how to set you free from that clod of a workman who trapped you into wedlock!'

'He didn't, Archie. You're mistaken!'

'Oh, you're too scrupulous in your notions of justice to him. He's betrayed you, Jenny, he doesn't deserve any kind of defence from you. You should rid yourself of him once and for all. What's he ever done for you? Made you unhappy, left you alone for over a year, and now he's living out there with his light o' love –'

She shook her head, attempting to free herself of his arm about her shoulders. 'You've no right to say things like that about him.'

'I've every right. I've seen you growing more and more unhappy for months. It makes me angry. If I had that man here I'd – I'd –' Archie jerked his head in anger. 'Never mind, we'll deal with him. I've lawyer friends who can help. We'll shake him off once and for all. And then, Jenny my darling, you'll marry me.'

'What?' she gasped in astonishment.

'Marry me, Jenny. I love you. I'll spend the rest of my life making this up to you.'

'But, but – Archie –'

'I know you think I'm a lightweight kind of a chiel. It's true I've frittered a lot of my time away. But I've changed, dear, you must have seen that I've changed. And you've let us become friends.'

'Friends, yes. But marriage; that's an utterly different thing, Archie. I've never even thought of it –'

'There was a time when you did, Jenny.'

'Ah yes. Yes, but that was ten years ago, lad. And even then, if the truth must be told –' She broke off, flushing painfully. 'I didn't love you. It was my duty to make a good marriage and everyone agreed you were the best man for me. So I worked for the match, I admit it. But there was never any love in my feelings.'

'But there was something. You wouldn't have thought of marrying a man for whom you felt nothing. You *did* like me, Jenny.'

'I . . . well, I suppose I found you . . . pleasant, good fun, well-informed . . . But now those seem like a very poor basis for a marriage.'

He tightened his grasp about her shoulders, pulling her closer so that he could touch their cheeks together.

'It's enough, Jenny. And I'll make it more – I'll make you love me. I'll make you forget the unhappiness that's come on you since then. Everything'll be different. I understand you better now, I know how to be at ease with you, and you'll learn to be at ease with me, dear heart, heart of my heart . . .'

Murmuring endearments, he turned her towards him and was about to kiss her on the mouth. She felt herself melting in the warmth of the moment, lips soft and yielding.

Then she felt him stiffen.

He was looking over her shoulder. His grasp relaxed. She turned to look at what he was seeing.

In the open doorway of the drawing room a small figure in a smocked flannel nightgown and bare feet stood watching them with sleepy eyes.

Chapter Seventeen

In the open doorway behind Heather, Baird appeared, hair in curl papers and dressing-gown dragged about her.

'Mistress, I'm sorry — her footsteps padding across the floor woke me but by the time I'd got out of bed she'd gone.'

Jenny and Archie had sprung up, Jenny in concern and Archie in alarm. Being stared at in silence by a tousle-headed moppet was a new experience.

'There now, my precious,' Jenny said, hurrying to stoop over the child. 'Was it a dream again?'

The little girl's head made a solemn nod once or twice. She twined her arms round her mother's neck and hid her face.

'Come along now, darling, it's the middle of the night, Wee Willie Winkie will be looking for you. Come along.' Jenny picked her up. Already sleep was exerting its influence over her again. She lolled like a rag doll in her mother's arms.

'Let me take her, Mistress Armstrong, and let you go back to your conversation.'

'No, no, Baird. It's time the house settled down for the night.' Jenny, in the hall, beckoned to Thirley, who came forward with Archie's coat and hat. The horse could be heard worrying its bit on the drive outside as it waited in the shafts for the welcome journey home.

'I'll away, then,' Archie said. He wasn't sorry to be going. The tender moment with Jenny had descended into bathos and he didn't think he could reconstruct it. 'I'll leave you to think on what we've been saying, and I'll come back some time tomorrow to continue our discussion.'

She made no demur. He bowed and took his leave.

As he drove home he was in a mood of exaltation. She would divorce Ronald Armstrong, she would be free and they would be married. He would take her to live at The Mains Farm. The furniture and decorations there were still according to the taste of his late mother, but Jenny should have a free hand, she could redecorate exactly as she wished.

As for continuing her interest in Waterside Mill, he wouldn't stand in her way. From Bowden to Galashiels in his Stanley gig was only an hour — she could be driven into town two or three days a week or, indeed, he himself would drive her, it would be a pleasure to do so, they would chat to each other as they drove, she about the weaving, he about the estate.

Her friends would come to The Mains, his circle would be enlarged by friendships with the new, enthusiastic men in the world of textile engineering and design. He would bring her the acquaintance of lawyers and bankers and landowners. They would be sought-after, the best host and hostess in the Borders.

He would even — he stiffened himself inside his carriage coat as he came to this thought — he would even take on the little simpleton. She was a pretty enough child. No doubt a good, patient governess could make something of her even if she never caught

296

up with others of her age group. She might never marry, of course. Well, then, he would provide for her. He wouldn't be a hard, uncaring stepfather. He wouldn't hold it against her that she looked like Armstrong, with her tawny hair and wide-set hazel eyes.

And he and Jenny would have children of their own. He would have a son to inherit the lands his own father had handed on to him. At this point in his scheming, an unexpected wave of sadness engulfed him. He could have had all this ten years ago — all of it, and without the little halfwitted child to mar the perfection. Jenny would have come to him then a happy, eager bride.

But he hadn't had enough sense to know that he had heaven in his grasp. His mother had always told him he was a fool but he had laughed at her in secret, calling her a silly old woman.

But she had been right to call him fool. He had wasted ten good years.

Jenny too was thinking of waste. Too wound up to go to bed, she sat by the side of her sleeping child and thought about what had been said to her that evening.

Divorce? But that was a waste of what had gone before. Their marriage — hers and Ronald's — had had value and meaning. How could she end it without losing more than she gained?

It was easy enough for Archie to say, Divorce him, he's no good. Archie had never been married. He had no experience of the tie that grows between two people who live together in day to day harmony, who love and disagree and laugh and mourn together.

He had swept her along with his words. For a moment she had almost given in to the comfort of his arms. To be loved and cared for — it was so enticing, a siren song that called her. She was tired, so tired, of being alone without a man. She was no weakling, but she needed someone to walk beside her on this sometimes thorny path through life.

She had recognised honesty and truth in his tone as he urged her to turn to him. He really loved her. How strange that was! How the gossips of the district would adore to be told what had passed between them that night! Archie Brunton in love — trapped at last, they'd say. And not by some speckless maiden with a great dowry, no, no. By a married woman with a witless child and a husband who had deserted her.

As the night hours wore on, her thoughts roved over her past. She saw herself in her girlhood — the strict Huguenot home in Edinburgh, her father's hands opening the family Bible to read a passage before they retired for the night.

Her upbringing was totally against any idea of marrying another man while her husband was alive — her real husband, the man with whom she had taken the vows in church. In all the Huguenot community there had never been a divorce. True, the matter wasn't regarded throughout Scotland with the severity it aroused in England, but it wasn't approved of. And by Huguenots it was unheard-of.

Jenny wasn't herself deeply religious. She had preserved the appearance because it was socially desirable, but often she found herself disagreeing with things the minister said in church. Nevertheless, she had been brought up to believe that a vow taken 'before God' couldn't be lightly broken. To Archie it might seem an easy thing to do — he might even feel that resentment or anger would carry her forward into an action for divorce.

But she didn't feel anger or resentment against Ronald.

What did she feel? She was bewildered, stricken, unhappy. Frightened, too – frightened that her life had gone awry totally and completely. She was lonely – lone and bereft. Even Archie, with all his passion and his longing to help, hadn't warmed the arctic cold of her loneliness.

Common sense cried out at once against this self-dramatisation. She wasn't alone – she had Heather, and she had friends, and her work. She had more, much more, than most people. She was independent, mistress of her own fate – Mistress Armstrong, the moving force at the best mill in the Scottish borders.

But courage is hard to shore up in the middle of the night. She heard the wind whining in the trees on the hill outside, she heard the barn owl call as she hunted from the coach house tower, she heard a train steaming out with night mail from Galashiels station. Few souls were awake, and fewer yet with cares like those that weighed her down.

She was wakened by a gentle touch on her shoulder. Baird was at her side.

'Mistress, why are ye no in your bed? It's four in the morning.' It was a whisper, so as not to rouse Heather. The maid had wakened and come to check on the little girl, only to find the mother still sitting by the bed.

'Oh.' Jenny rose slowly, stretching her stiff limbs and her aching neck. 'I dropped off.'

'And no wonder. Come now, mistress, come along to your room. I'll help you out of your dress –'

'No, no, I can manage –'

'Ach, you're fair dropping with weariness. Come now, let me help you into bed.'

Dazed and drowsy, she allowed herself to be led to her own room. Baird stirred the dying fire in the grate to give a little warmth. Then she came to Jenny, unhooked her bodice, helped her step out of her crinoline. With deft hands she folded the underwear — chemise and drawers of French lawn, stockings of pale grey knitted silk, petticoats of taffetas edged with lace. She unpinned Jenny's hair, brushed out the ringlet curls.

'I'll just fetch you a wee milk toddy,' she murmured, after helping her into a quilted dressing-gown.

She tiptoed down to the kitchen. There the range was damped down for the night, and she hesitated to open it up, for the sound would bring Cook to see what was afoot. She used a small spirit stove to heat milk. She spiced it with cloves and added an egg-cup of whisky.

As she carried it carefully upstairs in its silver holder, she was saying to herself, I'll not let them wake her at the usual time, she's to sleep in, she'll be the better of a good sleep, for God knows she looks as if she needs it these days.

Jenny was sitting close to the tiny red glow of the fire. Her dressing-gown was wrapped closely about her. Her face was pale, dim in the glimmer of the lamp turned low. She looked up as the maid came in. Her dark eyes were fixed on her.

'Baird,' she said in a small, firm voice, 'would you come to Australia with Heather and me?'

The toddy, glass and holder went down on the Brussels carpet with a little clatter. Baird threw her hands up to her mouth to stifle a cry of horror.

'Australia!'

'I'm getting out as soon as ever I can arrange it. I'll take Heather — I couldn't leave her, it would be terribly bad for her to part from me —'

'You're going out to settle there with him? Mistress, I'd do almost anything in the world for you and the wain, but I canna give up my native land, not at my age!'

'It wouldn't be for good, Baird. I must have worked it out in my mind while I was asleep just now. I was so perplexed, so baffled. And now it all seems clear to me. I have to go there, to Sydney, to see him. I have to talk to him. I've been told things that . . . if they're true . . . But I have to hear it from his own lips.'

'Guid sakes, can you no just write him a letter?'

'Letters! That's what makes it so awful — nothing but letters, that don't really say anything, explain anything! Set down on paper, things can seem so — so convincing. But before I give up hope for my marriage I owe it to my husband to —'

'Ach, now you're blethering, if you'll allow me to say so,' Baird said, in a tone that dared Jenny to tell her to stop. 'Your man went away and then he decided he wanted to stay away — and *he* never felt it was his duty to see you and talk it over.'

'This is different, Baird.' She hesitated, on the verge of telling her maid what Chalmers had reported. But she had always had a horror of women who gossiped with their servants. 'All I can tell you is that it's very serious to me, and I want to talk to Mr Armstrong — I need to talk to him. But I promise you this: whatever the result, we'll come back to Galashiels. This is my home, this is where my work is.'

She had come to this unconscious decision. She

would speak to Ronald face to face, and hear the truth about this other woman. If he wanted to remain in New South Wales with her, she would divorce him so that he could remarry.

As for herself, she would come home. She would devote the rest of her life to her daughter and her work. These would be her consolations, her compensations. She would not marry Archie Brunton — she didn't love him, she never had, and it would be wrong to take shelter with him from the malice of gossips.

She slept for four hours, then woke for a late breakfast and two hours' work at the factory before lunch. Heather went with her as usual, much intrigued at the idea of Mama staying in bed till eight-thirty and having to apologise for being late when she met Mr Gaines.

Gaines was summoned from his own cubbyhole of an office for a conference.

'I'm going away, Mr Gaines. I want you to take complete control while I'm gone.'

'Oh aye, mistress? How long for? Will it be for the New Year?' For some of the mill owners went to Glasgow or Edinburgh for the festivities.

'It will be at least six months, perhaps nine.'

'Eh?' gasped Charlie Gaines.

'I'm going to Australia, to join my husband for a visit.'

'A visit?' He sounded as if it was unheard-of.

'You'll move into this office and take charge. Everything is tidy for the present. Orders are coming in for our spring patterns, so you'll just carry on filling those —'

'But Mistress Armstrong!' yelped Gaines. 'Mrs Armstrong! I canna manage the mill without you!'

'Of course you can.'

'Of course I canna! When I took this job, it never entered my head I'd have to do it without you there at Gatesmuir to turn to.'

'But you'll manage fine, Gaines. You know all there is to know —'

'Aye, aye, if it were any ordinary mill. But this is William Corvill and Son. Standards are higher here, the volume of work —'

'But it runs smoothly even so. We're within our capacity. And you need only just keep things going.'

'But what if anything goes wrong?'

'If it's to do with finance, you speak to Mr Dolland at the bank. If it's to do with leases or contracts, it's my lawyer Mr Kennet. Anything to do with the machines, you know better than I do how to handle it, and the foremen can manage most minor problems. If it's anything really serious you'll have to turn to the suppliers of the machines for their mechanic — but that's not likely, now is it?'

'We-ell, no . . .'

'I have confidence in you, Mr Gaines.' She looked at him with her fine dark eyes and smiled, and Mr Gaines felt his opinion of himself rise in consequence. She said he could do it, so he could do it.

But he was still stunned at the notion. 'When do you think of going?'

'I've started inquiries now for a berth. I hope to leave within a fortnight.'

'But Mistress Armstrong — you'll be travelling at the worst time of year and the weather when you arrive will be the midst of their hot season — would you no put it off till the spring?'

'I can't, Mr Gaines. It's important to go now.'

'And here,' he said, struck by a terrible thought, 'what about the new patterns? What are we to put in the book that's due out in March?'

'I've some designs ready, you can use those. Some samples have already been woven and I'll get others ready before I go, to see if they'll do. They won't be enough, I agree, but you can include some from former books — it's time to repeat the Bewsley check and the one with the grey and green background, the Forester. As to the rest, I'll be working on the ship, so I'll send back a packet of designs from our various staging points.'

'My lordie, you've thought it all out!'

'Yes, I'm trying to do so.' It surprised her how much she had planned even since waking this morning. Already she was looking ahead to the day of embarkation, what must be done before she left, what absolutely must be signed and agreed and contracted for.

'And by the way, Mr Gaines.'

'Yes, mistress?'

'There'll be a commensurate increase in salary for taking on this extra responsibility.'

He blushed with pleasure. A much married man, he had five children to provide for. The promise of extra money was a great boon.

'Is it to be telt to the workforce?' he asked as he turned to go.

'I think so. They'll have to know sooner or later so you may as well mention it now. I hope to leave at the beginning of December. If anyone asks, I'm taking my daughter and my maid.'

From her little chair by the window, Heather looked up at the mention of 'my daughter'. She rose, came to stand by the desk, not intruding but looking from one to the other as Jenny spoke to the manager.

'The trip should last until about June, but that isn't definite. As I've explained, I'll send back designs and instructions, and I'll write to you at suitable opportunities to give you news of my plans.'

'Right you are, then,' he said, and went out to spread the word.

When he had gone, Heather put a small hand out between her mother's gaze and the papers on the desk. Jenny knew this signal well — it meant Heather wanted her attention.

'Yes, darling,' she said, 'we're going to Australia.'

Heather hesitated. Then she went to find one of the books that were kept on a shelf by the window, to amuse and educate her while she was in the office with Jenny. She brought it to the desk. It was a large illustrated volume called *Our Colonies*. She opened it, looking for a particular picture. When she had found the page, she laid it questioningly in front of her mother.

The picture showed a tumbledown hut made of rushes and branches by the banks of a wide stream. Outside stood two or three black figures, the men in a travesty of white men's garb, the woman in a skirt of coarse cloth and holding a cooking-pot. The title below read: 'Aboriginal mia-mia — typical living-place.'

'Oh no,' Jenny said with a laugh. 'This is where we're going.' She flicked over the pages until she came to a panoramic view of Circular Quay in Sydney. 'Here you are, lambkin. And look, this is like the ship we'll sail in.' She pointed to the spars of a sailing-ship seen distantly among the smoke-stacks of the local shore steamers.

Under this picture Heather had printed in rather limping letters, 'Papa is here'.

She now put a finger under the name.

'Yes, Heather, we're going to see Papa.'

A long pause. Then, satisfied that she knew all there was to know about the venture, Heather nodded and returned to her sum-book by the window.

Jenny had only resumed her desk-work for ten minutes when the hall porter came in to say that Mr Brunton had arrived. Sighing, she asked to have him shown in.

'Good morning, my love,' he said cheerfully as he entered, stripping off his gauntlet gloves. 'How are you today?'

'I'm well, thank you, Archie,' she said, hiding a frown at his term of endearment. She hoped the porter hadn't heard it as he closed the door.

'You do in fact look better,' he agreed. He was looking well himself, his fresh skin glowing from his drive in the crisp November air, his eyes sparkling with expectation. He had dressed with care – a light tweed jacket over a fine flannel shirt tied with a loose satin cravat of blue, and dark brown dogtooth trousers. Elegant and well-bred, a fine figure of a man: just the man any woman would want for a husband.

'Sit down, Archie. Can I offer you some refreshment?'

'Thank you, dear. A glass of something would be welcome after the cold outside.'

'Madeira? Whisky?'

'I'll take Madeira, I think.' He watched her contentedly as she busied herself pouring the wine.

She realised with dismay that he had settled everything in his own mind to his own satisfaction.

He took it for granted she was going to say yes to his suggestion of last night.

She went to Heather by the window. 'Go outside, darling, and see if you can find some moss among the stones at the back of the yard. I need it for a colour-match later.'

Heather sprang up. She loved to be sent on errands. Taking up the little oilskin bag in which she brought home such treasures, she ran out, pulling her outdoor cape around her shoulders.

'Well done,' said Archie. 'Now we can talk in private.'

'Yes — and what I have to say can be told in a few words.' She drew in a breath. 'I'm going to Australia, Archie.'

The expectant smile washed off his face. He looked at her in total dismay. 'Jenny!'

'I can't do anything else. I need to talk to my husband.'

'But that's absurd! He —'

'Everyone is only too anxious to tell me what 'he' did. But he and I are the only ones who know the inner side of our marriage.' She paused. It was impossible to explain it to a bachelor like Archie. 'I have to go.'

'No!' He felt he must prevent her. His hold on her was precarious — only since that moment of weakening last night. 'No, why should you undertake —'

'It's the only thing I can think of.'

'But what about the child?' he exclaimed, snatching at the only objection that might have some weight. 'She'd miss you.'

'I'm taking her with me.'

'Surely it will be very bad for her?'

307

She made an uncertain gesture. 'I don't know. She's been cowering here in a corner of Galashiels for over three years now. Perhaps it's time to take her out into the world.'

'But on a journey of that length!'

'I know, but I can't leave her.'

'Why must you go at all? It's a foolish venture. What will it gain you except heartache when you see him with his doxy? Think of the embarrassment, the indignity —'

He was using weapons that had edge to them. Jenny had pride: to be made to look foolish would hurt her.

But she simply closed her lips firmly and shrugged.

'And you really mean you'd leave all this' — he gestured at the busy-looking little office, a gesture that took in the humming sound of the busy mill — 'to grab at a man who's grown tired of you?'

She disregarded the cruelty of his words. She knew he was floundering for some hook with which to hold her. 'I'm not going for ever,' she said. 'I'm coming back.'

'Ah.' That at least was something. 'What if he says he won't come back, he wants to stay with this woman?'

'Then I'll come home without him.'

He didn't want her to go. If she was absent from him he could easily lose her. The confidence of last night oozed out of him. She didn't love him, he knew that. He had relied on the fact that she was lonely, wounded, unhappy. But now she was exerting herself and taking control of her situation — and her need of him, if it had ever existed, was diminishing like a snowman in spring.

'Don't go, Jenny,' he said. 'You'll only regret it.'

'My mind is made up.'

'But you haven't done anything irrevocable. Change your mind —'

At this moment the door of the office opened and the hall porter came in. 'Telegraphic message, mistress. The messenger's waiting for an answer.'

She opened it with a quick flick of the fingers. 'Cabin available price eighty-four pounds sterling aboard clipper *Larksong* sailing 8 December please confirm immediately consolidate by writing with fare Baines Shipping Liverpool.'

She picked up a pen, wrote on a pad from her desk. 'Confirm cabin booked collect fare from Agent N. Luker North Street Liverpool pp Corvill and Son send boarding instructions Mrs Armstrong Galashiels.'

She handed it to the porter with money to tip the messenger. He touched his cap and went out. She turned to Archie. 'That was the notification that there's a passage available. I've accepted it.'

'No, no, this is too rash —'

'I know what I'm doing, Archie.'

'I forbid it!' he cried, catching her by the arms and almost shaking her. 'I forbid it, do you hear!'

She did nothing. She stayed absolutely motionless in his grasp, looking at him with troubled eyes. After a long moment he let her go.

'I'm sorry,' he muttered, stepping back. 'I have no right, of course.' Now he found he couldn't face her. He knew tears of disappointment and loss were gathering in his eyes. It was unmanly. He didn't want her to see him like this.

'This had better be our leave-taking,' she said after a moment. 'I'm sorry that you've been involved in my problems, Archie —'

'Don't,' he begged, feeling as if he were suffocating. 'Don't. It's my fault, I've been too late all along. If only I'd . . .'

But he couldn't finish the sentence. He saw only too well that he had missed all his chances. 'Goodbye, then, Jenny. I wish you a pleasant voyage.'

'Thank you.'

'If things don't go well . . . If when you come back . . .'

'No,' she said, with a gentle shake of the head. 'No, Archie, it's better to tell you straight out. It never could be. You see, I love my husband.'

She listened to him drive off. But behind that sound she heard the echo of her own words.

I love my husband, she thought. And I'm going to the other side of the world to fight for him.

Chapter Eighteen

To the utter astonishment of Jenny and her maid, Heather revelled in the rail journey to Liverpool. Trains she had seen before. She had even become blasé about them, for a goods locomotive came into the loading yard at Waterside Mill.

But travelling in a train, in a reserved compartment, was exciting. So was changing at Carlisle, with a short stay in the first class waiting room with a bright fire to warm them, and having hot food in a basket brought to them at one of the stops so that they were picnicking while the countryside rushed by. The docks at Liverpool alarmed her. She hid herself against her mother's side as they followed their porter through the noise and bustle. Jenny had to carry her aboard the *Larksong*, her face turned inward against her mother's shoulder. Jenny's heart sank. It had been a bad mistake to force this experience on the little girl.

But once Heather saw their cabin, she was enchanted. They could see she thought it was a new way to play doll's house. And certainly the cabin, eleven feet by nine, was small enough for such a notion.

There were two bunks, one above the other, and a low fixed bed along another wall. They had a large stern window which could be opened for air and had a reed blind against the sun. There was a private water closet. This was truly a luxury cabin.

Heather's happiness was obviously complete when she was told she was to have the upper bunk. She took this to be a special favour. In fact, it was to save Baird the necessity of having to clamber up past a sleeping child.

After the confines of the cabin, the saloon was capacious and handsome — more than thirty feet by fifteen. It was surprisingly well furnished, with upholstered sofas and mahogany fittings. Here the cabin passengers would take their meals and pass their time when not on deck enjoying the sea views or the games.

Seasickness set in while they were beating up the Irish Sea. Two days later, both Jenny and Baird were on their feet again. Heather had not been affected at all. Jenny, who had heard many travellers' tales from her business friends, was relieved and pleased. Too soon. The frightfulness of the Bay of Biscay came upon them.

This time everyone was seasick except the crew. Groans from the *Larksong* could have been heard in Guyenne and Gascony. But they passed into the lee of Finisterre, and the sea calmed, and the world righted itself. Essence of peppermint was put away, likewise rum potion and barley water.

There was plenty to occupy the passengers if they wished to be occupied. There were games of quoits and spillikins on deck, there were innocent card games in the saloon during the afternoon and less innocent games among the men at night. There were three ample meals a day — breakfast, luncheon and dinner, none less than four courses. There were guessing games, sewing bees, religious services. There was livestock to visit in coops on deck — cows for fresh milk, chickens for eggs, geese and turkey for meat. The ship's longboats held boxes of soil in which grew lettuce, cabbage, carrots.

When the ship anchored to take on supplies, mail or fresh water, shore parties were formed. They visited Cape Verde, and after that aboard ship there was the ceremony of Crossing the Line, in which new crew members and male passengers were summoned by King Neptune, shaved roughly, and toppled into a bath of sea water. Such children as wished could also undergo the ceremony. Three little boys and one little girl volunteered, but Heather avoided the invitation of Neptune's trident.

Then came Cape Town, and Mauritius. After that it was the long crossing of the Indian Ocean with the southern trade winds blowing first from port and then starboard as the ship tacked to fill her sails. They didn't make a record voyage, but they had done the trip in a respectable time of eighty days when they entered Sydney Harbour on the 25 February 1869.

Ferryboats were plying to and fro. Coastal steamers were discharging cargo at the jetties. Beyond lay the town, nestled among greenery. The government buildings on Garden Island gleamed in the sun. The sky was a hard cobalt blue, the sea reflected back the colour. The breeze smelt of strange flowers, of fruit for which Jenny had no name as yet, of the smoke of steamers and factory chimneys. On deck the heat was so intense that the deck planks felt hot even through her shoes.

'So here we are,' Baird observed, looking about with a wary gaze. 'Is there anyone to meet us?'

'I sent word by the pilot boat to Mr Chalmers.'

'And to the maister?'

Jenny moved restlessly to hide her embarrassment. 'I asked Mr Chalmers to send word to him.'

'What for could you not send word direct?' The question seemed artless, but Baird had her own opinion of how things stood between husband and wife. On the voyage, Jenny had tried not to confide her troubles, yet only the most insensitive could have failed to see there were great uncertainties about the forthcoming meeting.

'I . . . there is some . . . some doubt concerning his whereabouts.'

'But I thought he had lodgings near the Quay?'

'Perhaps. His last letter certainly gave that address – but I've reason to believe he's gone from there.'

Reason to believe: a long interval without a letter from Himself. What could the gowp be up to? 'Humph,' Baird said, and turned to accompany Heather on a round of farewells among the surviving livestock of the *Larksong*.

Heather had stood the long journey well. She had soon become accustomed to shipboard life, had made friends with the animals, had been kept to her lessons at set times and, moreover, had taken them sometimes with the six other children on board.

These other little passengers had accepted Heather's silence as part of the strangeness of travel. Everything was different on board ship, so why shouldn't there be a little girl who didn't speak? She took part in games on deck, she shared in the cosseting of the ship's animals, she did her lessons under the kindly supervision of one or other of the mothers who never scolded when she shrank from reading aloud. The eldest of the children, a girl of eleven, had taught her to knit and crochet after a fashion and was now in tears at the thought of leaving Heather and sailing on by coastal steamer to Melbourne.

Jenny had been greatly relieved at how things went. At first she had been very worried: first the seasickness and then the sticky business of fitting the child into the pattern of shipboard living. Yet there had been no return of the nightmares of four years ago, no problems other than what could be expected from being cooped up for eighty days in meagre accommodation.

But now they would soon be ashore. Jenny was in a turmoil of emotion — first a mere physical longing for space, for unhindered activity, for the sight of trees and flowers and the sound of a running stream. And beyond and above that, longing to see Ronald, to look at his face and hear his voice.

There was apprehension too. What would he say when they met? If Mr Chalmers had been able to contact him, what had he felt at the news of her arrival?

Mr Chalmers, when he came aboard to greet them, was a surprise to Jenny. His letters had led her to picture him as a slender, willowy, rather poetic creature, earnest and easily made anxious by his own defects. In fact he turned out to be rather portly and red-faced, perspiring freely in his Norfolk jacket and sponge-bag trousers as he hurried in the wake of the purser to be introduced to her.

'Mrs Armstrong, ma'am! Welcome to Sydney!' he gasped, raising his brown bowler.

'Thank you, Mr Chalmers. You received my note, I see. Did you carry out my instructions?'

'Ah, yes, yes . . . That's to say, as regards the hotel,

I've sent to reserve a suite of rooms for you. As to the other . . . er . . .'

'You sent word to my husband?'

'Ah, no . . . not yet. I presumed, in fact, you would rather do so yourself. Ah . . . you see, he's off in the Riverina somewhere.'

Jenny drew in a deep breath. 'At what address?'

'Well, that's uncertain. He . . . perambulates a lot. But he can be reached, I believe, in care of Daniell's farm. I thought, since it's some distance away and a few hours' delay could make no difference . . . you'd rather . . . ah . . . communicate yourself.'

'I see. Thank you.' Her manner was completely calm, although her feelings at this strange landfall were acute. It seemed quite clear that Ronald had given up any pretence of looking after the interests of William Corvill and Son. He was off by himself somewhere — and if one wanted to cut oneself off from the rest of society, there was no place better than the Australian bush, she imagined.

But why, why? Was it to be with a woman, or was it to find something he had lost in the humdrum routine of running the mill? Adventure, she knew, could be enticing. Was it only that? Or was he in the arms of someone else?

She didn't pursue the matter of his whereabouts. 'Will you see to our luggage, Mr Chalmers?'

'Of course, of course. Permit me. How many items?'

She gave him her list so that he could check each trunk and hamper, then went to disburse tips among the crew. Baird and Heather joined her. They went down the gangplank, and set foot for the first time on Australian soil.

Circular Quay was busy. Bales, casks and crates were being unloaded. Nets swung from gantries. The cargo holds were open, releasing strange smells of machine oil and chemicals. Bags of mail were being carried ashore.

Men in cotton drill trousers, baggy check shirts and wide-brimmed hats were heaving on pulleys, wheeling trolleys. There were one or two black men, and a black woman in a shapeless cotton gown selling flowers from a basket — strange flowers, some of them, yellow acacia blooms, a pink blossom that looked something like a rose, crimson waratahs. But among them were familiar things from Europe: irises, potentillas, even the humble marigold.

'This way, this way. The luggage can be brought on a cart. Would you like to walk? After months at sea — exercise is so beneficial. The hotel is not distant . . .'

Heather was holding firmly to the hands of the grown-ups. Yet it was encouraging to Jenny to note that the child wasn't hiding her face against her mother's side as usual, but was looking about, scared but interested. Much as I feel myself, Jenny thought, with inward amusement.

They picked their way among the crowd on the Quay. She saw that their appearance caused curiosity. The inhabitants of Sydney were avidly interested in each new arrival, for it meant perhaps a useful addition to the workforce, a trade they needed, money to be spent in their industry or commerce, fashions to be copied.

Henry Chalmers led the way, talking with his mixture of hesitation and verbosity. The remains of a fine classical education could be heard in his choice of words, but his original Scottish burr had been overlaid with the narrower vowel sounds of Australia.

He pointed out the Tank Stream. 'This was the fresh water supply for the First Fleet. And here is the Bank of Australia, ma'am, although of course we use the Australian and Scottish Commerce Bank.'

The city was surprising to Jenny. She had of course seen photographs of Sydney but had always imagined these to show the more impressive buildings: she'd felt sure the rest would be timber shacks, much like the towns of the American West. Not so, however. Handsome sandstone office buildings and houses lined George Street, and moreover there was gas street-lighting and a good array of shops.

The Australia Hotel proved to be in Lower George Street, a two-storey building with a canopied verandah and blinds drawn against the mid-morning heat. Opposite, Chalmers informed her, stood the oldest business establishment in Sydney, Mitchell's Marine Store.

There was something of the maritime town about the whole street, so that she was prepared to find the hotel full of old sea-dogs. But though there were one or two seafaring types smoking over copies of the *Star* in the lounge, the housekeeper who came forward to greet them couldn't have been more sedate and proper.

'This way, ma'am, I've given you rooms at the back so as not to be disturbed by the traffic — wagons and carts go up and down even at night because of the shipping. My name's Mrs Welland. How are you, ma'am? Did you have a good voyage?'

As she led the way upstairs she was glancing back over her shoulder, drinking in details of Jenny's bonnet and the trimmings on her pale green linen gown. And more especially, of her white kid gloves. It was the dream of every Australian woman, Jenny was to learn later, to have an endless supply of white kid gloves − and the leisure in which to wear them.

The rooms were capacious and cool after the glare outside. Furniture was sparse, made of woods Jenny couldn't identify as yet. The floor was polished planks with rugs at bedsides and in front of sofas. Both rooms were bedrooms; there was no sitting room to the suite, and in fact the rooms could only be called a suite in that they had communicating doors.

'I'll put in a small bed for the little girl if you'll tell me which room she's to go in,' said Mrs Welland.

Jenny turned to Baird for her opinion.

'The bairn and I had best have the lesser room, you have the one with the corner windows, mistress. You'll need the bureau for a desk for business.'

The housekeeper looked faintly startled at this statement, but contained her curiosity. 'Now, can I fetch you anything? Tea? A glass of ale or stout?'

'Tea, please,' begged Jenny, thinking of the pleasure of having it made with pure fresh water.

'I'll send it up in a moment −'

'No, no, please, Mr Chalmers is waiting for me downstairs. Is there somewhere I can have it served?'

'The back verandah? There are shade trees there to keep it cool.'

'Very well, in ten minutes or so − tea for two on the back verandah. Baird and my daughter will take theirs up here.' To Baird she said, 'When the luggage is brought, begin on the unpacking. I'll be back within half an hour to help.'

Chalmers accepted tea but looked more ready for talk. 'I must tell you, ma'am, I was quite confounded when your note came on the pilot boat. I had no idea you were intending to make the voyage.'

She explained that there had been no ship sailing in time to bring him forewarning.

'An express message — ?'

'I preferred not to use that method. There is something terse about an express message, something impersonal. This didn't seem to be a time for being terse or impersonal.'

'No, ma'am,' Chalmers agreed, clearing his throat in embarrassment.

'This girl — what can you tell me about her?'

'Ah, well . . . the girl . . . People say her name is Dinah Bowerby. I myself have not seen her, nor am I cognisant of much concerning her . . . ah . . . antecedents. I believe she was brought up at the Female Orphan School. Her mother was Euphemia Bowerby, now deceased. Her father is, ah . . . unknown.'

'She lives in Sydney?'

'No, ma'am, she is a servant on a sheep station near Rankin's Springs. I comprehend that a post was obtained for her when she left the school at fourteen but consequent on some disagreement she removed and took employment further off — Larkin Springs is really a long way away, towards the Lachlan River.'

Jenny shook her head. 'I have no idea of the geography of the area, sir.'

'If you care to come to my office I can show you the map. Unfortunately it is not perfectly accurate, though it will demonstrate to you some of the problems — for instance, there are no bridges over the rivers and some of the valleys are very deep. The roads are poor. In the present season travelling is feasible but once the rains come — if they come, which is not always certain — the routes become quagmires.'

It sounded very formidable, yet, after all, what else had she expected? This was a young country, still trying to put the flesh of civilisation on the bones of the pioneering effort.

She returned to her former point. 'What is the girl like? I know you say you have never seen her, but what do people say of her?'

'Ahem, she . . . ah . . . I believe she is known for her pulchritude and also for her temper. It's said she flies up in a rage over nothing. Yet on the whole she has a good reputation — a hard worker and very honest. The upbringing at the Orphan School, you know — good precepts are instilled there.'

'And she is how old?'

'I think in her early twenties.'

'Young and pretty, and still unmarried?'

'She was betrothed, so I am reliably informed, to a young man who worked with horses — very rash and bold. He was killed in a horse race for a five-pound prize. It took her some time to recover from the loss. I have heard that she has been offered the married state at least once since then but has refused.'

Jenny's heart sank. A pretty girl in her early twenties — and not some simpering daughter of one of the Sydney families, but a hardworking girl with a mind of her own. This was a rival who might be difficult to defeat or even equal — for Jenny needed no reminding that she was into her thirties now.

'Do you think my husband is at the farm to which his letters are directed?' she asked.

'There is no way of telling. He comes and goes. He *has* been in Sydney two or three times in the last six months but he made no call upon me — he and I are not on good terms in consequence of his . . . ahem . . . activities.'

'I should like to go to the farm,' she said. 'Is it far?'

'Not far by the standards of the colony, ma'am. About fifty miles. But you don't think of going immediately?'

'Oh no! My little girl needs time to get her land legs, and so do my maid and I. But, let me see, today is Sunday — shall we say next Friday?'

'Friday,' said Mr Chalmers, making a note in a pocketbook.

'You'll hire a carriage for me?'

'Easily done, ma'am. In the meantime, I hope that after you've rested you'll let me show you round some of the sights of Sydney. It is a very delightful place, Mrs Armstrong, with some very picturesque scenery within easy reach.'

'I should like that. I'd also like to drop in at your office to see the map you mentioned, and to look over some of the reports and accounts.'

'Certainly,' said Mr Chalmers, looking faintly alarmed. 'You will find everything in . . . ah . . . apple pie order.'

'I'm sure I shall. Now, if you will excuse me, sir, I have unpacking to do, and my daughter probably needs my attention.'

'I wondered if . . .?'

'Yes?'

'If you would care to sup with me this evening, ma'am?' He went on hastily, 'We eat our evening meal early here, because we start the day early. Six o'clock supper — or tea, as many call it. My landlady is not . . . ah . . . a culinary expert but she . . .'

'Thank you, sir, but I believe it will be best if I and my little girl spend this first evening quietly together.'

'I quite comprehend.'

'Tomorrow morning I will come to your office —'

'The address is —'

'I know it well, Mr Chalmers.'

'Of course,' he said, blushing. 'Ask anyone, they'll direct you.' And still very pink, he bowed himself off the verandah and away.

Upstairs, Baird had the trunks unlocked and was throwing the wide skirts of the crushed gowns over beds and chairs to air them. Heather was helping by laying her own belongings on a sofa. The tea tray stood on a table almost hidden by shawls and scarves and underwear.

'There's no enough room in the presses, I'm thinking,' Baird remarked. 'And the moth have got at your worsted jacket forbye. I've askit the chambermaid to loan us an iron but the glaikit besom doesna seem to me to be speakin' the Queen's English.'

Jenny smothered a smile. Then she hugged her maid in affection. No matter if she was at the far side of the world, she had stalwarts to support her.

When they had made some progress with the unpacking they went downstairs for the midday meal. Baird went off to find her place in the kitchen and scare some discipline into the untrained chambermaid. Jenny found she and Heather were to sit down to a communal table, a long trestle covered with a white cloth.

Introductions were made. There were two sea captains and a coastguard, a farmer and his wife from the Cunningham Plains, and a fruit grower from beyond Camden. Jenny wanted to learn all she could about the country but there was no opportunity at that first meal — everyone wanted to know about 'home'. 'Home' meant Britain, no matter how long the immigrant had been in New South Wales or even if he had been born there.

Jenny recounted all she could recall of social and political matters but kept reminding her listeners that it was all four months out of date, and that in any case she came from a small town in the Scottish Borders, not the hub of great affairs.

'We love to hear about home,' insisted Mrs Clively. 'Every time a ship comes in there's a rush for the newspapers and the mail, and we all pass them around among us, but oh, it's such a long way off.'

'Yes, indeed,' agreed Jenny, her heart suddenly tightening at the memory of the hills above her dear town, the frost on the grass, the cool breeze along the brown waters of the Gala.

In the afternoon sleep overcame them all. They had been up since the middle of the night in expectation of their first glimpse of the landfall, and since then there had been the leave-takings, the disembarkation, the new surroundings — and the heat.

'Aw, this is nothing,' the fruit grower, O'Dowd, had assured Jenny. 'Why, the heat's dying away now. You should have been here in December — everything baked dry as a biscuit and the temperature up to a hundred.'

Baird had made inquiries and been told much the same, but had also been told of practical measures to help live with the heat. Ice was available in plenty, thanks to Mr Mort's ice factory, so that cool drinks could be had. Locally made orange flower water was cooling to the forehead and the back of the neck.

Fewer petticoats were worn here than in Britain — and no one thought the wearer flighty. Shady hats, although not as fashionable as bonnets, were the rule in daylight hours. Bedspreads were not used at night during the summer — they merely decked the bed in the daytime for the sake of neatness.

It was all very strange, especially to visitors from the cool Border country of Scotland. By and by, Jenny supposed, they would come to terms with it. And as the year wore on the temperature would go down in this topsy-turvy country.

The result of the afternoon siesta was that they were wide awake after tea at six. They went out to look at the city, but very little was happening. Some citizens were going to evening service, some were reeling about around the taverns. The shops were closed, of course. Only at the wharves was there much activity.

There, porters and stevedores were still unloading from the *Larksong* and from other lesser vessels. Jenny and Baird walked along with Heather between them, sometimes attracting stares — for, after all, what were an elegant lady, a well-dressed elderly woman, and a little girl doing here in this man's domain?

Jenny paused. Perforce Baird and Heather did the same. 'What is it?' Baird asked in surprise.

Jenny breathed in. 'Smell,' she said.

Baird took a deep breath. 'What?'

'Wool. Can't you smell the lanoline? These must be the wool-stores.' She led the way up a narrow lane. A set of wide doors faced onto the road at the top. 'You see? The wool comes in here, off the waggons, and then it's stored here until the auction. Then when it's been bought, it can be shipped straight on board by gantries on the Quay.'

'Mph,' muttered Baird, who knew nothing of commerce.

'No work today, of course, because it's Sunday. I keep forgetting which day of the week it is. I must come here tomorrow after I've seen Mr Chalmers and take a look at what's going on.'

'Oh, aye, I'm sure it's vastly entertaining,' observed her maid, and urged her back towards the hotel. It was close on ten o'clock, time all good people should be indoors.

Most of the hotel guests were on the verandah enjoying the cool of the night and the delicious breeze off Sydney Cove. At last Jenny was able to get some information about the vast country behind the seaport.

'The Riverina, is it?' said O'Dowd. 'Sure it's some of the best land in the world, but difficult to get at because parliament won't do a damn thing — beg your pardon, ma'am — for the farmers. The area only returns four members, you see. Can't get things moving on their behalf. That's why I've never tried moving further out. It's easier to get roads built around Sydney or Melbourne than out in the bush.

'Speaking for myself,' interrupted Mr Clively, 'I haven't got the time to set up for parliament. I've got my farm to run. Us selectors —'

'Excuse me, what is a selector?'

The farmer grinned. 'Anybody can tell you're a new chum! Us selectors are one of the main topics of conversation here! A selector takes up a parcel of land with the encouragement of the government and with the aim of improving the grazing, the wool-growing and the wheat-growing. But the hard fact is that big landowners use some of us to get the land. They pay men to sell out to them — some of the big holdings are —'

'But they need to hold great expanses,' interrupted the coastguard captain. 'You can't run sheep economically on some of the land unless you've got miles of it. Some areas it's one sheep to the acre — '

'Surely the grass can't be as scanty as that!'

'I assure you, ma'am, some districts of the Riverina are close to being desert. But on the other hand — '

'On the other hand, some of it is fine and dandy, and you could make a go of it if only the government would get off its behind on things like transport and mail delivery.'

'You won't get a damn thing done while this bunch of landowning twisters is in power — '

'Now, now, gentlemen, there are ladies present.'

'This government knows what it's doing, Clively. If it gives in to the pastoralists all along the line, soon it'll have the radicals demanding — '

'An eight-hour day! Did you ever hear anything so crazy? How can you run a farm on an eight-hour day?'

The men had forgotten Jenny and her questions. But she was content to sit in the darkness of the verandah listening to them, trying to gather some idea of the area into which Ronald seemed to have disappeared.

She gathered it stretched for miles, cut through by slow rivers on the banks of which the Aborigines dwelt. The soil varied from reedy sand to rich loam, from dry plains to fertile pasture. Strange vegetation grew there — eucalypt, acacia, mulga, saltbush and cypress pine. Homesteads were at great distances from each other. Life wasn't easy, and the farmers always had an eye to the heavens for there was evidence of previous severe drought. Fortunately the rainfall of the last few years had been ample.

When she went to bed at last she dreamed of vast

327

meadows of wiry grass among which leapt and bounced the strangest of all God's creations, the kangaroo. Far off among the trees a farmstead glimmered. And there, under that roof, was her lost husband.

Next day she visited Mr Chalmers, inspected his office, and learned why he wasn't the best of all possible wool agents. His heart was in the theatre. His walls were covered with theatre posters.

'It is my passion, I admit, ma'am. I came to Sydney originally to be a teacher in a small school with a view to earning a partnership. But the number of families who wish their boys to learn Greek and Latin is not large, so the school closed down.' He sighed, then brightened. 'I then played with Mr Salack's company at the Royal Victoria Theatre. Alas, Thespis found me an unpromising pupil and I was dismissed. So that is when I was lucky enough to be engaged by Mr Mort as a clerk in his woolstore and from there graduated to take charge of your office.'

Privately Jenny decided she would try to find someone else, but a few years ago it had been hard to engage staff. Most of the male population of Sydney had flooded out of the city to take part in the gold rush. Although now many of them had returned it was still difficult to get workers who would stay. Any rumour of gold in the outback sent them rushing off in search of El Dorado. Mr Chalmers had not been a gold-seeker. His love of the theatre had kept him here, and therefore made him available when she needed a wool agent.

But he was the kind of man who was easily distracted. When she questioned him about the hiring of a carriage to take them to the Daniell farm, he dithered and looked flustered. In the excitement of getting his office shipshape for her visit, he had forgotten to do it.

'But it's simple to arrange. You can go by train to Parramatta and thence by road to Koobalong. What are your plans? Do you intend to remain there long?'

'That depends whether there is a hotel at Koobalong –'

'Dear me, no, no such thing. A beerhouse, perhaps, where the shearers may stay overnight if they don't want to camp. But quite unsuitable for a delicate female with a child.'

'It will be impossible to go and come back in one day?'

'Oh, utterly. The road is not good. But Mrs Daniell will put you up if you so wish – I imagine she will be only too delighted to have female guests. Women are somewhat isolated on the farms, you know.'

'But we can hardly . . .'

Chalmers looked at her, puzzled. She could see he didn't understand her hesitation in expecting to put up at the same farm where her errant husband might be staying. Here in New South Wales, travellers took hospitality for granted, and whoever else was at the resting-place, there was a kind of unspoken truce.

For the next few days Jenny moved around Sydney, visiting the woolstores and the warehouses. Little activity was going on, for the wool had mostly been sold, shearing having been completed in the Australian spring. Some of the wool, however, had been slow to reach the port, and so Jenny was able to watch the auctions.

Her presence caused an enormous stir. A woman among the buyers? She didn't bid, but at first by

329

merely being there she put everyone off their stroke. But when she went up to the top of Mort's woolstore to examine the wool under the fine soft light from his glassed-in roof, they began to accept her. She knew what she was doing, that was clear. Her fingers feeling the wool, her head bent to look at the twist — they could tell she was no silly female wasting her time.

By the end of that day she discovered they had worked out who she was. 'She's the wife of that feller Armstrong, the one that's gone bush,' the men muttered to each other over their big tankards of beer.

'What, the one that went shack-up with the Bowerby gal?'

'Yeh, that one. This is his missus.'

'Gee-*up*!' they grunted in surprise. 'She's a looker. Why'd he go after somebody else?'

'Cos the somebody else was here and the missus was in Pommy, you mutt.'

She became such a focus of interest that she was glad when Friday came so that she could leave without appearing to be running away.

Mr Chalmers escorted the party of Jenny, Heather and Baird on the little wooden-box train to Parramatta. Outside a carriage was waiting, a strange contraption something like a four-wheeled brake with built-up sides and windows along the upper part. Inside there was a padded bench to seat four, and the rest of the space was presumably for luggage or freight. The driver was a gaunt man called Gunder who proved to be extremely taciturn.

He loaded their suitcases aboard, helped them up, and waited for Chalmers to mount.

'I'm not travelling, just the ladies.'

'Um. Paid in advance.'

'Half now, half when you bring them back.'

'Nah. Paid in advance.'

'I told you in my message —'

'Paid in advance.'

'Pay him,' Jenny broke in, thinking they would be here forever listening to the same refrain.

'But if I do he'll more than likely turn round the minute you set foot in Koobalong —'

'If he does he'll be a fool, because I'll pay a good bonus if I'm well served.'

Mr Chalmers pursed his lips and shook his head, but Gunder looked at her with admiration.

'Yair,' he said. 'Too right. Paid in advance, bonus when you get back.'

'It's a bargain,' said Jenny, offering him her gloved hand.

He stared at it, rubbed his own on his trouser seat, and shook.

Mr Chalmers handed up the picnic basket. Depending on circumstances they might reach Koobalong by afternoon, but the midday meal at least would have to be taken en route. A wooden box full of sawdust and ice held liquid refreshment — a bottle of Australian sparkling wine, lemonade, and cold tea. Gunder had his own provision of beer in a box under the driving seat outside.

'Au revoir,' said Chalmers, raising his hat, 'and bon voyage.'

'Thank you. I expect to be back in a few days — by next Tuesday, probably.'

'If you send word to me from Parramatta I will come to escort you home.'

'Thank you.'

'Mrs Armstrong —'

'Yes?'

'Are you sure you ought to go like this? Would it not be better to take a legal adviser with you?'

She shook her head with vehemence. 'We're not at that point yet, Mr Chalmers, and I hope we never shall be.'

'In that case, good luck.'

'Goodbye.'

The journey was bone-shaking. The springs of the brake were poor, and the road was even poorer. They had soon left the houses and the few factories of Parramatta. Tended fields fell behind. Soon it was difficult not to believe they were simply in the wilderness.

Now and again a house would appear not far from the road. Often a man on horseback would ride up to watch them go by. Sometimes he waved, sometimes not. On two occasions a file of black men stood silent as they rumbled past.

The heat was intense. During her stay in Sydney many of the inhabitants had told her the temperature was like that of Naples in Italy. Jenny had never been to Naples but she was sure it was not as baking hot as this terrain. Heat shimmered over the ground, making what looked like lagoons of water on the plain. Heather found it magical. She knelt with her face pressed against the glass.

The two horses were good beasts and if the road had been better they might have made as much as seven miles an hour. But in the end the journey to Koobalong took them from eight in the morning until six in the evening.

Koobalong proved to be a township of four wooden buildings: a beershop, a provision store which acted as mail office, a dwelling house with pigs, chickens and geese in a large compound, and an office with living quarters above on which a board announced, 'Wool Forwarding Agency, Jno. Myers, Druggist and Dentist, B D Cohen, Religious Service Held First Sunday Each Month, Pastor Barnley.'

'She's right,' announced Gunder, apparently meaning, 'We're here.'

Thankfully they all got out, to ease their bruised limbs and breathe the fresh air. Doors had already opened at the sound of their wheels. Although there were only four buildings, at least twenty people seemed to be present in a moment.

'Goodday!'

'Come out from Syd?'

'Why, it's Gunder — ha're you, cobber?'

There was a babble of voices. Hot tea appeared as if by magic. Offers of hospitality were being made before ever they asked for names or any other information.

'We're looking for Daniell's farm,' Jenny told them.

'Ah, another four miles, lady — but stay where you are, I'll give you and the kid a bed —'

'Thank you, but we should like to get to Daniell's by this evening.'

'Yair,' agreed Gunder.

'You their relative from Adelaide?'

'No, I'm from Scotland. My name's Armstrong.'

Glances were exchanged. A woman in a sunbonnet said, 'Miss Armstrong?'

'Mrs Armstrong.'

'Any relation to . . .?'

'His wife.'

There was a silence that seemed almost startled.

'He's married, then,' someone remarked.

'Looks like.'

'Yair.'

'Is Daniell's farm difficult to find?' Jenny inquired, after sipping tea for a moment to let the news sink in.

'Nah, two miles on, then there's the Beejera Creek, and there's a track goes off to the east, among the rocks, and there's a spinney of woollybutt trees you take on your left. Farm's across the medder. Can't miss it.'

Privately Jenny thought she could, but she had faith in Gunder. 'Thank you,' she said.

'They know you're coming?'

'No, it's a surprise.'

'Yair,' said a sardonic voice.

Baird collected the thick mugs in which the tea had been offered and handed them back. Their owner said, 'Well, ta-ra, then. Best of luck.'

'Thank you,' said Baird, with some misgivings.

The remainder of the journey took them another two hours. It was growing dark when they saw the glint of lamplight across a large paddock. Once again, they had still some distance to go when the door of the farmhouse was flung open and a man and a woman almost fell out, holding aloft a lantern.

'Hiyah? Who's there? Is that you, Tom?'

Gunder gave a cry like a wolf. 'Yah-yah-yah,' he called.

'Is that Gunder?'

In a moment they had rolled up to the gate of the farm. In the gloaming it was difficult to tell but it seemed as if there was a garden. Jenny could smell lavender and other flowers. A woman opened the door at the back of the brake. They all stepped down again.

'Goodday,' the settler's wife said. 'Visitors!'

'Who is it, Mabel?'

'She's right, Bob, we've got company. Come in, come in — where you come from? Gee, a little 'un — Bob, here's a little girl. My, and she's sleepy. Need your bed, duckie? Come on in then, we'll soon see you right. Gerrout of my way, Bob, can't you see the folk want to come in?'

Talking hard all the way, Mabel Daniell led her unexpected visitors into her house.

It was a large plain room they entered, but pleasant because of its bright colours. The inner walls had been washed with bright blue distemper, the floor had rugs made from rough dyed wool. A hanging lamp shed good light over a couple of shabby easy chairs. A harmonium took up a corner, with a vase of wild flowers on it.

'Gunder, you want to see to the horses? The stable's round the left side. I'll get some grub going. You'll kip down there afterwards, I suppose? The blankets are in the box inside the stable door.'

Gunder grunted and disappeared.

'You know him?' Jenny said in surprise. 'He had to ask for directions —'

'He ain't been here before but we've seen him around. Now, missus, what can I get you?' asked Bob Daniell. 'Whisky? Port? Tea?'

'You're very kind. I wonder if I could take you up on the offer of a bed for my little girl.'

'Too right. Mabel, take them through the back.'

They were led into a small plain room at the back of the one-storey building. Its wooden walls were painted in the same way as the main room, but were a reddish pink. There were two beds, one against each wall.

'Ain't much,' said Mabel, eyeing Jenny's clothes with some awe, 'but most folk manage to make out.'

'Thank you, it's lovely. And it's so kind of you —'

'Rubbish, what else d'you expect? Always a bed for a traveller. Same everywhere. But you're a new chum, I reckon.'

'I only arrived in Sydney a few days ago.'

'So what brings you here, Missus . . . er . . .?'

'Armstrong,' said Jenny.

The welcoming light suddenly waned on Mabel Daniell's broad face. 'Mrs Armstrong?'

'Yes.'

'You mean, Ron's wife?'

'You didn't know he was married?'

A pause. 'He never mentioned it,' said Mrs Daniell. 'I see.'

Baird had busied herself undressing Heather, who was practically asleep on her feet. Mrs Daniell led the way back into the living room.

'Bob,' she said, subdued, 'this is Mrs Armstrong.'

'Yuwah?' said her husband, turning from the bottle and glasses he was setting out.

'Ron's wife.'

'His wife?'

'Yair.'

'Oh,' said Bob. 'Oh, Jesus.'

Clearly it was a surprise to both of them. Jenny said in a small voice, 'I'm sorry if I've given you a shock.'

'Nah, I suppose we should have thought of it,' said Bob with a shrug. 'But hereabouts you never ask a feller what's his past and any of that. He never mentioned a wife so we just took it he was single.'

'Of course.'

'Listen, missus, I don't know if you know . . . I mean to say, there's an awkward thing . . .'

'You mean about Dinah Bowerby?'

'Jesus,' said Bob again, blowing out his breath.

'That's why I'm here.' She hesitated. 'Where is my husband, Mr Daniell?'

'Ron? He's off camping with the Abos.'

'With the . . .?'

'The blacks — I got a family of Abos, the men work as herders and so on, the women cook for them. Ron's off staying with them for a few days.'

'But what on earth for?'

'Trying to get some secrets out of 'em, about how they dye their cloth.'

Suddenly Jenny smiled. That sounded like the Ronald Armstrong she knew. He hadn't been utterly changed by this new land or this new woman, after all.

'If you're wondering,' Mrs Daniell put in, 'Dinah isn't with him. She's got a job at Durrumurra, about eight miles away.' She hesitated. 'Couldn't have 'em together here. Wouldn't have been right.'

'No,' said Jenny. 'I understand that.' She sat down on a wooden chair against the wall. 'And the camp where the Aborigines are — is it far?'

'Nah, five minutes on a horse, longer if you walk.'

So in the morning at first light Jenny set out after being shown the way by Bob Daniell.

And there on the bank of a stream, sitting between two coal black bodies daubed with red clay, she saw at last the familiar figure of her husband.

Chapter Nineteen

The next few moments were the most heart-stopping in Jenny's life.

She came to a standstill among the sharp-scented grasses. She was about sixty or seventy yards from the group, who sat facing her. Ronald had his head bent towards one of the black men, to whom he was speaking earnestly.

The breeze flirted the skirts of her muslin gown, one that Ronald had always been fond of, filmy grey over green. The movement caught his attention. He turned to look.

Blank astonishment swept across his face. Then disbelief. Then, frighteningly, she saw horror — and was stricken until she realised it was horror at what he thought was a phantom, horror at the idea he was having delusions.

But then the attitude of the other men reassured him. One was staring in impassive silence at her, the other had raised his arm and was pointing, saying something in a low voice.

Ronald gave a wild yell of delight. Next moment he was splashing through the shallow stream. He ran to greet her, streaks of weed and yellow mud on his canvas boots.

'Jenny! Jenny! Are you real?'

She held out her arms. The next moment they were twined together, rocking with the momentum of his arrival, hugging each other, laughing and crying, one spirit in two bodies that had been apart too long.

When he let her go she was too breathless to speak but he was full of tumbling words. 'The blackfellows have been saying for days that someone was coming to me. But you − ! How could I ever have guessed? Jenny, I can't believe it!'

She leaned against him. 'I'm real, I'm here. Ronald, I've had such a journey to find you!'

'My dearest, sweetest girl − what on earth − when did you arrive?'

'A few days ago. I've come from Sydney. Heather and I −'

'Heather? Here?'

'Yes, I brought your daughter −'

'But I thought she couldn't −'

'She's survived the journey very −'

'All the way from Galashiels! What ship −'

'The *Larksong*. I was lucky enough to get a cabin just when I needed one −'

'But why? My dearest Jenny, why?'

She stood away from him so she could look up into his face. She said, after a moment of serious silence, 'You know why, husband.'

'No, indeed I −' He broke off. He frowned. 'Ach!' he exclaimed in disgust. 'Someone's been gossiping.'

'Now, Ronald man, don't get angry about it. What did you expect − that because I was so far off I would never hear of it? You ken fine that folk like to spread bad news, and so I heard about the other woman −'

'Henry Chalmers, I suppose!'

'It doesn't matter who. What matters is, that I came

340

here to find out whether you and I had a marriage left, or whether you wanted to be free —'

'Free?'

'Aye, of course, to wed Dinah.'

'My God,' he groaned, shaking his head and letting his hands drop from about her shoulders, 'you even know her name!'

'Well, my love, you haven't exactly made a secret of it,' she rejoined. 'One of the first things the Daniells said to me was that my arriving was a little awkward because of Dinah.'

'Dinah isn't here!' he said sharply. 'I want you to understand —'

'Yes, and I want to understand, husband. You and I must talk it through from beginning to end. So let's go back to the farmhouse so you can meet your daughter again, and then we'll plan what to do next.'

He turned to look back, but the Aborigines had vanished. He muttered, 'I'll never get them to talk so long again.'

'What was it you were talking about?'

'Colours. They make a rough kind of cloth with wool they find on bushes and so forth. They colour it some strange shades. Ah well, I've lost that chance. They'll probably be gone if I come back here again.'

'What did you mean when you said they told you someone was coming?'

'They've been saying that for about three days.'

'But how could they possibly know?'

'Oh, they know, I canna tell how. I think they pick up vibrations in the air, tremors in the stones. It's uncanny . . .'

They fell into step together. She said, 'You look different, Ronald.'

'In what way?'

'Well, your face and arms are so tanned — don't you ever stay in the shade?'

'Och, you soon get used to the sun if you move about this country. And I've moved about. I've seen some strange things, Jenny. I first began to travel the district to get some idea of the wool situation. It's complex — the big wool stations send their wool to the docks and it's already bought by the big merchants, so it never goes to auction and the only chance to get at it would be when it reaches the London —'

'I gathered as much when I went to look at the woolstores on the Quay —'

'You've been there? Trust you to go straight to the heart of the matter!' He laughed. 'Oh, Jenny, I'd forgotten what it was like to talk to you! There's never any need to labour a point with you.'

He gave her a little hug of appreciation, and she took advantage of it to stay leaning against him as they walked. Mention of Dinah Bowerby's name had separated them from their first close contact. She was anxious not to let anything keep them apart even in minor ways if she could possibly avoid it.

'I soon understood that only the small wool growers sent their clip to market at the ports, and I soon found that for many of them, it was easier to get the loads to Melbourne than to Sydney. I've been to Melbourne three times, Jenny — a fine town, and at first I thought it was likely to become the queen of wool exporting.'

'You don't think so now?'

'Well, it's hard to say. There's a lot more going on in Melbourne than in Sydney at the present moment. But when you compare the opportunities for shipping . . . Sydney must be the best harbour in the world, I

342

imagine. It seems only logical and inevitable that in the end it will take over Melbourne's present position. So if you've come to invest in Australian property I'd advise you to buy into a Sydney woolstore.'

'I've other things on my mind at the moment,' Jenny said rather drily.

He nodded without speaking. They walked on in silence for a moment.

'Why did you stop writing, Ronald?' she asked.

He seemed to be studying the wattle flowers they were passing. At length he said, 'When I wrote that letter asking you to come out and make a new start here, it was a kind of . . . I don't know . . . a sort of plea for you to understand.'

'To understand what, my love?'

'I don't know, something . . . I felt we had gone wrong somewhere in the past and might do so again if I went back to Galashiels. But out here, where nobody cares who you've been or what you've done, I thought we could begin again. And then your reply . . .'

'Yes?'

'You didn't understand.'

She sighed. 'I'm sorry.'

'You wrote all about money and who owned what and whether it was good business . . . That wasn't what I hoped to hear, lassie. I hoped you'd say, I'll come as soon as I can.'

'And here I am, Ronald — later than you hoped, but not too late. Say it's not too late, my dear.'

He stopped at her words, turned her to him, and kissed her with passion. And for the moment, that was answer enough.

When they reached the farm, Heather stood with

Baird in the shade of the canopy over the door. Baird had dressed her in a crisp little dress of white duck trimmed with dark blue. Her tawny hair was held at both sides with bows of matching blue ribbons. She looked a picture.

Ronald left Jenny's side to walk slowly up to the child. He stooped, put his arms about her, and drew her close. Heather's arms didn't twine about his neck as they would have done had it been Jenny who embraced her. But after a long hesitation Ronald heard a tiny whisper in his ear.

'Papa?'

'Yes, my wee sweetheart, it's Papa! My, how you've grown! What a big girl you are! And here you are after coming in a big ship and trains and in a country cart — what a big adventure for a big girl!'

He picked her up and swung her round. Any other child might have screamed in delight, but Heather let her head sink back to see the sky wheeling above her, and made a little singing sound of pleasure.

Baird came forward to steady her as Ronald put her down. 'Well, maister, it's yourself.'

'Aye, and how are you, Baird?'

'None the worse for seeing the family together again.'

'Blunt as ever, I see. I'm surprised you came — I'd have thought nothing would get you on a journey like this.'

'It was Herself,' Baird said in a low voice. 'I couldna let her go alone and she was bent on it. "I will come again, my love, though 'twere ten thousand mile." '

Ronald looked at her in surprise at the quotation. He had never thought of the maidservant as a reader of poetry. Baird held his eye, then nodded. Next moment she had turned her attention to Heather.

Breakfast at the Daniells' was a strange meal that morning. Usually Bob was off and out long before this to visit his flocks and herders over long distances. But politeness and curiosity had held him at home. His wife had prepared large quantities of the usual breakfast dishes — eggs, lamb chops, porridge, sourdough scones. There were mountains of butter and huge jars of wild honey. The tea was strong and dark like plug tobacco.

The talk was general. Mrs Daniell tried to tempt Heather into speech by talking of the ponies in the back paddock. 'Would you like to see them? There are two foals, one's speckled on the flanks like a thrush from the Old Country.'

Heather nodded eagerly. She went off between Baird and Mabel Daniell without a backward glance. Bob went out to speak to his jackaroo and then said he had to go to the east creek where the water seemed to be drying up.

'You'll be right, though, Mabel will give you a meal at dinnertime if you want it, or you can take some tucker out as usual, Ron.'

'Thanks, Bob, I think we'll do that.'

Jenny took no part in the arranging. She was content to let Ronald lead the way. About nine o'clock, with the sun already very strong, they set off in a little trap drawn by a wiry pony with a picnic basket under their feet.

They drew up in a little clearing at a different point on the stream Jenny had seen already. There was a lean-to in the shade of the trees, constructed from woven twigs. Blankets were rolled at one end of a couch made of springy boughs and dried fern. There were the ashes of previous fires, a small pile of dry wood, and some bags and boxes hung from tree branches.

'My country house,' Ronald explained, ushering her forward. 'The bags and boxes are my emergency supplies — dried beans, flour, smoked fish.'

'You *live* here?'

'Sometimes.'

She stared up at him. This was a new Ronald Armstrong. 'I didn't know you could do this kind of thing.'

'Och, it's a throwback to my childhood — I used to camp out in the wilds sometimes when I went on fishing trips with my father.' He grinned. 'It's a lot more comfortable here than in the Ochills — warmer and a lot drier.'

There was a fallen log with two or three yellow-breasted birds picking up insects from the bark. As the two humans approached, the birds looked up, then flew without haste up into the trees.

'Yellowbobs,' Ronald remarked. He fetched a blanket which he spread on the tree trunk. 'The best chair for the visitor,' he added, bowing Jenny to her place.

They sat side by side for a while in silence. The yellow-breasted birds flew down after a while to look at them. Off in the woods, other birds called harshly. A resinous smell hung heavy in the air. The sun glimmered through the leaves. The water in the shallow stream purled over the stones.

'Why did you come?' Ronald asked at last. 'I mean, what brought you to the decision?'

'I'll tell you. Archie Brunton came back to Galashiels and proposed to me.'

'Archie Brunton! What the devil was he up to, proposing to a married woman?'

'He wanted me to divorce you, my love. He —'

'You never thought seriously of marrying *Archie Brunton*?'

'No,' she agreed, 'and I knew why when I thought about it. It was because I could only have one husband and that was you, Ronald lad.'

'There now,' he said. He took her hand in his. 'And I'd come to the same conclusion — that I had only one wife and it was you, Jenny lass.'

'So what have you to tell me about Dinah Bowerby?'

She felt his fingers tighten round hers. He took a long moment to frame a reply.

'I don't want you to think I'm excusing myself. I've behaved badly, and I'm ashamed. But the fact of the matter is, though I like and admire the girl, there could never be anything lasting between us.'

'But you've been lovers.'

'Yes.'

'And now?'

'Now I'm sorry for it, and I've tried to explain it to Dinah, but she . . . she's a passionate creature, is Dinah. She won't listen to what she doesn't want to hear.'

'You mean she won't let you go?'

She was watching him with a steady glance, and at this question she saw him colour.

'You see, I thought you were off at the other side of the world, and from the way you answered my letter it seemed as if we had nothing in common any more —'

'Ronald!' She was sharp. 'I don't want to condemn, but you couldn't have forgotten we have a child!'

He gave a sigh of regret. 'Aye, I forgot that — or at least I wouldn't let myself remember. You have to realise, Jenny, that she had gone so far from me even before I left home. She seemed not to like me, and wouldn't speak to me —'

'But she never speaks to anybody —'

'And people were saying she was weakminded and I . . . I was ashamed of her. So I was glad to forget I had a daughter.'

The painful honesty of this touched Jenny. She said with gentleness, 'I understand. Go on.'

'I met Dinah when I was on my travels in the Riverina. It's a big country, and she was working at a sheep station up by Hay. The shearing gang had come in, there was a fight, and the best thing seemed to be to get her out of there, so when I left next morning I took her with me.'

He stopped. He moved restlessly, let go Jenny's hand, then resumed his grip. 'I never thought I'd ever be discussing this with anyone else, let alone my wife,' he muttered.

'I need to understand, Ronald.'

He nodded. 'Well, on the journey we became lovers. She seemed to regard me as a sort of Sir Galahad — it's flattering, you know, to have a woman much younger than yourself fall into your arms. And she's . . . she's very pretty.'

'So I heard. I heard she was renowned for her pulchritude.' Jenny was smiling.

'Oh, that's Chalmers — I can hear him say it. Aye, renowned for her pulchritude — a lot of men have wanted Dinah Bowerby and she's always held herself aloof.'

'Until now.'

'Yes, until now.' He felt for words. 'You must understand that at that time Dinah didn't know I was married. I'd never said anything about it to the people I met during my travels in the bush. Afterwards . . .' Once again he coloured up. 'After she'd given herself to me she took it for granted we would be married. I had to tell her then that I had a wife in the Old Country.'

'And what did she say?'

'At first she was shocked. She was strictly brought up, you understand − in an orphan school where they talked about hellfire and so on. In taking a lover she felt she had sinned in some degree. Having slept with a married man was like . . . like asking for eternal damnation.'

'Poor girl,' sighed Jenny.

'It was partly because she was so overset that I told her you and I had drifted apart, that I'd decided to make a new start. She was content with that.' He paused. 'Out here, you see, it's what you are and what you do *here and now* that counts. I'll wager there's many a man doing well in some little settlement with a new wife and family who left a wife or a fiancée in England. There's a sort of tolerance − not for wrong-doing among your friends and neighbours because you have to be able to depend on those, and they on you. But for what you may have done in the past that you've left behind − there's a suspension of blame on that.'

'Was that why you asked Chalmers to buy a family farm for you? You were going to set up anew with Dinah?'

'Oh, don't, Jenny! It sounds so . . . so impossible when I hear you say it in that soft Scots voice of yours!' He sighed. 'That's one of the things it's marvellous to hear again — your voice is as beautiful as your face. I've missed that sound . . .'

Jenny knew at once that Dinah Bowerby had an unattractive speaking voice. She condemned herself for finding that very cheering.

'The farm was for you and Dinah, though?'

'I suppose so. I was trying to decide what to do. Then I got a terse message saying you had no interest in buying a small farm. At first I was very angry. "What does she mean, telling me what I can do and what I can't do" — you know how it is. And then I thought how awful it was to think of buying a farm for my mistress when I would have to use money from William Corvill and Son. It brought me up short. I think it was that, almost more than anything else, that made me draw back.'

'Did Dinah know about buying the farm?'

'Oh yes. And when I put it off she was very distressed. She said I was trying to get rid of her, and I of course tried to reassure her, and instead of making things better it made them more confused. But the Daniells, for whom she'd been working, began to get worried, so she moved off to a place about eight miles up the road near Murramurra — she cooks for them.'

'You go to see her?'

'Last time was ten days ago. We had another quarrel . . . though she coaxed me round before we parted.'

'A fine fix you're in, Ronald Armstrong.'

'Don't I know it.'

'And what do you intend to do now?'

He nodded to himself. 'I'll go and see her. When I tell her my wife has come, she'll understand it really is over. I don't want to use you as an excuse, but nothing else seems to convince her. She's . . . she's not a clever woman, you see, Jenny. She takes a stand and then she can't listen to reason. But I mustn't put the blame on Dinah. It's all my fault.'

'Ach, it will come out all right, so long as we really love each other and want to keep our marriage. You do love me, Ronald?'

'Oh, Jenny . . . ' He took her in his arms and began to kiss her with a longing that had something of desperation in it. Her response was as deep and eager as his.

The couch of ferns cradled them. Around them the bright birds piped in the trees, grasshoppers trilled a descant. The world whirled around them to become a haze of colour and sound and scent, coalescing at last into a jewel point that glistened with the ultimate reward.

'I love you, Jenny. No matter what I may have done, I only ever could love you.'

'Yes, Ronald my joy, I know it. And you're the only man for me.'

'No one is like you, Jenny. To me no woman on earth is your equal.'

'Hush, man. I'm no marvel, God knows. But if you love me, that makes me special.'

They lay for a time renewing vows that had been forgotten. Then passion took them in her grasp once more. This time there was no slightest apprehension to mar their unity. She held him in her arms and took his body to her with every sinew, every nerve, every wish and hope of her soul.

Spent, they slipped into languor. But it was hot and they grew restless. Jenny half sat up, reaching for her clothes.

'No, come along,' Ronald protested, seizing her hand. He drew her to her feet and pulled her with him. Half-running they made their way along the river bank until they came to a bend where the water had formed a pond. He put his arms around her, overbalanced them, and they fell into the cool yellowish-brown pool.

Jenny gave a shriek of alarm. But almost at once she found her feet and stood up. The water was only waist deep. They bathed and splashed like children playing truant from school. Ronald amazed her by catching a fish with his hands, scooping it up to throw it on the bank.

Later, clad in only the minimum of clothes, he grilled the fish over a fire of dry twigs. They ate it with their fingers, and drank water from the stream.

Then they lay down in the shade to while away the heat of the afternoon. They slept, woke to kisses and caresses and the long pleasure of making love, with the wilderness beating to the same pulse that measured their heartbeat.

When they returned to Daniell's farm, they found Heather being led round the back paddock on a sturdy little pony. The pony was being held by Mabel Daniell, with Baird plodding grimly in the rear.

Heather waved as they came up. She was beaming with delight.

'So you're a horsewoman!' cried Ronald. 'That's a good thing — it's one of the most useful talents in this country.'

'She's a natural,' said Mabel. 'She's got no pony at home, Mrs Baird tells me.'

'No, she never seemed to want to . . . But then the coachman was the one who tried to put her up, and she shied away from him.'

352

'She can take lessons on Goodie, if she wants. The jackaroo can teach her.'

'The jackaroo —'

'That's the apprentice boy, Harry — he does all the odd jobs around the place,' Ronald explained. 'A bit simple but good with the livestock.'

'I don't know . . .'

'I'll keep an eye on her, never you fret,' Baird said. 'If she wants to learn . . .?'

'Aye, she should be encouraged.' Every change in Heather, every improvement, was important. Bringing her out to meet the real world was one of the most important things Jenny had to achieve.

Bob Daniell came home in time for tea. 'The blackfellows over the ridge were saying they'd seen Mrs Armstrong,' he remarked.

'You talked to them?'

'Yair. Off to Tarrabinna Spring, I gather.'

'I never got the whole story from them about the plant that gives the tan dye —'

'You might catch 'em up at Hoke's place. They like to stop there, there's honey in the woods just above it. But I reckon they won't tell you much about the dyes. I don't think they know themselves how they do it.'

'Do they just wander about as and when they please?' Jenny inquired, struggling with the mountain of food Mrs Daniell had piled on her plate.

'Right. Nomads, that's what they are. You give 'em employment, they stay a few weeks or months and then one day you go to their camp and they've gone. Still, they spread the news around the district. By now everybody within a radius of ten miles knows Mrs Armstrong has arrived.'

She met Ronald's eyes. The unspoken question was, Would Dinah know? He nodded imperceptibly. He sighed, and she too felt a moment of unhappiness.

'Besides,' Bob added, grinning, 'Gunder's gone off visiting. He'll be spreading the word.'

'Gunder? He scarcely opens his mouth,' Jenny objected.

'But he nods and shakes his head when folk question him. Oh yes, I reckon everybody knows you're here, Mrs Armstrong.'

Later, after he'd said goodnight to Heather and spent some time in farming chat with Bob, Ronald set off for his camp by the stream. There was no room in the house for him to sleep without turning out Baird to a bed in the hayloft.

Jenny walked part of the way with him. 'Come out to me, if you're lonely,' he said in a whisper as they said goodnight.

She gave a low laugh. 'What, into the wild Australian bush?'

'It couldn't be any wilder than we were today. Besides, we still have a lot to talk about.'

She hesitated. 'I'll come,' she said. 'After everyone has settled down.'

The moon was high when she slipped out of the door. Scattered on a slate-blue sky, the stars seemed larger and brighter and with a softer glow than in the northern hemisphere. She had no difficulty following the path to the stream. Ronald came to meet her as she parted the brush near his lean-to.

They sat for a long time on the fallen log, each with an arm about the others shoulder, listening to the quiet breathing of the night.

'I want to talk to you about Dinah,' she said at

length. 'It's clear she knows by now that I've come. What is best to do next?'

'I'll have to go and see her, tell her that it's really over —'

'Ronald, I think I should go.'

'What? Certainly not! It's my mess and I'll clear it up!'

'I think it would be better if I spoke to her. You see, I know what she's going through.'

'I don't see —'

'You don't know all that's happened to me. There was a time, when I was even younger than Dinah, that I was in love with a married man. I had to give him up but the parting was so cruel that it left a scar — I still shudder when I think of it. So I'd like to be the one to speak to Dinah. I have a fellow-feeling.'

'I absolutely forbid it!'

But by the time she rose quietly in the dawn light to go back to the farm, she had convinced him it should be left to her to see Dinah Bowerby.

She made the trip next day, leaving Heather happy in the care of Baird and Harry the apprentice boy. She borrowed a little trap with a lively, stringy pony. The road was easy to follow — you had only to look for the tracks of other wheeled vehicles on the dry ground.

Eight miles off was Durramurra, a station on the southern slope of a long, shelving hollow. The selector here had been lucky — the streams were shallow but still ran with energy despite the long dry spell, and the grass, though patched with scrub, was holding up under the searing heat. There were fences of carpentered wood and wire, not thorn brakes. The house itself proved to be much larger than Daniell's, part of it even having an upper storey.

She drove up. Guard dogs barked and cavorted. A blackfellow ran up to hold the pony. She stepped down, and was greeted by Mrs Fowler, wife to the owner.

'You'll be Mrs Armstrong,' she said at once.

Jenny didn't say, How did you know? She said, 'How do you do,' and held out her hand. Mrs Fowler looked at the kid driving glove with admiration, and shook hands.

'Been expecting you,' she said. That was clear, for she had on what looked like her best gown. 'Come in and I'll give you a cup of tea. Hot, isn't it?'

Jenny went thankfully into the cool of the house. It had more elegance than Daniell's, with lace-edged antimacassars on the chair-backs and lace curtains at the inner windows. Coolness was retained by a wide verandah all round the house with windows shaded by holland blinds.

The scene was almost bizarre. Mrs Fowler had set out her best china on an embroidered cloth, and there was even a silver cake-stand with scones and two kinds of cake. 'Do you take milk and sugar?' Mrs Fowler inquired, lifting a Wedgwood teapot.

'Milk, please, no sugar.'

And so they conversed in genteel tones until Jenny had drunk a cup of tea and sampled a scone with home-made quince jelly.

'You want to see Dinah, I suppose,' Mrs Fowler said as they set down their teacups.

Jenny nodded.

'Now, I don't want you to think I approve of her goings-on just because I gave her a job. But I can't manage this place on my own and the Abo girl I had

356

just upped and went. So I was glad to get Dinah, for she's a good worker and the men like her grub. And in any case I thought it'd be sorted out by and by when the two of them got married.'

'I understand,' Jenny said faintly. This forthright interest in someone else's affairs was totally unlike the hints and nods of the townsfolk of Galashiels.

'You could have knocked me down with a feather when Gunder said the lady who'd turned up was Mrs Armstrong.' Her hostess surveyed Jenny with great interest. 'Is that corded cotton, your dress?'

'It's a fabric called repp. The weave is used in silk and wool too.'

'Is that right? And the hat — did you bring that from the Old Country?'

'No, I bought it in Sydney. Bonnets at home have narrow brims.'

'Narrow brims,' said Mrs Fowler, recording it in her memory.

'If you could tell me where to find Dinah?'

Mrs Fowler took her to the door and pointed. 'She took to her heels the minute Marty — that's the Abo — said you were coming. You'll find her in the dairy, that's the shed at the far end with the stone walls. She's probably making butter — working off her energy on the paddle.'

'Thank you.'

She knew Mrs Fowler stood and watched her until she reached the door of the dairy. She opened it and walked into the cool dimness.

At first, after the glare of outdoors, she could make out almost nothing. Then she saw a figure sitting next to the butter churn at the far side of the shed. She was tall and well-made, clad in a faded high-necked print dress. Her hair gleamed, a rich light chestnut.

Jenny had come all across the world to confront her. For this was the other woman.

Chapter Twenty

Dinah Bowerby kept her head turned away.

'If you've come to tell me I'm a wicked woman, don't bother. I've heard it all from Ma Fowler.'

Jenny hesitated. 'That's not why I came.'

'Why, then?' The girl looked at her at last. The blaze of anger was in the dark blue eyes. 'What are you here for? If you want my Ron, you can't have him.'

Jenny looked around for something to sit on. She didn't want to stand over the other girl like a scolding schoolmarm. She saw a wooden box by the whitewashed wall, dragged it over, and sat.

'I've come a long way to meet you,' she remarked, 'so let's try to talk sensibly.'

'I can't understand why you're here!' Dinah cried, forcing the handle of the butter-paddle up and down in the churn with fierce energy. 'What made you come? You've given up all your fine life back home and it's not as if you really care about him!'

The voice was without modulation, rather nasal in tone. Jenny understood what her husband had been hinting at. It was strange that a girl so beautiful to look at should be so unpleasing to listen to. It was strange, and sad.

She ranted on, banging the paddle up and down in the narrow wooden tub, turned away so that she couldn't see her listener. 'And you didn't want him when he was home in Scotland so why −'

'What makes you think I didn't want him?'

'It's plain to see, ain't it? You were all taken up with your business concerns, hadn't time for your man −'

'Did Ronald tell you that?'

The thud of the butter-paddle stopped. 'It was easy to read between the lines of what he said −'

'The trouble with reading between the lines is that you can imagine what you like in the blank space,' Jenny said. 'Did he ever speak about our little girl?'

Dinah sat back on her stool. 'He never mentioned even you, until . . . until . . .'

'Until you began suggesting a wedding.'

'So you've discussed it with him!' It was almost a snarl of resentment.

'Of course. I had to know how matters stood. After you'd been to bed together and you wanted to get married, he told you he already had a wife. That's right, isn't it?'

'You've no need to be so tart about it −'

'I don't mean to sound tart. I'm not blaming you or him. He told you he couldn't marry you because he was already married, and spoke about me − that's clear because you've got some impression of me, no matter how wrong I think it is. What I asked was, did he speak about Heather, our daughter?'

Dinah let her hands fall loosely into the lap of her gown. She stared at them. 'He said he had a little girl. I told him it didn't matter.'

'We lost her −'

'What? When?' There was genuine shock in the harsh tone. 'Last time he spoke about her, he took it for granted she was still alive −'

'No, no,' Jenny broke in, quickly trying to put it right. 'Heather is alive. I meant it literally — we lost her, she was stolen away.'

Dinah frowned. 'You're joshing me.'

'No, truly. I don't want to go into a long story about it, but Heather was missing for almost a whole year. When I got her back she took up my entire life. She was so . . . so changed, so scared and shocked, I couldn't think about anything else.'

'Why are you telling me this? Is it some kind of trick to get sympathy?'

'It's the truth. If you like you can ask Ronald. He'll tell you it's why he and I began to drift apart.'

'Who's supposed to have taken her away, then?'

'What difference does that make to you, Dinah? I'm only telling you so that you'll understand that our marriage struck a very big rock. And I handled it badly. So when I come here to talk to you, I know I've no one but myself to blame. That's what I meant when I said I hadn't come to reproach you.'

After a moment Dinah looked full at Jenny and said, 'This is the truth? About the little girl?'

'I swear it to you.'

'I thought the trouble had to do with you being rich and only interested in making money.'

Jenny coloured. 'He *couldn't* have said that!'

'No,' said the other girl, with unwilling honesty, 'I reckon that's what I wanted to believe. He said . . . he told me . . . you had the best cloth mill in Scotland and were famous, had met the Queen. So I reckoned you must be grand and high-hatted.' She broke off, and sat looking at Jenny with her head on one side. 'I never imagined you'd be the kind to come and corner me in the dairy!'

There was a wry humour in the remark. Jenny let a little silence fall. Then she said, 'Now that we're face to face, we have to be honest, haven't we? I want you to understand that I don't hate you or despise you — nothing like that. But you have to accept that it's over between you and Ronald.'

Dinah shook her head so that the chestnut hair gleamed in the narrow sunbeam from between the shutters. The harsh animosity was back in her voice. 'Never! He's mine! Ron and I were meant for each other!'

'No, you must give up that idea —'

'He loves me!'

'No.'

'Yes he does, he does! A woman knows when a man really loves her —'

'Dinah, you're talking yourself into it, just as you did when you made yourself believe I was some kind of ogress. I'm Ronald's wife. He has a six-year-old daughter who needs him —'

'*I* need him —'

'Not as much as we do.'

'But you've got so much: a famous name, an important job to do, a whole world of your own! I only have Ron . . .'

'You're talking about someone who doesn't exist!' Jenny exclaimed. ' "Ron" — that's not his name. He's Ronald Armstrong, my husband and the father of our child. He's well-known for his ability with dye-stuffs — his name is a byword for excellence all over Scotland. He doesn't belong here where he can't use his talents. He doesn't belong with you —'

'But I love him!' Dinah sprang up, throwing up her head in proud protestation. 'Don't think you can take

him away from me by using clever words! I know
you've got education and all that, but he belongs to
me and I won't let you have him −'

'Dinah, Dinah −'

'I tell you I love him −'

'Do you think I don't?'

'That doesn't matter to me! All that matters is that
since I met Ron everything's been different for me.
And I'm going to keep him −'

'But you can't. Don't you understand that? He
doesn't "belong" to you in any sense that means you
can keep him against his wish −'

'His wish is to stay with me.'

'No, Dinah, you're wrong −'

'You let him go, more fool you. Finder's keepers,
that's what they say, don't they −'

'But you can't keep him if he doesn't want to stay.
And he doesn't, Dinah.'

'Yes he does, I know he does. What can you know,
suddenly arriving out of nowhere −'

'I've talked to him. We talked for hours. I know
what he feels, and you must face it.'

'You talked him round! I'll make him see that
you've tricked him − he'll listen to me. And no matter
what you say, I'll never give him up!'

'What will you do? Follow him around for the rest
of his life telling him you love him? It's just
foolishness, my poor girl −'

'Don't you patronise me! Don't you dare patronise
me! Just because you've got prettier clothes and −'

'And a daughter, and a wedding ring on my finger.
Don't forget those, Dinah.' Jenny put firmness into
her tone. 'You're coming between husband and wife.
We made vows in church, before God − and you can't

set it aside just because you think you want him for yourself.'

'I do want him! I love him! I love him far more than you do.'

'Oh, Dinah . . . That's childish, childish.' She sighed. 'I'm not entering into a competition to prove who loves him the most. That's not the question. The question is whether Ronald loves you. If I truly believed that he did, I'd not stand in the way of your being happy together. He could have a divorce if he asked me. But he hasn't asked me, and he never will.'

'You're not saying he loves *you*!' Dinah cried with incredulity.

'I think he does.'

'That's nonsense. Just because you came back all sad and pathetic and asked him — what else would he say?'

'I'm not talking about words, Dinah!'

Dinah's face went pale under the golden skin. 'What do you mean? Not words? You mean you and he . . . that you've been . . . ' Her harsh voice faltered into silence. She walked to the window, pulled the shutters wide, and turned to stare at Jenny in the full sunlight.

'You've slept with him?'

'Yes.'

'He wouldn't do that. He wouldn't be unfaithful to me!'

Jenny stilled a little gesture of irritation. 'Why won't you think of someone other than yourself? Unfaithful to you? He's *my husband* —'

'But that's all over —'

'Yesterday we were husband and wife together, just like when we were first married. I know with every fibre of my being that Ronald loves me, no matter what's happened between the two of you. I can't be mistaken in this. The old tie between us was still as strong as ever.'

'That's easy to say —'

Jenny shook her head. 'I don't find it easy to say. I don't talk about things that are important, intimate — it's distasteful, it somehow reduces them. But it seems nothing else will convince you. Don't you understand, Dinah? Ronald and I are husband and wife — in law, in our need of each other, in the happiness we find when we're together. You can make claims on him until the heavens fall but it won't change anything — my husband loves me and I love him.'

Dinah stood in the shaft of cruel sunlight. Her lovely face looked pinched and weary. She fought against what Jenny had said. But as they faced each other the unassailable truth could be read in Jenny's gaze.

'But what about me?' Dinah wailed, childlike.

For a moment Jenny was tempted to offer her money. Enough to let her make a new start somewhere else, find an easier life. But instinct warned her that it would be a cardinal error.

'You're young,' she said. 'And independent. You'll survive.'

'What would be the point, without Ron?' Tears gathered in the great violet-blue eyes. 'You don't understand,' she faltered. 'I've put all my hopes in him. It was going to change my life, being Mrs Ron Armstrong. He would have taught me all he knows, told me about the places he'd been — in Europe and everywhere. I'd have been something better than just a girl from the orphan school.'

'But you could learn all about that — better yourself — without depending on anyone else.'

'But I don't want to!' It was a wail of misery. 'Besides, you don't know what it's like here on the stations. If you want to better yourself they say you're an upstart, and a woman in any case ain't got a chance; you have to settle for a husband and kids or being a servant all your life, an old maid that they'll just sneer at –'

'I understand, Dinah. I do. I had to struggle for what I've got –'

'But it's different back Home. There's great ladies there who've done something themselves – Ron told me – there was one travelled all over foreign places, Turkey and everything –'

'Lady Mary Wortley-Montagu.'

'That's the one, and Miss Nightingale – I forget the others. But you've never heard of a woman out here who's been let do anything.'

'But Dinah, the colony's so new –'

'And it's not even as if I want to do anything clever or anything, I just wanted to *be* somebody – and now you're taking all that away from me.'

Jenny didn't know how to answer the reproach. It was useless to try reasoning, to say that to 'be someone' simply because of your husband wasn't Jenny's idea of achievement. After a long hesitation during which Dinah's stifled sobs were the only sound, she said, 'Is there anything you'd let me do for you? Could I send you books? Pictures?'

'What good'd that be, with no one to help me understand them?' Dinah said in bitter rejection. 'There's nobody out here –'

'The school-teacher?'

'The nearest one's about a hundred miles away. And besides, what kind of a mug d'you think I'd look, asking old Mr Percher to help me? It was different with Ron — he didn't laugh when I asked questions, and he'd talk about all different things — not just about livestock or the station but about plays, and the shops in Melbourne . . .'

'Why don't you move into the city, then? Get a job in Melbourne or Sydney? You don't *have* to stay out-country if you don't like it.'

'Nah,' the girl said, shaking her shining head. 'When Mrs Daniell said I had to leave their place, Ma Fowler made me promise I'd stay here at least a year or until I got married. That was the condition for the job. Reckon I got to stay here.'

'I'm sorry,' Jenny said, meaning it. 'It's a hard life here, I can see that. I wish I could —'

'Well, I don't want your pity, so don't put yourself out, Mrs Big-Hearted. There was only one thing in the world I wanted and you're taking that away from me so the less we have to do with each other the better.' Dinah was taking refuge in pride and anger. It was understandable, and it made her more beautiful as her dark blue eyes glowed and her chin came up. 'Just take yourself off, Lady Jane, back to your kid and your husband and all the fine friends that are waiting for you. Don't you bother your head about me, 'cos I'll forget about you the minute you've walked through that door!'

Jenny knew better than to protest. She smiled helplessly, half-shook her head, and went out. As she closed the shed door she heard the outburst of wild sobbing that followed on Dinah's defiant farewell.

Mrs Fowler was waiting for her in the shady verandah of the house. 'How did it go?'

'Not well, I'm afraid. I feel . . . Mrs Fowler, I feel so sorry for her!'

The older woman shrugged and folded meaty arms across her satin-clad bosom. 'She's not the first to get in a pickle like this. Don't you worry about it, Mrs Armstrong. I'll stand as her friend until she's over it. Of course, she'll come in for a lot of teasing — folk were all saying they were surprised a man like Ron Armstrong would take up with a girl from the orphan school and now they'll say she had ideas above herself —'

'It would be better if she could get away.'

'I can't spare her, Mrs Armstrong, and that's the fact. 'Sides, what good would it do for her to run away? No, no, she threw her cap over the windmill without asking first if the miller was free to catch it. She's got to face the consequences of her own rashness.'

'But it's so unfair, Mrs Fowler! The man gets off scot free!'

Mrs Fowler pursed her lips. 'Reckon so? I think Ron'll have his hard times for a while.' She glanced at Jenny. 'You thinking of going home soon?'

'Well, pretty soon, I imagine, though there's some business to be attended to.'

'Seems to me it'd be easier all round if you and your husband cleared out. The whole thing will die down all the sooner, and it'd certainly be easier on Dinah if Ron were out of the district.'

Jenny nodded agreement, and held out her hand. 'Thank you, Mrs Fowler. You've been very understanding.'

'Oh, lor, I haven't done much.'

'You've been kind to Dinah.'

'I'll go on being kind so long as she keeps her temper with me,' Mrs Fowler said with a grin, 'but she can be a tartar when she's roused up. But I'll do the best I can for her.'

'Goodbye, then.'

'Goodbye, all the best.'

The boy had brought the trap to the garden gate. Jenny mounted and drove away, her thoughts busy with what had happened.

She wasn't exactly proud of herself. She had used weapons that she would rather not, against an enemy for whom she felt nothing but pity. What a victory . . .

She reached Daniell's farm in good time for tea. Ronald had gone riding out to look for the Aborigines with whom he'd been talking when she first saw him. Heather was being bathed and made ready for bed after a long day outdoors, learning to ride in the morning and doing lessons in the shade of an ironbark for part of the afternoon.

To Mrs Daniell's half-expressed queries Jenny merely replied that everything was now cleared up. 'Is Gunder around? I hope to be heading back to Sydney tomorrow or the next day.'

'Will Ron be going with you?'

'I hope so. We'll discuss it when he comes back. When do you expect him back, Mrs Daniell?'

The other woman looked uncertain. 'Who can tell? Depends how far he follows the Abos. They wander a long way, you know — seems to us, without rhyme or reason though I guess they know why they do it.'

'But he'll be back tonight?'

'Did he say he would?'

'No,' confessed Jenny, 'I just took it for granted . . .'

But when she thought about it she understood that Ronald was probably feeling embarrassed and shamefaced about the whole business with Dinah Bowerby. She couldn't blame him for absenting himself until the first gossiping interest had died down.

He made no appearance that evening. When she went down to his camp by the stream after the meal, there was no sign of him. Next day the same. Jenny spent the morning watching Heather trot carefully round the paddock on Goodie, the tough little pony which had come to be regarded as hers. In the afternoon she wrote a letter to her factory manager in Galashiels, which was to be sent with a packet of designs left in her hotel room in Sydney. She had expected to be setting out for Sydney by now, but she couldn't think of leaving without first speaking to Ronald and if possible taking him with her.

Because she knew Henry Chalmers would be getting worried, she sent Gunder back to Sydney next day with a request to send on her letter to Scotland. She enclosed a note to the hotel manager asking him to give to Chalmers the packet of designs he would find on the bureau in her room. These were to be despatched with the letter. Gunder was to return as soon as these tasks were accomplished.

She had fallen into the habit of going to Ronald's campsite each morning and nightfall. When she had been a week at the Daniells' farm, an elderly black woman met her on the path. She held up a hand to stop Jenny, then addressed her rapidly.

The language had a vague resemblance to English, but it was too difficult to follow. Jenny invited the old woman to accompany her, took her back to the farm, and there got Mrs Daniell to interpret what was clearly a message.

'She says your husband is with a group of distillers up at Langa — '

'Distillers?'

'Eucalyptus distillers — '

'But how did she know the message was for me? She's never seen me before.'

'Don't ask me, dear. They're a mystery. Ron says he's found his friend who has the information about colours for cloth and he hopes to be back in a day or two.'

'But where is he?'

Mrs Daniell made the inquiry. The black woman turned to face the northwest, made a vague outward movement of her arm, and turned back.

'My God!' Jenny said. 'This place is like a hall of mirrors — people appear and disappear in a moment.'

'Yes, it's a great place for getting lost in,' Mrs Daniell agreed with faint irony.

'Tell the lady thank you from me.'

Mrs Daniell translated and paid her for her services with a sugared almond. To Jenny she said, 'You don't mind having to wait a bit longer?'

Jenny didn't say, I waited a lot longer than this already. Instead she asked, 'Is it convenient to have us here so long?'

'Good heavens, only too pleased! I love having Heather here. Reminds me of when my own young 'uns were still around.'

'She loves the pony. You're so kind to lend it to her — '

'Nonsense, always plenty of ponies and brumbies around. And she seems to be doing well on it.' She looked at Jenny. 'Doesn't she ever speak?'

'Almost never.'

'Something wrong? Vocal cords damaged?'

'No, we don't know exactly why it is. She had a bad time when she was little.'

'Sick, you mean?'

'In a way.'

Mrs Daniell's curiosity was kindly but Jenny didn't want to go into long details about past sorrows. She wanted to think about tomorrow or the next day, when Ronald might be back and she could talk to him about the future.

She found him at his campsite the following evening. His borrowed horse was cropping the grass by the streamside, its saddle and harness over a bough. He had clearly come in only a short time ago, for he was stripped to the waist and shaving himself preparatory to coming to the farmhouse.

At the sound of her footsteps he put his head round the canvas which formed the door of the lean-to for the moment. 'Jenny! You got my message?'

'Ronald, you've been gone five days!'

She cast herself upon him, heedless of the shaving soap on his chin. He threw his razor into the bowl and wrapped his arms around her. 'Well, this is what I call a welcome,' he laughed.

'I wanted you here, Ronald. I needed you.'

'Yes, lassie, I know.' He kissed the top of her head. 'You wanted to tell me about Dinah.'

'Yes.'

'What happened?'

'She . . . she accepts that it's all over. But Ronald, she's such a sad girl.'

'Sad?'

'Yes, hoping and longing for something she hasn't the ability to get for herself. It's such a waste! As beautiful as she is, she ought to have the world at her feet.'

He said nothing, and she understood that he couldn't discuss Dinah in that way. He saw her as a mistake in his life, one he wanted to put behind him. He might be sorry for her, but he knew there was nothing he could do about it.

This masculine wisdom had to be adopted. Dinah Bowerby might be talked about but only as something in the past. Her future was her own, to make of it what she could. If Jenny had fellow-feeling for her, it was better not to speak of it.

While he finished his shave and put on a clean shirt, she talked to him about possible plans. 'I sent a message by the driver so we're not expected back at once. But I ought to get to Sydney, Ronald, because I kept our hotel rooms there – '

'But that's not important, is it?'

'No, but I want to keep in touch with which ships are sailing – '

'Surely you don't want to rush straight back to Galashiels?'

'I left the mill in the hands of Charlie Gaines, Ronald.'

There was no need to enlarge on that. Ronald understood how inadequate Gaines would be except in the most everyday situations.

They fell to discussing the mill, its problems of the moment, its prospects. By the time they had strolled up to the house they were deep in a discussion of percentage costs per bolt for export.

Bob Daniell was back from his day's work. At the sight of Ronald he at once began asking for news, the main interest of every dweller of the outback. Ronald told of his stay with the blackfellows, shook his head over the chances of getting supplies of the herbs and barks they used for cloth-dyeing, and then went on to talk about the eucalyptus distillers, men known to the Daniells through occasional visits.

'Albert was saying, they'd be packing it in in a day or two, as soon as that batch had run through.'

'Whaffor?' Daniell said through a mouthful of mutton stew. 'There's always a demand for eucalyptus oil.'

'Yes, but they were telling me, there's been gold panned-out on the Lachlan.'

Mrs Daniell paused in offering more potatoes and frowned at her husband. His face creased up in dismay.

'Oh, Jesus,' he groaned, 'that means half the stockmen in the district will take off for the Lachlan.'

'What's the matter?' Jenny asked. 'Someone's discovered a gold mine?'

The men began explaining both at once. In the end Daniell, who knew more about it, took up the word. 'If anybody wants my opinion, gold is the curse of this country! All the men go rushing off after it, and who the devil's going to look after the stock and the harvests if they're all off searching for El Dorado? And you weren't here, of course, but eight or nine years ago they had to call in government troops to keep order at Lambing Flat — I can tell you, that was something, seeing armed troops riding past the farm!'

'But that was because of the swindling that went on in the gambling tents, dear —'

'That's what I mean — all kinds of bad things come after gold-hunting. You see, Mrs Armstrong, after somebody boasts of picking up a nugget or two, hordes of fellers come crowding after him. The trouble is, surface gold is easy — alluvial gold, found near or in the rivers. It's washed down from some vein somewhere and at first everybody's splashing about with pans trying to pick out "colour" .'

'Colour, that's enough gold to mean it's worth going on,' Ronald put in. 'I hear there's often traces even in British rivers — but it doesn't mean there's any gold worth prospecting for.'

'After a bit,' Bob Daniell resumed, 'all the easy gold's been picked up or panned and then the mob starts looking for the vein it came from. Naturally, the first man to find the vein and stake a claim might turn into a millionaire, and they all lose their heads. At first they were happy with a nugget or two or some gold dust, enough to buy themselves a house and some land. But the craze takes them, and they want the source of the gold, and they hang around digging and searching, and then they get bored at night, and they play cards with the nuggets they've pocketed, and they lose them — and that's where all the trouble starts.'

'But that doesn't have to happen, Bob,' Ronald protested. 'It's all perfectly orderly and well-managed at Parkes —'

'Yes, because they've gone on to reef-mining there with a properly organised mining company. You should have seen Parkes when the first news broke about the fortunes waiting to be picked up in the soil.'

'Albert and Dave said they'd talked to a fellow who picked up a nugget worth two hundred pounds.'

'I'm sure,' Bob said, nodding. 'And if that feller had the sense to go home at that point, there'd be less harm done.'

'So you believe there really is gold?' Jenny asked,

half-incredulous at the talk. Finding gold was the kind
of thing that happened at the other side of the world
from her home — to be actually close to a goldfield
seemed unbelievable.

'Aw, there's gold on the Lachlan all right,' Bob
agreed. 'But what I'm trying to say is, the real future
of this country is in farming — wheat and wool and
beef. So long as men keep running off to make a quick
fortune, we won't build up the farming industry.'

'All the same, I can understand the fascination,'
Jenny said. 'Gold is romantic. Farming isn't.'

'You wouldn't think it was romantic if you'd seen
the gold camps I have,' her host grunted. 'Dirty,
stinking, immoral muckheaps.'

'Now, Bob, don't lecture us,' his wife soothed.

'I'll tell you this — if Tim or Limpy pick up their
swag and run off in the next day or two, they needn't
ask for their jobs back when they turn up broke in six
months. And the same goes for any of the men on the
north pasture.'

Mrs Daniell coaxed him into talking about the
problems over stockmen for his square miles of
pasture. Jenny found it impossible to come to terms
with farms measured in square miles rather than acres.
She listened with awe to his tales.

'The worst worry is rain. The creeks dry up and the
sheep get desperate for water. Of course, the farm here
is on a bore-hole — there's plenty of water below the
surface hereabouts, you can always get it by digging.
But that's no use to cattle and sheep, at least not at
present, though the time may come when we'll
construct tanks with water pumped up every day to
trickle into troughs. But that costs money.'

'How long since it last rained?' Jenny inquired. In

these high temperatures and dry winds, she found herself longing for the cool soft air of the Scottish Borders.

'Not a drop all summer — but that's all right, we'll get by until the winter rain. Clouds'll start building up in a week or two. Usually we get the first good downpour at the end of March.'

When she'd helped clear up after the meal, Jenny went for a stroll with Ronald. They went back to the conversation they'd been having earlier, about Waterside Mill. Jenny was eager to involve him in its problems again. The more he could be made to think about them, the more ready he would be to go home. She'd been a little alarmed at his demurring when she spoke of finding out about sailings for home.

Gunder came back the following day. He found them standing at the rail of the paddock watching Heather learning to put her pony into a canter. 'Done all you told me, missus,' he reported. 'An' I got somethin' for you.'

He had brought a manila envelope. Inside was a note from Henry Chalmers saying he would send on her designs and her letter as soon as possible. With it were two letters from home.

She opened the more important one at once. It was from Charlie Gaines. He began reassuringly by saying all was well at the mill for the moment. Then came the worrying part.

'I regret to tell you that your lawyer Mr Kennet has been stricken by a paralytic stroke and has had to retire unexpectedly. I do not wish to imply that there is any urgency in the situation and as far as I know there are no legal problems, but I thought it right to let you know that the personal supervision of Mr Kennet is not now available. His chief clerk is handling the business until the practice is sold.'

'Trouble?' asked Ronald, watching her face.

She handed him the letter. He read it while she opened the second one. It was from the London factor who marketed tweeds and tartans on behalf of William Corvil and Son. Nothing urgent, but it contained news she ought to act on as soon as possible.

'The Marlborough House Set now contains a young American millionairess who saw and liked the plaid worn by the Princess of Wales at the launching of a ship recently. Miss Reinmann has ordered my entire supply of your plaids to be sent to her father in Chicago. He is the owner of a chain of stores. This lucrative connection is being pursued by me as vigorously as possible but it would be a useful compliment to Miss Reinmann if you could design a plaid for her exclusively. I remain Yours Etc, Donald M. Wilson pp Wilson & Co., East Dockhouse Road, London.'

'Oh!' exclaimed Jenny, refolding the letter and pushing it into its envelope. 'How can I design a plaid for a woman I've never even seen? Men are ridiculous!'

Ronald had just finished the letter about Kennet. 'Charlie sounds as if he's getting cold feet.'

'There's no need. Nothing needs doing about contracts or leases. Poor Mr Kennet . . . And poor Mrs Kennet. I wish I were there to help comfort her.'

Ronald moved restlessly, then set off towards the house. 'You're longing to go back, aren't you?' he said over his shoulder.

'Longing . . . No, it's not as bad as that. But I do miss it all, Ronald.' She hurried to catch up with his long stride. 'Do you think you might want to start for home in the near future?'

His long narrow face took on a stubborn slant. She felt anxiety rising within her. She, of course, saw Galashiels as home, the place of comfort, happiness and safety. But to Ronald it held painful memories — of a marriage gone wrong, of family quarrels and constraints.

'There are still things here that need doing, Jenny. I came over to sort out the best way to buy our wool —'

'Yes, of course, we ought to go into that, but perhaps it needn't take too long —'

'But where's the hurry?'

'Well,' she ventured, uncertain how it would be received, 'Mrs Fowler out at Durramurra said it would be better for Dinah if you packed up and left. She said the story would die all the quicker if you weren't in the district.'

His glance darkened. 'You mean I've got to run away with my tail between my legs.'

'Oh, Ronald lad, it's not that at all —'

'I don't give a damn what the old tabbies say about me —'

'No, but think of Dinah — it's always worse for the woman —'

'That's not my doing. It's the way people look at it.'

They had come to a standstill as the argument began to gain pressure. She could tell that he was unsettled, ready to take offence.

'I know people can be unfair, but all the same it would be better if you weren't here —'

'So I'm to go back home and settle down into the old rut, is that it?'

'Ronald!' She was hurt at the expression. 'I didn't think you felt like that – '

'How do you expect me to feel? Dammit, what am I, when you come to examine the situation? I'm a paid employee, that's all – '

'But darling, you made your own terms with Ned when you first – '

'If I'd known what it was going to be like, I'd have started out differently! You don't really think I enjoy being referred to as "Miss Corvill's husband", do you?'

'Nobody calls you that.'

'Not to my face, no. But everybody is well aware that you have all the money – '

'I haven't, Ronald! You know I haven't a penny of my own, really – it all belongs to Ned, that's the way Father left it in his will.'

'All right then, I'll rephrase it. All the money is on your side of the family. I contribute nothing except my work – and that puts me on the same level as any other charge-hand in the mill.'

'But that's just your way of looking at it. Nobody else thinks like that – '

'No? You haven't heard the kind of jokes that go round the Galashiels Gentlemen's Club! If you think I want to go back and be just the man who married you for your money, you're mistaken, Jenny.'

She swung round, away from him. 'I don't know how to talk to you when you're like this!' she cried, her hands up to her mouth as if to check an outcry. 'What is it you *want*?'

He made no reply, and the pause went on for so long that at last she turned back in concern.

He was standing with his hands in the pockets of

his drill trousers, his head bent, the sun glinting on his tawny hair.

At length he looked up. 'I want to have something of my own,' he said.

'But what does that mean?'

'I want to have funds to use as I see fit. I'm not sure how I'd use them but I won't be tied to William Corvill and Son by a paypacket any more. So I'm going to the Lachlan.'

'What?'

'I'm going to look for gold on the Lachlan River.'

Chapter Twenty-one

It was as if the breath were knocked out of Jenny's body. She stood as if struck to stone.

Ronald, who had looked away as he spoke, walked on. She stared at that tall spare figure moving away from her, and something like rage engulfed her. She ran to him, seized his arm, dragged him round to face her.

'Stupid, stubborn, wrong-headed fool!' she cried. 'Did I come all this way just to lose you again?'

She began to hammer at his chest with her fists. Amazed, he fell back a step. She hit out at him blindly. 'I hate you, I hate you!' she shouted.

He captured her flailing fists, then dragged her arms down to her sides. 'Jenny!'

She glared up at him, eyes wide with anger, like a cat waiting to spit at him. 'I hate you, do you hear me!'

'Good God, lassie, what's come to you —'

'You can ask me that? When you've just said you're going away again — without even discussing it?'

'There's nothing to discuss —'

'Oh, you're so stiff necked and proud —'

'Surely it's easy to understand? I don't want to go back to Galashiels with the same few pounds in my pocket —'

She seized on that. 'If that's the reason,' she begged,

'if you don't want to go back — we can stay here, we can get some land —'

'Stay here?'

'You wanted to buy a farm —'

'But that was for Dinah —'

'I could learn to farm, do the things that Dinah could do.'

'But why should you? What was it you called her — a "sad girl". Why should you dwindle away to be a "sad girl" lost in the farmlands, your name forgotten, your talents wasted? The sacrifice would make you hate me before too long.'

'I'd never complain, Ronald —'

'And I would never forget,' he said, shaking his head. 'You weren't meant by nature to live in a pioneering country where women have to take second place. It would change you, and we'd both regret it.'

She sought about for some other argument. 'You don't have to go to the goldfield. There must be some other way —'

'Jenny, I've thought it all out. I didn't sleep much last night, I had too much on my mind. Out on the Lachlan, I'll just be a man who's looking for his good luck. When people here mention me, they'll say, "I hear Armstrong went out to the goldfield," instead of, "I hear Armstrong's wife had to extricate him from that affair with Dinah Bowerby." '

'Oh God,' she groaned. 'And I thought I was being so clever!'

He gave her a wry smile. 'You were, my love. I don't believe I could have got Dinah to see reason. All the same, it makes me look a fool, doesn't it?'

'No —' But she broke off. Perhaps she had made things more difficult for him by coming in search of

384

him. He had pride — how could he let himself be dragged off home at his wife's apron-strings?

Yet she knew if she hadn't come she might well have lost him. This long journey round the world to him had been the proof he needed that she really loved him. And now she had to give him yet another proof — by letting him go again.

'It's so far,' she mourned. 'And Mrs Daniell says it's half-desert. A friend of hers settled there about seven or eight years ago and was driven out by drought.'

'It's not as bad as all that. I've talked to men who've been there, and some of the blackfellows have described it to me. The river gets low sometimes, of course, and there are forest fires —'

'Forest fires!'

'No, now, calm down. Winter's coming, the rain will damp it all down. And as for it's being so far, it's only a few hundred miles to the northwest —'

'A few hundred miles! That's the length and breadth of the British Isles!'

He shrugged, giving up the pretence that it was an easy trip. 'It's not a cosy little district like Berwickshire back home,' he agreed. 'But people have settled and raised sheep there, and got the wool back to market. From what I hear, it's not so bad getting to Forbes. From there it should be possible to travel by boat.'

'But you heard what Mr Daniell said about the diggers' camps —'

'You have to make allowance for his religious scruples. It's true that the camps aren't exactly halls of virtue, but men have gone to the diggings and come back quite safe and sound. And some have come back with a pocketful of gold.'

385

It dawned on her that it was a lost cause. He was determined to go, for subtle reasons that couldn't be gainsaid.

She took his arm and began to walk with him towards the house, and after a moment asked him when he thought of going and what he would need to pack.

'I'm setting out tomorrow.'

'Tomorrow?' It was a gasp of dismay.

'No reason to delay — Daniell will sell me the horse I've been borrowing and I can get a packhorse at Forbes along with any other equipment I need.'

'Shall I look through your clothes? There may be things that want mending.'

It was wifely — patient, subdued, gentle. He had loved and admired her as his equal but in that moment when she showed understanding by accepting his decision, he loved her more than ever in his life before.

When they made love that night it was with a deep and returning passion. In Jenny's heart there was a whisper that said this might be for the last time. She wouldn't let herself hear it, but her body was aware of the hidden fear. She responded to Ronald's demands with a desperate ardour.

Early next morning he put his neatly rolled gear — his swag — on his horse behind the saddle. He sent messages of goodbye to the people still asleep at the farmhouse. 'Tell Heather I expect her to be a champion jockey when I get back.'

'When you get back . . . Ronald, how long do you think you'll be gone?'

He looked down at her in the dawn light. 'Three months? Four?'

She pressed her lips together to keep them from trembling. 'Take care.'

'Of course. You too — keep busy and don't worry.'

'Yes, Ronald.'

A last kiss and a hug. He pulled his wide-brimmed hat over his tawny hair, swung up on the horse and rode away in the long lazy canter he had learnt from the people of the outback.

She stood still outside the lean-to, listening until the hoofbeats on the parched ground had died away. Then she stole back in her nightdress along the path and into the sleeping house. She found her dressing-gown in the room she shared with her daughter and Baird, pulled it on, and sat on the verandah steps in the cool of the morning.

Only when Mrs Daniell got up to open up the kitchen range and start the bread-dough did she move. And one glance at her face was enough to keep Mabel Daniell from saying so much as good-morning to her.

At some point in her thinking it had come to Jenny that she ought to go back to Sydney to attend to the various matters of business that waited there. Yet she hated to leave the farm, because it was the place to which Ronald would return.

When she tried to explain her feelings to Mabel, she was greeted with protests. 'No need to think you're leaving! Your room's always there — why don't you leave your things in it? You can come back here any time.'

Baird seconded this. 'I've nothing against Sydney but living in a hotel is no sort of life for a wee lass. Heather loves it here. Why do you not just let her stay here with me, mistress?'

'Do you think she would?' Jenny asked, surprised.

'We can ask her.'

Heather was sitting under the ironbark wrestling with the six-times table. She looked up with relief when her mother came to her with Baird.

'Heather, Mama has to go back to the city.'

The little girl looked attentive.

'Baird says you would like to stay here —'

She shook her head so that her honey-coloured hair bobbed about her ears.

'Wait, let me finish. I'd be back again in a day or two. You could stay here and go on with your riding lessons.'

This time Heather looked solemn. She put her slate pencil in her mouth and sucked it thoughtfully.

'I'd be here,' Baird put in. 'You and me could go for walks thegither, and help Mrs Daniell make the pastry.'

A pause.

'Well, Heather? Would you like to stay?'

The child hesitated. Jenny knew it was anxiety about the separation. She picked a leathery leaf from a nearby shrub. 'I'll be back before that leaf has withered,' she said.

Heather took the leaf, studied it, then looked up and nodded.

It was settled. Heather would stay, Jenny would go. It was the first separation between them except for the two days when Ronald had left from Liverpool — and the child had been so poorly with chickenpox that she didn't remember it. So it was a great decision, a great step forward.

The drive back to Parramatta reinforced Jenny's anxieties about the country to the northwest. The road to Parramatta wasn't good but it existed — this was considered 'easy country'. What it must be like beyond the settlement at Forbes she didn't care to consider.

But her husband had told her to keep busy and not to worry. The first was simple enough. Henry Chalmers welcomed her with news of wool auctions due to take place in the following week. Moreover, at her hotel, notes and invitations awaited her. The society leaders of Sydney had 'discovered' her — she was asked everywhere.

'Mr Chalmers tells me that you have actually met the Queen?'

'That's quite true — and the Prince Consort before his death.'

They were delighted with her. She had brought new fashions with her, new topics of conversation. Almost every evening for the next few weeks she was out, in the surprisingly fine houses on the shores of Sydney Cove. The gardens here were superb. Although the harsh dry weather continued, water was easily available to hose the precious flowers every day. Nothing was more pleasant than to sit on a lamplit terrace after dinner, with the scent of blossoms and the sea mingling on the breeze.

To the businessmen she presented an opportunity to make money. After about a month of looking at the wool still on sale at Circular Quay, she began to see the good sense in having control of the original product. The best clip had clearly been sold at the very beginning of the season, and before any outsider had a chance to bid for it. What was now coming to market was good, but it was not the best of the crop.

Her murmurs about buying a sheep station and having it managed by an experienced man were listened to with interest. She was taken to the Camden Park

Estate to see what the Macarthur family had done for sheep-rearing. It was impressive, but as she remarked on the fifty-mile drive back to the city, 'It's more than I want to do. I don't want to raise a prize dairy herd or lease out farms to other breeders. I just want to be in control of my wool supply.'

Over the next few weeks she went to look at several farms. Mr Wolfe, a wholesale merchant of Maitland and a very shrewd speculator in wool, eventually recommended the farm that she decided to buy. It lay about eighty miles north of Sydney, consisting of about ten thousand acres. The present owner had poor health and no children to leave it to. His manager, a married man with one child, very much wanted to remain in his post. When offered a share in the profits in addition to salary if he would take sole charge, he agreed almost without negotiation.

Mr Chalmers recommended a Sydney law firm, Lionel and Martin Hignett. Contracts were drawn up, and the deal was done. Jenny arranged a small celebratory dinner. The guests were Henry Chalmers and an actress friend of his from the Royal Victoria, Mr Wolfe and his wife, Mr and Mrs Lionel Hignett and the former owner of Giddiring Station.

Although astounded at being asked to lay on a business dinner by a lady, the landlord of the Australia Hotel made a special effort. He hired out a recently repainted parlour at the back of the ground floor. His housekeeper even produced some silver épergnes in which to make floral decorations for the table.

It was an agreeable affair. The actress, Lisette Barron, pretended to be a French comédienne, but the occasional slipping of her accent betrayed London origins. Nevertheless she was a lively lady, full of gossip which she heard through a multitude of men friends.

'You know Joseph Mallory — ze reporter for ze *Morning Herald*?' she remarked, after her fourth glass of wine. 'He tol' me *quelque chose de très intéressante* at lonchtime.'

'Really? What?'

'If it's about Susan O'Farrell we don't want to hear it,' Mrs Wolfe put in. 'I'm sick to death of reading about what a marvellous horsewoman she is —'

'No, zees is somesing really new — eet only came in zees morning. 'E was, how you say, writing it up for tomorrow's *journal*.'

'Well, what, my dear?' asked Mr Hignett, the lawyer.

'You know ze goldrush camp up by ze Lachlan Rivaire?'

Henry Chalmers sat up and looked at Jenny with some apprehension. Tales from mining camps were generally salty. Jenny waited eagerly for the gossip.

'What about it?' she urged.

'Joe says eet has been burned out.'

'What?'

'Wait,' Jenny said faintly. 'I didn't quite catch it because of your accent. The camp of the gold-diggers has been burned?'

'*Mais oui! Quel drame, n'est-ce pas?*'

'Was anyone . . . anyone hurt?'

'But yes! Many dead, and some very badly burned. It was, how you say, *un feu-forestier* —'

'Cut it out, Miss Barron!' Mrs Hignett said with unladylike sharpness. 'Mrs Armstrong's husband is up on the Lachlan.'

'Oh!' cried Lisette, real distress superseding all the

pretence. 'Oh, poor dear — I'm so sorry! If I'd known I wouldn't for the world —'

'Do you know any more?' Jenny asked in a faltering voice. 'Did your friend have a list of . . . of the dead?'

'He only had the bare bones of the story. I'm sorry, Mrs Armstrong, the news just came in with an ox-cart team who arrived in the morning. They'd heard it from the Abos.'

'When did this happen?' Mr Hignett took up the questions that Jenny couldn't utter.

'I think about a week ago.'

'Look, Mrs Armstrong,' said Mr Wolfe, 'the Lachlan's a long river. There's no proof that this particular camp is the one your husband is at.'

'But it's where the gold was found — that's right, isn't it, Miss Barron?'

'Well, yes . . . Joe said it was the diggers' camp.'

'But the news could have been exaggerated —'

'To be sure, that can transpire,' Chalmers agreed. 'There is a regrettable propensity to magnify events.'

'When does the paper come out?' Jenny asked, trying to regain her sense of the practical.

'Oh, as to that,' Chalmers got up. 'I'll go and ask Joe what he elicited. He'll either be at their office in Pitt Street or at his lodgings.'

'I'll come with you,' Jenny said, half-rising. And then, recalling that she was hostess to the party, she sank down again. 'Oh, I'm sorry —'

'Not at all, Mrs Armstrong — you go — don't stand on ceremony.' The men were on their feet, pushing back their chairs, clearing a way for her to the door. Jenny, after a momentary faltering, took them at their word. She seized Henry Chalmers' arm and went hurrying out with him.

The stars were out, the breeze from the sea seemed much cooler. Jenny, in her thin dinner-gown of paper silk and lace, shivered. It was colder — winter was coming. Even to sunny Sydney, winter was coming. Or perhaps it was just fear of what she might learn that made her feel cold.

In the hall of the *Herald* the porter said that Mr Mallory was still in the building, down by the printing presses where the last of the news was being set up. He was inclined to argue when Chalmers headed for the stairs down to the printing office, but the glint of silver changed his mind.

The noise in the printing department was deafening. Accustomed though she was to carding and weaving machines, Jenny almost cowered back from the presses. A tall skinny man with a shock of black hair was leaning over a flat bed of print with an aproned man by his side. He had to be tapped on the shoulder before he was aware he was wanted.

'Can we go outside?' Chalmers shouted in his ear. 'We need to ask you something.'

'I'm busy, Henry!'

'This is important. *Important*!'

Unwillingly Mallory left his work and went with Chalmers to the door where Jenny hovered.

'This is Mrs Armstrong,' Chalmers said, in his anxiety forgetting proper form. 'Tell her what you know about the fire on the Lachlan, Joe.'

'It'll be in tomorrow's edition.'

'Come on, my friend, show some consideration. Mrs Armstrong's husband —'

'Oh yes, I heard he'd gone up there . . . I'm sorry, ma'am, there's almost nothing I can tell you. The men with the wagon team had stopped at an Abo camp on

393

their way in. They said the Abos told them there had been a big fire — they heard of it from some of their tribe who were out hunting and saw the smoke.'

'You mean that's all — they didn't go into the camp themselves?'

'Didn't need to. They climbed a tree and had a dekko. You know what their eyesight is like. They said there were a lot of bodies lying about and some men crawling as if they'd been hurt.'

'Didn't they go to help?' Jenny broke in, aghast.

'Well, ma'am, I daresay they were scared — there are fellers in the bush who set upon miners in their camps for the gold they've found. White men get up to some funny tricks and if the Abos get in their way, the Abos tend to come off worst. 'Sides, they had freshly killed game they wanted to take back to their womenfolk.'

'So all we are cognisant of,' Chalmers said, 'is that the camp has been burnt and men are hurt or . . . or . . .'

'Or killed. Yes, that's about it.'

'When will we hear more?' Jenny asked.

The reporter looked at her with surprise that changed to pity. 'Gee, ma'am, news comes in from places like that more by chance than intention. It might be a coupla weeks before we hear more.'

'But isn't anyone going — ?'

'Yes, I reckon there'll be a rescue party. The *Herald* is putting up fifty pounds towards medical supplies and equipment — you'll see it in the paper tomorrow. There'll be an appeal to the readers for help.'

'Dr Vance will volunteer,' Chalmers said.

'I reckon. He's generally first to offer — can't settle down to doling out cough syrup to old ladies.'

'Where does Dr Vance live?' Jenny demanded.

'Where? In York Street, on the opposite side to the Market Sheds. You going to offer him funds for the first aid party?'

'I'm going with him.'

'You what?' said Mr Mallory, shocked. 'Listen, lady, that's not the kind of thing a woman ought to —'

'Don't be absurd,' Jenny said curtly as she turned away. 'If there are injured men they'll need nursing, won't they?'

'Yes, but —'

'Will you show me the way to Dr Vance's house?' she said to Chalmers, leaving the reporter's protests behind her as she led the way out.

Dr Vance proved to be a young man with a face much battered by his love of boxing, wrestling and steeplechasing. When he heard the news from his unexpected visitors, he immediately began opening cupboards in search of items he ought to take with him to the Lachlan. 'Fifty pounds from the *Herald*?' he muttered. 'We ought to be able to buy plenty of bleached cotton and laudanum after we've paid for the wagon and food supplies —'

'I'll pay for the wagon,' Jenny broke in. 'I was going to travel tomorrow in any case — I try to visit Daniell's farm every week or ten days so I had made arrangements.'

'Good on you,' enthused the doctor. 'We'll take the wagon you were going to use — you can get something else for your trip easily enough —'

'Just a minute. I mean, you can use the carriage and take me on the trip.'

Dr Vance let his broad-lipped mouth fall open. 'Oh no!'

'Oh yes. I'm going, Doctor, whether I actually travel with you or follow along behind you. Wouldn't it make more sense if we rode together?'

'Now look here, Mrs Armstrong, I quite see that you're anxious about your husband, but believe me, it's not the kind of thing a woman should —'

'Oh, how can you talk such nonsense!' Jenny cried. 'Miss Nightingale and her nurses went to the Crimea — was that the "kind of thing a woman should do"?' She banged a fist on his desk. 'I'm going to the Lachlan River. I ordered the carriage to be waiting for me at Parramatta at nine, so get your supplies to Redfern Station tonight so they can be put aboard first thing in the morning. We'll transfer them to the cart as soon as we get to the other end.'

'Look here —'

'Shall I come with you, Mrs Armstrong?' Chalmers inquired meekly.

'You don't mean you agree with this?' Vance exclaimed in indignation.

'I've come to realise that Mrs Armstrong knows what she's doing. And what she says makes sense — Gunder and his carriage will be waiting, you can get your necessities aboard in ten minutes, and who knows how long it might take if you started on your own hiring a wagon from Coffill's —'

'Well, that's true, but all the same —'

'I won't be a nuisance,' Jenny promised, modifying her tone to one of quiet good sense. 'I'm used to travelling —'

'But we don't want to waste time going to Daniell's —'

'No, no, I quite understand. I'll send a note to my

little girl's nurse to let her know I shan't be coming for a while.'

It was arranged that Chalmers should approach a widow-woman of his acquaintance to go too — a capable soul who had taught school in the outback and knew how to deal with emergencies. Next morning they set out with boxes and hampers loaded in the luggage van of the train. At Parramatta Chalmers and the doctor hired horses while the porters and Gunder loaded the supplies on the cart. Jenny had already written to Baird. She gave the letter to a travelling haberdasher to deliver, with a florin for his trouble.

By nine-thirty they were on their way. The weather was cooler though not cold by Jenny's standards. A strong gusty wind blew, dust rose up to plague them and get in their eyes, their nostrils, and in the food they ate when they stopped for a breather. Mrs Gray showed Jenny how to eat with her back turned to the wind and her dish held in the protective lee of the cart.

It was almost a week's travelling — long hard days and cool nights by a welcome camp fire. Jenny tried to contain her anxiety to be getting on. She knew it was no use overstraining or injuring the horses by useless effort in failing light. It was the month of May — Jenny kept trying to envisage what the countryside would be like around Galashiels now, the lush young grass springing in the river valleys, the trees in new leaf, the Gala Water rushing in its bed in full flood. How different from this vast terrain.

After Parramatta with its orchards, tilled fields and extending railway line, they had passed through undulating country and the flat meadowlands of the Central Tableland. Cowra was to the south on the upper Lachlan, but the camp towards which they were heading was northward, beyond Forbes.

Forbes was a surprise to Jenny. She had expected some little settlement, but instead she found a town – a town of canvas and bark humpies, but a town nonetheless. Thick scrub came up to the very flaps of the tents, with paths walked through it as if for a 'main street' and side roads. There were pubs, cook-shops, gambling saloons, money-lenders, provision stores, a tailor, a laundry, a barber, a horse-coper and farrier, a fortune-teller – all in makeshift premises and all doing a roaring trade.

Dr Vance thought it unwise to stay overnight in the town in view of the theft and pick-pocketing that always went on in the mining settlements. They therefore camped outside the town on the banks of the Lachlan. In the morning Vance made inquiries about the fire. Yes, said the inhabitants of Forbes, they'd heard there'd been a fire, could smell burning on the west wind a couple of weeks ago – some stupid galah had set fire to the bush, no doubt. They showed little concern. They had too many troubles of their own, mostly about how to find gold or how to latch on to a man who had already found it.

But the main direction of the search for gold was to the northwest, up along the river towards Willangra Billabong. That was where the furthest camp was sited and that, they admitted, was where the smoke seemed to come from.

'How far to the camp?' asked Vance.

A shrug. Eighty miles? A hundred? 'It's in the North Riverina country . . .' And then with anxious inquiry, 'Why you so keen? You got inside information about the gold there?' But when they learned that the travellers were solely concerned with the safety of the miners, the inhabitants of Forbes decided they weren't worth wasting time on.

Inquiries about possible river transport were treated with scorn.

'Only get an Abo canoe along that damn stream,' said the people of Forbes. 'It's never much use but with the lack of rain you can wade down it faster than you can row.' So any faint hopes of transferring to water transport were dashed, and they repacked their gear on Gunder's cart.

From now on it was hard travelling with no occasional encounters with ox-wagons to reassure them they were taking the best route. The river ran down a gentle but definite incline towards the plains but now there were no distant sheep stations and no sheep. 'Nobody's squatted on this area so far,' Dr Vance explained. 'Somebody'll take it on if the railroad ever gets to Forbes — easy transport for supplies then, and less of a haul getting the wool to market.'

Jenny stared from the cart at the countryside. The grasses were tan-yellow from lack of rain, and the dark pine scrub spread all around like a sea under a wintry sky. Their wheels made a track through the bush, winding hither and thither as Gunder sought for an easy patch. But always they were headed along the bank of the Lachlan, heading northwest.

Two days later, as they were watering the horses in the early afternoon, Gunder raised his head. 'You smell anything?' he asked.

They breathed in. There was the smell of dry soil, of eucalypt, of saltbush and mulga. There was the smell of the river water, a mixture of weed and mineral. But then, faintly, Jenny caught the whiff of something else — acrid and piercing, but gone in a moment.

'What is it?' Chalmers asked. 'I can discern nothing.'

'Wait,' said Dr Vance. 'Burnt wood? Scorched grass?'

'The camp!' gasped Jenny.

She clambered aboard the cart, and the men mounted up. Soon they found a distinct track, worn not long ago by hooves and wheeled vehicles. They pushed on as fast as they dared. The smell grew stronger — unmistakable, the smell of burnt wood doused with water, burnt cloth and — perhaps — burnt flesh.

Round a knoll, they came upon a patch of twisted blackened wood, like a witches' forest. The short trees were dark skeletons, the bushes had been razed to the ground, here and there pieces of iron and steel implied man-made tools.

It was an area about two hundred yards square. Beyond it was another area, where the scrub was battered down. Then a clearing, with fourteen roughly-made wooden crosses, some bearing pieces of bark with names scratched on them, some unnamed.

This was all that was left of the Lachlan River camp.

Chapter Twenty-two

They sat staring at the scene.

'But the survivors?' Jenny faltered.

'They had to move camp, hadn't they?' Gunder replied. He leapt down from the driving seat and splashed into the river, which came up to his knees. 'Gone upstream, o'course — wouldn't go downstream.'

He waded against the current. After a moment's consideration Dr Vance urged his mount after him. Chalmers sat in his saddle, gazing around. 'Funny business.'

'What do you mean?'

'Well, it wasn't a bush fire in the way it's normally meant. It's such a small area —'

A call from Gunder stopped him. 'He's found them,' Chalmers said.

Jenny and Mrs Gray got down from the cart. Chalmers barred her way. 'No, wait till we hear what he's got to say.'

They were looking towards the water, but it was by land that Gunder returned, from behind some unharmed bushes and bringing with him a stranger in a dirty torn shirt and dungarees.

'Goodday,' said the stranger. 'Damn glad to see somebody.'

'The new camp's about seventy yards upstream,' explained Gunder. 'A ruddy mess —'

'Listen, mister, considering how much was lost in the fire, that camp's pretty fair.' He looked at the women with embarrassment, running his finger round the inside of a shirtband that was clearly too small for him. 'The name's Skinner, Albert Skinner.'

Jenny offered her hand. He looked at his own, which was filthy dirty, and smiled instead of shaking. His face was pale under the grime, and lined with weariness. 'Any more folk coming?' he asked. 'We could do with help.'

'How many of you are there?' asked Mrs Gray, beginning to unfasten packages on the cart.

'There's nineteen of us fit, and twenty-two with bad burns — the doc's stopped to see what he can do for them. There's four or five gone off to try to find the horses — fat chance! They've probably joined up with a bunch of brumbies by now.'

'What exactly occurred?' Chalmers said.

'Listen, mate, you don't happen to have any baccy with you? I'm fair dying for a smoke.'

'I . . . ah . . . have some cigars.' Chalmers produced them. Skinner took one and drew in smoke with avidity when Chalmers lit it for him.

'Well, see, it was one of those unfortunate coincidences,' Skinner began. 'A feller called Kinnear and his mate Lefty had struck it lucky about sixty miles north of here, and came back to boast about it. At the same time a couple of Clever Joes arrived from Forbes with a load of stuff to sell us, and most of it was booze — begging your pardon, ladies, I mean strong drink. Naturally Kinnear and Lefty stood their shout and then again and again, until they were more than a bit tipsy. In fact, we all were — drunk as lords. God knows what was in them bottles — some kind of gin, I s'pose, but it didn't half have a kick.' He paused, shaking his head over the recollection.

'Go on,' prompted Jenny.

'Dunno as it's fit for you to hear, missus. These bushwhackers tried to trick Kinnear out of his poke, and a fight started, and knives came out and then somebody used a pistol, and there were men all over the place fighting and mauling. It was dark by then, you understand, so we couldn't rightly make out who was who or what was going on.'

'So those graves aren't for burn victims?'

'Oh, yair, burns and God knows what. It was this way, see — men stumbled over their fires and sent sparks flying and the bush caught, and before we knew it we were surrounded by flames, but the wind was blowing towards the river so if we'd had our senses we could have escaped into the water easy enough — it's a natural firebreak. But we were all roaring drunk and didn't know what we were up to, and the long and short of it is, eight men died in the fire and the rest in the next few days of bad burns.'

Mrs Gray shook her head a little and made a sound of disapproval, which died away as Chalmers frowned at her. This was no time for moralising.

'Some of the crosses have no names on them,' Jenny said quietly.

'Yair, we ain't particular about names in the first place and some of these fellers was in such a mess . . . Well, I won't go on about it, missus, you wouldn't care to hear it, but we couldn't recognise some of 'em enough to be sure. I'm trying to get a list of names of the men still here, but some of them are pretty crook, out of their heads, so they don't answer up when you speak to 'em.'

'Is there a man called Armstrong here?'

'Armstrong?' He considered, then shook his head. 'Can't say I know the name.'

'Ronald Armstrong — Ron — a tall thin man with fairish hair.'

'Means nothing to me, missus. But people were coming and going all the time. And a lot of the time fellers answer to nicknames. Somebody else might know.'

'I'd like to come and speak to some of your mates —'

'Well, lady, it's a fair mess, as you can imagine. We mostly lost all our possessions and none of us have been too good — I got sick on account of inhaling a lot of hot smoke and others are the same. And we ain't got no soap or clean clothes or anything.'

'That's all right,' said Mrs Gray. 'We didn't come here expecting a picnic.' She had unpacked towels and soap and coarse sheets from one of the hampers. She gave an armful to Skinner, who pinched out his cigar for future enjoyment and led the way.

Despite her stout words, Mrs Gray faltered for a moment as they came to the new camp. There were no tents and only one piece of canvas seemed to have survived. It was strung between two stakes, as a roof over a row of brushwood beds. Four men lay on them, still partly clad but with rough bandages on limbs or round chests or heads. These men were motionless.

Others were tossing under lean-to shelters of bark and woven twigs. As Jenny and her companion moved from place to place they could see the injuries were extremely serious. Dr Vance was on his knees, at work on a man wrapped in parts of an old linen dust-coat. He looked up at their footsteps.

'Go back to the cart and get my medical bag,' he commanded. 'And you'll see a small square tin box – bring that too, it's the opium. I've got to give some relief from pain or they'll exhaust themselves.'

Jenny went back on the errand. Chalmers was already unloading some of the boxes of supplies. When they returned to the camp they found Mrs Gray trying to remove the filthy garments that clung to the burns. With scissors Jenny helped cut away the cloth and gently cover the wounds with bandages.

Although Jenny devoted herself to the work, she couldn't help looking about as she moved from one patient to the other. And none of them was her husband. She saw in her mind's eye the crosses on the scarred ground down-river. Was he lying under a cross with no name on it? She clenched her teeth against the need to weep at the thought, for her attention was wanted here, with men who were still living.

So they laboured on until darkness fell, Chalmers fetching and carrying from the wagon, Gunder building more extensive shelters against the strong breeze, Dr Vance giving pain-killing drinks where the patient could swallow. They spoke little. The only sound was the moaning of the injured and sick men and the rustle of dry twigs and small trees in the wind.

By lantern light it was difficult to be of help to Dr Vance – bandaging a man in pain was too hazardous. Instead they moved from pallet to pallet, trying to soothe those who couldn't be given any sedation and those whose heaving chests troubled them due to smoke inhalation.

It was clear that many of the men were in fever. 'The

burns are infected,' Vance said, when he paused for a can of hot tea and a bite of bread. 'I suppose the clothes they were wearing were stiff with dirt in the first place — miners don't bother too much about washing their gear.'

'Have you medicines to counteract the infection?' Jenny asked.

He shook his head. 'There's no medicine I know of for that. You must have seen it yourself — some people recover quickly from an injury, others develop poisoning of the blood and die or lose a limb.' He sighed. 'That's going to happen to some of these men.'

'Don't say that!'

'It's true, Mrs Armstrong. But at least our arrival has reduced that number — and if the follow-up team arrives soon we can carry back to Forbes those able to be moved, where they can be in greater comfort. There's surgery to be done, and I'd rather it were done in Forbes.'

Jenny repressed a shudder. Forbes was better than the wilderness, but only a little so.

'I think we should send Gunder back in the morning,' the doctor went on. 'He can guide the follow-up team — and bring back more food supplies. For, as I see it, we're going to be here two or three weeks before the bad cases can leave.'

They took turns on watch each night. Jenny sat under the canvas ceiling where the worst of the injured lay, trying to keep them quiet, soothing them with words when the supply of drugs ran out. She would move quietly through the camp, speaking to those who were unable to sleep. Out on the plain she could hear the call of the mopoke in the night, a monotonous sound that seemed to travel over long distances on the wind.

She soon ceased to ask for news of Ronald. Partly it was because she feared to hear a definite sentence of death: 'Yes, he's under the fourth cross from the left.' But one day in the camp was enough to show her that the men had almost no recollection of who had lived and who had died. There had been no organisation, no attempt to manage the original camp as a community. Every man for himself had been the rule.

Moreover there had been an endless coming and going. Newcomers would arrive, eager, avid, asking questions about gold finds which no one would answer. If a man had had luck he took it in two ways — either he was uproariously proud and happy, or he hugged his secret to himself in the hope of going back, uncovering yet more gold. Such a man might drift silently out of the camp in the night, his place empty at 'brekker', his humpy neglected until some new hopeful took it over.

Those who were well enough to talk of the wild night that ended in the fire could remember little. The drink had been strong, plentiful, raw on the throat — alcohol distilled in some shack in Forbes, perhaps with some impurity that had driven them wild. Shame, too, hampered their recollections. Only a few had appreciated what was happening or tried to save their camp-mates.

Then there was the problem of names. 'Monickers', they called them. They referred to each other as Slim, Baldy, Mulehead. Jenny couldn't quite understand why they were so keen to lose their real identities under nicknames, unless there was something in it of shame, a feeling that in their real lives they wouldn't have been so rapacious, lawless, dirty, coarse . . .

Yet there was kindness in them, gratitude too. They appreciated everything that the two women could do, though Jenny felt in herself that it was very little except to sit with them.

After she came off watch she would drink some of the meat tea they made for the patients, and then lie down. Sleep sometimes eluded her, but sometimes it was like falling into an abyss of weariness. When daylight came there were duties to be performed — cooking for both the sick and the fit, makeshift laundering to ensure a supply of clean wrappings, and eternally trying to keep things free of the dust that drove before the never-ending wind.

'I thought it was supposed to rain here in winter?' she asked Gunder when he came back, grey with fatigue and dust, from Forbes.

'Thank your stars it don't,' he grunted. 'This camp'd be a mudbath in no time. And the roads'd vanish — bad enough when it's dry but rain bogs down everything.'

She was sitting up with a very sick patient one night when she heard the sound of horses carefully picking their way towards the camp. She came out of the shelter. In the flickering light of the campfire Dr Vance was crossing the clearing to see who was coming. 'It must be the other team from Sydney,' he called to her over his shoulder.

The fit men came running. Mrs Gray crawled out of her nest of dried ferns half awake.

One of the miners shouted, 'It's Dick Traherne!'

A shabby, weary horse plodded into the clearing. Hung on his back rather than riding, a scarecrow of a man could be seen. 'Dick!' his mates called. He roused himself, looked about, and slithered off the horse.

But there were other hoofbeats. One of the miners walked into the thicket and called back, 'Here's some of our horses, by God — that's Skinner's bay with the white sock. You've brought back our horses, Dick!'

Dick was shaking his head and murmuring faintly that he hadn't done it. Then the last of the party appeared, using the ends of his reins to drive a quartet of exhausted beasts ahead of him.

'Good on you, mate!' cried Skinner, running up to put a twitch of plaited grass round his horse for a bridle. 'We've been waiting for days to get some transport back — where'd you find 'em?'

'What the devil's been happening here?' demanded the newcomer. 'The old camp's a shambles —'

'That's Sandy, isn't it? Sandy, is that you? Where'd you find the nags?'

'In a gully up by the Willandra. You could see they'd been running — what happened?'

Jenny had hurried to join the group of laughing, shouting men. She tried to elbow her way through.

'Did Dick bring you in?'

'No, I found him lying in some rocks — I think he fell and cracked some ribs. He can't talk without hurting himself. What in God's name has been happening?'

'We had a fire, Sandy,' said an embarrassed voice.

'A fire?' The speaker advanced into the firelight. He was looking about with dismay. 'Where is everybody?'

'This is all of us that can walk, mate. We've — we've lost a few chums, you see.'

Jenny had reached the front of the group. 'Sandy?' she said in a faint voice.

'Yes?' He turned. Then he bent forward in the uncertain light. 'Who's that?'

She couldn't mistake that tall spare figure, even in silhouette in the dimness.

'Ronald,' Jenny said, scarcely above a whisper.

'Great God in heaven,' said her husband in total disbelief, 'it's Jenny!'

Chapter Twenty-three

If anyone had told Jenny Armstrong that there would be constraint in this reunion, she would have thought it outlandish. But this tall gaunt man in the flickering light, bearded and grimy, was even more of a stranger than the man she had found by the stream at Daniell's farm. And in front of the jostling, shouting onlookers, she didn't know how to react.

She held out her hand. He took it. But at that moment a scream of terror split the air. Jenny jerked her hand free and ran to the canvas shelter.

Tom Seeley in his nightmare delirium was thrashing about on his bed of brushwood, tearing at the wrappings she had so painstakingly put around him that morning. He was shrieking in pain and horror. Jenny knelt beside him, trying to restrain him. After a moment one of the diggers came to help.

Dr Vance set about binding up Traherne's cracked ribs. Mrs Gray stirred the fire to start some food for the newcomers. The fit men took the horses to picket them. The camp settled down again.

When Jenny was relieved of her watch she stole to the fire, looking about for her husband. She knew each man's sleeping-place. The newcomer had thrown a canvas sheet over the bough of a low tree, pegging it to make a windbreak. He was lying as sleep had caught

411

him, with the empty tin plate at his elbow and his other
arm sprawled across his saddlebag. She put a hand on
his shoulder to shake him awake. But then she
bethought herself of the long ride with the fractious
horses and an injured companion.

She fetched her cape, wrapped it about her, and lay
down at Ronald's side.

When she woke the sun was shining and the camp
was up and about. Ronald had gone from his place,
but the buckle of the saddlebag was undone, showing
a few clean clothes and a hair-brush. Jenny sat up,
stretching. She had grown accustomed to a hard bed
but never got used to finding herself in her clothes
instead of a nightgown. She longed for a bath, for time
to brush out her hair and feel it smooth against her
skull. But this wasn't the time or the place.

Ronald strolled up, holding a tin mug of the strong
tea which formed the basis of every meal. He held it
out to her. Now she felt she knew him — the beard
was gone, the shabby jacket had been replaced by a
clean shirt.

'Good morning, wife,' he said.

'Good morning, husband.'

'Chalmers told me how you come to be here. I hear
you've been doing wonders.'

She shook her head. 'Not enough. Things are very
bad here, Ronald.'

'So I see. I went to the old camp at firstlight.
Fourteen graves . . .'

'And some with no names,' she said. 'I thought one
of them might be yours, lad.'

He folded himself neatly to sit cross-legged beside
her. 'I left the old camp about, let me see . . . it must
be over a month gone by. Didn't they tell you?'

She looked at him with eyes rimmed with tears. 'Ach, husband, how can I keep track of a man who has so many different names? They called you Sandy last night.'

'Yes.' He ran his hand over his hair. 'And of course I'm a Scot. It's a natural choice for a nickname.' He patted her shoulder. 'Drink your tea, lassie.'

She gulped down a mouthful, but it met a rising sob she couldn't prevent, and the result was a coughing fit that lasted until the emotion of the moment had passed. When she recovered Ronald had taken the mug of tea from her and was holding her close with one arm.

'Now, now, my bonnie dearie, there's nothing to cry over. You're here and so am I, and we'll go back to Daniell's farm to pick up Heather and Mrs Baird and then we'll be off to Sydney for the first ship to England.'

'Ronald! You mean it?' Delight and disbelief struggled for first place.

'Aye, it's time to go home, I believe.'

'Does that mean . . . Did you find what you were looking for, laddie?'

He studied her and smiled. 'There's two questions there, I think. The answer to both is yes. I found hardship enough to make me appreciate what I'd turned my back on. And I found gold.'

'Ronald!'

'Ssh,' he said. 'It's hardly decent to triumph over it in this place, where so many men have given their lives and not found it. We won't speak of it to anyone, Jenny. But there's a pouch in my saddlebag with eighteen hundred pounds' worth of gold nuggets in it.'

She covered her mouth with her hand to prevent

herself exclaiming aloud. In a low tone she said, 'Where did you find it?'

'In the roots of an upset tree! I was riding by, and something glinted, and I thought, Shall I bother to go back? and almost rode on. And then I thought, after all, I'm not expected anywhere so why not go back? And there they were — eleven nuggets, one that must weigh almost eight ounces and the rest smaller, but pure gold.'

'From a vein in the rocks?'

He shook his head. 'I think they must have been washed down in some landslip during a rainy spell years ago. They caught in the tree roots, and then perhaps last year or the year before, the tree fell over during the winter weather.'

'But don't you want to look for the seam?' she asked, surprised.

He hesitated. 'I looked about, and could see that there wasn't a gold vein near. I went up the slope and spent a day looking for it, I admit. But when I'd bedded down that night I got to thinking. I remembered what Daniell said — that the craze can take hold of you and you can spend months searching, and end up wasting what you found in the first place. So, I decided to be satisfied with what I'd got. And thank God for it, because if I hadn't turned back when I did, Dick Traherne would be making bones among those rocks where I found him.'

She hardly dared to speak. In the midst of the dirt and misery of this camp full of sick, injured and penniless men, she and her husband had everything — happiness, plans for the future, and above all, each other. 'I'm glad, Ronald,' she murmured.

'Aye, we've much to be glad for, Jenny my love.

So off you go to the river and wash some of the tear-stains away, and then we'll think what's best to do.'

As to that, there was really no argument. They couldn't leave the camp when every able-bodied person was needed to nurse the sick. Ronald added himself to the party of fetchers and carriers who went back and forth to Forbes for supplies. At the end of a week, the long-awaited group rode in from Sydney, with additional drugs and cleansing materials.

But they were too late to save some of the patients. Tom Seeley died the day after Ronald first rode into the camp, and that same day an old man known only as Mitts slipped away. When at last the area was cleared and the remaining patients were put aboard the wagons to go to Forbes, the graves at the old camp numbered nineteen.

Once the wagons had been unloaded in Forbes and the patients settled under the care of the nursing staff who had come out from Sydney, Jenny felt free to think about setting out for Daniell's farm. Gunder had decided to stay on, lured by hints that 'colour' had been found in a creek to the southwest. He consigned his cart to them, to be sold when they eventually got back to Sydney, the money to be put into the bank for him to draw on.

Ronald took turns driving with Henry Chalmers. Dr Vance had stayed with his patients, as had Mrs Gray. Jenny travelled in the back or sometimes rode, for they had Chalmers' horse and Ronald's mount and his pack-horse trotting along at the tailboard.

But now the winter rain had come at last, and sometimes all three had to be on foot, pushing and dragging to keep the vehicle moving. The horses were plastered with mud at the end of each day. It seemed an endless task to groom them before making camp.

It took longer to get back along the route than it had on the outward journey. At the end of six days the rain eased off, the sun came out, and the landscape sparkled. Fresh green glimmered on the tableland, there was no dry dust in the air. But the mud remained.

At Cowra they at last turned northeast. They lost the track entirely but a team coming out from parramatta with the mail put them right. Ten days after they had left Forbes, they sighted the first of Bob Daniell's sheep, munching contentedly among the sprigs of new grass.

It was mid-morning. They trundled over the muddy terrain, Jenny on the driving seat beside her husband with Chalmers riding alongside.

The sound of their approach set the dogs barking. The farmhouse door opened. From behind the farm a pony trotted, with a small figure on its back. The pony approached the thorn fence that separated the back paddock from the farm garden. The rider rose in the stirrups to stare.

Then Goodie was turned away from the fence, taken back a few paces, and set at it once again.

'No!' cried Jenny in alarm.

But Goodie rose in the air, jumped the fence, and landed with neat certainty among the shrubs.

'Yee-hah!' screamed the rider in triumph. 'Mama! Mama!'

Next moment the pony had leaped the front fence and was trotting to the carriage-side. Heather beamed at her mother and waved in excitement. Ronald put on the brake, Jenny slithered down to the muddy earth, and her daughter was in her arms.

'Mama! Mama!'

It was a strange little voice, a cracked treble that seemed unsteady in its pitch. But the word had been spoken aloud, not in a whisper. And when Heather let go to turn to her father, she spoke audibly. 'Papa,' she said, and held out her hand to be shaken.

'Well,' said Ronald uncertainly, 'I said I expected you to be a champion jockey — and so you are!'

Mrs Daniell came flying down the path to greet them, with Baird in pursuit. In a moment they were a muddle of hugs and handshakes, with Heather somewhere in the middle laughing and crying all at once.

'Come in, come in — my, you do look bedraggled.' Mabel Daniell shooed them before her. 'But isn't it great the rain's started? Saved our pasture — we were getting really worried. Well, so I see you caught up with each other on the Lachlan! How thin you are, Mrs Armstrong! You need a good meal, I can see that.'

'I need a bath and a hair-wash a lot more,' Jenny said.

'I'll go and see to the hot water,' said Baird, rushing towards the house.

Later, Jenny sat in the little room having her hair brushed. It wasn't Baird who was doing it, but Heather.

'How long have you been able to jump the pony?' Jenny asked.

'About a week.'

'The jackaroo taught you?'

Heather nodded. 'Can I have a pony when we get back to Gatesmuir?' she asked in her strange, creaky little voice.

Jenny looked at her in the small mirror on the

dressing-stand. 'Yes, my darling, you shall have a pony.'

The little girl smiled. In her delight she let her attention wander from the hairbrush, which was rather too big for her hand. 'Oh dear. I'm afraid your hair's harder to brush than Goodie's mane . . .'

'Let me,' said Baird. She took over and with skill disentangled the brush. 'Go and see if dinner's ready, Heather. Your poor mother is probably as hungry as a hunter.'

Heather darted off on this errand. Jenny said, 'When did she begin to speak?'

'We think it was about a month ago. Harry — the apprentice boy, you know? — he heard her talking to the pony while she was grooming him. So he told me and Mrs Daniell, and we decided it might be a good thing to see if she would speak to somebody other than Goodie.'

'How did you manage it?'

'Mrs Daniell sent the jackaroo to the other side of the farm to do some chores. When it was time for the bairn's riding lesson, Harry was nowhere to be found. Bob Daniell's forbidden Heather to ride unless Harry tightens the girths for her — she can't do it well enough herself. So she went hunting for him about the farm, and finally had to start calling for him in the barns and the woolshed. When he came down from the hayloft at last he said, "What time is it, Heather?" and she said, "Time for my ride" — and since then she's been almost conversational.'

'It's wonderful,' Jenny breathed. 'But what a strange little voice!'

'Aye. I don't think she's ever going to sound like anyone else, and aiblins she'll never be a bletherer — but she's come out of the silence at last.'

Heather reappeared to announce that the meal was just going on the table. They went along to the kitchen where steak and potatoes and a large dish of fresh spring greens awaited them.

Ronald and Henry Chalmers did full justice to the food. Chalmers was full of questions about what had been happening in Sydney during his absence. Mrs Daniell supplied such news as she could. Heather even chimed in to remind her that Mrs Vincent, passing by, had said the new steamer mail service was about to begin between Sydney and Colombo.

Although she was hungry, Jenny found she couldn't eat. She was too taken up with the sensation of being with her family again — Ronald and Heather and that old friend Baird. She listened to the flow of talk, but scarcely took in any of it. She had a sense of being blessed, of being granted a great boon after years of unhappiness.

After lunch the rain came down again. They sat in Mrs Daniell's parlour telling her all that had happened on their trip to the Lachlan. Mrs Daniell at last asked the question that had so far been forgotten in the drama of the fire and its aftermath.

'Did you turn up any gold, Ron?'

'As a matter of fact, yes.'

'You did! How much?'

'Enough for a pony, Papa?' his daughter put in.

'Yes, enough for a pony and a bit over. I've got plans for the rest of it when we get back to Scotland.'

Mrs Daniell raised her eyebrows. 'You're going, then?'

'Yes.'

'Was a time I thought you'd settle here,' she murmured.

'Yes, but that was when I still believed I couldn't set right what had gone wrong back home. Now I know better, Mabel.'

'Yes . . . When you have to face a hard time, it teaches you something, I reckon.'

'That's what I found.'

'So you're going back to pick up the threads, like,' she suggested.

Ronald looked at her in surprise. 'That's very apt, Mabel. You know, in the weaving trade, sometimes a thread will break while the cloth is being made. Then the machines have to be stopped and if the weaver knows his craft, he mends the broken thread so well that it scarcely makes a mark in the warp and weft.'

Mabel understood perfectly. 'Took a long time to mend up this broken thread.'

'Yes. The question is, whether it will leave a big blemish on the cloth.'

Later, when the downpour eased off, Jenny and Ronald went for a walk to the stream where she had first found him when she came to the farm. The path was slippery. He put an arm round her to keep her from falling. She let herself lean on him more than was strictly necessary.

When they reached the stream it had changed greatly. Bright water was pouring along the channel, lapping over the bank. Rich green grass and reeds were springing up at the verges. The trees were putting forth blue-grey leaves.

'You know,' said Jenny, 'those colours would make a fine plaid . . .'

'Blue, grey and green?'

'With a brown line, perhaps. I wonder where my watercolours are?'

'In your hotel room in Sydney, I imagine.'

'I suppose so. I haven't thought of them in weeks. Nor of what's happening at the mill. I ought to write to Charlie Gaines to tell him . . . to tell him . . .'

'To tell him what?' he prompted.

'To tell him when to expect me — us — back.' She faltered into silence. She held her breath, waiting for Ronald's verdict.

'Don't you remember? I said we'd take the first ship.'

'You really want to go?'

His arm about her shoulders tightened. 'In a way I want to stay. I like it here. But you know, when Mabel said something about it being midwinter here, I suddenly longed to see frost on the grass — like midwinter back home in Galashiels.'

She nodded, and let her head rest against his shoulder. The rain resumed, and they had to put on the hats they had been carrying and fasten their oil-cloth coats.

'We'd better get back or we'll get drenched.'

'Yes.'

When they reached the farm Ronald led her to the men's bunk-house, where he and Chalmers would sleep tonight. Leaving her on the shaded verandah, he ducked inside, returning a moment later with the canvas pouch from the saddlebag.

'We never had a chance before,' he said. 'I thought you'd like to see.' He opened the bag and took out a lump of gold as big as his fist. Jenny stared at it. 'Impressive, isn't it? I'll have it assayed when we get to Sydney.'

He shook the bag. She could hear the other nuggets rattling together. He put back the large piece, drew the strings close, and weighed the bag in his hand. 'I'm no expert, of course, but I've seen gold other men brought in. I think there's about seventeen or eighteen hundred pounds there.'

After a moment she said, 'And what about the future? You said at dinner that you had plans for that gold.'

'Well, I'm certainly not going to waste it.'

'I would quite understand if you wanted to strike out for yourself, Ronald. You left Galashiels in the first place because you were dissatisfied.'

He gave a grin of amusement at the term. 'I may get "dissatisfied" again,' he agreed. 'I can't guarantee I'll be as "good as gold". But I think I may put up with things if I can buy a partnership in William Corvill and Son.'

'A partnership!' The idea startled her, because all her life the weaving trade for her had been William Corvill and Son — nothing else.

'I don't expect to be equal with Ned,' Ronald said quickly. 'It's his firm and however unjust I may think that, I don't argue with it because I know you want to respect your father's will. But there's no law that says the firm can't accept an investment from someone else.'

'I suppose not,' she admitted, trying to come to terms with the notion. 'But whether Ned would agree . . .'

'You've still got power of attorney, haven't you?'

'Well, yes.'

'You could accept as junior partner someone who wants to invest eighteen hundred pounds?'

'I . . . suppose I could . . . ' She thought about it. 'But Ronald, we couldn't change the name. Corvill and Armstrong wouldn't have the same prestige as William Corvill and Son.'

'I'm not troubled about what the firm is called. I just want it known and acknowledged that I've got a share in it.'

It was a matter of pride, *his* pride, the stubborn stiff-necked pride that had parted them in the first place. She gave in without further argument. It mattered little to her who actually owned the firm so long as she was permitted to see to the making of the cloth, the fine cloth that had made them famous. Let it be financed by money left by her father, let it be financed by money earned by Ronald's hardships in the outback — the important thing was that they should make good cloth.

Already, now that she had Ronald with her again, her thoughts were reaching out to new ideas, new shades she had seen here on this strange continent. Her mind teemed with new patterns that would combine the soft grey-blue of the gum-trees, the yellow of the wattle, the rose-pink breast feathers of an Australian robin, the reddish-brown of a native cat glimpsed by the poultry coop, the thunderous silver-grey of the rain clouds sweeping over the tableland.

And there were the pigments Ronald had gathered on his outings with the Aborigines. Perhaps when he got home and could analyze them he might find usable dyes — new, original, challenging.

Bob Daniell rode in at nightfall, wet, tired, but full of eagerness to see them. The blackfellows had told him strangers had arrived at his farm and he had guessed their identity. That night he sat up late with the two men, listening to the story of the burned-out camp and toasting Ronald's success as a gold digger.

They stayed a week at Daniell's farm, resting and waiting for the road to improve. Baird entertained herself by trying to repair and refresh the clothes Jenny had almost ruined during her stay on the Lachlan. Heather spent all the time she could with the pony, well aware that soon she must part with him.

Before they left, Jenny had a private word with Mabel Daniell. 'Is there any news of Dinah Bowerby?'

Mrs Daniell shrugged. 'I heard she'd had a quarrel with Mrs Fowler and walked out. Somebody said they saw her on the mail coach for Newcastle but I don't know how true it is.'

Jenny thought it likely. She remembered trying to encourage Dinah to get out of the rural environment where she felt so trapped. Newcastle, she recalled from a short visit to that town, was a busy centre for the shipping of coal, just like its counterpart in Britain.

'What would she do in Newcastle?' she asked Mrs Daniell.

'Oh, Dinah can always get a job. The problem is whether she'll stay in the job she gets. She's a difficult girl, you know. She's got ideas above herself.'

Jenny smiled ruefully. That was exactly what Dinah had said people thought about her. 'She has a right, you know,' she ventured, 'to want to better herself —'

'Now it's not for you to bother your head about Dinah Bowerby,' Mrs Daniell scolded. 'She got herself into a stupid situation and you sorted it out —'

'But only so that Dinah came out worst —'

'Good lord, what other way was there? She'd got herself involved with a feller without first seeing the wedding band on her hand. That was bad enough — my man was very upset about that —'

'Yet he didn't turn Ronald away. It was Dinah who got the rough deal — ',

'My dear, you know as well as I do that it's always the woman who suffers in that kind of thing. And besides, don't forget that we know Dinah. There isn't a doubt she threw herself at Ron — you should have heard her go on about him, as if he were some knight on a white horse who'd come to rescue her.'

'But even if she was a bit headstrong, that was no reason to put all the blame — '

Mabel Daniell sighed. 'I don't know why you're worrying about her!'

Jenny almost said, Because I know what it's like to be in love and find out the man is already married. But that was far away in her past, and it was certainly not a thing to be confided to Mabel.

'Do you think she'll be all right in Newcastle?'

'Dinah's free to make her own choice. If she wants to work in Newcastle, that's her affair.'

'I wondered if I — '

'If you what?'

'If I could leave some money with you . . . so that if you ever hear she's in need . . .'

Mabel shook her head with almost angry emphasis. 'Don't you take that on. It's not *your* fault that things happened as they did. You don't have to make amends.'

'No, but all the same, I feel somehow responsible . . .'

'Nonsense,' said Mrs Daniell with all the force of common sense. And Jenny had to let the matter drop.

The travellers set out when a few days of drying wind and intermittent sunshine had produced a better road surface. Heather said goodbye to Goodie with many tears. Jenny couldn't help thinking that only a few months ago the sight of her daughter crying would have put her in a panic. Now she was able to view it as a part of ordinary life, where partings between children and their pets were inevitable.

When they reached Parramatta Henry Chalmers sold Gunders carriage for him. Jenny ordered fancy goods from the best shop in the main street to be sent to Mrs Daniell as a present before they boarded the train for Sydney.

The city was almost overpowering to them after their sojourn in the wilderness. It surprised Jenny to recall that when she first arrived here she had thought it a sleepy little place. Now it seemed like a metropolis.

She had half expected some embarrassment in arriving at the hotel with a husband. But everyone was agog for news of the events on the Lachlan, and for hard information about the supposed gold finds.

Ronald let it be known he had been lucky. The news would have got out, in any case, when he went to the assay office. As he had foretold, no one thought of him as the missing husband of the lady from Scotland. He was Ron Armstrong, who had come home with a poke of gold and who had helped save the lives of the injured in the gold field. In their first afternoon in Sydney, more people stopped him to talk about gold than had ever spoken to him before.

It was strange to prepare for bed that night. For the first time in nearly two years they were husband and wife in the old way, in the same room, with Ronald helping to take the combs out of Jenny's hair and Jenny shaking out his jacket for him before hanging it up.

'Well,' Ronald said, sitting on the edge of the bed,

'this is different from the lean-to by the stream.'

She gave a trembling laugh. 'So why are you wasting time talking about it, husband?'

He ruffled her dark hair and turned out the lamp. The moonlight streamed in upon them but, though it was beautiful, they had other things to think of.

Next day they went to inquire for berths on a homeward-bound ship. To their delight they found that the new steam-clipper mail service would be arriving in a few days and leaving again for Britain within a week. They booked passage, though Baird was dubious about it. 'How do ye ken it winna run out of coal halfway?' she wanted to know.

'If it does, they can always use the sails.'

'Ye mean it's got baith sails and a boiler?'

'Yes, Baird.'

Baird gave a grim smile. 'It must have been invented by a Scotsman,' she averred.

There was business to attend to. The first item on the agenda should have been to find a replacement for Henry Chalmers, for nothing was ever going to make him efficient as a shipping agent. But in this small colony, men with any business training were very scarce indeed: most immigrants wanted to own land or raise sheep or find gold, and were very unwilling to be employed in office work.

Besides, Chalmers had been such a tower of unexpected strength on the trip to the Lachlan that to dismiss him would have seemed downright ungrateful. Jenny and Ronald contented themselves with giving Chalmers the fullest instructions about future contracts, and begging him to be more to the point and less flowery in his correspondence.

That done, they paid a visit to the newly purchased

Giddiring sheep station so that they could give final instructions to the manager, Arthur Newbold. Heather at once went to the stables to talk to the horses, and though they only stayed overnight was granted the boon of a morning ride.

'What kind of little girl is this?' Ronald inquired, laughing, as she was unwillingly lifted down from the pony to start on the return journey to Sydney. 'Are we raising a little centaur?'

'What's a centaur, Papa?'

'A mythical creature, half-horse, half-human.'

'What's missical?'

'Imaginary, like in a fairy tale.'

'Mmmm,' said Heather, and leaned out of the carriage to wave goodbye to her recent friend. Some miles up the road she remarked, 'It would be nice if centaurs were real.'

'Why, my love?' Ronald inquired.

'When you talk to a pony, he'd answer.'

Her father was delighted. It was the first time she had ever volunteered to start a conversation — hitherto, though she had found a voice, she had only responded when spoken to.

He turned to Jenny, saw in her face that she too had noticed one more step forward in their daughter's recovery, and instinctively held out his hand to her. She took it. They sat holding hands in complete happiness for the next hour.

The day came when they must board the *Cumberland*. All their goodbyes were said. Jenny had had long conversations with Henry Chalmers, giving him instructions as to the conduct of their wool shipments, the overseeing of the sheep station, and how to treat its manager. 'Bear in mind, Mr Chalmers, that Newbold is an experienced man. Leave him to his own ways unless anything extraordinary occurs.'

'Yes, Mrs Armstrong.'

'And there is another matter, Mr Chalmers.'

'Yes?'

'The young woman . . . Miss Bowerby . . .'

'Yes?'

'I . . . er . . . would never wish her to suffer unduly because of . . .'

'I comprehend,' Chalmers said, pursing his lips and puffing out his plump cheeks.

'I was told she had gone to Newcastle.'

'So I heard also.'

'Have you heard whether she has employment?'

'Some tidings in the greenroom at the theatre lead me to understand she is working in a restaurant.'

'Waitress?'

'So I heard.'

'But that's such hard, tiring work . . .'

'My dear Mrs Armstrong, Dinah Bowerby is accustomed to hard work. Please relieve your mind of anxiety on that score.'

Jenny sat silent for a moment, listening to the clatter from Circular Quay which came in through the half-open window of the little office. 'Mr Chalmers, I have made a sum of money available to you at the bank,' she said with some abruptness. 'If ever you hear that Dinah Bowerby is in need −'

'In need of what?' Chalmers asked in bewilderment.

'I don't know, I just don't like to think that she might be suffering hardship, and no one to turn to.'

'She would never think of turning to *me*.'

'No, of course not, but this is really a very small community − quite quickly everyone seems to learn what everyone else is doing. Mr Chalmers, if ever you hear that Miss Bowerby is in difficulty, you will make use of the money I have left with Mr Sumner at the bank. It is a special deposit, under the title Extraneous Expense — Mr Sumner is empowered to give you up to a hundred pounds on your written application giving details of Miss Bowerby's need.'

'This is very generous, Mrs Armstrong. Unnecessarily so.' And very foolish, his tone implied.

'I don't ask you to approve, Mr Chalmers,' she said with asperity. 'Simply remember this instruction, which I don't wish to set down on paper along with the others. And please don't mention it to anyone.'

He raised an eyebrow. She met the quizzical gaze and nodded. 'Not to anyone,' she repeated. They both knew she meant her husband.

It wasn't the kind of information he was likely to volunteer to Ronald. 'By the way, sir, your wife made monetary provision for your ex-mistress . . . ' No, no. He wouldn't mention it to anyone and especially not Ronald.

Jenny spent two afternoons writing thank-you letters to all who had been kind and helpful to them. She made a round of the shops buying items to take home as presents — articles made of the beautiful Australian woods, dried flowers, opals from the Riverina, fans of multi-coloured feathers, combs for the hair made from glowing shell, and a few landscapes by artists of varying ability.

Her own sketches, made for the purpose of recalling colours when she reached home, she carefully parcelled up in oiled cloth against the hazards of sea travel. She had some new designs ready to try out on the loom the moment she got back to Galashiels — delicate

checks of misty grey and soft umber, bolder squares
of cream and brown.

She had had some wool threads dyed by the methods
Ronald had gleaned from the blackfellows, but
whether the process could be replicated in the Scottish
Borders was another matter. These might be strands
that could never be used — truly broken threads. As
she sat with the yarn spread between her fingers, she
thought of Ronald's words. Broken threads can be
mended — but some perhaps are never meant to be
woven into the fabric of life. All the same, she wrapped
them carefully, already thinking ahead to the dyes she
might try at Waterside Mill.

It was a grey day of rain, the Australian winter
giving a demonstration of its wish to retain its hold
although already people were talking of 'spring'. Jenny
was sad. She would have liked her last view of this
beautiful day to be one of bright sunlight, more typical
of what she remembered of her stay.

The purser came to greet them. He was aware that
they were people of consequence who in due course
would take a seat at the captain's table. Their cabins
were the best on the ship, adjoining rooms which
though small had 'every comfort', as the ship's
advertising brochure announced.

Baird took charge of seeing their luggage properly
bestowed. Heather was taken off by one of the
stewards to make the acquaintance of the ship's
livestock. Ronald and Jenny, after a stroll through the
public rooms and a brief and rather frightening
glimpse of the engine room, went on deck to shake
hands with Henry Chalmers and one or two others who
had come to see them off.

It was a relief when at last the bosun called for

visitors to leave the ship. The gangplank was run on board, chains began to rattle, and the sails filled a little as the *Cumberland* turned into the faint breeze. Once out of the harbour the engines might be called up if the breeze didn't freshen. A faint trickle of smoke from the long thin stack told of the leashed power below, but for the moment the captain had no need of it.

The ship's siren sounded a farewell call, dripping ropes were tossed and coiled. Gradually the gap between the rail and the jetty widened.

The rain streamed down. The little crowd on the cobblestones waved handkerchiefs which soon wilted in the downpour. Grey-green water swirled as the helm turned. 'Goodbye, goodbye, safe journey!' voices called. Umbrellas were tilted so that those under them could look up at the funnel, but were straightened as the hoped-for cloud of black smoke failed to appear.

Jenny stood with her cloak and hood wrapped close to keep out the rain. She longed to give one last wave and go below. But Ronald was still calling last messages to his Sydney friends.

Jenny's eye was caught by a figure standing alone on some bales of wool further up the quay. It was the look of loneliness that drew her attention.

She gave a little start of surprise. But no — it was easy to be mistaken — someone wearing a long loose raincoat of oiled cloth and a wide-brimmed felt hat. It could be anyone. Yet she knew with certainty who it was. Dinah Bowerby had come to see them off.

The girl was standing in a nook made by a stack of bales awaiting loading. She had climbed one row up from the cobbles of the quay so that she had a vantage point. She was staring at the departing ship with an unobstructed view over the heads and umbrellas of other wellwishers.

Jenny gazed at the girl. But Dinah's eyes were fixed on Ronald, who had moved a little apart from his wife to call through his cupped hands to Chalmers.

The steam-clipper moved off, turning a little to head out of the cove. The people on the quay began to seem smaller.

The girl on the wool bales clambered up one more row, to the top of the stack. She stood holding the brim of her hat off her face with one hand, so that she could catch without hindrance the last glimpse of those on deck.

A gust of wind swept along the jetty. The wet, heavy oilskin coat was pulled back by its force. The coat clothed her for a moment like a second skin. In that moment, Jenny understood. Dinah Bowerby had come to the docks to say a last goodbye to the father of her child.

She was obviously pregnant. Not perhaps noticeably so when moving about in normal circumstances and in the loose wide skirts that were usual in farming country. But at that moment when the breeze folded her coat against her body, her secret had been revealed.

Jenny turned to grasp Ronald's arm. He was out of reach for the moment, waving and calling farewells for one last time.

'Ronald!' called Jenny.

'Just a moment, my love.' He moved farther off, to lean over the rail at the point still nearest the land. 'Keep after that joiner making the woolpress for Giddiring!'

On the pier Chalmers held up palms helplessly, signifying he couldn't understand.

'Giddiring! Woolpress!'

Chalmers pantomimed non-comprehension. Ronald went as far aft as he could, cupped his mouth, and shouted his last instructions. It was useless to try for his attention elsewhere.

Perhaps that was as well. Perhaps it was better that he shouldn't know.

Dinah had not wanted him to know. She had made that clear by disappearing from the Fowlers' sheep station.

Jenny understood her feelings. What good would it do? To reproach him, berate him, demand something from him — and what? What could he give?

He certainly couldn't give his name to the coming child. He could have offered money, of course, but Jenny knew in her heart that Dinah would have thrown it back in his face. She herself, in making her arrangement with Chalmers, had tried to do it so that if it was needed the money could be made to seem impersonal, brought from a bank, from some businesslike fund.

She stood holding her cloak about her, racked by indecision. Should she fetch Ronald, point the girl out to him, tell him what she had seen?

Heather ran up from the far side of the ship. 'I nearly didn't see us leave!' she panted. 'I was talking to the sheep.'

She was hatless, her bonnet having fallen off while she leaned over the sheep pen. Her honey-coloured hair was beginning to be darkened by the rain but even so, it suddenly occurred to Jenny, she must be clearly recognisable to the girl on the jetty. Recognisable as Ronald's daughter.

434

Jenny looked towards her. She was just in time to see her staring at mother and daughter before she turned away in angry despair.

'Mama, they've got some lovely little rabbits in hutches. Mr Gatton says I can take them out and hold them sometimes.'

'That's wonderful, Heather.' She put a fold of her cloak round the child to keep the rain off. 'Look,' she said, 'it's all fading out of sight in the cloud and rain. Say goodbye to Sydney, dear.'

Obediently the little girl waved her hand in the direction of the harbour. But already her mind was losing the picture of Goodie and the rides on the Fowlers' station, the travels on the strange little train to Parramatta, the room at the hotel she had shared with Baird. She was thinking of the voyage, the livestock who would become her new friends, walks on shore in strange ports where there were strange animals such as camels and elephants, lessons in the saloon with other young travellers, perhaps a party soon for her birthday.

The jetty dwindled and was lost in the rainstorm. Sydney was gone, blotted out by the downpour. On either side the shores were only intermittently visible as the wind drove the squall.

The ship sounded its siren in farewell.

Goodbye to this strange wild country, to all that had happened here. It was behind them now, Jenny told herself. Even this great secret which she had been allowed to learn by chance — it was behind them.

She would say nothing to Ronald. What good could it do to tell him? Yet more guilt to bear as a burden . . . And he had enough already, for she knew he would never forgive himself for the affair with Dinah.

If he had loved her deeply — if it had been born of something more than proximity and restlessness — that would have been different. But she recalled his embarrassment when he tried to describe how he felt about Dinah. And it might come between them in their new life. She had tried by every means to show him she forgave him his unfaithfulness, understood how and why it had happened. If she were to say to him now, 'Dinah is having your baby,' she might find it hard to add, 'and I forgive you that too.'

Worse, it would shatter him. To fall momentarily in love with a beautiful farm girl who soon proved boring was one thing. To leave her with a baby coming was quite another. He would see himself as a scoundrel. Which would be unfair, because once Jenny came on the scene Dinah with her strong religious principles had felt so much in the wrong that she herself gave him up.

It would harm their day-to-day relationship as husband and wife if she had to tell him what she had learned. Especially here in the crowded confines of a ship. No, no! If she were ever to tell him Dinah's secret it would be once they were home, safe in the workaday wonders of making fine cloth, busy and confident in their natural surroundings.

But it would be better to say nothing, ever. It was not her secret to tell, it was Dinah's. Perhaps she would write when the baby was born. Perhaps she would preserve her silence. Whichever she chose, Jenny vowed to herself, I will abide by that decision.

She sighed. She had looked forward so much to this home-going. For weeks in her mind's eye she had had the picture of the hills around her home-town — the rich green of pasture, the coming purple of the heather, the cool pale blue of the sky, the sparkling brown of the water in the hillside burns. But now it was all blotted out by her memory of that lonely figure on the wool stacks.

Ahead lay the ocean, the long voyage round the world to the life where she and Ronald belonged. On that journey she must come to terms with what she now knew, make it part of the fabric of the past. It was an unhappiness, but unhappiness and joy go together through human existence, she had learned — twining and inter-weaving, first one taking priority and then the other.

She must pick up the threads of their life again, mend those that had been broken, strengthen and protect those that carried joy. They were the threads that led into the future.

KAY STEPHENS

WEST RIDING

An absorbing saga of love and ambition in the Yorkshire hills

Rhona Hebden is the daughter of a mill owner in the West Riding of Yorkshire, a girl whose pretty heart-shaped face and tumble of auburn hair disguise a strength of will and character that surprises even herself. When she inherits shares in Bridge House Mill from her late father, she leaves her home in the familiar row of back-to-back houses in Halfield town and determines to break through the Depression years of the 1930s to make the knitting pattern and yarn business a going concern.

When civil engineer Wolf Richardson announces a plan to flood the beautiful Halfield valley in order to create a reservoir, Rhona's Yorkshire pride comes to the fore and she sets out to thwart his scheme. But Wolf is a hard man to win over and Rhona finds that she has more than met her match. Moreover, she realises that she is disturbingly attracted by his dark, brooding looks and fiery ambition. Then the war intervenes, bringing unpredictable tragedies, and Rhona is swept up by the effort to fight and survive. During a weekend leave, she hastily marries an old childhood friend, only to find herself longing once more for Wolf. Whilst battling against the heartbreaks of war, Rhona discovers that her greatest struggle is that of her own conflicting emotions and the desire to give up all for love.

Full of passion and ambition, WEST RIDING is an absorbing novel rich in emotion and infused with the spirit of the rugged Yorkshire countryside.

'A nicely crafted love story' *Yorkshire Evening Post*

FICTION/SAGA   0 7472 3330 6   £3.99

MALCOLM ROSS

**An enthralling Cornish saga from
the bestselling author of
ON A FAR WILD SHORE**

A Notorious Woman

Johanna Rosewarne is an extraordinary young woman
– not just in her looks, though her clear blue eyes draw
people to her like moths to a candle flame. Nor in her
unselfconscious manner, for she is not in the least
vain. No, Johanna is just a completely unconventional
woman living in the most conventional of times – the
repressive years of the Victorian era.

Orphaned at an early age, she is treated by her aunt
and uncle as little better than a servant. And when she
catches the eye of the suitor intended for her cousin,
Johanna is cast into the role of wanton seductress and
can no longer call their home her own.

Taking a post as companion to a rich young widow,
Johanna meets Hal Penrose, a handsome young man
just off to seek his fortune in America. It is love at first
sight. But determined not to compromise Hal, Johanna
doesn't reveal that he has left her pregnant, and she
finds an unusual way to earn a living for herself and
her unborn child . . .

A NOTORIOUS WOMAN – the story of Johanna
Rosewarne's fight for independence in the narrow
society of mid-nineteenth-century rural Cornwall.

A selection of bestsellers from Headline

FICTION

THE DIETER	Susan Sussman	£3.99 ☐
TIES OF BLOOD	Gillian Slovo	£4.99 ☐
THE MILLIONAIRE	Philip Boast	£4.50 ☐
BACK TO THE FUTURE III	Craig Shaw Gardner	£2.99 ☐
DARKNESS COMES	Dean R Koontz	£3.99 ☐

NON-FICTION

THE WHITELAW MEMOIRS	William Whitelaw	£4.99 ☐
THE CHINESE SECRET SERVICE	Faligot & Kauffer Translated by Christine Donougher	£5.99 ☐

SCIENCE FICTION AND FANTASY

MAD MOON OF DREAMS	Brian Lumley	£3.50 ☐
BRIDE OF THE SLIME MONSTER Cineverse Cycle Book 2	Craig Shaw Gardner	£3.50 ☐
THE WILD SEA Bard III	Keith Taylor	£3.50 ☐

*All Headline books are available at your local bookshop or newsagent,
or can be ordered direct from the publisher. Just tick the titles you want
and fill in the form below. Prices and availability subject to change without
notice.*

Headline Book Publishing PLC, Cash Sales Department, PO Box 11
Falmouth, Cornwall TR10 9EN, England.

Please enclose a cheque or postal order to the value of the cover price
and allow the following for postage and packing:
UK: 80p for the first book and 20p for each additional book ordered up
to a maximum charge of £2.00
BFPO: 80p for the first book and 20p for each additional book
OVERSEAS & EIRE: £1.50 for the first book, £1.00 for the second
book and 30p for each subsequent book.

Name ....

Address ....

....

....